The Witching Hour

The Witching Hour

ELIZABETH MACNEAL
LAURA SHEPHERD-ROBINSON
STACEY HALLS
ANDREW MICHAEL HURLEY
IMOGEN HERMES GOWAR
NATASHA PULLEY
SUSAN STOKES-CHAPMAN
JESS KIDD
STUART TURTON
KIRAN MILLWOOD HARGRAVE
BRIDGET COLLINS
CATRIONA WARD
MICHELLE PAVER

SPHERE

SPHERE

First published in Great Britain in 2025 by Sphere

1 3 5 7 9 10 8 6 4 2

Copyright in the contribution as follows:
'The Doll's House' Copyright © Elizabeth Macneal Limited, 2025
'The Second Witness' Copyright © Laura Shepherd-Robinson, 2025
'23 Bridge Street' Copyright © Stacey Halls, 2025
'The Bugle and the Drum' Copyright © Andrew Michael Hurley 2025
'Two Go Together' Copyright © Imogen Hermes Gowar, 2025
'The Signal Bells' Copyright © Natasha Pulley, 2025
'A Midnight Visitor' Copyright © Retter Enterprises Limited, 2025
'An Artful Curse' Copyright © Jess Kidd 2025
'An Age of Evil' Copyright © The Adaverse Limited, 2025
'Feast' Copyright © Kiran Millwood Hargrave, 2025
'The Terror By Night' Copyright © Bridget Collins, 2025
'Macaw' Copyright © Catriona Ward, 2025
'Dr Thrale's Notebook' Copyright © Michelle Paver, 2025

The moral right of the authors has been asserted.

Illustrations Copyright © Dawn Cooper

All characters and events in this publication, other than those clearly in the public domain, are fictitious and any resemblance to real persons, living or dead, is purely coincidental.

All rights reserved.
No part of this publication may be reproduced, stored in a retrieval system, or transmitted, in any form or by any means, without the prior permission in writing of the publisher, nor be otherwise circulated in any form of binding or cover other than that in which it is published and without a similar condition including this condition being imposed on the subsequent purchaser.

A CIP catalogue record for this book is available from the British Library.

ISBN 978-1-4087-3466-7

Typeset in Garamond 3 by M Rules
Printed and bound in Great Britain by Clays Ltd, Elcograf S.p.A.

Papers used by Sphere are from well-managed forests and other responsible sources.

Sphere	The authorised representative
An imprint of	in the EEA is
Little, Brown Book Group	Hachette Ireland
Carmelite House	8 Castlecourt Centre
50 Victoria Embankment	Dublin 15, D15 XTP3, Ireland
London EC4Y 0DZ	(email: info@hbgi.ie)

An Hachette UK Company
www.hachette.co.uk

www.littlebrown.co.uk

CONTENTS

The Doll's House – Elizabeth Macneal	1
The Second Witness – Laura Shepherd-Robinson	39
23 Bridge Street – Stacey Halls	79
The Bugle and the Drum – Andrew Michael Hurley	115
Two Go Together – Imogen Hermes Gowar	151
The Signal Bells – Natasha Pulley	187
A Midnight Visitor – Susan Stokes-Chapman	225
An Artful Curse – Jess Kidd	257
An Age of Evil – Stuart Turton	297
Feast – Kiran Millwood Hargrave	339
The Terror By Night – Bridget Collins	371
Macaw – Catriona Ward	405
Dr Thrale's Notebook – Michelle Paver	433

THE DOLL'S HOUSE

Elizabeth Macneal

Verity was given the doll's house just before her Papa left on his expedition. His furs, boots and velvet-lined box of silver instruments were already on board *The Virtue*; she had pressed the needle of the compass against her finger and watched as a tiny globe of blood formed. When she placed the tool back in the case, it had left a rusty smear on the fabric. If that small trace of her travelled with him, she told herself, he would return home safely.

On his last day at home, Verity had listened at the top of the stairs as her mother's voice had risen from her father's study. Her mother had a ghastly feeling about it all: he would not return. *You must not go!* A wail had broken from her throat. Verity had sucked on a strand of hair. She had not thought her mother had it in her: that she too could spill over, her voice and fear filling the hallways of the house.

Later, her governess had tried to extract Verity from his study. *These Latin verbs won't conjugate themselves*, she'd said brightly, but when Verity felt a hand on her shoulder, she had screamed just as her mother had. She gave herself fully to the sound, her lungs emptying with a feeling akin to glory. Nobody moved. Verity had closed her mouth and waited.

Would she be punished, reprimanded? But her father had held out his hands helplessly, as if to say it was pointless, it was in nobody's power to silence her; then he had chuckled. Verity had thrilled at the idea that she existed beyond everyone's control, and she had smiled at the governess as she left and thought, *I wish you would die.*

Later, her Papa had led her to her bedroom. 'Just wait, Vee,' he said. 'Just you wait and see what I've made you.'

There was a square object in the corner of the room, shrouded in a pair of old curtains.

'Here,' he said. 'Let's do it together.'

His hands were tanned, rougher than hers. Verity held her breath.

'Hurry, then,' he said.

But she did not move. The cloth twitched under her hand. Perhaps she could hold him here for ever, waiting for the moment the curtain lifted. The days would turn and the ship would sail without him, and here they would remain.

Her Papa tutted his impatience and pulled the curtain for her.

'Well?' he asked. 'What do you think?'

It was a neat box of a townhouse exactly like theirs. Immaculate painted bricks, carved stucco, glossy black railings.

Her eyes stung with the effort not to cry.

'Here, look,' he said.

He opened the door, and every detail of her life was tucked inside: her own bed with its pink hangings; a little spaniel warming itself by the fire. There were dolls, too. The Verity doll was reading a book under the table in the scullery, her pale hair unravelling from her cap, tiny flecks of mud on her hem. Her mother was in the sitting room with the governess, hand resting on a sampler. And her Papa was in his study, as she knew he would be. A pair of fur gloves dangled from his fingers. His other hand pointed to a map of the Antarctic Peninsula on the wall behind him, each sea and island carefully labelled. *Weddell Sea, Elephant Island, South Orkney Island*. His would be the first expedition to cross the South Pole on foot, to add new names to the map. *Verity's Peak*, he had once suggested with a laugh.

'Look,' he said. 'I even made a little journal, just like the one I will take with me.' He reached into his tiny study and held up a leatherbound book, the size of a coin. He flicked through it, the pages so white and empty. 'You can think of me, writing in it each day.'

It was too much. The tears dripped silently from her chin. This house was where she would be contained, confined, just like her mother. While her father traversed mountains, she would cross the hall. He would touch the far edges of the globe; she would lift a teacup to her mouth.

'You like it, my best girl?' he asked, but he did not seem to notice her silence. He was already elsewhere, in towering shelves of ice, watching whales breach the surface of the ocean.

⚮

For a whole year, the doll's house sat untouched, the curtain flung over it. When Verity went to bed, her eyes slipped past it, moving from the chest of drawers to the mirror in the corner. Sometimes, she lay awake for hours and became convinced she could hear a low whispering in the room, like wind whistling across the brim of a chimneypot.

Letters arrived from Madeira, Montevideo and Buenos Aires, informing them that relations between the crew were cordial, and they had met whalers with a deep understanding of the Antarctic region, who had much to share. There were no lines to read between; everything was matter of fact, bleached of life.

Whalers, Verity thought. If she had written the letter, she would have described how a dead whale smelled. She would have determined the sound it made as their harpoons caught in its flesh, and whether the whalers heard it in their dreams.

I miss you and Verity terribly, the letter continued. *I often imagine that Vee and I are picking plums in the orchard. Might I humbly petition that she turn this year's crop into jam for me? I bitterly regret that my greed has got the better of me, and I have already eaten the five jars I brought with me.*

Another season began. Verity's Mama busied herself with a revolving door of visitors, whom Verity endured in silence. The scones were dry and churned around Verity's mouth endlessly, her saliva turning the dough to putty. Nobody asked her anything. Her fingers seemed to twitch no matter how still she held her hands. She challenged herself to see how long she could last without blinking. Sometimes, she caught her reflection in the mirror and began to see a little of the strangeness that she knew lurked within her, that sent the other girls careering away from her, that made her governess afraid to meet her eye.

Late one night, she stole one of her Papa's letters from her mother's bureau and took it to her bedroom. The house was quiet. She turned it over in her hands, breathed it in. Perhaps she was imagining it, but she felt sure that she could smell him faintly: peppermint and pipe smoke. Half a year before, the ink would have been wet, his pen scratching out each hope and wish. *Do tell me what games my dear Verity has played with her little house. Has Winston been a beastly puss and stolen one of the glass pears? You must tell her I have found a perfect treasure for her in the market here: a little bear stitched from the skin of a seal pup.*

She placed the letter under her pillow. The clock chimed eleven, and still she couldn't sleep. The chasm between her and her Papa seemed unbridgeable. Sometimes, when he was at home, she would tiptoe down to his study and see a line of candlelight under his door. 'Can't sleep either, my best girl?' he'd ask. Rather than rebuking her, he would pat the seat of his armchair and she would sit for hours, watching him write letters and articles, his pen creaking against the page. He would murmur aloud as he wrote. *The glaciologist and geologist will study ice formations – magnetic observations will be taken –* Sometimes he might fetch her a piece of ham from the kitchen and they would eat it as delightedly as a pair of street children, sucking the fat from their fingers. She would usually wake in her own bed, and faintly recall the pressure of his arms as he'd carried her upstairs.

But now the house seemed shelled of him, an absence none of them dared name. The doll's house sat sadly in the corner. A shame crept over her. He had made every piece in this house just for her. He must have spent months paring tiny pieces of wood into tables and chairs, sewing dresses from little offcuts of fabric, fashioning a barrel from a bobbin. *Ungrateful*, she hissed. *Ungrateful wretch!* Her fingernails shaped half-moons into her wrists. Then she climbed out of bed. The floorboards were cold as she kneeled in front of the little house, lifted off the curtain and unhooked the door.

Everything was exactly as she had first seen it. There was her doll, hiding under the table. Her Papa was in his study, gloves in his hand. It occurred to her that he might have made this house on his most recent voyage. Just as she longed for a widening horizon, he might have longed for a familiar scene, conjuring each tiny detail before him, walking the rooms of the house in his mind. Toast cooking on the stove, the bellows by the drawing-room fireplace with a little chip in the wood. His daughter and his wife, patiently awaiting his return. His Penelope and Telemachus – or Telemacha – he had once called them, until her mother had spat the names back at him in a particularly violent row. *Don't you dare, Alfred, don't you dare make light of it – do you know what it is to wait and hope? One day you will return home and I will be gone. You will not find me as constant as Penelope.*

Verity flinched at the memory. She positioned Papa doll

at his desk, his journal in front of him. She made Verity doll tiptoe down the hallway. Her porcelain fingers pattered on the door. Faintly, she could hear the grandfather clock downstairs chiming twelve; the tiny clock in the doll's house was also set to midnight.

Verity doll and her Papa conversed a little. *Come in, my best girl*, her Papa doll said. *Sit as quiet as a mouse in the corner and you may stay as late as you like. Here, why don't you draw in my journal? I will find you a pen.*

She reached for the tiny journal and opened it, her fingers looking so big and ugly against it. She was about to place the book back on her Papa's tiny desk when a flash of ink caught her eye. The candlelight shuddered and it was difficult to see. She peered closer.

'How?' she whispered.

Each page was filled with tiny handwriting. This was just like her Papa: he did nothing by half measures. But when he'd shown her the journal, hadn't the pages been blank? It was puzzling, even more so once she'd retrieved her magnifying glass. The writing was impossibly minute. Even a nib made of an eyelash would be too thick.

༄

25th February, 1890. I am glad that our month in South Georgia is at an end. It shall be weeks until I am able to forget the stench of decaying whale carcasses, the greasy mounds of offal cast into the harbour, meat slipping from bones. It put a chill through me to see how the blood of those great beasts turned the sea around Grytviken red.

It might be an ordinary sight for a whaling port, and yet it has charged me with unease. In one of the inns, I drank with a captain who was incredulous that we would venture to the Antarctic Peninsula at this time of year. He said that the ice had come far north that season, and our only chance of making it through the pack was by postponing our arrival until September next year. Half a year lost, I exclaimed. A whole six months more until I see my wife and daughter again! Aye, that or your life, was his retort.

I confess I was unsettled by this, but when I relayed what I had heard to Paulson, he called the man a dunce and a drunkard. It was envy speaking, he said, with a dismissive wave, that we should make such discoveries. A postponement of the expedition was tantamount to relinquishing it for ever. I am ashamed that Paulson and I quarrelled, but naturally his decision was final.

So now we find ourselves at sea once more. Our ship is loaded with more provisions; we even have two live pigs on board. Verity would love to name them, I am sure, but if she did I would be unable to eat them. I write this in my cabin as sleet bashes the sails, and I wonder – will our expedition make heroes of us all? Or will we be known only for our folly, and we are a company of doomed men, sailing in what will become our coffin?

༄

Verity read it again, more slowly this time. Her nostrils flared, her eyes unblinking. The date was that day's. Her heart began to beat very fast. It was so different from the flat letters he had sent to her Mama, stripped of worry or concern.

She reached into the study and lifted out her own doll. It looked the same as ever, her porcelain face the same insipid white, her eyes a vacant blue. She pinched the doll's cheek. There was no echoing pain on her own face. Carefully she replaced it. Was anything else out of the ordinary? When she noticed the map on the wall, she felt bilious, her belly churning. There, smaller than a grain of rice, was a tiny little galleon, just like her Papa's. It had just left the port of South Georgia, its nose pointed at South Sandwich Island.

It was a ruse, she told herself. It had to be. But she knew, the excitement stirring within her, that it was not.

Her mother was breakfasting in the parlour with the governess when Verity hurried through the door, still in her nightgown.

'What is the meaning of this, Verity?' her mother asked. 'Why aren't you dressed?'

Verity took it all in, panting a little from the effort it had taken her to run down the stairs. Her mother's startled expression, her governess whose knife clattered to the floor, the vague sense she had of hands slipped away and out of sight.

'I – I—'

Her voice stuck in her throat. The ludicrousness of what she had seen struck her anew. Where was she to begin?

'Miss Verity,' her governess said. 'I will call for Anna. You can't be running down the hallways in your nightgown, like a girl straight from the wards of Bedlam—'

'I – I have heard from Papa,' Verity burst out. 'He is uneasy since he left South Georgia, and he and the captain have quarrelled.'

Her mother stood too suddenly, sending a teacup clattering to the floor.

'But the post has not yet come. Let me see his letter at once.'

'It is not—'

'You should not have opened it, Verity.'

'I – I did not open it. Or at least – it was not a letter.'

Her mother stared at her, brow creasing. 'I do not understand, child.'

'It is – oh, Mama, you must believe me.'

'Believe what? And what is that frightful bruise on your face?'

Only then did Verity notice the pain in her cheek; so too did she register a low, persistent ache at the back of her skull.

'Please, Mama. Please come with me. I don't know how, but Papa found a way to write to me.'

'Where?'

'Somehow he – he wrote to me in – in the book in my

doll's house. You need only see it, and then you'll believe me. *Please. Please.*'

'In the book in your doll's house?' her governess repeated, shaking her head. 'What nonsense is this?'

'You must believe me!'

She clenched her fists, tried to master herself. Perhaps it was the desperation in her voice. Perhaps her mother was anxious to hear from her husband and would try anything. Regardless, she allowed Verity to lead her upstairs.

'This is nonsense,' the governess repeated, but she followed too.

When they were in her bedroom, Verity ran towards the house. 'Here,' she cried, fumbling for the catch, opening the door. She seized the book, opened it.

The pages were blank.

She must have been mistaken. She thumbed through them once more.

'It was – they were—'

Her mother shook her head. 'Verity.'

'It was here! I swear it, Mama, I—'

Nobody could have removed the pages. The binding was pristine, finely stitched.

She scrabbled for the map, almost ripping it. The ship was gone. The sea was a placid blue.

'It was here. It was all written in his hand. I swear it.'

'It is a grave sin to lie,' her governess said.

'I didn't!'

'You might miss your father, but to fabricate a *quarrel* with the captain! Your father would never be so rash,' her mother said. Then, seeing Verity's expression, she added weakly, 'Perhaps it was a dream.'

'It was all here! You must believe me!'

But she knew it was hopeless. She flung herself on the bed, hands covering her face.

'Don't touch me!' she cried when her mother reached for her. It was like her blood was boiling within her, rising up her gullet.

'Verity, please,' her mother begged. 'Verity. Don't do this again. I can't bear it.'

'If she wants to have hysterics, let her,' her governess said. 'She is like this because we all pander to her.'

The door slammed shut. Verity was alone. She panted on the bed, her pillow damp, her lungs squeezed flat of air, her hair rumpled around her. She raised her hand to her cheek and felt that bruise, blooming like a plum.

༄

27th February, 1890. Only three days after leaving South Georgia, we have already passed numerous bergs and reached the edge of the pack ice. We inch our way between floes carefully, slowly, the ice at the edge of the pack softer and more easily broken.

Well, Paulson, said I; do you see the whalers were right?

But we are all determined and set on our course. What other choice do we have, save for a shame-faced retreat? And truly, my fear is matched only by my awe. These are sights indeed. I wish

I might bottle them and bring them back to show to Verity: the radiant, still mirror of the sea, the bergs floating like lily pads on a pond. Blue whales lift from the water, sea leopards sun themselves on bergs. Yesterday, we moored to a floe and exercised the dogs. Mercury slipped her muzzle and fell into a pool, but I was able to haul her out. How contrite she was then, shivering and whining. She has been mated but we do not yet know if she has caught. We joke she is the only one satisfied among us all, a ship of men.

Tonight is Paulson's birthday and we are promised a veritable feast: turtle soup, jugged hare, with rum and stout. It is difficult to believe we are not dining at White's, that I might not return home tonight to my wife and Vee, and hold them against my chest.

༨

'And to think that they will be among the first men to cross Antarctica from sea to sea! They must almost be at Vahsel Bay.'

Verity and her mother were sitting in the drawing room, taking tea with several of the women whose husbands were also aboard *The Virtue*.

'They are not,' Verity said calmly, barely looking up from her sampler. Her satin stitch was a series of knots; her French knots, meanwhile, were unravelling. 'Their ship makes slow progress and has been hampered by ice floes.'

Verity felt her mother stiffen.

Mrs Paulson laughed. 'And how, pray, do you know this?'

Without even looking at her mother, Verity could sense that her hackles were rising.

'Well, Miss Verity? What else might you tell us about our adventurers?'

'Some of the men have quarrelled with Paulson,' she said, leaning forward. 'The whalers warned him about the pack ice in the Weddell Sea, but he dismissed them.'

'My own husband act in a foolhardy manner!'

'It is true!' Verity exclaimed, putting aside her hoop. 'I have tried to tell Mother. I have tried to warn her, but nobody will listen!'

A ripple spread through the room. It was only then that Verity realised she had been shouting. Suddenly, there was laughter. Her face turned hot, an itchiness spreading across her chest.

'Have you heard this?' Mrs Paulson demanded, whacking her friend across the knuckles with her fan. 'Miss Verity is entertaining us all with wonderfully vivid stories. I warrant she's as knowledgeable an explorer as Franklin himself!'

More laughter. They looked at her in that familiar way: heads on one side, half fascinated, half repelled by her.

Verity's needle stabbed in and out of the sampler.

And from the next day onwards, her mother freed her of these interminable afternoons.

Every night, Verity lay awake, listening to the clock ticking in the hallway. The closer it grew to twelve, the more agitated she became, until at last the clock chimed, and she sprang forwards and there were her Papa's words, for one glorious hour.

Her eyes glittered. Her fingers trembled. The light from her candle cast long, jaundiced shapes onto the rooms of her house. She existed in that single hour between midnight and one.

It did not matter that she barely slept.

If she shut her eyes, she too could feel the shiver of the boat as it collided with the ice, hear the low, rumbling crack as a wedge was formed, as the ship steamed into the small passage. She tasted the oily fishiness of stewed seal that the men had clubbed, chuckled over the tiny puppies whelped by Mercury. But above all, she felt wonder: at the deep indigos of the sea, at the emperor penguins, slipping on and off the ice floes. As the months passed, she watched the slow, cautious creep of her Papa's ship towards Vahsel Bay. She tried to ignore the alarm in his account, how the crew were anxious and shifting, the weather turning bitter, the bergs multiplying in number and size. Soon it would be July, midwinter. In London, the sun blazed for days, turning Richmond Green to straw. The horses panted up the hill, greasy and shimmering with sweat.

↝

28th June, 1890. I was awoken in the night by raised voices, by shouts. The seas were rough, a gale ripping through the skies, my bedsheets damp from a leak overhead. Some of the men were drunk; one had Paulson by the throat.

'Ease up, ease up,' I called, and pulled them apart, the men spitting and snarling.

'Can't you see this is madness?' one said.

I waited to see if Paulson might recognise the truth of it, if a flicker would pass across him. He was like a dog with a bone; he would not give it up.

'We are only eighty miles from Vahsel Bay,' he retorted, straightening his cuffs. 'And if you touch me again, I will shoot you.' He retreated to his cabin.

The character of the pack has changed, growing thicker and more difficult to break through. Ice pressure against the rudder is a grave concern. Each night, the pack closes tighter around us, threatening to seal us in.

How small our boat is; how unfathomably deep the horizon, the ice, the ocean.

༄

'Am I imagining it, or has Verity grown ... peculiar?'

Verity crouched behind the door, her eye staring through the keyhole. She must not blink.

Her governess frowned. 'More than usual?'

'I wish she would stop with these senseless lies. I know it's all make-believe, but she makes it sound so – so real. So *ghastly*.'

'She thinks nothing of you and the pain it must cause you.' The governess clasped her mother's hand.

'She has missed her father before, but this is something different. It is easy for him to be the favourite when he's never here. I've always felt so – so *unnecessary*. He would die for her, Jane. He would die in an instant. Isn't that what a parent ought to do? And sometimes I worry that I – I would not do the same for her.'

Verity bit down on her thumbnail, felt that glorious rush of pain.

Her governess spoke quietly, gently. 'I've said it before. Some men are filled with the need to wander. And as for Verity, she can be so sweet when she chooses, so eager to learn. But plenty of children live in circumstances far harder than hers and *they* do not frighten their guests and tell terrible lies and drift around the house like halfwits.'

Verity knew her mother would not defend her, and so it did not disappoint her when she didn't.

'Perhaps, my dear,' her mother replied. 'Perhaps.'

18th July, 1890. It is as we feared; we are held up in the ice. The temperature has dropped; the floes are cemented together and show no signs of relenting. What are we to do? The notion of spending the season here is unpleasant to all of us. The cold needles us. Our supplies may not sustain us. We have done what we can: we have travelled over a thousand miles through the ice in the past six weeks.

And now we have nothing to do but to wait to see if nature or God will release us.

◊

When Verity's Papa spent summers at home, he would lift her on his shoulders and they would roam through the orchard, picking fruit from the low branches of the plum trees. Together they would invade Anna's kitchen and make bubbling cauldrons of jam, the hot liquid shining like amber. It was important, he told Verity, that a gentleman learn the fundamentals of cooking, just as he knew how to sew. If he was stranded on his expeditions, he would have to fend for himself.

The morning after her Papa became trapped in the ice, Verity stared out the window on to the orchard, watching the mounds of fruit rotting on the ground. Her mother was poorly; the governess was tending to her, and Verity paced the walls of her bedroom. She tried not to think of her Papa. The heat of the Surrey summer felt grotesquely decadent. She wished she could punish herself with a cold winter of her own, with no fire and no covers, as though by doing so, her own body might absorb some of his pain.

Verity watched her hand, the way she commanded it to flex. She had to be calm, reasonable. She would not burst into the dining room in a flail of limbs and hair.

'Verity,' her mother said, all delight, when Verity sat down in the chair opposite her, her dress newly pressed, two neat plaits weighing heavy on her shoulders. It was a relief to find her mother alone for once.

Her mother reached for the toast. 'I thought I might visit Smith's this morning, to see what heavy winter fabrics he has in stock. You do not mind missing a morning's study, if I am to prevail upon your governess's time.'

Verity's breath was shallow. 'Mama,' she said. 'Mama – there is something of the utmost urgency I must discuss with you—'

'Do not try me, Verity.' She raised a finger in warning.

'Mama, please,' she said, trying to keep her voice level, trying to swallow the queasiness that turned her mouth acrid. 'You must listen to me. Papa's ship is locked fast in the ice. There is no recovering it. They are marooned, their supplies dwindling. I can give the coordinates. Without rescue, they will certainly die.'

Her mother gripped her teacup, tighter and tighter. 'You must stop this, Verity.'

'It is true, Mama! You must send a ship. You are his only hope!'

'That is enough!' Her mother shook her by the arm. 'Why do you tell these lies? Do you have any idea how much they frighten me?'

'Please, Mama. You must send a ship. If you don't, Papa will die! How can't you see it? He will die, Mama. He will die! And it will be all your fault.' She seized hold of her mother in turn, as though she were drowning, as if she might shake the truth into her. She dug her fingernails into her mother's arm and the flesh felt as soft as fruit.

'Stop it! Get her off me, Jane, get – her – off—'

Hands were grappling her, pulling her back, and still Verity fought, still she writhed and begged and screamed. Fabric shrieked, her own voice pulsing in her ears, *He will die – he will die—*

And then she was in the hallway, and it was her governess who was pulling her backwards, who was dragging her up the stairs by the wrist.

'Let me go! Let me go! Mama – Mama – you must listen—'

On she was pulled, up to her bedroom, where her governess flung her onto the floor.

'You are a foul little liar,' she spat. 'If you had any idea how you torment her, how you sicken her—'

'He is stuck in the ice!' Verity cried. Her breath was coming in sharp gasps; she had to master herself. 'You must believe me. You must help send a ship—'

'And where is she or I to find this ship? Are we to sail it to Antarctica ourselves, and find ourselves stuck, too?' Her governess took a step back. 'I have never seen your mother like this, in all the years she has been my dearest friend—'

'Friend?' Verity scoffed, pulling herself to her feet. 'You are her servant!'

The slap sent her sprawling across the room. Still she did not cry.

Her governess reached for the door. She cast one final look at Verity. 'It is little wonder that your father always leaves you.'

Verity fell back against the floorboards.

It was a thought that had lurked in the distant corners of her mind, that had eaten at her when the house was quiet and she was half-asleep. If she had been better, more exceptional, or even just more ordinary, her Papa would never have left.

※

19th July, 1890. The pack ice is shifting, carrying us further from Vahsel Bay, from the sight of land. I think of my wife and my daughter, and it sustains me, like a small lantern in the dark. In a month, the ice may melt and free us from this glacial prison. The men dig trenches around the ship. Mercury nuzzles me, her pups grown now, bearing the rounded bellies of brigadiers. There is hope, is there not? There is always hope, always a chance we will live.

※

That night, Verity sat in front of her doll's house, waiting for the strike of twelve. She felt like an ogre, a god, a demon. Here, she could hold sway over her own small world, however imperceptibly.

She thought of her mother's hand covering the governess's, how quickly it was withdrawn. *My dearest friend.* The way it had been spoken. *Jane.* The intimacy of first-name terms. When had such familiarity begun, when had the governess first sat at her father's place at breakfast, handling his cutlery, carving the bacon with his knife? *You will not find me as constant as Penelope.* A thousand small things adding up to this: a dark shape she could neither understand nor name, two figures in a doorway.

When midnight chimed, she gripped the governess doll. Her Papa had glued on her hair so carefully, scraping it into a little bun. Perhaps it was rabbit fur, or another small mammal he had skinned on his travels.

Verity raised her hand and smacked that tiny china head against the chequered hallway tiles. The crack made her flinch. A single shard of porcelain skittered across the floorboards. Verity placed the doll at the bottom of the little staircase and smiled.

ஒ

At first, the pain in Verity's head was so sharp that she couldn't remember what she had done. It was the same *stab-stab-stab* she'd felt on the day she'd bruised her cheek.

The recollection was slow, glugging, like floating to the surface of the water.

Anna did not come that morning. Nobody came. Verity sat in her window seat and watched the doctor's coach draw up, him and his assistant taking the steps to the house two at a time. She tiptoed to the top of the stairs.

'Is she alive? I cannot lose her. I cannot.' Her mother's frantic voice.

'We are doing what we can, Mrs Edgars.'

'She must have slipped. She must have fallen down the stairs. Anna found her this morning. Oh, it's too awful.'

Verity felt a coiling in her chest, as though a serpent were slipping towards her heart, sinking its fangs into the meat of her.

୬

18th August, 1890. And so we begin another day with little hope. Great plates of ice grind and explode around us, sounding for all the world like the boom of artillery. We ate the last of the pigs yesterday. Last week, Purcel shot three penguins, and we were so famished we might have eaten them raw. Their skins fuel the galley stoves. Our stores of blubber are nearly at an end. The fact is this: we are marooned on an island made of pack. What the ice has eaten it will not easily disgorge. Soon our ship will be ground apart. It is a strange thing, to realise there is no hope of rescue, to think what a small speck you are in the world. Nobody knows where we are. If only a ship might come, ploughing across the horizon. A distant mast, how we would race across the pack and greet it.

I am without Mercury, a loss I feel as strongly as the grief for any human I have known. We did not think Paulson would command it, but perhaps it takes strength to issue an order like it. This morning, in a break between snow flurries, he instructed four teams of dogs to be shot, twenty-eight in total. We could no longer keep feeding them; their food store would be allotted to the men instead.

I gave Mercury a last meal of blubber and led her outside. I am glad, at least, that the task did not fall to me. There are men

I would sooner have shot than those dogs. We all flinched with each crack of the rifle, the whine and howl of the dogs awaiting their turn. When it fell silent, I stared at the ground, my vision blurred.

And then Smithson turned to me. 'Lucky bastards,' he said, as the snow beat down on us and the endless, endless ice stretched out. 'Lucky bastards, all of them.'

༄

For months, the governess lay insensible in Verity's mother's bed, her head bandaged. Every day, Verity's mother spooned soups and stews between her lips. The season passed without a single visitor. Anna ferried away the dirty sheets, the stink of shit filling the hallways.

On the rare occasions her mother left the house, Verity would let herself into the bedroom. There she would sit, watching the spasms of the woman's eyelids, the drool running from the edge of her lips. The veins on her hands were furrowed, like small blue worms.

Verity could not look at her. The snake in her heart twisted, coiled itself tighter.

༄

5th November, 1890. We must face it with fortitude. The chances are, we will die on this ship. Many men are gravely ill. Our ship is raked by squalls and storms. We are down to our last bricks of lard, oatmeal and sugar, rations which were intended for our trek across the pole. There are men who say we ought to have eaten the dogs.

What does it mean to die? To admit I will never balance my daughter on my shoulders once more, and witness her delight as she selects the ripest plums? Oh, what I would give to see her for one more evening, to embrace my wife for the final time. To never set foot on a wretched ship again. Rather, to pack myself into Verity's little doll's house, with the curtains drawn tight, and the fire in the grate. What a gift life is, and how cheaply I have held it.

The doctor had visited. The governess's condition had worsened; there was no hope for her. He expected that she would die in the night.

Verity did not leave her bedroom all afternoon. Her days had grown grey, as cold as gruel. The whole house seemed stultified, servants drifting from room to room, her mother's sobs seeping out from under her bedroom door.

The clock ticked. Nine o'clock chimed. Ten. Eleven. Verity had begun to dread midnight, and when the twelfth hour rang in the hall, she lay in bed for a full five minutes. What if she went to the journal and found it blank? But what if, too, she missed the last entry her Papa ever wrote, his last cry to the world?

Slowly, she inched her way across the floor, her candle gripped in her hand. When she opened the doll's house door, nothing seemed out of place. There was her governess with her cracked china head; there was the journal in her Papa's study. She bit hard on her lip, opened the book. There were words there, new words!

A small hope bloomed in her heart. For now, the world still contained her Papa; his heart still beat in this life. She snatched the map from the wall, studied it. The Antarctic Peninsula was the size of her finger. If only she could pluck him out of the ice, lift his ship as easily as an ant. Verity rubbed the ship with her finger.

She leaned closer. She could have sworn she saw the mast flickering. Could it have been the candlelight, or her tired eyes playing tricks?

Her eyes narrowed. Her finger pinched the mast, tried to drag it. A pain crackled through her and she almost cried out. But sure enough, the mast flinched again, the ship shifting incrementally. Just a fraction, but wasn't that something? She pressed and pressed the ship, but she could do no more. It would loosen no further.

He must live. He must.

She was about to shut the house when she saw the broken governess doll. She ground her eyes with her fists.

What a gift life is, and how cheaply I have held it.

Soon the clock would strike. She had to be quick, but her limbs felt so heavy. The honey sandwiches which Anna had brought her for dinner were still untouched by the door. Verity dipped her finger into the sticky honey and dabbed it around the jagged edges of the doll's skull, pressing the missing shard into place. Tenderly, she smoothed that grey hair over the join.

Little sooner had she placed the doll in the house than sleep dragged her under. She lay in front of her house, her head resting on the cold floorboards, her arms splayed in front of her as though in hopeless prayer.

☙

The word echoed.

Miracle.

Miracle —

'What did you say?'

Her head throbbed, a dryness in her mouth. She could only catch the vague shapes of things, like peering through grimed glass. Anna, bringing her pottage in bed, smiling.

'Don't you sicken just as your governess recovers. It's a miracle, the doctor's saying. A miracle.'

The pap was sweet and hurt her teeth.

'Your Mama found her in the sitting room, picking out a book to read. Walking and talking and entirely herself! Can you give credence to it?'

Verity sat up a little. Her head; she let out a moan. Pain flinched in time with her heart. It grew sharper and sharper, a spiked egg pressing into the back of her skull.

'What is the time, Anna?' she whispered.

'Eleven o'clock, Miss. You were sleeping so deeply there was no waking you.'

She only had to endure the slow ebb of thirteen more hours. What if she had accidentally shattered the ship, ground it against the ice? What if it had been nothing more than an illusion?

Her Mama came and fussed around her; her governess even knocked on her door and thanked her for the solicitude she was told Verity paid her during her convalescence; and still time dragged its heels.

At last, midnight came, and when Verity read the journal, her relief was only fleeting. This was just the beginning.

It was the map that preoccupied her, the map that she gripped in her fingers so tightly she might have torn it. She sat before her house, her limbs convulsing, her eyes bulging. She did not blink. The noise that filled the room was not the grinding of ice, but of teeth, her lips flared in a frightful gurn, her fingers pushing, pushing, pushing.

7th November, 1890. I can hardly explain it. I scarcely dare write it for fear I am delirious. I will tell it only as I understand it; I will strip it clean of hope, of fearful anticipation. In the middle of the night, I was woken by a ferocious thundering, as though the very fabric of the world were being rent in two. In moments I was out of my cabin, fearing the worst. We would be crushed; we would be buried alive. Stay below deck! Paulson raged, holding us all back. And then we saw it. Great chunks of ice cascading around us, taking bites from the deck. Each shard glittered in the moonlight,

ground off the great bergs that glowed, blue, around us. Where did this come from? The ice holds many secrets and yet there was no storm, not even a puff of wind. When the sound passed, we dared to climb on deck, to pick our way through the great hillocks and mounds of ice. The ship swayed, tilted.

She is freed!

It was Paulson who said it first, quietly, then with more joy. A great cheer went round, but I know what it is to hope and to have it dashed. A small image crossed my mind then, I could not help it – these hands lifting my daughter to seize a ripe plum, just out of reach.

But that was not all. A small channel of water gleamed beyond us, as though it had been carved from the ice just for us. Without a moment's pause, we angled our ship down it, heaving on the ropes, the wind filling the sails. We dropped anchor before we reached the channel's end, to avoid the ice surrounding us once more.

So why, when this is all so good, do I feel myself hounded by fear, with a sense that the universe is a place of such perfect balance, that somehow we must have tipped the scales elsewhere?

Besides, this means nothing, I tell myself. It means nothing. There are hundreds of miles yet to pass through. Have a hold on yourself, Alfred. You are far from saved.

༄

She would not stop until she had freed the ship, until she knew it was safely out of the ice. Weeks passed and Verity did not rise from bed until midnight. Every ounce of strength was reserved for when the clock struck twelve.

There were days when she couldn't move it far, when a black stillness descended on her, when her skull felt as fractured as the doll's had been. But it was her Papa's account that spurred her on. His journal brimmed with optimism, with thanks to God, with avowals of love for his wife and daughter, with incredulity that his life was saved.

On the first day of my return, Verity and I will take a boat on the river and row all the way to Kew Gardens –

She did not care that the doctor was summoned, that pain was such a constant she moaned and thrashed and tore at her hair.

A different doctor was summoned, this time from Mayfair.

All that mattered was the tolling of the clock, those twelve clear chimes.

The doctor's words sounded distant, unmoored from her. *I fear she will die.*

She expected to be afraid, but it was triumph that filled her. Her Papa would soon be freed. Nothing else mattered. Just Verity sitting in front of her house, the clock striking twelve, the tiny map creasing under the strain of her fingers, a bright fire raging in her eyes.

16th June, 1891. Never did I think I should be glad to see the harbour of South Georgia once more! I walk about in a state of

airlessness, each ring of my boots on the cobbles a joy so extreme I can find no words to express it. Even the smell of dead whale is as sweet to me as nectar. I read that back and laughed; what do I think I am, a tuppenny Byron? I think my relief has addled my wits. When we docked last night, many of the men grew outrageously, uproariously drunk, and who can blame them? For myself, I wanted only a small booth in the corner of the inn, a mediocre sherry and some writing paper. I hope to beat my missive home; we are like a jostling hive of bees, desperate to be on the seas again, to see the shores of England once more. As I sit here, I feel that hand at my throat, a curious certainty that I was destined to die, but cheated death in some way. I lift my hand against the lamplight to check my shadow still falls against the wall. I dip my finger in wax, and there it is, clear: the dimple of my fingerprints.

༄

'She mutters such things.' Her mother's voice was a whisper. She must have thought Verity was asleep. Verity kept her eyes shut, her hand limp against her chest.

'What things?' the governess asked.

'About – about his ship. She seems to think –' Her mother gave a brief, derisive laugh, as though she was already contradicting its possibility. 'That – that she can rescue Alfred's ship. That she has – oh it's too absurd.'

The governess was silent. A blackbird trilled, far away.

'I came up here a week ago. I heard a sound. It was midnight. And – and she did not hear me at the door. I saw her before the house. The doll's house, I mean. Her whole body was rigid. She was muttering strange things about – about harbours of blood and pack ice and shot dogs and – oh it's too ghastly! Even when I came to her to touch her, to hasten her to bed, she did not notice me. There was a blankness to her. A – a *possession*.'

Verity did not move. She kept her fingers very still, very flat.

'No matter how ill she has seemed by day, every night since I have heard the creak of the boards at midnight. But I have not dared to come up. I cannot bear to see her like that. It – it frightens me.' Verity's mother seemed to recall herself, to quieten her voice. She added, in such a low whisper Verity could scarcely catch it, 'I ask you, Jane, do you think she is mad?'

༄

Time slipped past; Verity could not say how many weeks or months. The only constant was pain. Her skull was red hot, branded. Some days she was able to open her eyes and see the way the wind puffed up the curtains. In her ears she heard a hissing, and she parsed it, her lips forming the sound. *Ice – ice – ice.*

A cold metal instrument was often pressed under her tongue, against her heart. Murmurings seemed as faint as the breeze.

Will she live?

Ice – ice – ice –

A woman crying, sharp as glass.

Ice –

Her hand grasped, kissed. A fire lit in the grate each day. Bitter things forced into her mouth.

She might have torched cities with the fire in her head; it was bright enough to set the whole world ablaze. She moaned and wailed, thrashed her head.

Hopeless, a man's voice said. *She grows weaker by the day. Her heart scarcely beats. It is a miracle she is not already dead. See how cold her hands are, her feet.*

She almost smiled. Opened her mouth to speak the word.

Ice. As though her whole body were encased in it, slowing to nothing, to the barest human impulses. To twelve, when for an hour, her pain eased, watching the now steady track of the ship across the ocean. He did not need her any more. He was saved.

Muffled words. *Her heart is failing.*

The night slipped away. New mornings arrived, grey, muted, each as worn as the one before.

He may not arrive in time.

Who? she wanted to ask. In time for what? But her mind drifted away, a slowing within her.

༼

26th February, 1892. Paulson came to me in my cabin. Unease was writ on his face, and at first I feared there was some great ill about to befall us. A mutiny, an approaching storm, a problem with the masts. He settled himself at my escritoire. Alfred, he said. I cannot understand it. It is scarcely possible. Such a phenomenon is not credible, by the bounds of science. The ice broke only for us. A channel opened before us. The floes seemed to melt away.

Like Moses, I said with a laugh. We are blessed.

Well. He drew his hands over his chin. It is not so unlike it. How could it have happened? As a man of science, not religion, I find myself baffled. It feels almost – he paused – malevolent.

Malevolent? I cried. It is the contrary! Question nothing, my good sir, be glad only that within a week we will be holding our wives and children once more. Within a week, sir! I repeated, and his face broke into a smile.

Yes, Alfred, he said. You are right.

But when he left, that word stuck like a thorn. Malevolent. An unease has begun chipping away at me, a feeling of things out of their natural order. It is a feeling I have done my best to deny. What spirit can be working on our behalf, what could possibly force entire bergs to break apart? I cannot square it. I cannot tie these threads together.

All is well, I tell myself. All is well.

୭

Quick footsteps on the stairs, a voice crying out, 'My best girl!'

A weight was pressing down on her chest, stopping her breath.

Papa – Papa –

She should greet him. She should throw her arms around him, have him waltz her around the room as he always did on his return, until they were both so giddy they toppled to the floor, laughing.

'What's wrong with her? What's happened? Verity? Her skin is so grey – her eyes – they are blank and – what has happened? She is a skeleton—'

Her Papa's panic, filling the room. She could not breathe.

'What's happened? What's wrong?'

Her mother's voice. 'Oh, Alfred. You're just in time.'

He was home; that was all she'd wanted. She felt a slackening within her.

The ice – the little house – I did it – Papa –

The strength it took her to say the words, for her lips to obey her.

'What's she saying?' her mother asked. 'Did you hear her?'

A cold quiet seemed to descend on the room, like the stillness on a grey day before the heavens opened. And then, all was flurry, movement. There was a splintering of wood, a crash.

'Alfred! What are you doing? Stop! This is madness!'

Verity tossed her head from side to side.

'No,' she cried. 'No, Papa, not the house, not—'

She opened her eyes, saw her Papa hunched over the fire, feeding in great chunks of wood. Hungry flames licked up the roof, the walls, a small lacquered cabinet. All gone, turned to ash. She half-expected to see her own skin charred to the bone.

'No,' she wept, but he did not seem to hear her.

When Verity woke, the pain was gone. Sunshine gleamed through the curtains. Her mother was reading a book in the armchair beside her.

There was a space next to her chest of drawers where her doll's house had once sat. The fire, her Papa's fury; it all came back to her.

'Mama,' she said, and her mother glanced up. Her eyes were red and swollen. 'Might you send in Papa, when he wakes? I suppose he is terribly tired after his voyage.'

'Verity, darling.' Her mother took her hand.

'I feel well, Mama. I think I shall rise. Papa and I might hire a boat. He said we would row it all the way to Kew.'

Her mother shook her head.

'What is it?' Verity asked brightly. 'Whatever is the matter? I'm better, aren't I? I shall live. You needn't cry any more, Mama.'

'Oh, Verity.' Her mother was holding a letter in her hands. Her voice cracked. 'The expedition was hopeless.' She dabbed at her eyes, fresh tears running down her cheeks. 'Everybody perished.'

THE SECOND WITNESS

Laura Shepherd-Robinson

J onathan Barnard opened his eyes with a start. Shadows pressed in around him, and seemed to constrict his racing heart. For a moment, he fancied he was tucked up in his own bed in Chorleywood. But as the fog of sleep receded, and he made out the heavy black shape of his travelling trunk in a corner of the room, it all came back to him. Hampstead. The draughty old mansion. His thwarted investigation. His failures danced around him like little black sprites.

Then he heard it. *Knock, knock, knock.* Coming from the room next door. The elusive charlatan was at it again – and in the middle of the damn night! Pretending to be the ghost of Lady Marsham! Rising from his bed, his legs becoming entangled in his nightshirt in his haste, he crossed the room and opened the door as quietly as he could. He took a few swift strides along the hall, and threw open the door to Lady Marsham's bedroom.

Half-blinded by the light of a candelabrum, he drew up short at the sight of a dark-haired woman in a blue silk dress knocking on the wall. She had her back to him, but he could see that she was not slender enough to be Miss Marsham, and the lady's-maid, Frances, had blonde hair. Yet being a rational man, Barnard did not for one moment contemplate the possibility that this woman lacked corporeal form – that she was the ghost of Lady Marsham, who had passed from this earthly realm three weeks ago, and was commonly believed to be haunting this room.

'What is the meaning of this?' he demanded. 'Explain yourself, madam.'

The candles flickered in the draught as she turned. 'You must be Mr Barnard.' The lady studied him rather intently. 'My name is Miss Amelia Hayes. Like you, I am a guest in this house. I arrived yesterday afternoon from Stoke Newington.'

Barnard frowned. He didn't remember a carriage arriving. And yet sometimes he got lost in his work, and he'd tried very hard to shut out the sounds of all the unwanted visitors who called daily at the house. Yet this one, it seemed, was invited. Barnard wondered why no one had seen fit to introduce them.

'What were you doing?' he said, rather tersely. 'I saw you knocking upon that wall.' She couldn't possibly be the one responsible for the past three weeks of chicanery, given she'd only been in the house half a day – but her behaviour was suspicious, decidedly so.

'I was trying to summon the ghost,' she said brightly. 'This is the best time to do it. The witching hour.' She rapped again on the panelling. *Knock, knock, knock.*

'Balderdash.' Barnard couldn't help himself. They made his blood boil, all these credulous fools, eager to encounter the ghost of Lady Marsham. Men and women in the grip of superstition, who refused to embrace the new ways of thinking. They might as well be living in the Dark Ages, rather than the 1780s.

'You dispute the significance of the witching hour?' Miss Hayes said. 'I assure you that my studies confirm that ghosts most commonly manifest at this time.'

Her studies? Barnard restrained a sigh of frustration. 'It is the existence of ghosts that I dispute. My own studies—' He broke off. 'Hayes? Amelia?'

She smiled broadly. 'It has all been rather a tilt, has it not? A broken lance here and there, but no mortal wounds inflicted. I have rather enjoyed our correspondence, sir.'

Barnard stared at her. For over three years now, he had been locked in spirited combat on the letters pages of the *Public Advertiser* with one A. A. Hayes of Stoke Newington, whom he'd imagined to be a middle-aged gentleman much like himself. Hayes had not only cited the usual tripe about unhappy souls wrenched from the body, he had claimed that ghosts could be summoned at will, and might even be induced to improve the sum of human knowledge. Their correspondence had attracted supporters on both sides, culminating in Barnard publishing his views in a pamphlet entitled *An Historical Essay Concerning Ghosts*, to which Hayes had responded with *A Vindication of the Possibility and Reality of Spirits*. It seemed inconceivable to him that his adversary could be this slip of a girl – surely not more than twenty-five – with her pale, rather plain face, and large green eyes that sparkled with amusement.

Trying to muster a little dignity, despite his nightshirt and hairy legs, he bowed stiffly. 'Can I ask why you are here in Hampstead, Miss Hayes?' Though he feared he already knew.

'To investigate this ghost,' she said. 'To investigate this murder. If indeed that is what it is.'

Why on earth would Sir Robert have invited her here? It made no sense. 'An investigation is already in hand,' he told her, rather coldly. 'I have been asked by Sir Robert to prove this ghost a fraud.'

'So I hear,' she said. 'Only you don't seem to have made very much progress. It has been suggested that I might lend a new perspective.'

The worst part was that it was true. Barnard was no nearer to solving the mystery than he had been ten days earlier when he'd arrived in Hampstead, full of confidence that it would all be done and dusted by the end of the week. He had come by carriage, in a hired vehicle sent by the master of the house, Sir Robert Marsham, a newly widowed baronet of the fourth generation. As Barnard had alighted from the carriage on Holly Bush Hill, the small crowd gathered around the gates of the old red-brick mansion had peered at him feverishly.

'Are you here to see the ghost of Lady Marsham, sir?' one fellow called out to him, as he struggled with the latch of the gate. 'They say her husband poisoned her. Better watch your step.'

A gravel path led through a frost-rimed garden to the front door. Rooks protested his approach from the skeletal branches of specimen trees. As Barnard neared the pillared portico, the door opened, and a young gentleman in a black frockcoat emerged. The pale winter sun on his head of golden curls made him shine with an otherworldly aura. Barnard gazed at the man transfixed, his sleek profile and ease of movement recalling a time in his life before the grey and the aches and the torpor of spirit that had since settled upon his soul. His dearest friend, David, had once possessed such beauty – and towards the end of his life, the same coldness of gaze.

'You are Barnard, I suppose,' the young man said, as they drew level, and the crisp air filled with his musky scent. 'The man my stepfather hopes will make all this go away.'

Barnard bowed. 'You have the advantage of me, sir.'

'Sebastian Coke,' the young man said, not troubling to return the bow. 'Lady Marsham was my mother.'

'My condolences,' Barnard said sincerely. 'You don't want it to? All go away, I mean.'

'I want the truth,' Coke said. 'If there was more to my mother's death than meets the eye, then I want to know it. I won't stand by and watch you collude in hushing it up.'

He brushed past Barnard rather roughly, forcing him to step aside onto the grass. A woman was watching them from the door. About twenty years of age, her fair hair was pinned without adornment, no stones or frills or lace embellishing her black dress. The lady's-maid, Barnard guessed. Sir Robert had said in his letters that all of the other servants had fled the house when the knocking began.

'My name is Barnard,' he told her, as he reached the portico.

She dipped a curtsey. 'If you'll come this way, sir.'

The oak-panelled hall was deathly quiet, each creak of his step upon the floorboards a statement of intrusion. The maid watched him surreptitiously, as he divested himself of his overcoat, hat and gloves. They waited a minute for the coachman and guard to carry his trunk up from the carriage, and then he followed the maid along a corridor hung with Dutch oils. A door opened a crack as they passed, and Barnard caught a glimpse of another young woman peering out at them. Gaunt cheeks, unpinned dark hair, one rather wild, dark eye meeting his gaze, before the door closed again, just as abruptly.

They continued along the corridor, past a dining room and a parlour, until the maid halted and knocked at another door. 'Enter,' a commanding baritone said.

Barnard walked into a room lined with books. The maid announced his name, and Sir Robert rose from behind his desk, extending a hand in greeting. 'I am glad to see you, sir. Very glad.'

About fifty years of age, Sir Robert still possessed a broad, athletic build. A Roman nose, thick dark brows, and a purple house-robe combined to put Barnard in mind of a painting of Mark Antony that he'd once viewed at the Royal Academy. Marsham had been an army officer, he recalled, and had served under Wolfe at Quebec. Vigorous, martial men normally made him painfully aware of his own physical inadequacies, but Marsham's bloodshot eyes and the dampness of his palm were a testament to the baronet's desperation.

Marsham dismissed the maid and offered Barnard brandy from his decanter. 'This is a bad business, sir. A very bad business,' he said, once they were settled in a pair of wing chairs before his fire. 'When I walk into the village, my neighbours cross the street to avoid me. Rotten eggs have been thrown at my carriage. They say I am a murderer. That I killed Eliza. Even the magistrate has started to look at me askance.'

Barnard's gaze drifted to a large oil over the fireplace. Sir Robert and Lady Marsham, hands joined, in a portrait clearly painted to celebrate their marriage. That happy event, only two months earlier, had been swiftly superseded by tragedy, when Lady Marsham had succumbed to a violent griping of the guts, said to have been caused by an adulterated pickle. Artists were known to flatter their subjects, and this one had chosen to omit what the newspapers referred to as Lady Marsham's 'great tragedy': the smallpox scars that had turned a celebrated beauty into an object of pity. Her wide blue eyes gazed up at her husband adoringly, one finger resting upon a tortoiseshell box embellished with silverwork, presumably meant to symbolise her wealth. That fortune, left to Lady Marsham by her first husband, an East India man, had figured large in all the newspaper accounts of the ghost. The journalists had also made veiled allusions to the tavern rumours that Sir Robert had a mistress he loved – that he'd married Eliza Coke for her money and then done away with her.

'The knocking began only three days after Eliza died,' Sir Robert said. 'It is heard only in her room, at all hours of the day, and I have been unable to ascertain any natural cause of it. I am a rational man, sir, but I find myself wondering if it might indeed be Eliza's ghost. Yet the physician who examined her had no suspicions about the cause of her death – and so I cannot understand why she would be haunting us.'

'Whoever is responsible for the knocking,' Barnard said emphatically, 'I am quite certain that it is not your dead wife.'

His conviction seemed to buoy Marsham's spirits. 'Then who?' he cried. 'Frances was my wife's maid for over five years. I cannot think she would make a mockery of her memory like this. Sebastian, my stepson, was close to his mother and mourns her deeply. The idea of him playing such a cruel trick is simply unthinkable. As for my daughter, Becky, she is just fifteen years old.'

In Barnard's experience, youth did not preclude a malevolent mind. 'There is nobody else it could be?'

Marsham shook his head. 'Many have witnessed the knocking. The magistrate, the rector, several friends and neighbours too. But since the rumours of murder began, I have admitted few visitors. Most of the time when the knocking is heard, we are alone in the house.'

Three suspects then. At least that would keep things simple. 'I will need to interview them all,' he said, 'and I will also need to examine the room in question. Do not look so distraught, sir. I will soon find the person responsible and prove your innocence in this matter.'

Such misplaced complacency! Over the course of the past ten days, Barnard had interviewed and he had examined. He had consulted his books, and written letters to his fellows in the business of disproving ghosts. He had witnessed the knocking himself, on half a dozen occasions, and yet he'd been left just as baffled as Sir Robert. As the days had passed without progress, the baronet's expression had grown darker – until Barnard's humiliation, three days ago, in an incident he could hardly bear to think about without wincing. And now here was Miss Hayes, with her sparkling eyes and her foolish opinions, come to make hay out of Sir Robert's misery and his own failure. Well, he wouldn't stand for it!

'I cannot think Sir Robert will want you in this house – not once he knows what you are about,' he addressed her sternly.

'Sir Robert understands entirely what I am about,' Miss Hayes replied crisply. 'I cannot say he is happy to have me here, but I was invited by the Hampstead magistrate, Mr Fry. He was rather surprised by my appearance too, but my credentials are impeccable, and he soon reconciled himself to my sex. Ghost or no ghost, he wants to get to the bottom of this matter. In short, sir, he would like us to work together.'

Which was just about the worst idea that Barnard had ever heard.

Having taken himself back to bed in a temper, Barnard slept fitfully that night. The following morning, when he emerged, bleary-eyed, from his room, he heard voices in the hall below. Sir Robert and his strange, wild-eyed daughter, dressed in fur-lined cloaks, presumably heading into the village. Barnard thought about going down and having words with the baronet about Miss Hayes, but if it was true that she had been invited here at the magistrate's behest, then Sir Robert was just as powerless in this matter as he was himself.

More voices carried to him from Lady Marsham's bedroom. The door stood ajar and Barnard pushed it open with a creak. Miss Hayes greeted him with a smile, but Frances, the lady's-maid, who was sitting opposite her at the tea table, flinched and looked away. The last time he had spoken to the girl, Barnard had stepped up his interrogation, convinced that her nerves betrayed some secret she wasn't telling. But Frances had stuck to her story resolutely, insisting that she knew nothing of any fraud, and he had only succeeded in making her cry. She had avoided him ever since, scurrying away whenever he encountered her in the hall.

There being no other chair available, Barnard took up a position next to the window, his arms folded, determined not to let Miss Hayes use this fraud to promote her foolish theories.

'You were the first to hear the knocking, I believe?' she addressed the maid.

Frances nodded, biting her lip. 'Three days after Lady Marsham died. I was stripping the bed when I heard it.' She rose and went over to the four-poster. The blue-and-white toile de Jouy curtains had been tied back, and she pointed to a spot on the oak panelling just above the headboard. 'It was coming from here. At first, I assumed it must be someone in the guest room next door. Only when I went to see, there was nobody there.' She gave a little shiver and returned to her seat.

'What happened then?'

'The knocking had unnerved me, and so I fetched Sir Robert. Soon it started up again.' Frances tapped an irregular rhythm with her nails on the tabletop. 'It is a tune from an opera. Lady Marsham used to hum it sometimes when she was embroidering – and sometimes she'd tap along with her thimble. "Lady Marsham," I cried out. "Is that you?" Well, Sir Robert turned on me then. Very red in the face, he was – and he ordered me out. He said it must have been a bird stuck up in the chimney, though it plainly wasn't that. Then the following day, Bess, our housemaid, she heard the knocking when she was dusting. She summoned Master Sebastian, who heard it too. The other servants all left not long after that, but I stayed on account of the family.'

Miss Hayes inclined her head. 'Your loyalty is commendable.'

Barnard had heard this tale three times now, and his attention had wandered to a scene outside the window. An alleyway ran behind the garden wall and Sebastian Coke,

Sir Robert's fair-haired stepson, was walking along it in the company of two shabbily dressed men. Coke halted to say a few words, his face contorted with what looked like rage. Remembering his humiliation at the hands of the younger man a few nights earlier, Barnard's fists clenched. Despite the evidence pointing to Coke's innocence, he'd been unable to entirely shed his suspicions of the man, and he wondered if this interaction might pertain to motive. The trio moved off again, heading around the corner of the house, where he lost sight of them. Yet Barnard's own room had an aspect on that side, and so he headed for the door. In his haste, as he passed, he dislodged a sheaf of Miss Hayes's papers from a side table, which made the maid jump and elicited a slight frown of enquiry from Miss Hayes.

When he reached the window next door, he saw that the trio had drawn to a halt again. One of the shabby men gripped Coke by the collar and slammed him up against the wall. A heated discussion ensued, Coke still pinioned to the wall, until his interlocutors released him and walked off down the alley. Coke waited a few moments, apparently collecting himself, before heading towards the main entrance of the house on Holly Bush Hill.

As Barnard was returning to Lady Marsham's bedroom, Coke came through the front door. Barnard lingered a moment to watch at the top of the stairs. The young man leaned against the door, taking a silver flask from his coat pocket, from which he drank a long pull. Barnard's frisson of cruel pleasure at his adversary's evident distress was swiftly superseded as a most peculiar sensation crept over him. It raised goosebumps on his flesh, and made his head spin. He heard a faint exhalation of breath behind him, and he wheeled around. The hall was empty. His heart pounded unaccountably. Was he getting a fever? Gad, he couldn't afford to be ill.

Having mopped his brow with his handkerchief, and taken a moment to catch his breath, Barnard returned to Lady Marsham's bedroom. Frances appeared, once again, to be fighting back tears.

'Lady Marsham complained of a pain in her stomach,' she was saying. 'Another hour and she was vomiting and voiding her bowels like water. Her pulse was weak and her brow hot. I put her to bed and Sir Robert sent for the physician. After the doctor examined her, he said that her illness was probably caused by copper adulteration. Lady Marsham had consumed a green pickle at supper, you see, the day before her symptoms began. The doctor did his best, but she died not twelve hours later.' The girl dabbed at her eyes with a scrap of lace.

'You were close to Lady Marsham?' Miss Hayes asked.

'I never had anything but kindness from her lips. I told Mr Barnard that.' She raised her chin defiantly.

And so she had. Again and again. Cited it as proof that she could never have done anything so wicked as inventing this ghost.

'Thank you, Frances,' Miss Hayes said. 'That will be all for the time being.'

Once the girl had gone, Barnard knelt to collect up the papers that he had knocked to the floor.

'Frances seemed terrified out of her wits,' Miss Hayes said. 'Jumping at shadows.'

Barnard hardly heard her, staring at the papers in his hand with a mounting sense of outrage. This was his report, the one that he'd given to Sir Robert four days ago, chronicling his investigation to date. A plan of the house. Interview notes. Records of all the dates and times that the knocking had been heard, listing those who had been present on each occasion. Background on similar cases, such as the Cock Lane Ghost, which had subsequently been proven to be elaborate frauds.

'Where did you get this?' he cried, waving the papers.

'From the magistrate,' Miss Hayes replied. 'He ordered Sir Robert to hand it over.'

Consumed with indignation that the baronet hadn't troubled to tell him any of this, Barnard considered walking away. Leaving Sir Robert to face the magistrate and the hostile crowds and the newspapers alone. And yet his sense of professional pride would not permit it.

'I think, in his heart, that Sir Robert believes in the ghost,' Miss Hayes said. 'Naturally, he maintains his innocence in the matter of his wife's death. But if Lady Marsham is haunting this room, then there must be a reason for it.'

'Stuff and nonsense,' Barnard said crossly. 'There isn't even any evidence that she was murdered. The physician still maintains that a bad pickle is the most likely explanation.'

'Yet he has a motive for defending his own diagnosis.' Miss Hayes turned a few pages of her notebook. 'I am told that several poisons can produce symptoms similar to Lady Marsham's. Arsenic for one. It is regrettable that the cook threw away the contents of the jar of pickles, or an apothecary might have been able to give us a definitive answer.' She studied his face. 'What do you make of Frances? She says that you questioned her rather vigorously.'

Barnard bristled at the implied criticism. 'Sir Robert tells me that she was devoted to her mistress, and I have no reason to doubt it. Yet she is twitchy and ill at ease – as you yourself remarked. It made me wonder if she was keeping something from me.'

'She is afraid of the ghost,' Miss Hayes said. 'Though that could be the product of a guilty conscience. How about the daughter? I have yet to speak to her alone.'

Another twitcher. And yet, by all accounts, that was simply Rebecca Marsham's manner. When Barnard had questioned her, she had professed herself fascinated by ghosts, apparently taking delight in her stepmother's supposed inability to rest in peace.

'She is frank to the point of peculiarity. I judged her to be not entirely right in her wits. That was also her stepmother's conclusion. I was told by the apothecary in the village that Lady Marsham was trying to convince Sir Robert to have her sent away for treatment at a madhouse.'

Miss Hayes raised her eyebrows. 'Now there's a motive for murder.'

Barnard considered. 'I am prepared to accept the possibility of foul play,' he said magnanimously. 'There was certainly no love lost between Rebecca and her stepmother. But she plainly adores her father, and if she was indeed responsible, I cannot see why she would have implicated him by inventing this ghost.'

'Unless the ghost is real, and Lady Marsham simply seeks justice.' Without giving him an opportunity to respond, she pressed on: 'Why did your principal suspicions fall upon Sebastian?'

Then she had heard about his humiliation. Barnard supposed that he shouldn't be surprised. 'He was hostile to my presence in the house from the very beginning. Sir Robert says he was close to his mother and his grief appears genuine. I struggle to believe that he would have killed her. But whether Lady Marsham was murdered or not, Coke had a better motive than anyone for implicating his stepfather in a capital crime.'

'You mean the money?'

Barnard nodded. 'Under the terms of his own father's will, Coke received two-thirds of his estate, with the remainder – five thousand pounds – bequeathed to his mother. That latter sum became Sir Robert's when he married her. But if Sir Robert hangs for his wife's murder, I was told by a lawyer of my acquaintance that it was highly likely the courts would settle that money upon Mr Coke.'

'Isn't he already a very rich man?'

'I'm not so sure. My correspondents say there are rumours

about town that Coke has already squandered his own inheritance at the hazard table. Perhaps much more.' Barnard told her about the scene he had just witnessed in the alley. 'If Coke owes money and is being threatened, then that's a powerful motive.'

'Desperation can certainly drive people to great extremes,' Miss Hayes agreed, with some feeling. 'What led you to accuse him?'

'I didn't. Not exactly.' Barnard felt blood rush to his cheeks, and he hastened to check his emotions with rationality. 'Normally, in a fraud like this, the evidence points to one person. A suspect who is conspicuous by their consistent presence at the scene of a supposed haunting. That was the case with the Cock Lane Ghost, where the girl responsible was found to be surreptitiously scratching on the wall with a wooden implement. A little distraction and legerdemain were all it took to convince half of London that the house was haunted. Alternatively, a "ghost" can sometimes be contrived by a person in an adjacent room or outside a window. I investigated one such incident where the rogue responsible took himself out on a roof to moan down a chimney. In these cases, the suspect is consistently absent from the scene. But neither was the situation here. No member of the household was consistently present, nor consistently absent when the knocking was heard. It made me think that the culprit might be utilising a combination of those two methods.'

If Miss Hayes had any views upon his reasoning, then she kept them to herself. 'Go on, sir.'

'Four days ago, shortly before I questioned Frances, I was in my room when I heard the knocking again. I hurried in here to find Coke hunched over his mother's bedside table. When he saw me, he slipped his hand into his pocket. I thought he might have been holding some sort of implement. The knocking has a metallic edge to it, as I'm sure others have told you.'

'Lady Marsham's thimble.'

Barnard rolled his eyes. 'I asked Coke to empty his pockets, but he refused. So I called for his stepfather. When Sir Robert came, he ordered his stepson to turn out his pockets, but all Coke had upon his person was an ivory locket.' He recalled the young man's flushed face, the tears of grief and rage in his eyes. His own embarrassment at being wrong-footed in front of Sir Robert. 'Coke said his father had given the locket to his mother when they were courting and that he'd merely wished to have it as a keepsake. As he was telling us this, we all heard it: more knocking. Coke had his hands out in front of him, and he was standing several feet from the wall. It appeared impossible that he could be responsible.'

Barnard broke off, remembering how Sir Robert had stared at his wife's bed with an expression of bewildered terror. 'Forgive me, lad.'

But Coke hadn't been in the mood for reconciliation. 'I shall do nothing of the kind,' he'd said. 'That you would listen to the accusations of this *person* confounds me.' He turned on Barnard, his handsome face a sneer. 'As for you, I have seen the way you watch me, sir, like a man obsessed.

Well, why don't you go play with the other Ganymedes down at Birdcage Walk. We have no truck with your sort and your perversions here in Hampstead.'

Shame flooded through Barnard at the mere memory of those words. Nothing would have induced him to repeat them in front of Miss Hayes. 'Sebastian was furious with me and with his stepfather,' he settled on saying. 'He said that up until now he had held his tongue, despite all of his misgivings. But after this effrontery, he was prepared to do so no longer. That he was convinced his mother was murdered, and that Sir Robert and I were trying to conceal that crime. Then he went off to see the magistrate – and his father blames me for it.'

Sir Robert had barely spoken to him since, and were it not for the baronet's desperation, Barnard sensed that he would have been dismissed from the house. Yet now, with the arrival of Miss Hayes, they'd both lost control of the situation.

She jotted a few notes down in her book. 'Did you never once stop to consider the possibility that the ghost might be genuine?'

For one brief moment, Barnard recalled that odd feeling that had just come over him on the landing. That powerful sensation that someone had been standing right behind him. His skin prickling again, he spoke harshly to discount it. 'Never.'

A little smile played about her lips. 'You were ever the sceptic, sir. But between your reason and my belief, I am convinced that we shall soon find the answers we seek.'

Her confidence, so reminiscent of his own when he'd arrived at the house, raised Barnard's hackles. 'And how exactly do you propose that we do that?'

Her smile broadened, revealing a row of crooked teeth. 'First, I think we should talk to the ghost. Lady Marsham appears to need a little more encouragement.'

৯

It was shortly before midnight, but the household was awake. The witching hour approached: one of those old superstitions that should be consigned to the midden of history, along with all the charlatans who propagated such ideas. Barnard's resentment towards Miss Hayes, who seemed to him to embody all of society's most foolish notions, was the more marked for the presence of the magistrate and the rector, neither of whom should have given this plan a moment of credence. Miss Hayes bustled about, lighting candles and positioning people around Lady Marsham's bed, everyone deferring to her authority.

Only the maid, Frances, had refused to join them. Sebastian Coke and the rector had tried to persuade her otherwise, on the grounds that her mistress's decision to first manifest in her presence made her far more likely to do so again. But she'd refused, her body shaking, her face perfectly white.

'I feel the ghost everywhere now,' she'd cried. 'In my mistress's bedroom most of all. I'll leave this house for good, before I will set foot in there at night.'

If it was all a performance, then the girl was a better actress than any Barnard had seen at the Theatre Royal. Of course, none of the family wished to be deprived of their only remaining servant, and in the end, Frances had consented to be locked in her attic bedroom, in order that there could be no question of her interfering with the summoning.

Miss Hayes exchanged a glance with the magistrate, a short, rather pompous gentleman named Gideon Fry. Some unspoken piece of communication seemed to pass between them, making Barnard worry that she had already won the magistrate round to her belief that the ghost was real. It made him think of his friend David, as he so often did in situations like these. How David had listened to all those charlatans who had told him they could communicate with his dead wife – for the right price. How he had ignored Barnard's appeals to reason, and how David's delusions had led to angry words about Barnard's motives. How the death of their friendship had presaged David's own death, in a backstreet lodging-house, penniless and alone.

'Come further in, if you please, Sir Robert,' Miss Hayes called, 'and close the door.'

The baronet glowered. 'I wish my objections to these proceedings to be registered most strongly. What qualification does this girl possess to order me around in my own house?'

The magistrate regarded him evenly. 'Many eminent gentlemen have testified to Miss Hayes's authority on the subject of ghosts. I am told that she is adept at summoning the spirits of the dead, and learning why their souls are unable to rest.'

Miss Hayes had spent most of that day putting her preparations in place. In the absence of the cook, she had baked Portugal cakes, apparently a great favourite of Lady Marsham's. The room had been sprayed with her perfume, and prized possessions laid out on the tea table: a miniature of a dead lapdog, her two wedding rings, and a volume of poetry she had treasured.

'It is important that Lady Marsham's spirit feels welcome in this place,' Miss Hayes said. 'She must sense no danger here, no rancour at her presence.'

The scent of the Portugal cakes mingled with the perfume and Sebastian Coke's musky scent, making Barnard feel rather sick. He wanted to support Sir Robert's objections, but he was afraid of drawing attention to himself. The last thing he wanted was Coke repeating his vile allegations in front of the magistrate. So he kept to his position by the window, in the shadows of the room, from where he could keep careful watch upon his suspects.

'How did you come to learn the art of summoning ghosts?' Rebecca Marsham asked Miss Hayes rather breathlessly. Someone, presumably Frances, had attempted to tame her abundant dark curls, securing them with a silver comb. Her dark eyes shone with a feverish intensity in the candlelight, so that in her white muslin gown she resembled an adept at a Grecian temple.

Miss Hayes spoke with a slight catch to her voice. 'I am

afraid it is rather a tragic tale. When I was eleven years old, my mother was waylaid and murdered walking home alone from the local village. There were no witnesses to the crime, and the culprit went unpunished. My father, in his devastation, became convinced that her spirit could not rest. At first I scorned the idea, but one night, during the witching hour, unable to sleep with the pain of my own grief, I saw her ghost from my bedroom window, outside on the lane, heading for the very place where her body was found.'

Barnard listened to this tale aghast, his heart going out to Miss Hayes. As for her father, he'd like to have taken a horsewhip to the man, for compounding his daughter's loss with this surfeit of nonsense.

'I said just now that there were no witnesses to the crime, but of course, that is never truly the case,' Miss Hayes went on. 'There is the murderer, for one, who can be accounted a witness, though his testimony is rarely forthcoming. But there is always a second witness too: the victim of the crime. I knew that my mother wished to tell us who had killed her – and yet I did not know how to elicit her testimony. Three years after her death, the magistrate arrested a man for killing a young girl in another village, and on the day of his hanging, he confessed to murdering four more women and girls, including my mother. I was haunted by the knowledge that if I'd known how to communicate with her, then I might have prevented those other deaths. Which was when I resolved to devote myself to the study of ghosts. I have since solved five murders through my methods.'

'But my wife was not murdered,' Sir Robert exclaimed. 'Nor do I believe that she haunts this room.'

'How can you say that?' the rector said. 'When we have all heard the knocking with our own ears?'

Barnard eyed him with contempt. A white-haired septuagenarian, he had, according to Sir Robert, been a malign influence from the start, the man who'd convinced the magistrate to take this whole business seriously.

'Mr Barnard's failure to prove the ghost a fraud should definitely give us pause for thought,' the magistrate said, making no effort to mince his words in Barnard's presence.

'His reputation has certainly taken a tumble,' Coke declared cheerfully.

'Sebastian,' his stepsister exclaimed, the only one who appeared to have a regard for Barnard's feelings.

Again, he wrestled with the urge to defend himself, but his memory of Sebastian's cruel tongue and his own shame confined him to silence.

'Enough,' the magistrate declared, with a frown. 'Let us see if Miss Hayes can provide us with better answers.'

'I concur.' Sebastian Coke took out his watch. 'Miss Hayes, it is time. The witching hour.'

She stepped forward with an air of ceremony and rapped her knuckles upon the panelling over the bed. In the hushed silence that followed, Barnard felt a waft of cool air on the back of his neck. Though his rational self knew that it must be a draught from the window, it felt so much like a person's breath that it occasioned him a prickle of unease despite himself.

Knock, knock, knock, knock, knock, knock... His head jerked up. That same metallic tap, that same rhythmic beat. Mozart, he had learned from Sebastian Coke: *The Marriage of Figaro* – which Lady Marsham had seen performed two years ago in Vienna.

Sebastian ran his hands through his golden hair. There was surely no physical way he could be responsible for the knocking. 'Is that you, Mother?' he cried.

Miss Hayes held up a hand. 'One knock for yes, Lady Marsham, two knocks for no.'

Knock.

Miss Hayes turned to face those assembled in the room. 'You will observe that the knocking appears to be coming from this point here on the wall, just above the bed. Mr Lansgrove,' she addressed the rector. 'Will you please step next door and confirm that the guest room is presently unoccupied?'

The rector reappeared a moment later. 'There's nobody there.'

Coke drew a breath and Rebecca Marsham clutched herself with what appeared to be excitement. 'Dear God,' Sir Robert murmured.

It must be the maid, Barnard thought, going back and forth between his suspects as he had during his entire time in that house. Yet he had stood in this very room, together with Frances, and witnessed the knocking in her company. Nor could he explain how she could be tapping on that wall, when she was locked away upstairs.

'Is there a reason why your soul cannot rest?' Miss Hayes said. 'Is there something you wish us to know?'

Knock.

'Ask her if she was murdered,' the magistrate said.

'Did you die a natural death?' Miss Hayes asked.

Knock, knock.

Rebecca gave a little cry. 'I knew it,' Coke muttered.

'I will recite the letters of the alphabet,' Miss Hayes declared. 'If you knock once when we come to a letter, then I shall write it down. That way you can tell us what we need to know. Do you consent?'

Knock.

'How did you die?' Miss Hayes went through the alphabet, all the way to the letter P, when there was a knock. Slowly, by means of this laborious method, a message took shape: P-O-I-S-O-N

Despite his lack of answers to the mysteries before him, Barnard remained firm in his conviction that he was witnessing an act of fraud. Yet it was plain from the tense faces around him that he was alone in this belief. Miss Hayes was still reciting the alphabet, though everybody else was watching Sir Robert.

I-P-O-I-N-T

'Ipoint?' Coke exclaimed. 'What's that? Latin?'

'I point,' the magistrate said. 'At whom? At the murderer?'

'Do you know who killed you?' Miss Hayes asked.

Knock.

'Will you tell us their name?'

M-A-R-S-H-A-M

'What the devil!' Sir Robert cried. 'This is preposterous.' All the colour had drained from his face.

'He is innocent,' his daughter cried. 'I know he is.'

Her stepbrother's fists were clenched. 'How could you, sir? How could you?'

The magistrate laid a restraining hand on his arm, though his gaze was hard as he contemplated Sir Robert.

'Is there anything more that you can tell us?' Miss Hayes asked.

Silence greeted her words and though she asked several more questions, no more knocking was heard. Eventually, the magistrate stepped forward to halt the proceedings.

'Thank you, Miss Hayes,' he said. 'I see that I was right to permit you to come. Sir Robert, I think we'd better resume our discussion downstairs.'

'You're not going to arrest him?' Coke cried, his face darkening.

'Silence.' The magistrate's uncertain face belied the authority of that word. Barnard could see he was convinced of Sir Robert's guilt, but he would need more than the testimony of a ghost to secure a conviction in court. Presumably his next step would be to try to elicit a confession.

As her father and the magistrate left the room, Miss Marsham burst into tears. The rector drew her into the hall to comfort her.

'I point,' Miss Hayes murmured. 'What did she mean by that?'

Barnard thought about holding his tongue, not wanting to lend credence to this piece of theatre. Yet someone would surely work it out sooner or later. 'Isn't it obvious?' he said, with a sigh. 'The marriage portrait.'

Miss Hayes turned, her eyes widening with comprehension. 'Yes, of course. Sir Robert showed it to me yesterday.'

'What was that?' Coke demanded.

But Miss Hayes was already striding to the door. Barnard followed hard on her heels, down the stairs to the hall. They caught up with Sir Robert and the magistrate, as they were entering the former's study.

'Didn't I make it plain?' the magistrate said. 'I wish to speak to Sir Robert alone.'

But Miss Hayes slipped past him to gaze up at the portrait. 'I point,' she announced, pointing herself at Lady Marsham's extended index finger. 'Where is that tortoiseshell casket, Sir Robert?'

Sebastian Coke, who had followed them into the room, answered for him. 'Right there on that shelf,' he said.

The magistrate retrieved the casket, and carried it to the desk. Barnard watched, with a despairing sense of inevitability, as the magistrate lifted the lid and took out a small glass bottle. He held it up so that they could all read the label: ARSENIC.

'I've never seen that before in my life,' Sir Robert exclaimed. 'Someone else must have put it there.'

Coke addressed the magistrate. 'You said that you required evidence, sir.'

'Indeed I did.' The magistrate nodded grimly. 'Sir Robert, I am arresting you for the murder of your wife.'

༄

Barnard stood at the top of the stairs, watching Sebastian Coke pacing the hall below. He was plainly trying to listen to his stepfather's conversation with the magistrate in the drawing room. The rector had gone to fetch Hampstead's lone constable, the magistrate unwilling to escort the arrested man to the watchhouse by himself. Occasionally, Sir Robert would exclaim loudly, but indistinctly. Miss Marsham was weeping in one of the other rooms, and Miss Hayes had gone upstairs to release the maid from her confinement in order that she might attend to her.

Still unable to shed his suspicions of Coke, Barnard was suddenly struck by a moment of clarity. Astonished that he hadn't thought of this theory before, he was trying to follow the new chain of logic, when he was overcome again by that strange, head-spinning feeling of vertigo. Again, he felt a cool breath on the back of his neck, and he whirled around. 'Who's there?'

The hall was empty, and he stared into the shadows, his heart beating wildly.

Hearing footsteps on the stairs that led down from the attic, not wanting Miss Hayes or Frances to see him in this disordered condition, Barnard hurried into Lady Marsham's bedroom. He was just tired, he told himself, trying to breathe more evenly. Imagining things. Hadn't he been woken in the middle of the night? He was hungry too, couldn't remember the last time he had eaten.

Dimly, he heard Miss Hayes exchange a few words with Frances, and then she entered the room alone. 'Mr Barnard, are you quite well? You look rather white.'

'Was the maid still locked in her room?' he asked, rather roughly.

'Yes,' she replied. 'Sir Robert says that I have the only key.'

'It must have been her,' he murmured, more to himself than to her.

'You still refuse to believe?' Miss Hayes said. 'Despite all that you have just witnessed?'

In his state of unease, Barnard struggled to rein in his temper. 'Do you really think Sir Robert would have kept that incriminating bottle in his casket, when he might have disposed of it at any time in the past three weeks? Someone is implicating an innocent man in a murder – and through your reckless indulgence you're helping them do it.'

Miss Hayes was silent a moment, perhaps seeing the logic of his words. 'I suppose it's possible that he is innocent,' she said at last. 'Perhaps whoever put that bottle there also killed Lady Marsham, and that is what the ghost is trying to tell us.'

'There is no ghost,' Barnard exclaimed, his memory of David's pig-headedness still so very vivid. 'If you would only open your mind, then you would see it.'

A spark of challenge lit her green eyes. 'Very well, Mr

Barnard. Let open minds be the order of the day. I will listen to your arguments – accept that this ghost might be a fraud – if you will do the same, and accept that it might be real. What do you say?'

So his opponent's resolve was faltering at last! Barnard didn't hesitate. 'I think I know how they are doing it.'

She studied him curiously. 'They?'

'Frances and Sebastian. I think she was the one knocking just now. And I think she was knocking the other day when I confronted Sebastian. But on other occasions, when Frances was in this room, it must have been him.' Barnard went to the tea table and started rooting through his papers with a new frenzy of determination. 'Look,' he cried, having found the papers he sought. 'Frances was present for six of the so-called hauntings and Sebastian for four.' He scanned the list again. 'But both parties have never been present at the same time.'

He had always known it. Sebastian Coke, his enemy – who had thrown those vile accusations around to slander Barnard's name and unsettle him.

'You think Coke killed his own mother?' Miss Hayes asked.

Barnard shook his head. 'I don't think we're dealing with a murder at all. Sebastian's grief is the only genuine thing in this whole business. But after his mother died, I think he saw a path to solving his financial problems.' He searched through the papers for the plan of the house he had made, and studied it thoughtfully. 'Frances's room is directly above my own.'

'What of it?' Miss Hayes frowned. 'The tapping is coming from halfway down the wall in this room, not from the ceiling in your own.'

'I'm not sure.' But Barnard was certain that it had a bearing on this matter. 'Come, let's take a look while the coast is clear.'

His vertigo occasioned him less unease, now that he felt so close to an answer. When he returned home to Chorleywood, he would consult his physician and all would be well. Down in the hall, he could hear Frances murmuring solicitously to Miss Marsham, who was still weeping. They mounted the stairs to the attic as stealthily as they could.

Frances's door was unlocked, and when Barnard opened it, he saw that her bedroom was of a medium size, befitting her position in the servants' hierarchy. A narrow bed with a quilt, an armchair before the fire, and a chest of drawers under one of the dormer windows. A row of cupboards had been built under the eaves along the length of one wall, and their position drew Barnard's attention.

'What are we looking for?' Miss Hayes whispered.

'Anything out of place, anything that points to her guilt.'

While Miss Hayes searched the chest of drawers, Barnard opened the central cupboard. To the right, a number of shelves held items of clothing, while a taller compartment to the left held a jumble of possessions piled on top of one another: a carved wooden box of exotic design, a folded blanket, an ear-trumpet, several old newspapers, and two parasols propped up in the corner, next to a gentleman's walking cane.

Barnard examined this last item, testing its weight in his hand. Sturdy, made of Malacca, with a brass ball finial. An odd thing for a lady's-maid to own. Now that the cupboard was empty, he saw that Frances had pinned a map of the environs of London to the wall at the back, near to the floor, which struck him as a very strange place to put it.

'It's just stockings and linen in there.' Miss Hayes closed a drawer. 'I did find this though.' She crossed the room to hand him a small package. 'It's soap.'

'I don't see the significance.'

She showed him the label. 'It's from an apothecary in Islington. That's quite a walk from here, especially as Hampstead has a perfectly good apothecary right here in the village. Perhaps Frances bought something else there too.'

Barnard smiled. 'Like that bottle of arsenic?'

'I merely state it as a possibility – in the interests of keeping an open mind.'

In a moment she'd have to admit it. Filled with anticipation, Barnard leaned forward and tore the map from the wall – to reveal a large hole in the lathe and plaster. Gesturing to Miss Hayes to pass him a candle, Barnard awkwardly manoeuvred his head into the cupboard to look into the hole. He found himself gazing into a six-inch gap between the vertical timbers that supported the walls. By craning his neck, he could see right down inside the house! Grabbing the walking cane, he inserted it into the hole, through a maze of beams and joists, until his entire arm was extended. He moved the cane back and forth. *Knock, knock, knock.*

Triumph flooded through him. He withdrew the cane and grinned at Miss Hayes, determined to be magnanimous in victory. 'My guess is that with the aid of that ear-trumpet, you can hear everything that is said in Lady Marsham's bedroom.'

Miss Hayes inclined her head, looking less disappointed than he'd thought she'd be. 'It seems that in this tilt, the victory is yours, sir.'

Barnard gazed around the room. 'I wonder why Frances was prepared to do all this for her mistress's son. A misplaced sense of loyalty, perhaps?'

'This might provide an answer.' Miss Hayes had opened the carved wooden box, and she held up an ivory locket.

'That's the one Sebastian took from his mother's room,' Barnard cried. 'He said his father gave it to his mother.'

Miss Hayes opened it and showed him a lock of golden hair tied with a ribbon. 'It looks as if Sebastian gave it to Frances.'

'So she helped him out of love?' Barnard shook his head. 'He probably told her that he'd marry her once he got his hands on the money. I must say, I don't rate her chances.'

He paused for a moment, still revelling in his victory. Perhaps now Miss Hayes would recant her foolish theories? If he could convince her to do so in print, a heretic reformed, then others might be spared David's anguish. He was still contemplating this exciting possibility, when his eye fell upon a headline in one of the newspapers he'd found in the cupboard.

INVESTIGATOR OF GHOSTS FOUND DEAD IN HAUNTED HOUSE.

Frowning, Barnard picked it up.

The newspaper was dated two days ago. Barnard's eyes skittered over the sentences. *Prominent sceptic of ghosts, Jonathan Barnard, aged 52, was yesterday found dead with a broken neck after an apparent fall down a flight of stairs . . . believed to be no suspicious circumstances, but the accident has heightened fears that the house may be haunted . . . Sir Robert Marsham dismissed speculation that the ghost might have been involved, but others have opined that Mr Barnard might have angered the spirit with his investigation . . .*

A small cry escaped his lips. Miss Hayes was watching him, her eyes soft and sympathetic. 'I have to ask you if it is true,' she said. 'That there were no suspicious circumstances, I mean. I worried that there might be, you see, when I heard about your accident, which was why I convinced the magistrate to let me look into this matter. I felt I owed it to our correspondence over the years.'

Everything crowded in on Barnard all at once. His attacks of vertigo at the top of the stairs, how nobody save Miss Hayes had seen fit to speak to him in days, how the maid flinched every time that he went near her.

'Frances seems to sense your presence,' Miss Hayes said, as if reading his thoughts. 'She nearly jumped out of her skin when you knocked over those papers. You said you spoke to her on Monday afternoon, not long before the accident happened?'

Barnard was struggling to think through the fug of his thoughts. 'I questioned her,' he heard himself say, in a quiet listless tone. 'I made her cry.'

'Where was this?'

'In Lady Marsham's bedroom.' Barnard swallowed dryly. 'Why didn't you tell me?'

'Sometimes the realisation can be a dreadful shock. It is better for it to happen gradually. I didn't want to risk you losing your memories.' Miss Hayes paused delicately. 'Did Frances follow you out of the room that day? Could she have pushed you down those stairs?'

Barnard closed his eyes, trying desperately to remember. 'No, I followed her. I watched her descend the stairs. I suspected that she was keeping something from me.'

'And then?'

Hot tears were creeping from beneath his lids. He didn't want to be dead. He didn't want to be wrong. 'There was a scent on the air, a trace of musk. I felt a breath. And then . . . I remember very little . . . until you came.'

'I summoned you,' Miss Hayes said, 'at the witching hour. Justice will be served now. I promise you that. Frances will give up Sebastian to save herself.'

In that moment, Barnard could only think of David. Of all the things they'd said to one another in good times and in bad. Could David's dead wife really have been haunting him? Was it possible that she had borne a grudge against him? Had she believed that David's heart was engaged elsewhere? The possibility moved Barnard profoundly, and in the light of it his failures seemed to diminish. He gazed at Miss Hayes earnestly. 'I feel so very tired. As if I could sleep for a thousand years.'

'You may rest now.' She laid a hand upon his arm. 'I am very glad to have known you, Mr Barnard.'

23 BRIDGE STREET

Stacey Halls

My house and Winnie's were exactly the same. Two upstairs bedrooms, a narrow staircase slicing the house sideways in two. Two parlours – front and back – and a kitchen overlooking a paved yard with high brick walls. We were at number 21 and Winnie was next door at number 23. Her front door was black, ours was brown. Many times I'd opened hers thinking it was ours, only to realise when I was already down the passage. Sometimes I stayed anyway, especially when Doris was making mince and dumplings. Doris was a brilliant cook, and never minded having another mouth to feed.

We lived halfway down Bridge Street, a row of terraces with houses on both sides. Woods at one end, a farm and allotments at the other, hills beyond that. We'd lived on Bridge Street all our lives, both of us born in our houses, and our mothers were best friends. We said we'd be like them when we were older, and have baby girls at the same time. We'd put on our mothers' headscarves and house coats, tuck her ginger cat, Clarence, into drawers with tea towels for blankets. We'd stir empty pans and chide imaginary husbands home from work, counting the coins they gave us.

Our little village was barely even that: just a few streets of houses built for the mill. There was a reservoir, a Christmas tree farm, and farms higher up, on the hills, where endless footpaths criss-crossed to nowhere. There was a school, a Sunday school, a church, a shop and a pub. There was a river.

In our village the houses were more or less the same. From fifteen everybody worked at the mill, making slippers. We all went to the same church, knew each other's families. Our fathers drank in the Buck, read the *Free Press*, were members of the poultry and bowls clubs, played football on Sunday afternoons. Some had come through the war; some had less than they started with: an eye, a leg, a mind. Our mothers worked on the production line, stitching soles to felt, sharing sweets and cigarettes and advice on mysterious, unknowable things. Everybody hung their laundry in the back alleys. There was nothing extraordinary about anything or anyone.

October was warm that year, and then November came. The nights were freezing, and every morning was like waking up inside a cloud. I'd wipe condensation from my window, which overlooked the yard and alley, and Winnie's yard next door. I'd run through to Mum and Dad's room and dive into their bed while they protested. 'You're getting too big, Nelly,' Mum said, but then Dad would go and make us a cup of tea and we'd all sit under the covers, trying to warm up.

It's funny, isn't it, how the days when everything changes are the most ordinary of all. Tea in bed, bread and dripping for breakfast, fat spitting and crackling in the pan. Mist over the hills, pooling in the streets. Late for school, a dash upstairs to make my bed, Winnie waiting outside with the hat I didn't even know I'd lost. We fell into step wordlessly, no greeting necessary, picking up where we left off the night before, Winnie's younger sister Dot scurrying behind us. Dad left for work early: it was his job to get the machines going, making sure the production line ran smoothly. As Mum locked our front door Doris came out of theirs: like us, they waited for each other, and made the few minutes' walk last a whole cigarette each, lingering at the mill gates until they'd finished, like two schoolgirls. Like us, they sat next to each other, and somehow managed to talk over the din of the factory floor. We could hear the clack and rattle of the machines from school, though the mill windows were always closed, to keep the moisture in. The mill was where all of us would end up, and often I wondered what the point was, of learning Latin and algebra and Tennyson, when all we'd do with our lives was keep people's feet warm indoors.

After school we walked home past the woods. Winnie said: 'Do you think God goes everywhere with you?'

'What do you mean?' I asked.

'Does he go to school with us then come home again? Or does he follow everyone back to their houses all at once?'

I thought about it. 'I don't know,' I said eventually. 'He surely can't follow everyone home every day from every school. There'd have to be hundreds of him. Thousands, even.'

Winnie was always asking profound things that had

no clear answer. Last week it had been: 'If you woke up in somebody else's body, do you think you'd make the best of their life and do all the things they do or try and get back to your own?'

'Bloody hell, Winnie,' I said. 'I don't know. I just want to keep waking up in my own body, thanks.'

I asked my parents what they thought they would do. Dad laughed and said Winnie ought to be a philosopher, and Mum laughed and said, 'A philosopher!', as though he'd suggested she become a dolphin.

A chill wind scraped dry leaves down Bridge Street, and it was dark by the time we got home. Dot was waiting outside their house without a coat on, looking up and down, her arms wrapped around her. I opened my front door, could smell potato pie cooking in the kitchen. Winnie smelled it, too. 'I might come to yours,' she said.

'You've to come home,' Dot said. Her eyes were unreadable behind her spectacles, which glinted in the light from the street lamp. Winnie shrugged, opened her black front door. A light was on in the front parlour. I'd think about this later, as it wasn't a room they used. We didn't even say goodbye. Why would we? We were never truly separated. She'd knock goodnight on her bedroom wall and I'd hear it in mine. I'd knock back: twice for goodnight. Three times for good morning. Three knocks in the day: are you there? One for yes. Three more for come over. 'You two are like bloody Navy subs,' Dad said. Sometimes she carried the gramophone upstairs and played music to me through the wall. Jack had bought one from a man in the Buck after a few too many ales and Doris never forgave him for it. Still, it was Jack's pride and joy. Christmases and birthdays he'd pass round little glasses of sherry and we'd all dance, our parents looking flushed and young and enchanting.

There was no reply when I knocked goodnight. I thought nothing of it. Sometimes Winnie and Dot and their two brothers stayed up drinking cocoa and eating sardines. I'd stayed there enough to know Winnie had to be told to go to bed a dozen times. She and Dot shared a bed, and when I stayed Dot slept on a pile of blankets on the floor like a cat. She didn't seem to mind; I knew she liked listening to us rambling on about school and teachers and the shopkeeper Mrs Barrow who always had a drip at the end of her nose that never seemed to fall, and whether the priest had been to Rome and met Jesus, and why Robin Ackroyd always picked on Winnie, even though we knew, and it made a part of my soul fall away, knowing she would belong to somebody else one day, like how our parents were still friends but belonged to each other.

That night there was only silence from the other side of the wall. I nestled down, trying to get warm, and soon fell asleep.

෨

The noise came all at once, like a gunshot. My bedroom door burst open, and in the darkness I couldn't see anything at first, but a figure flew towards me, frightening me out of my wits. 'Where are they?' she screamed. 'Are they here?'

'Doris?' I had never seen her like this: hair unkempt, a shawl around her clothes. As my eyes adjusted to the darkness I realised she was terrified. 'Where are they?'

'Where are who, Doris?'

She stalked across the room, looking in every corner and under the bed.

'Nelly, please tell me where they are.'

'I don't know. Who, Doris?'

She began crying. Loud, ugly sobs, as though she had already been crying for some time and now had begun again. The sound of it sliced me in two. Where was my mum? Why hadn't she and Dad come in? Before I could make sense of any of it, Doris left, slamming the door so hard a picture fell from its nail to the floor. It was a photograph of a carousel horse, a postcard we'd bought in Blackpool a few summers ago, when Mum, Dad and I had gone for the day on the train. I'd ridden the carousel twice, and cried when Dad said I couldn't go on a third time, but instead he bought me the postcard at a newsagent, and in a junk shop I'd found an elegant little green-painted frame that fitted it perfectly.

I lit a candle and looked at my grandfather's watch, which sat on my bedside table. The hands read 12.41 a.m. I sat up in bed for a long time, until the candle burned down, listening for any sounds next door, but there were none, and Mum and Dad didn't come. I hardly slept that night, and when I woke up in the morning the carousel horse looked up at me from the floorboards. There was a tiny crack in the corner of the glass, like a spiderweb.

Mum and Dad weren't in bed when I went in for our cup of tea. The bed was made, the curtains open, looking over the quiet street. Downstairs, Mum stood looking out of the little kitchen window at the yard. There was a strong smell of burning.

'Mum,' I said, staring at the stove, where the pan had been left on the heat and the fat from Dad's bacon sizzled black. Absently Mum took it off, as though she hadn't even noticed the smell. Dad's breakfast things were still on the table, half eaten. A full mug of tea had gone cold, coated with a pearly film of milk.

'Mum?' I said again, but she'd gone back to looking out of the window. 'Did Doris find them?'

She turned then. Her face was pinched and strange. 'Find who?'

'I don't know. She came in looking for someone last night. I think she thought Winnie was here. Did you not hear her?'

Mum stared straight through me. 'What?'

'Doris. Is she all right? Did something happen?'

Mum stared and stared. I moved Dad's breakfast things to the sink, buttered a piece of bread, spread it with jam and ate it standing up as Mum came to her senses. She filled a kettle for the sink and scraped Dad's breakfast into the waste.

We left together as usual. When we stepped onto the street Annie Payne came out of her house with her children and gave Mum a strange look, one I couldn't read. Mum ignored her, locked the door, bundled me under her arm and marched me up the road. 'I need to wait for Winnie,' I said, struggling out of her grip.

'Not today, love,' she said.

༶

Winnie wasn't at school. The desk beside me sat empty, and all morning I kept looking at it, as though a note might appear at any moment explaining her absence. When the bell rang for breaktime and everybody filed out, I opened Winnie's desk. There was nothing new inside: dictionary, thesaurus, chalk, slate, pencils, exercise books. A couple of conkers. A pretty oak leaf. Sweet wrappers, unfolded and neatly pressed. The Bible her grandmother gave her for her tenth birthday. A photograph of her dad in uniform, years before in Egypt, a land that seemed as distant and exotic as a half-forgotten dream.

At the front of the classroom, Miss Naven was cleaning the board. She was a kind teacher, shy and clever. She'd recently got engaged to a man who drove the trams. 'Miss Naven, where's Winnie?' I asked.

She looked at me, then returned to erasing equations. A cloud of chalk dust shimmered between us. 'She isn't in today.'

'So where is she?'

But Miss Naven wouldn't look at me, and told me to go outside and play. I stood at the back door and looked out, combing the dark coats and hats for Dot and their younger brothers, Alfred and William. But I couldn't see them either. Winnie had been on holiday once in her life, to Southport, to spend a week with her grandparents. But that was at least two years ago, and now it was November, when nobody went to the seaside.

I looked all around the playground until I was sure none of them were there, and some of the children glanced back at me, for a little longer than usual maybe. Perhaps they could tell I was lost without Winnie. I decided they were ill, taken down with a bad cold and in bed at home. I walked back into the classroom in silence, and Margaret Hobbs passed me a stick of liquorice with a pitiful smile.

When the dinner bell rang I hurried home, and on the way bought a bag of pear drops from Mrs Barrow, who put her sleeve to her dripping nose as she wound the corners of the bag. I remember Mum saying pear drops were good for a sore throat, and I knocked on the door of number 23, going to open it when nobody replied, but it was locked. I went round the back, down the alley between the yards, opened their gate and went inside. The back door was locked, too, and there was nobody in the kitchen. I peered through the glass, but the table was tidy. Doris hadn't made dinner, or if she had it had been eaten, cleared and put away. My stomach was hollow, and I let myself in at our back door to make a tongue sandwich. I sat at the small table with only the tick of the wall clock for company, trying to connect Doris coming round last night with the fact none of them were in school today. Had they run away? That was impossible. Winnie would have told me. Besides, she'd never run away. I thought back to Dot waiting for her last night in the glow of the street lamp, the plain, neutral way she said 'You've to come home.'

I went upstairs and looked at the photograph of the painted carousel horse in the cracked frame, still lying on the floor. I didn't pick it up.

֍

That night, number 23 was dark. I knocked again at the black door after school but could tell that the house was empty. There was no thud of boots on the stairs, no closing of doors in the passage. Mum and Dad came home from work and we ate mutton stew in silence. Mum and Dad usually talked, gossiped, teased one another, and Dad sometimes read the evening paper, telling us interesting things that had happened, but tonight we sat like three strangers around the table.

'Winnie didn't come to school today,' I said. 'I couldn't see Dot or the boys either.'

Mum had that strange look about her, narrow and troubled, as though she was trying very hard to keep something inside. I watched her push onions and peas around her plate.

'They've gone away for a bit.'

'Who?' My stomach clenched.

'All of them.'

'Where have they—?'

'No more questions, Nelly. Eat your tea.'

'But—'

'Leave it, love, eh?' Dad smiled kindly at me as Mum put her face in her hands.

Winnie didn't come to school the next day, or the one after that. The windows next door stayed dark, the wall between our rooms silent. At breaktime I sat alone, watching carefree groups run and shriek around the yard, playing tig and bulldog. A few of my classmates invited me to join in, but to do so would have meant talking to them, and my heart wasn't in it. The bell rang and I walked back to the classroom just as Robin Ackroyd made a sound like a shell exploding, flinging his hands apart, entertaining the small crowd surrounding him with what appeared to be yet another exaggerated tale of peril and his own bravery.

'Robin,' one of the girls said, cocking her head at me.

They all stared at me. 'What?' I said.

And then I heard it: a whisper. 'She doesn't know.'

My head snapped towards the speaker, Leonard Buttershaw, a tiny wisp of a boy for one with so grand a name. 'Doesn't know what?' I demanded, but they all looked at the ground.

'Doesn't know what?' I said again, louder, but the headmistress appeared then and ushered us inside. For the rest of the afternoon I sat mute, not answering even when Miss Naven asked me a simple arithmetic question, feeling a kernel of something like panic turn and swell in my stomach.

That night was so cold Mum warmed my sheets with a brick from the fire. I lay awake, shivering, my mind turning, my stomach churning, until a sound made both stop instantly. A noise: a tiny noise. I lay still, my heart racing. There it was again. A keening, high-pitched sound, like a baby, or a cat ... A cat. I knew in my heart, in my soul, that it was a cat, that it was Clarence, and that he was next door. I flew out of bed, down the dark landing and staircase to the kitchen, where we kept, in a mustard box, the spare key for Doris and Jack's. It was still there, nestled among hair pins and broken pens and old keys whose locks were a mystery. With trembling fingers I retrieved it, went to open the back door – and realised it was already wide open. I hadn't noticed the cold because the house was freezing, and there was not a breath of wind, only the still, frosty air, the silent yard beyond.

Heart pounding, I slipped my stockinged feet into Mum's clogs and went quietly through our yard and into next door's. The sight of the dark, blank windows on these winter nights depressed my heart, and coming home from school that day I could barely look at number 23. No house had ever looked so lifeless. Our road was cheerful at this time of year, with lit parlour windows and steam pressing against the glass from kettles boiling, pans simmering, fires crackling. But

Winnie's was vacant, lifeless, like some of the men who'd come home from the front looking like candles that had been blown out.

Winnie would never have left Clarence. I knew that for certain. The kitchen was dark, exactly the same as it had been left a few days ago. I should have brought a candle, but the night was cloudless, the moon bright and clear. I looked again at the clean sink, not a pan or spoon in sight on the drying rack, the tea towel folded neatly by the stove. It was as though they'd tidied up after themselves, made a deliberate decision to leave everything presentable for whoever found it next. But then all their things were still there: Doris's pinny on the back of the kitchen door; a drawing one of the boys had done of the family and Clarence; the posy vase of artificial carnations in the centre of the table that always made their kitchen seem glamorous, like a café. Wherever they'd gone, they'd surely need their cooking things, Doris's pinny, memories and keepsakes. Unless they were coming back?

I went through to the back parlour, disturbed by how cold it felt. It was always warm in there, with so many people and a fire going and the wonderful smells and steam from the kitchen. It, too, was neat: cushions plumped, newspapers and magazines tidied into the bamboo rack, the grate swept, the brass scuttle filled with coal beside the hearth.

There was a creak upstairs. I started, my breath coming shallow, and listened. Swallowed. I moved through to the dark passage, where the front parlour door was closed. 'Too pricey to heat,' Jack always said about that room, so it was where they stored Doris's mending and the boxes from Jack's parents' house when they died. Winnie and I had combed through her grandparents' things like scavengers, putting on dusty ancient gowns and posh voices and sitting down on the rug with the old-fashioned tea set. But then Jack came in and his face fell, and Winnie and I had felt cruel even though we'd only been joking, and hastily we took off the dresses and put everything away.

I waited at the foot of the stairs, listening, then slowly climbed up. The top floor was silent, and I stood for a moment on the tiny landing. On the left was Doris and Jack's room, on the right the children's. Both doors were ajar. 'Clarence?' I whispered.

A *thunk*. To my delight and relief, the marmalade cat slunk through the doorway of the children's bedroom and rubbed against my legs. I picked him up and nuzzled him, noticing how thin he felt, how noticeable his ribs were beneath his gloriously warm fur: a miracle on this freezing night. I pushed open the bedroom door, saw the two beds that the children shared: Winnie and Dot by the wall connecting our rooms, the boys on the other side of the room, squeezed between the window and the fireplace. Moonlight streamed in. The beds were neatly made, but their teddies – Winnie's little brown bear, Honey, and Dot's threadbare grey mouse – were gone. With great trepidation I walked across to the wardrobe in the corner and opened it. All the shelves were empty.

And then came another noise: one that turned my arms to gooseflesh. A quiet, hushed sobbing, a woman crying softly, as though she was trying to hide it. All the hairs on the back of my neck stood up. Was it coming through the wall, from my house? Was it Mum? Or was it ... was it coming from *inside* Winnie's house, Winnie's empty, dark, cold house? I didn't want to move but knew I had to. I closed the wardrobe door, feeling a pang of pain and sorrow at the familiar scent of mothballs and Doris's washing powder, feeling tears stinging my own eyes as grief and fear and confusion collided, and with halting steps I crept across the room to the landing, towards the source of the noise. Perhaps it was the house on the other side, I thought, the old lady who lived with her son. But no: the crying was coming from Doris and Jack's bedroom, and when I pushed open the door, Clarence stiffening in my arms, heart drumming, blood pounding, expecting, hoping, to find Doris sitting up in bed, sobbing into her handkerchief ... Of course she wasn't there. The room was empty. The crying stopped, and the house fell once more to silence.

The kitchen was silent when I came down the next morning with Clarence in my arms. Mum was wan and drawn; I knew she hadn't been sleeping because I heard her creaking around at night, and at three in the morning I'd gone to the top of the stairs and seen a light on in the parlour, smelled cigarette smoke drifting up the stairs. At the sight of Clarence Mum went even whiter.

'Where did you find him?' she asked.

'In Winnie's house. He was crying in the night. He was locked in. They must have left him. But they wouldn't have, would they?'

'Hang on,' Mum said. 'You went in the house? When?'

'Last night. And the back door was open. Our back door.'

A muscle twitched in Dad's cheek.

'Dad? They wouldn't have left Clarence. Where have they gone?'

'Nelly,' he said.

'All their clothes are gone. I looked in the wardrobe.'

And then I burst into tears. Mum came straight to me and folded me in her arms. Her familiar smell – flour, smoke, talcum – only made me cry more, and she held me until it had passed. She leaned down, put her hands on my shoulders and looked closely at me.

'Promise me you won't go in again.' She hugged me once more, fiercely, then went to the mustard tin on the shelf, took out the key I'd returned the night before and pocketed it. She gave my dad a look I couldn't read, and Dad returned to his breakfast.

Clarence began to squirm in my arms. I realised he would be starving if he'd been at home alone for days. The idea of him being trapped in there with no food, no family ... I put him on the kitchen floor, opened a tin of sardines and scraped it onto a saucer. He began eating before I'd even finished, lapping the silver scales with his little pink tongue. There was something neat and pleasing about watching a cat eat. I poured milk into a teacup and he drank as I stroked his fur.

'There was something else in the house,' I said. 'A noise. A woman crying. But nobody was there.'

Mum had that glazed look again. Suddenly there was a burning smell. From the corner of my eye I saw bright orange flames.

'Mum!'

Mum had left the tea towel too close to the burner. She picked up a corner with her thumb and forefinger, opened the back door and threw it outside, but before it reached the ground she screamed.

'What is it?' Dad leapt up from his seat and I hurried after them. There, on the doorstep, was a dead mouse, left right in the centre like a present.

'Bloody cat!' Mum shrieked. She grabbed her cup of tea and upended it over the tea towel, which smouldered to stillness, smoking and steaming in the damp air. I knelt down to look more closely at the mouse. Clarence was still going at his sardines and wasn't interested.

'It wasn't Clarence,' I said. 'He's been with me since I brought him home.'

'Well, it wasn't me,' Mum snapped. 'Who else could it have been?'

'If he'd killed a mouse he would have eaten it. He's been starving for three days.'

Mum swept it up with the dustpan and brush and took it straight to the dustbin. She flung the lid closed with a clang and stalked back into the house, closing the door firmly and locking it.

'And why was the door open last night?' I demanded, meeting Mum's rush of indignance, feeling angry now, that she could be so het up by a dead mouse when our best friends had disappeared.

'I must have left it open,' Dad said, turning the page of his paper. 'Why don't you go and get ready for school?'

'I haven't had breakfast.'

'Mum'll do you some toast. Go on, love.'

↭

That evening we were sitting in the back parlour. Mum was sewing, Dad and I were playing dominoes. The fire was on and Clarence was asleep on Mum's lap. She was humming along to an old tune, absorbed in her work, a cup of tea going cold at her elbow.

'I like this one,' I said. 'Reminds me of the seaside. Do you think we'll go to Blackpool again next year?'

'Maybe,' Mum said through the needle between her lips, holding her work to the firelight to inspect it. Then she stopped. 'Where's that coming from?'

'Where's what coming from?'

The tune she'd been humming: she'd been *accompanying* it, for the music was playing softly somewhere. We didn't have a gramophone. We all looked at each other, and suddenly my heart lit up like a thousand flashbulbs.

'Next door,' I shrieked, scrambling to my feet. 'Their music's on, they're back.'

'Arnie,' Mum said, 'Could you go and look?'

Dad had already got to his feet.

'I'll come!' I said.

'No,' said Mum. 'Arnie, please.'

Mum went to fetch the key and I listened to the back door open and close, then Mum and I sat in silence. The music played on.

'They must be back, Mum.'

She said nothing, only looked into the middle distance with the tight, anxious expression she'd worn the last few days.

'Do you think they—'

'Shush, Nelly.'

The music stopped. Just then Clarence looked towards the kitchen door. He rose, stretched, yawned, padded to the doorway and began winding in a figure of eight, as though somebody had walked in and he was nuzzling their ankles. I don't know if Mum noticed, because a moment later Dad came in holding a pile of records and a key. He gently set the records down on top of the sideboard. I knew from the way he did it that the house was empty still. Dad lit a cigarette and said he was going to the pub.

༄

Another mouse arrived, this time on the front doorstep. I found it while fetching the milk, and so it wouldn't disturb Mum took it by the tail, carried it to the end of the street and threw it over the wall into the allotments.

Mum sent me to the shop for butter and flour, and outside there was a news board advertising the *Free Press*, which stopped me in my tracks. The headline screamed 'ACCIDENT INQUIRY', and beneath it, in smaller type, 'AT KEARNS MILL'. As I stood looking at it, the shop bell trilled and old Miss Jones stepped out.

'How's your mum doing?' she asked, snapping her purse shut and then fumbling again at the clasp. 'Here you are.' She passed me a penny. 'Get yourself some sweets. Cheer you up.'

I thanked her, closing my hand around the cold coin. Miss Jones lived at the big house at the top of the lane. Each one of the large windows was decorated with pale and delicate orchids that she watered with a little brass can. She'd never married, and was an only child like me. The poultry club counted her as its only female member and for thirty years she ran the Sunday school.

'What happened at the mill?' I asked her, nodding at the sign.

She looked at me with bright blue eyes, as though she wanted to tell me something. Then she opened her purse again.

'Tuppence will get you a nice bit of coltsfoot rock,' she said, handing over another coin. 'Good for the lungs with all this damp.'

Back home, Dad was sitting on the back doorstep polishing his shoes, blackened newsprint spread out beneath him. I glanced down, trying to look at the stories, and he smiled and shifted his feet so the papers creased.

That afternoon I left the house without telling my parents, fastening my coat against the raw November wind and walking up the lane towards the mill. The tall blue-painted gates were locked, the windows blank and empty. A brown paper bag skittered and whirled in a little eddy in the courtyard. The mill was open to the elements, a grey brick fortress on top of the hills. It was eerie on Sundays, unrecognisable from the lively, clattering place it was the other six days of the week. I walked around the side where the carts went in and out, and noticed the furthermost window at the top right-hand side was broken. Of eight panes, six were missing or jagged. I stared at it until the sky lowered and darkened, and the threat of rain sent me home.

That night I lay in bed listening to the muffled sound of weeping, but when I went into Mum and Dad's room they were both asleep.

༄

It happened before dawn, so loud I woke with a start and Clarence, who in the night had found his way to the nook behind my knees, scrambled from the bedclothes and leapt with a soft thud to the floor.

'What the bloody hell——?'

The music was deafening, as loud as if I'd fallen asleep with my ear to the horn of a gramophone. A jaunty, jazzy tune, it seemed to rattle the very house, and Dad came bursting in so fast the carousel horse swung on its nail.

'Where's it coming from? I cried, alarmed by the fear and confusion on his face.

He looked around for the source of the noise, as if I'd decided to have a party at six in the morning.

'Helen?' he called, hurrying out. I took the picture off the hook and followed him. Mum was wrapping her dressing gown around her. She lit a lamp and peered at us.

'What the hell is going on, Arnie?'

'It's next door again.'

'It can't be!' Furious, she scrabbled around in the shallow drawer of her dressing table beneath the window. 'Where's that bloody key?' A glint of silver; she held it up, triumphant. 'We've the only spare, nobody can get in or out, so how can somebody be playing bloody show tunes at this hour?' She noticed the green-framed postcard in my hands. 'What've you got there?'

I showed her.

'Arnie, will you go next door and sort it out? Smash it up if you have to. Sell it, I don't care. How'd this get broken?'

'Doris did it.'

Mum stared at me. 'What?'

'When she came in that night.'

'What night?'

'The other night. I told you the next day.'

Gently Dad took the picture from me. 'I'll fix it.'

At some point the music had stopped. The room was silent, the little flame sputtering in the corner.

'Doris came into my room, crying and shouting,' I went on, 'I don't know how she didn't wake you. She was asking where they were. And then the next day all of them had gone. I looked at Grandad's watch, it was twenty to one in the morning.'

Dad put a finger to the crack in the corner of the glass and pressed gently.

'I can't stand this, Arnie,' Mum said. 'What are we to do?'

Why did she sound so scared? Why was nobody telling me what was happening? And suddenly the music started again, a slower, mournful tune this time: a song to signal the end of the night, or goodbye, the type that people danced to holding one another close as the lights dimmed.

'For god's sake!' Mum looked really frightened now. 'There's an explanation for all of this. Nelly, you must have been dreaming.'

'I wasn't dreaming!' I never shouted at Mum, but now I did. 'It was real."

'She can't have come round!'

'She did!'

'Helen,' said Dad, putting his hands on her shoulders. 'Get back in bed. I'll make you a brew. And I'll take Nelly for a walk before school.'

He led Mum, who was trembling, back to bed, and like a child she climbed obediently beneath the covers.

'Nelly, love,' he said, his deep voice grim and hollow. 'Go and put your coat on. I'll meet you downstairs.'

༽

I waited in the back alley for Dad, who came out of Winnie's house carrying Jack's gramophone wrapped in a sheet. He opened our coal shed, set it down on the ground and shut it inside. We climbed uphill towards the reservoir. Daylight was just breaking, and we turned up our collars against the cold. I'd forgotten my scarf, so Dad took off his muffler and wrapped it round my neck. It smelled of him: tobacco, coal and oil, and I breathed it all in.

'Let's see how the Christmas trees are coming on, shall we?'

We turned into the field where they stood, attentive, elegant, like a troop of soldiers. They would be cut down in a month. Dad and I always chose ours and Dad carried it home on one shoulder, as if he'd shot and killed it himself. Meanwhile Mum waited at home, surrounded by boxes of decorations and, paper garlands trailing from the walls, two little glasses of sherry on the mantelpiece: one apiece for her and Dad. When we'd finished I'd go round to Winnie's and look at theirs, or she would burst in through the back door to see ours, marvelling at how neat and matching it was, with its shop-bought theme of red and green, compared to all their homemade decorations. With a pang I realised her birthday was coming up at the end of November. I didn't know if I'd ever see her Christmas tree again.

We walked slowly down the rows of firs as the wind cut through the branches. I felt sick, light-headed, like that time Mum had left the gas on by accident. I brushed my hands against the sharp needles, rubbing them between my fingers.

'Are you going to tell me what happened to Winnie?' I asked Dad.

At first he didn't reply. Then I heard his boots stop, and so I did, too, but I didn't face him, I stood with my back to him and braced myself for what was to come.

'Something happened at the mill, didn't it?'

'Yes. It did,' said Dad. 'Winnie has had to move away. Dorothy and the boys – they've all gone.'

'Where?'

'They've gone to live in Southport with Doris's parents for the time being.'

'Why?'

Slow, heavy footsteps. Dad came to stand directly behind me. Then he knelt down, took me by the arms and turned me so that I was facing him. I could hardly look at his face, so creased and worried, full of something unbearable.

'Jack and Doris died, love. There was a boiler explosion at the mill. Jack was working in the boiler room, Doris had gone up to talk to him, and ... it happened quick. They wouldn't have known about it.'

The ground bucked beneath me. Dad held my arms tightly. His eyes searched mine.

'We wanted to keep it from you, me and your mum. We didn't want you to . . .' He trailed off, adjusted his cap. Sniffed, rubbed his eyes. The Christmas trees sighed and shivered around us.

'Everybody knows,' I said. 'Everybody knew but me.'

'It was a tragedy,' Dad said.

I felt as though my mind had been scoured with carbolic. It was clean, smooth, white.

'So they won't come back?'

'They won't, love.'

'But I saw Doris that night. She was looking for them. Why was she looking for them?'

'You can't have seen Doris, Nelly. Sometimes dreams can feel so real they—'

'It wasn't a dream! She broke my picture. The one you bought me in Blackpool.'

Dad stood and straightened. 'Your mum's been on edge ever since it happened. She's been hearing things next door, we both have. The mind does strange things when it's in shock.'

That Doris and Jack were dead – it was unfathomable to me. But Winnie was *alive*, as alive as I was. My friend was still here, in this world, a tram and a bus and a train away in Southport. I remembered the broken window at the mill, Miss Jones's kindly look, the noise Robin Ackroyd made in the playground, like a shell exploding. And then it felt real to me: Doris and Jack were *dead*. We wouldn't look at their Christmas tree again, or play games in the parlour. I wouldn't eat Doris's dumplings and wash my plate at her sink. She wouldn't brush and plait my hair before church, or bring us cocoa in bed, or take off her slippers and crack her toes before resting her stockinged feet on the little pouffe by her armchair. Jack wouldn't tread down the passage, whistling, bring a baby rabbit home for us to pet, dance with Dot standing on his feet as his gramophone played softly in the corner. I felt as though I'd been winded, and Dad caught me before I folded in two.

'I'm sorry, love,' he said as I cried. All those memories at number 23, of warmth and light and family: they were over now. There would be no more. I thought back to the night we came home, when Dot was waiting outside the house, her spectacles hiding her eyes in the glow from the street lamp. If only I had seen her eyes, I might have known, might have been able to stop them from leaving.

'Their Aunt Sally took them away,' Dad said.

'She didn't say goodbye,' I sobbed.

'They weren't told about Doris and Jack. Sally thought it was too soon.'

I gripped onto the branch of a pine tree and snapped it off.

'Will I ever see them again?'

'I don't know, love. I don't know.'

႙

Knock knock knock. It came a little after midnight, and I was already awake, disturbed by Clarence, who had taken to sleeping with me every night. I listened in the silent, cold bedroom, but Clarence slept on, purring mildly.

Knock knock knock. Are you there?

I definitely hadn't imagined it. Blood pounded in my ears and my heart thrummed as I struggled upright. I waited, then drew my hand from beneath the warm covers and put it to the wall.

Knock. Yes.

It came back: *knock knock.* Hello? Goodnight? Come round? A little gasp escaped from my mouth and I sat upright, wide awake now. I had to know. I crept through to Mum and Dad's room and carefully retrieved the key from Mum's dressing table, making as little noise as possible. They slept on, curled together like question marks. I looked at Mum's face in the moonlight, pale and worn, the corners of her mouth turned down. I'd said nothing to her when Dad and I got home, only hugged her, and she cried. Then she set about putting the kettle on, tidying the washing-up away, as though that was that, as though Doris and Jack had ended, like a book we'd closed and put away on a high shelf.

But I couldn't close it, and it felt as though their house, their story, was seeping into ours, that the walls were thinning, vanishing, until our two houses became one. Our two families had been like one and now we were left alone, with only silence on the other side.

I let myself in through their back door into the silent kitchen, lit silver with moonlight. The clock ticked on the wall. Before I knew what I was doing I was pulling out a chair at the table, sitting at the lace tablecloth, as if waiting for one of Doris's meals. I began to cry. No more paste sandwiches. No more Friday-night fish suppers, mince and dumplings, hot cups of tea with the windows steamed up. I wiped my nose with the sleeve of my nightgown and in the brief silence heard a very faint hiss. A sudden spark, a ring of bright blue. The stove had caught alight beneath the kettle. I stared at it, and the empty kettle began to heat and rumble. I jumped up and removed it, and the gas ring continued to burn. I put my hand over it to check it was real, to feel its warmth. There'd been no match, no flame to begin with.

I moved the kettle off the stove and turned off the gas, stood once more in the quiet kitchen, listening. Was that a creak upstairs? I almost wanted it to be. I went through to the parlour, which smelled faintly of coal smoke, and the passage, and up the stairs. Winnie's room was just as I'd left it, just as she'd left it, and without thinking too much about it I pulled back the bedclothes and got in her bed. It felt warm, as though somebody had just left it, and I breathed in the scent of her hair on the pillow. My chest ached. I closed my eyes and the tears came again.

Knock knock. Goodnight. I opened my eyes. Our greeting again: this time from *my* house, as though another version of me was lying in bed on the other side. I knocked back, and then all was silent, until distantly I was aware of a soft sobbing noise coming from across the narrow landing. This time I didn't investigate, only lay in the dark, in Winnie's warm bed, until with surprising swiftness sleep came and stole me.

※

'Nelly? Nelly! My god.'

Mum was shaking me awake, and for a moment I was terrified. She looked half-crazed, her hair escaping from her headscarf. Behind her, Dad let out a huge breath and clutched the door frame.

'What the bloody hell are you doing in here?' Mum cried, pulling me out from under the covers. 'What do you think you're doing? You gave us the fright of our lives.'

'I heard knocking,' I protested. 'I took the key and came round, and the kettle came on and I heard the crying again—'

'That's enough!' Mum was half pushing me down the stairs. Dad was already at the bottom. 'I'll not hear any more. You are in so much trouble. Get home now before I box your ears.'

Mum had never laid a finger on me before and I knew she wouldn't now.

Suddenly a door slammed above us. We stared at each other, crammed into the dark passage.

'Who else is here?' Mum asked.

'Nobody. That I know of.'

And then the music started. It was faint, far-off, like a band was playing a few streets away.

'Arnie?' Mum said, her white face somehow going whiter.

'I moved it. I put it in the coal shed.'

'Then why is it playing?'

Clarence walked in then, through the parlour, and began winding and twisting beside Jack's armchair.

'What's that smell?' Dad said, lifting his nose. It was unmistakeable: gas. He hurried through to the kitchen and we followed. Both the burners on Doris's stove were alight. The music was louder in here, blasting out of the coal shed in our yard next door. I knew Dad had put all the records indoors, in the sideboard.

Mum turned the burners off, and seconds later the back door flew open with such force the little wooden clock hanging beside it fell from the wall to the floor. It lay face down and we all stared at it, and in a shaking voice Mum said, 'Arnie?'

'I saw it,' Dad said, swallowing hard. Slowly he reached down and retrieved the clock. The corner of the little face was cracked: a spiderweb of broken glass.

'That's what she did to my picture as well,' I said.

Mum stared at me, her eyes wide with terror. 'Who?'

'Doris! I told you.'

Cold air blasted in from outside, and as though to warm us, the stove caught alight again. The blue rings burned and hissed, and Mum and Dad stared at them.

'Arnie, we need to leave.'

'We can't leave her here,' I said. 'We can't leave Doris.'

'Nelly, she's dead! She isn't here!'

'She is, and she wants the children to come home. That's why she's putting the kettle on, warming the bed, playing music, crying and crying. She doesn't know where they've gone. Clarence can see her, can't you?' The skinny orange cat had appeared in the kitchen doorway and was looking up expectantly.

'Enough, Nelly!' Mum sobbed. 'She's gone, stop it, will you.'

'I'll stay, Doris,' I said into the kitchen. 'I'll stay with you.'

'You will not!'

The crying started up again, in the parlour this time, and I thought Mum would faint. She gripped the sink and Dad took hold of her arm. 'We're going home,' he said firmly. 'Nelly, come on.'

'I can't leave Doris.'

Briskly Dad ushered Mum and me out of the little kitchen and closed the door behind him. 'Key,' he said.

'It's upstairs,' I replied. 'I think I left it on the floor.'

'I'll get it later,' he said. 'And Nelly, you're not to go in there again.'

The Christmas trees were cut down, and Dad and I chose one to bring home. We dressed it with none of the usual fuss – Mum washed our clothes in the kitchen while Dad and I hung the decorations. Somehow the paper chains and baubles had their own air of gloom about them, as though waiting to be put away and left in peace for another year. One Wednesday, snow started coming down in little flakes like ash when I came home for dinner with Dad, who'd started waiting for me at the school gates so we could walk home together. Mum left our dinner on a plate, covered with a tea towel: a cold meat pie, usually, with some pickled onions or a bit of corned beef hash. More often than not, by the time we'd sat down she'd be home herself, hanging her hat and scarf on the peg by the door, her cheeks pink from her brisk walk down the hill.

Dad and I let ourselves in at the front door. In the hall, a single object waited on the doormat: a small, rectangular picture of a curious tower, cream-painted, with what looked like a serpent coiling round it. A helter-skelter: I'd seen one in Blackpool, and wanted to ride it, but Mum said it'd make me dizzy. Above it were the words 'Southport for mild winters'. Mouth suddenly dry, with shaking fingers I turned it over.

'What's that, love?' said Dad, closing the door behind us.

Dear Nelly, it read. *We are here. I will write soon. Love Winnie.*

I propped it against the salt and pepper shakers while we ate eggs and fried potatoes. I tucked it under my pillow that night. And the next morning at dawn, before Mum and Dad woke and the house groaned into life, I sneaked into their bedroom, stole the key, let myself in at number 23 and left the postcard on the mantelpiece so that Doris would know where her children were.

When I got back in bed, I heard a gentle *knock knock*. *Thank you.* I rapped my knuckles three times. *You're welcome.*

THE BUGLE AND THE DRUM

Andrew Michael Hurley

In those days, before the war, it wasn't unusual for fathers to expect their sons to follow them into a particular profession, whether they were suited to it or not. And it wasn't unusual for sons to agree, in order to make their fathers happy. But Howard Halliday quickly discovered that accountancy wasn't for him.

Not that he struggled with numbers or the intricacies of tax regulations. At twenty-one, he had a sharp mind and an inborn aptitude for arithmetic and, like anyone who excelled without effort, he found his work too easy, if anything. By ten o'clock in the morning, he was usually gazing out of the window.

To prevent the other junior clerks from being affected – or inspired – by his lethargy, he was extricated from the office under the guise of 'redeployment' and apprenticed to an avuncular man called Larkhill whose job it was to find new clients for the firm.

Now that things were picking up again after the slump earlier in the decade, the two of them travelled to mercantile conferences and commercial expositions in Manchester and Liverpool and Leeds and the like to make Halliday & Gatley known to those in the early stages of establishing their businesses, and 'get a foot in the door', as Larkhill put it.

At these meetings in so many municipal buildings and assembly rooms and cavernous hotels, Halliday found that he could strike up a rapport with more or less anyone he met. With bachelors, he spoke (and drank) like a bachelor. With fusty old conservatives, he could be sober and partisan. And he flattered family men by asking for their advice regarding marriage and fatherhood, though he had no interest in either. It was all about forging a personal connection. If these prospective customers felt as though they'd be dealing with a friend in whom they could have complete confidence, why would they go anywhere else? Persuasion, he found, was simple. If you told people what they wanted to hear, you had them eating out of your hand.

Laurence Mortimer had been no different. On the surface of things anyway.

Their paths had crossed in Bradford one day in mid-December about a year or so after Halliday had graduated from Larkhill's tutelage. Having secured contracts with several up-and-coming clothiers and importers in the West Riding, he'd been given his own patch in that part of the country and entrusted to keep on adding to his clientele. And yet, for all his success, he was becoming increasingly despondent. Indeed, success had only walled him in the more. It troubled him to think how soon a sense of *limitation* had befallen him, and that the confines he knew now would be all he'd ever know.

It had to be the same for a newly incarcerated prisoner when he realised how much of his sentence lay ahead. Decades of tedium, obedience, hopelessness and then, in old age, the cruellest of all punishments – the regret of a wasted life.

He owed it to himself to pursue his own ambitions. Quietly for the time being. He didn't want his father to think him ungrateful or scheming or – worst of all – idealistic. And so he continued to attend these conventions as an outwardly steadfast representative of the old man's company, while at the same time looking for opportunities that might afford him a means of escape.

He didn't recall seeing Mortimer at the manufacturing exhibition – but then it had been exceedingly busy – and they had only spoken by chance at the railway station much later as they whiled away the time reading discarded newspapers and watching the to-and-fro of other passengers.

When the two of them came to be alone in the waiting room, conspicuous to one another in the silence, for want of something to say, Mortimer asked, 'Were you there at the town hall too?' and caught Halliday by surprise. He'd taken the cloth-capped, middle-aged fellow sitting across from him with the case between his knees to be a working man off on his jollies for the weekend. But he was a toy-maker and had come in the hope of finding an investor. Without success, as it had turned out. It was the same everywhere he went, he said.

Well, was it any wonder? thought Halliday. The baggy suit and the old shoes didn't exactly inspire confidence. Still, he felt rather sorry for him, and since their trains would be another half an hour, he offered to buy him his tea in the station cafeteria.

The portmanteau that Mortimer lugged around with him contained samples of his work, or his *craft*, as he preferred to call it. And to Halliday, that seemed a word far more apt for the exquisite things of tin and wood and glass that Mortimer set down on the table between the cups and saucers.

Here was a little green racing car with automated gears, and a model train that really could run on steam. Here was a miniature biplane with an ingenious mechanism that kept the propellor spinning indefinitely and some apparatus for controlling its flight path via the emittance of radio waves.

For girls, he had made dolls of various Shakespearean heroines, which when tipped and righted again delivered their most famous lines from a speaker inside the head. And there was a clockwork ballerina that pirouetted and pliéd and was guaranteed never to fall down.

For younger children, there was a gadget he called 'Mother's Love' – something like a metal egg cup – through which Halliday could hear a soft disembodied voice singing lullabies when he put it to his ear.

'How do you contain the sound?' he said. 'How is it replayed?'

He shook the little contraption and then listened again.

Now it was 'Frère Jacques', and he laughed at being amazed for a second time.

'My son and daughter enjoy them too,' said Mortimer.

'I dare say they do. They're extraordinary,' Halliday replied, though he'd not imagined Mortimer to be married.

His wife had to be either especially loving or especially tolerant of a husband who touted his wares from town to town in a suitcase as shabby as his coat. She clearly didn't mind him going without a haircut either, judging by the dry grey curls that sprang from the edges of his cap. But perhaps she was holding out for the return of better times, for Mortimer spoke in a refined sort of voice that seemed to have lingered on from a more affluent past. It hadn't served him well, mind. The incongruity of accent and appearance was probably another factor in his lack of success. It wasn't all that surprising that these Pennine capitalists didn't know what to make of him.

Yet the man's talent was quite obvious and undeniable, and it struck Halliday as odd that no one had realised the fortune to be made from it. Yes, the cost of mass-producing what Mortimer had created might turn out to be high, but there was a healthy profit to be made by those bold enough to take a risk.

His father would have called it madness to throw good money at something like this, thought Halliday. But he had no vision. No guts. What safer career was there than accountancy? Only that of an undertaker.

Halliday had to admit that he was no expert when it came

to selling toys, but he was fairly certain that none like these existed. Once the designs had been patented and manufacture had begun, Laurence Mortimer stood every chance of becoming a wealthy man. By next Christmas, every child in the country might be clamouring for one of his playthings.

When Mortimer's train was announced with the clanging of a bell on the platform, Halliday put out his hand and said, 'I wonder if we might meet again?'

Mortimer took it as a pleasantry rather than a request and said, 'Oh, I've no doubt we'll run into one another somewhere soon.'

'No, no, I mean I'd like to have a more formal discussion,' said Halliday. 'About your business.'

'Oh?'

'That surprises you?'

'It's just that everyone takes me for a hoaxer,' said Mortimer. 'They believe that I'm showing them a trick when I demonstrate my toys. They laugh. *You* laughed.'

'Listen, regardless of what anyone's told you,' said Halliday, speaking confidentially as people moved past them, 'it seems to me that you're sitting on a gold mine here.'

Mortimer sniffed cynically. 'Well, you're the only one who thinks so,' he said, and stood up to put on his scarf, a startling home-knitted creation of daffodil yellow.

'Well, one person is enough if they have the capital, aren't they?' Halliday reasoned.

'And you *do?*'

'Hypothetically.'

Since Mortimer knew nothing about him, he could pretend to be whoever he wished to be, and he fell naturally — and convincingly — into the role of an entrepreneur with money ready and waiting to be spent.

'I'm genuinely interested,' Halliday said. 'I promise you.'

'Well then, we *should* talk again, most definitely,' said Mortimer, shaking his hand with more enthusiasm. He had surprisingly stubby fingers for someone so adept at building tiny machines.

As his train pulled in, he put away the toys, animated now, even overjoyed.

'And this is only a fraction of what there is, of course,' he said, as if what he'd shown was somehow not enough in itself. 'I have much more at home. All kinds of things. Prototypes. Most of them close to completion.'

It gets better and better, thought Halliday.

After closing the latches on his case, Mortimer gave him an address card and said, 'Look, why don't you come and visit me? Say, a week today. Then you can see everything for yourself. I'd like you to have the full picture.'

'I'll do that,' said Halliday. 'Thank you.'

Mortimer gripped his hand for a third time, left in high spirits, it seemed, and was soon swallowed up by the crowd getting on the six thirty-five.

Perhaps it was wrong to have let him go off buoyed with so much optimism when there was no actual substance to their partnership as yet. But Halliday assured himself that he wasn't being dishonest. He *did* have money to put on the table. That wasn't a lie. Being single, he'd been able to keep a fair bit aside for an opening such as this; enough to prove to Mortimer that he was serious, anyway.

For now, he'd go and recce what the man had to offer and if it still seemed a worthwhile prospect, he'd see about coming to an agreement – so much outlay for so much return. If Mortimer was eager to move things along, he might be willing to agree to very favourable terms. But however much he conceded, he wouldn't lose out in the grand scheme of things. These astonishing toys had the potential to make them both rich.

The following Friday, under the pretence of visiting a friend so as not to arouse his father's suspicions, Halliday travelled to the Lancashire mill town where Mortimer lived. Heavy rain and winter gales had brought down trees on the line here and there, making what was already a substantial journey even more delayed. It was after half past nine by the time he arrived.

He checked into a guest house close to the station, and after asking the landlady for directions to Ribble View, he went out onto the high street to find it virtually devoid of people. Those he happened to pass hurried by as anonymous shapes under their umbrellas.

Away from the centre, the streets that descended towards

the river were quieter still and the road that ran parallel to the water notably darker, as some of the lamps were out.

In the gloom and the downpour, Halliday struggled to see the door numbers as all the blandly identical houses were set back from the pavement and had been built in an elevated position to give them grandeur. But eventually he came to number fifty, opened the gate and made his way up through the concrete terraces of the front garden to the door with a growing feeling that after the effort of getting here it really had been a wasted journey. The drapes were closed and no light bled from around the edges. No smoke came from the chimney either, which on such a cold night was strange.

Since Mortimer had seemed so thrilled about the prospect of securing a backer, it would be peculiar of him to be out. Unless, having had so many rejections, he had become wary of false prophets promising – well – false profits. Maybe his initial excitement had cooled over the last seven days, and because Halliday hadn't appeared on time, he'd come to the conclusion that he was a charlatan and wasn't coming at all. Sick of waiting, he'd taken his family to the pantomime – or something.

Halliday rang again and was on the verge of leaving when he began to hear music of a kind coming from somewhere in the house. The tuneless blaring of someone mucking about on a trumpet and the irregular beating of a drum. It grew louder, and then when he rang for a third time it stopped and there was the sound of a heavy bolt being drawn back.

*

It was Mortimer's children, he realised, when they opened the door. A boy and girl, ten and twelve respectively, at a guess.

He'd evidently dragged them away from some dressing-up game in which they were putting on a two-person parade. They both wore black military-style uniforms, with braided caps and fringed epaulettes and brass buttons done up to the chin.

The big-eyed boy had been playing the drum, which hung from a piece of rope looped around his neck, while his sister, so very pale and freckled, held what looked like a half-sized bugle; something her father had made for her, perhaps.

'Don't you look smart?' said Halliday. 'Here, do you know "Good King Wenceslas"? You play and I'll sing. We could go from door to door and make a few bob if we're any good. What do you think?'

He liked children, he enjoyed being silly with them, and children on the whole liked him. But the boy gawped, and the girl stared at him impassively.

'Yes?' she said. 'Can I help you?'

She was so serious that Halliday had to smile. He thought she'd quite like it if he played up to the impression she had of herself as the lady of the house, and after taking off his hat he gave her a short bow.

'Miss Mortimer, is it? My name's Halliday,' he said. 'I've come to see your father. Is he in?'

'He's busy,' replied the girl, glancing behind her in the direction of the stairs which rose quickly into darkness.

'Can I speak to him?' said Halliday.

'From here?' she said. 'I doubt it.'

She was very dry for one so young.

'He did ask me to visit him,' he said.

'When?'

'When I met him last week.'

'Where?'

'Yorkshire.'

'Are you sure you have the right house?'

He found the address card Mortimer had given him and showed her, but she still wasn't willing to be swayed.

'Father says we've to be careful who we let in,' she said. 'He doesn't want anyone prying at his work.'

'It'll be fine, buttercup,' said Halliday. 'I come in good faith.'

He put his hand to her cheek, stepped over the threshold and closed the door behind him, half expecting Mortimer to have heard the conversation and be on his way down. But he didn't appear, and the girl said, 'I told you, he's busy. He's with someone,' as she slid the bolt back into its hasp. She was taking no chances.

'And your mother?' Halliday asked.

'Father says she's on her way.'

'Been out visiting someone, has she?'

It was a normal sort of thing for people to do at Christmastime, but the girl made it seem such an audaciously personal question, the way she frowned.

'Well, is there somewhere I can sit while I wait?' he said.

The girl indicated a hard wooden bench under a painting of the Last Judgement.

'Nowhere warmer?' he said.

'It has to be like this,' the girl replied. 'Father says so.'

It was little better indoors here than it was on the street. The air in the house was so deeply chilled that he could see his own breath. There couldn't have been a fire going in any of the rooms for days. Things were much worse than he'd thought. It could be that Mrs Mortimer was out working somewhere in order to make ends meet.

There were electric lights, but no bulbs in the fittings. They'd resorted to using candles, and even skimped on those. It was stumps in saucers. Along the hallway and into what was presumably the kitchen, the pockets of sallow light were so meagre and infrequent as to be interspersed with patches of near blackness. It was no wonder that the boy had such big eyes, like those of a deep-sea fish. And no wonder that he and his sister chose to play such an energetic marching game, since it kept them warm.

As Halliday sat down and lit himself a cigarette, the children started again, stamping away down the hall with the tread of Shire horses as they performed their horrible duet.

Hearing the instruments at close quarters, they didn't quite sound as they should for their size. The boy had what appeared to be a miniature snare, but it boomed and reverberated like the bass drum in a brass band. And when the girl blew through the mouthpiece of the bugle, it was almost painful to listen to, even though she was facing away from him.

Good god, Mortimer and his wife had to have the forbearance of saints to let their little darlings carry on like this, even if it did ward off the cold.

At the end of the hallway, they turned and strutted back to where Halliday sat and smoked, keeping their spines straight and their knees high. With the full force of the screeching horn and the hard erratic thumping coming at him, he put his hands over his ears.

Standing before him again, the girl and the boy stopped and smiled, looking pleased with themselves that they'd made him so unsettled.

'Would you like a turn?' the girl asked.

'Me? No. I'd be hopeless at it, I'm sure,' he said.

'It's not difficult,' said the girl.

Well, no musical instrument was *difficult* to play, he thought, so long as you were content to play it badly.

'Here, do you think your father might be ready to see me now?' he said, getting to his feet and rubbing his knuckles against his palm. How could they stand it being so bitter in here?

'I shouldn't think so,' said the girl. 'He always has a lot of questions to ask.'

'Who's he with, exactly?' said Halliday, sensing that he might have a rival.

'I'm not sure,' the girl said. 'Another man. They come and go. I don't know their names.'

More than one rival then, perhaps.

'Had lots of visitors, has he?' Halliday asked the boy, who continued to gape at him.

He wondered if he was a bit slow and had been given the drum because it required such little skill to play. Or it was because he liked to touch the skin. He seemed to enjoy the feel of it under his fingertips. Why, though, was hard to say. It was a grotesque thing made of mottled animal hide. There were still hairs in various places.

'Could you at least go and tell him I'm here?' said Halliday.

The girl proffered the bugle. 'Not until you've played.'

She was only keen for him to do so because she thought it might embarrass him or rattle him again, but the boy looked at him with such encouragement that he couldn't say no.

'Fine, all right,' he said. Children liked to strike these strange bargains sometimes.

After licking his fingertips to nip out his cigarette, he took the instrument off her. Thinking that he'd have to give it his all to make any sound – such was his assumption about playing a trumpet – he blew far harder than was necessary and produced a shriek much louder than the girl had managed. This delighted the children, especially the boy, who began to pound away at the drum again, gazing at Halliday intently and willing him to continue.

He did – for the boy was so earnest – but when a woman emerged from the kitchen, he stopped immediately and gave the bugle back to the girl, feeling a touch embarrassed that he'd be as much to blame as the children for the disturbance.

'Is it Mrs Mortimer?' he asked, but as soon as she came into a brighter ring of candlelight he could see that the woman was a domestic. Very elderly and sluggish, with a pinafore strapped tight to her squat, bosomy body. Mediterranean, he thought, from her complexion and her dark hair. Bleary-eyed, as if she'd just woken up.

'At last! There you are, Maria,' the girl said and took her hands. 'Make some biscuits, will you? We're ravenous.'

The woman, who wasn't much taller than the girl, peered past her at Halliday. Ah, that special look of inimical scrutiny these hoary charwomen perfected over the years. He smiled and nodded and said good evening.

'Biscuits, Maria,' the girl said, regaining her attention. 'Go on. For us.'

The woman looked at the girl and then the boy and began to speak rapidly in what Halliday took to be her own language, though he hadn't a good enough ear to place it precisely. He couldn't decipher the intonations, as her voice didn't rise and fall so much as spill. Its inflections were random and rhythmless, local to whatever far-flung village she'd come from and impenetrable to anyone else.

Or it was all just nonsense. She looked around as though she was confused, even distressed. It wasn't grogginess so much as incomprehension. Perhaps the poor thing wasn't quite the full shilling and that was why Mortimer kept her on. There had to be some reason. She was a luxury that he could ill afford. His compassion or his pity for her meant that they'd had to cut back on other things.

The temperature felt as if it had dropped even more, and the darkness edged in as the candles sagged and burnt inefficiently. And there were no decorations up, Halliday noticed.

Not a single bauble or a paper chain. It'd be a dismal sort of Christmas here. Even for the children of a toy-maker. A batch of biscuits their only treat.

'There's no need to get so worked up, Maria,' the girl said, as the woman talked and gesticulated. 'You'll soon remember once you get started. Butter, flour, sugar, ginger. Go on.'

She led this Maria towards the kitchen, sending her on by herself after a few steps. The woman went away muttering, checking her hands, discomfited by her colossal shadow on the wall.

'Well done you, Mr Halliday,' the girl said, going back to him. 'We've been trying to get her to come out for hours. Haven't we, Alex?'

The boy nodded.

'Out from where?' said Halliday.

'She sleeps a lot,' the girl said. 'We have to get her up, otherwise she'll do nothing.'

'I see.'

'She has to *work*,' the girl said, sensing Halliday's sympathies for the woman. 'That's what she's here for. She knows that.'

He began some riposte about the lady being old and, given that it was late, how the evening ought to be hers to do with as she pleased. But as he spoke, Mortimer made an appearance at last and came down the stairs saying, 'Alex? Dora? You've stopped. Don't stop.'

He was suitably dressed for his ice-box of a house in a

Russian-style fur hat, a pair of thick gloves and two woollen jumpers over his plaid shirt.

When he clocked Halliday, it was with a look of surprise. He'd forgotten about the appointment, hadn't he?

'I'm sorry I'm so late,' said Halliday, and he began to explain how he'd been held up on the train. But Mortimer brushed aside his apologies and turned to the children.

'Come on,' he said, clapping them into action. 'Off you go. One-two, one-two. Go round again. You'll get cold standing about like this.'

Without complaint, the girl fitted the bugle to her lips and blasted out a fanfare that squealed more raucously than before, cueing her brother to join in. She made for the stairs and together they tramped up into the dark. The cacophony was unbearable, but Mortimer was obviously used to it and was far more interested in the lady who'd been summoned.

'Ah, they managed to rouse Maria, did they?' he said and looked down towards the kitchen, where the woman, illuminated by a single candle in Renaissance chiaroscuro, seemed to have been stumped by the weighing scales and couldn't get them to balance.

'I think that was me, actually,' said Halliday. 'I didn't realise that they were trying to wake her up.'

'It was you playing the bugle, was it?' Mortimer said with intrigue now, properly acknowledging Halliday's presence for the first time.

'Briefly,' he said. 'Your daughter wanted me to try.'

'Yes, she can be quite demanding, can Dora.'

This he clearly considered to be an asset.

'She's got the poor lady making Christmas biscuits, I'm afraid,' Halliday said.

'*Is* it Christmas?' said Mortimer.

'Almost.'

'Well, well.'

He watched Maria turning a knife this way and that in the light.

'Fascinating, isn't it?' he said. 'The way she looks at things. What does she make of it all, I wonder? She can't tell me, of course.'

A clock somewhere clanged discordantly. Halliday looked at his watch. It was eleven already. Late for the children to still be playing.

'Come up to the workshop,' Mortimer said. 'There are things I'd like your opinion about.'

'You've finished your meeting, have you?' said Halliday.

'My meeting? Oh, yes, he's gone, he's gone,' Mortimer replied, gesturing towards the back of the house where there had to be another way out, as the man in question hadn't come down to the hallway.

He was a wily bastard, Mortimer. That story he'd told at the railway station about no one taking him seriously was what he told everybody. One by one, he was luring in the money men by making each of them believe that they alone had appreciated the true commercial value of his toys. And thinking that they'd got in first, anxious to capitalise on the exclusivity, they came here to see him as soon as they could, chequebook in hand.

At the top of the stairs, Mortimer halted to let the children go by.

'That's it,' he said. 'Good lad. Keep it up.'

He gave his son an affectionate pat on the back as he passed. This galvanised the boy into an even heavier assault on the drum skin, and Halliday missed what Mortimer said.

'It's the volume they get out of those things,' he repeated, closer to his ear. 'That's been the biggest surprise.'

'I can imagine, yes,' Halliday replied, raising his voice to be heard. 'Incredible for such small toys.'

'Toys?' said Mortimer, watching the children high-stepping along the landing. 'I'm not really sure I can call them toys any more. This way.'

He unlocked a white-painted door, held it open and Halliday walked into the pages of *Pinocchio*. Here was Geppetto's workshop no less, cluttered from floor to ceiling and lit by candles, just as it had looked in the book he'd had as a boy.

A large rectangular bench with a lathe and a vice at one end was littered with half-formed or half-dismantled wireless sets and cameras and typewriters, and other appliances of pistons and valves more ambiguous in their function.

Three of the walls were entirely taken up with shelves for tools and materials. Saws, hammers, planes, hand-drills, files, pliers and screwdrivers were strewn among lengths of wood and sheets of tin, stacks of sandpaper, bottles of oil, and demijohns filled with nails, cogs and springs. If there was some order to it all, then it was known only to Mortimer.

'Please, take a seat,' he said, leaving Halliday to find a suitable place by himself while he got back on the high stool by his bench, intent on recommencing work, it seemed, rather than talking business.

In front of him were what looked to be the component parts of the bugle and the drum that he'd fashioned for the children. He was in the process of making more. Several finished instruments sat to one side and the next on this rudimentary assembly line lay half completed.

'I've tried my best to reconstruct what I made for Alex and Dora,' said Mortimer, putting on a pair of glasses. 'I've done everything exactly as I did the first time, but none of these are quite the same. They don't do anything at all.'

He looked with irritation at his other efforts, but Halliday couldn't see any difference between them and the instruments the children were playing.

'Well, I'm sure that if we were to start manufacturing these things, a designer would make it all uniform,' he said. 'All the dimensions and so on.'

Mortimer didn't appear to be listening and held up a sketch-plan of the bugle and then the drum in the glow of the candle closest to him, trying to work out where he'd apparently gone wrong.

Outside, on the landing, the children came back to the head of the stairs. The boy hammered at the drum and the girl blew out a succession of screams before they made their way down to the hall.

'You said that you had more to show me?' Halliday said once he could hear himself think again.

Fixated on his drawings, Mortimer waved him uninterestedly in the direction of a glass-fronted cabinet where he kept his finished pieces. They were just as impressive as the things he'd shown at the station café.

Stroking the neck of a realistic life-sized parrot, Halliday set it squawking and flapping. Next to it, a miniature working guillotine allowed the more grisly-minded child to play Robespierre and put paid to an assortment of snooty-looking aristocrats. And there was a wooden windmill that made real flour, a hot-air balloon with a well in the basket for paraffin, and a nativity scene with angels that seemed to hover of their own accord above the infant Jesus in the crib.

Halliday bent down to locate the wires holding them up, but it was too dim to see. There might not have been any at all.

'If the instruments are giving you difficulty, which of the toys *would* be the easiest to replicate, do you think?' he asked, turning back to look at Mortimer to find him still engrossed in the puzzle.

'I can't work out if it's the diameter of the cup or the throat or the backbore that does it,' he said, squinting through the hollow of the latest mouthpiece he'd drilled out. 'Or if it's just how it's played by the individual. Either way, it must be something to do with the frequencies produced, mustn't it?'

'You've lost me, I'm sorry,' said Halliday, but it was a rhetorical question. Mortimer had already moved on to inspect a scrap of the pale hide he'd used for the drums.

'And it must be that the membrane sends out vibrations at a certain wavelength when it's struck,' he said. 'There must be a tension that's just right. I don't know. It was all accidental, you see. I'm not entirely sure how they work as yet.'

'I wouldn't worry about it,' Halliday reassured him. 'You've plenty of other things. This place is a gold mine. Like I said.'

Mortimer had a magnifying glass out now and moved it inch by inch to study the piece of skin.

'Perhaps the arrangement of the hairs makes a difference,' he said. 'It could be something as minute as that.'

'Look' said Halliday, sitting down opposite him. 'I don't know what the others have proposed to you, but I'm sure I'll be able to give you something closer to what you think all this is worth; what *you're* worth, more to the point.'

To gain Mortimer's full attention, he opened his cigarette case and passed it across the table.

'Tell me,' he said. 'How much more do you need? I'll top whatever the last man promised you.'

'The last man?'

'The one who was here when I arrived,' said Halliday. 'He must have presented you with a figure. What was it?'

Mortimer finally looked up and declined a smoke with a shake of his head. 'I didn't talk to him about anything so crass as money,' he said. 'Good lord.'

'What then?'

Downstairs the children suddenly stopped playing and Mortimer got up and shuffled around the table to get to the door.

'Carry on,' he called to them. 'It won't be much longer. One-two, one-two.'

The children re-started and he came back into the workshop.

'Mr Mortimer,' said Halliday. 'I'd like to make you an offer. The best offer, I hope.'

'Offer?'

'An investment.'

Mortimer shook his head. 'I'm not interested in anything like that. This is my work now,' he said, and resumed his examination of the parts in front of him.

'If it were me, I'd give them up as non-starters,' said Halliday.

'Non-starters?'

'There are at least a dozen things of yours that will sell far better,' Halliday went on. 'The plane, that little windmill, the earpiece that sings by itself . . .'

'None of those things matter any more,' said Mortimer. 'No one will care about them once they see what the bugle and the drum can do.'

'As far as I can tell, all they do is make a dreadful bloody racket,' Halliday said. 'No parent is going to thank you for that. They won't want to be woken up like your woman earlier.'

'*My* woman?' said Mortimer.

'Maria.'

'I haven't the means to employ a servant.'

'Who is she, then?'

'I can only assume that she belonged to a family that was here before us,' Mortimer said.

'And what?' said Halliday. 'She keeps coming back, does she?'

'Like the others do, yes.'

'The others?'

'Three of them so far,' Mortimer said. 'One fellow is about your age. Another's fifty, I'd say, like me. And tonight it was some ancient old boy with no teeth.'

'They used to be in service too, like Maria?'

'Not by the look of their clothes,' Mortimer replied. 'One or other of them might have been her employer once. I don't know how long ago they lived here. I don't even know if they're related.'

'But what is it they come back *for*?' said Halliday. 'I don't understand.'

'It must be that they're drawn here,' said Mortimer. 'By the sound of the instruments. I've yet to fathom out the process. I've tried to ask, but they have a different language, the dead.'

Halliday laughed.

'You've a dead woman making biscuits in the kitchen, have you?' he said, but Mortimer misconstrued what he was being sceptical about.

'I know,' he replied. 'We shouldn't really say *dead* any

more. It doesn't mean anything now, does it? There's only life. More life. A different form of life. We *endure*. We can be brought back. Isn't that marvellous?'

Halliday waited for him to crack and admit the joke of the whole thing, but he didn't. Well then, *he'd* expose it, he thought. There was one very obvious hole in the plot.

'This woman downstairs,' he said, with a smile in his voice. 'If she doesn't speak English, how do you know her name?'

'Oh, that was Dora's invention,' Mortimer replied. 'Maria's the housemaid in *Twelfth Night*, I think.'

'Making me Malvolio, I suppose?' said Halliday, laughing again by himself.

'Don't ask me to explain it to you,' Mortimer said. 'It's all rather beyond me. It might be beyond anyone at the moment, truth be told. But that's always been the way in science, hasn't it? Things *are*, but we don't know *how*. Not straightaway.

'I've no idea why Maria and the others speak as they do,' he continued. 'And I can only speculate about why they acquire form again when they're brought here to the house. It's as if they return to the state they were in when they were last alive. Maria had some senility. Well, you saw that. The old man here earlier could hardly breathe. And the one your age . . . he had these terrible sores . . .'

He trailed off and rubbed his neck. 'Perhaps they all came to the end of life in such suffering that they haven't quite moved on to where they ought to go.'

'What are you talking about?' said Halliday. 'Restless spirits? Come on.'

He couldn't have come up with a more hackneyed notion.

'It's a crude explanation, I agree,' Mortimer said. 'But I wonder if there's something we're supposed to do for them. Something that might alleviate their pain. Give them peace.'

After a moment in which he seemed to wrangle with some particular anxiety, he reached across the table and held Halliday's arm.

'You'd do the same, wouldn't you?' he said. 'If you thought it possible. Anyone would.'

'I don't follow.'

'I'd give anything to see her again,' said Mortimer.

'See who?'

'Iris. My wife.'

She hadn't died recently, had she? thought Halliday. It would explain the solemnity of the place, the lack of Christmas decorations.

'When did she . . . ?' he asked.

'Years ago,' Mortimer replied. 'She became unwell not long after Alex was born.'

Halliday passed on his condolences, but Mortimer wasn't after any commiseration.

'I mean, I've kept the house dark and cold, just as the others seem to like it,' he said. 'But she hasn't come. All I get are these strangers. And I wonder if she's somehow further away than they are and the children don't quite have the strength to make her hear them. Or they can't find the right pitch on the instruments. I don't know. I don't know anything.'

It wasn't uncommon, so Halliday had heard, to feel the torment of bereavement more keenly at this time of year, but the way Mortimer grieved for his wife was too bizarre to be understood or empathised with.

'I've obviously come on a difficult night for you. I'm sorry,' he said, standing up now. 'Why don't we talk again in the new year?'

By which time he might have put away his sorrow again and got over these delusions. These very cruel delusions. It was one thing for him to indulge them but another to involve his children. They were expected to be acquiescent to their father – he knew how *that* felt – but making them process around the house for hours, supposedly waking the dead: it was quite obviously mad.

Wherever the children were now, they were starting to sound fatigued. Mortimer slipped his thumb and forefinger under his glasses to rub his eyes.

'It's getting late,' he said. 'They must be exhausted. They really ought to go to bed.'

'And I ought to make tracks,' said Halliday. 'It was good of you to see me.'

Mortimer took his hand as offered and held it. 'Will *you* try to reach Iris?' he said. 'You got through to Maria much quicker than Alex and Dora did, after all.'

'I wouldn't want you to rely on me,' Halliday answered diplomatically.

'I'd be in your debt.'

'I think it's best if I go.'

'They've never known her, the children,' Mortimer said, clutching tighter. 'And I'm sure she must have been longing for them all this time. Stay,' he persisted. 'Dora will make up a bed for you here.'

Halliday hid his aversion to the idea with good grace.

'It's kind of you to offer,' he said, 'but I've a place in town.'

'Come back in the morning, then.'

'I have other things to do.'

'It's Saturday.'

'Even so. I'm sorry.'

He left the room with Mortimer close behind him, still pleading, and met the children as they came up the stairs. They'd taken off their caps and looked weary and morose.

'Maria's disappeared again,' said the girl. 'No biscuits. Are you going now too, Mr Halliday?'

'I'm afraid so,' he answered with a smile. 'My bed's calling.'

Mortimer must have given the children a sign or a nod to stop him from leaving, as the boy linked arms with the girl and she held tight to the banister rail, barring Halliday halfway down.

'Come on, you two,' he said. 'It's almost midnight.'

He went down another step and the girl looked at him impishly, daring him to push past. He turned to Mortimer, who now blocked the stairs behind him.

'Tell them to move aside, will you?' he said. 'The landlady will have locked me out at this rate.' He kept his voice light, not because any of this amused him but so that he didn't betray his unease.

'Give him the bugle, Dora,' said Mortimer, and the girl did as requested, forcing it into Halliday's hands.

He felt ridiculous, trapped like this by two children and a man more than twice his age. But there was no point in jostling Mortimer out of the way, because where would he go after he'd done so? And it would be too dangerous to barge between the boy and the girl. How would it look if they were to tumble and break a limb on the wooden stairs or the tiled floor of the hallway? He had little choice but to humour them.

'The drum, Alex,' said Mortimer, and the boy passed it to him.

After hanging it around his neck, he began a hard, steady beat that echoed in the enclosed space and was so loud that Halliday felt it in his heart as well as his ears. He looked at the girl and the boy and they stared at him until he began to play too.

As before, he conjured up a series of high-pitched squeals, horrific noises that made him think of pigs being slaughtered. Compelled by the insistent gaze of the two children, he continued in bursts for as long as he could stand it and then stopped.

'That's all I can do,' he said. 'I must go.'

He tried to give the bugle back to the girl, but she refused to take it and behind him Mortimer continued to batter at the drum.

'Again,' he said. 'You can't stop now.'

'Look, I've already stayed later than I intended to,' said Halliday. 'Nothing's happening, is it?'

'Then play louder,' said Mortimer.

All right, Halliday thought, he'd get such a howl out of the damn thing that even the children would beg him to stop. He blew as hard as he could, taking in a full lungful before each blast and directing every one of them at the boy and the girl. But this only excited them more, the way that children often enjoyed the excess of things, even dangerous things – *especially* what was dangerous.

The smirk on the girl's face made anger get the better of him and he tossed the instrument aside.

'Move, for God's sake,' he shouted and took her arm, meaning to wrench her from the banister, consequences be damned.

But she was quick and slippery and twisted out of his grasp and put her hand back where it had been. And each time he tried to hold her, she made the same nimble manoeuvre, thinking it a marvellous game.

As he tussled with her once more, the thud of the drum so forceful that it felt as if Mortimer was tenderising his brain, Halliday saw that the boy was shaking his sister's shoulder.

When she turned, he tapped his ear, the girl listened and then darted past Halliday to get her father to stop. With their sharper hearing, the children had picked up on the sound of someone banging at a door. Mortimer put down the drum and looked up in the same direction as them, to the floor above.

'Is that her?' asked the girl, and Mortimer motioned for her to be quiet.

A clock on the landing struck the hour by ringing out a melody on twelve dainty carillons and then a woman's voice came, making Mortimer short of breath, as though he was choked with happiness.

'Let me go and speak to her first,' he said to the children, and then after kissing them on the head in turn, he made his way up to the landing with a candle in his hand, calling, 'It's me, Iris. It's Laurence. Don't worry,' as he took the next flight of stairs.

In reply, the woman cried out again in the same strange language Maria had spoken. Not some dialect of Greek or Italian, but more an irregular sprinkling of notes. It was like listening to a blackbird broadcasting some feeling of distress, for she came down to the landing very much against her will, yanking at the hold Mortimer had on her wrist.

She was a tall, fair-haired woman. If she'd had any prettiness to her once, it had gone now, and she was terribly gaunt. Her neck was sinewy, with the bones of her clavicle protuberant under her almost translucent skin.

The large green dressing gown she wore looked to have been draped over her shoulders for modesty's sake, as all she had on beneath was a thin chemise. When she writhed in Mortimer's grip, and the robe slid aside, Halliday saw that her nightdress was stained down the front with yellowish vomit.

'It's all right, Iris. It's all right, my love,' Mortimer said to her. 'You're at home now. You're with us.'

Candlelight made everyone look pallid, but she had no

colour in her face at all, and even with the house so cold, she sweated and stank like someone with a fever or an infection.

As it had been for Maria, everything seemed strange to her, everything needed to be studied, and as she twittered out her words and tried to prise Mortimer's fingers off her arm, she stared at the pictures on the landing, the bookcases, her bare bony feet, then Halliday.

She looked terrified or furious, and certainly in pain. But Mortimer didn't see it, or didn't want to see it, and caressed her neck and lips with his free hand in ways that seemed too intimate with others looking on. For a moment or two, he was lost in his desire for her and revelled in her reluctance to allow it, as if recalling some erotic game of hard-to-get they'd once enjoyed. But then remembering the children were there, he held Iris by the chin and turned her face to look at them.

'See,' he said. 'Here's Alex and Dora. They're yours. Ours.'

He urged the children to come closer and smile and say hello. They did as they were told, but to them she could have been anyone, and Iris appeared not to recognise them at all. Even her own husband was unfamiliar to her, and she recoiled from his affections again with a string of inscrutable utterances and brought up the watery contents of her stomach. Blood with it this time.

'Christ, that's enough,' said Halliday. 'Let her go.'

But she didn't need his intervention. After wiping her mouth, she worked herself free and pushed past the children, knocking aside their ineffective attempts to keep her there.

And then thinking that Halliday might try to stop her too, she struck him in the jaw before taking the stairs, coughing and retching.

Down at the front door, she couldn't seem to turn the handle or work out the bolt, and as Mortimer came after her, begging her to stay, telling her how she was loved and missed, promising that he'd make her well again, she made off along the hallway, dashing the plates of candles to the floor to prevent herself from being caught.

The children picked up their instruments and followed, laughing, whooping, high on the thrill of a chase in the dark. But even as they reached the bottom of the stairs, Mortimer was already crying out, 'She's gone! Bring her back! One-two, one-two. Again. Again.'

As Mortimer searched about with a struck match and the boy and the girl started playing once more, Halliday took the chance to leave, and after slipping out he hurried down the wet steps from the house to the pavement. He'd be back at the guest house before he knew it. It wouldn't take long. Then in the morning he'd catch the first train home. What was that? Six or seven hours from now? He wondered if he might be able to get a drink somewhere. A stiff brandy and he'd soon see that it had all been a trick. Of course it had. Mortimer had said himself that people took him for an illusionist. The only mystery lay in the man's motivations for all this theatre.

With the sound of the bugle and the drum still audible, feeling as foolish and angry as a child for allowing himself to become a participant in such absurdity, hoping that his chin wouldn't bruise so badly that his father would notice, Halliday set off, but saw that there were others on the street now, heading towards him from both directions.

They were, from this distance, indistinct and innumerable, but he felt that there were more people out than there ought to have been at this hour of the night, especially in such filthy weather. Their noise came to him on the high wet wind. They were all gabbling, like a flock of birds coming home to roost.

TWO GO TOGETHER

Imogen Hermes Gowar

Owing as it does a debt to Jeduthan Hawley

Massachusetts, November 1718

The Death

Late it was, and so often that's the way: the dying choose to make their exit in those slim still hours after midnight, when things are different. I was used to a late knocking. That evening I had put the bar to the door with some intimation that I would take it off again before morning, and when the knock came at one-of-the-clock, my eyes were already open.

I sat up and touched Dorcas's shoulder where she lay beside me. 'A job,' I told her.

'Bless their soul,' she murmured, and turned over into the warm space I left.

Out into the passage I went. Stiff-legged, stiff-hipped, shivering. Flexing my fingers to get the movement into them. All this was easier when I was younger. Slid the bolt back and saw on my doorstep a figure, hunch-shouldered, thick-cloaked. Too dark to know more.

'I'm sent to fetch you,' he said.

He set off at once, and I followed. It was the sound of his breath that led me, and the stamp of his feet, for his hooded silhouette grew and shrank as he passed through the shade of alleys and tall buildings. When he turned a corner too swiftly I thought he vanished into air.

All my life I've walked the streets of Balaam by night, and should know it better than anyone, but in the darkness it is another town. The sounds fall differently in empty streets. The buildings lean differently. The town shows me things as if they were secrets shared. Raccoons frisking up and down the steps the Justice of the Peace strides. A snouty black bear slouching its round-shouldered way along the high street. Sometimes I see the humans of Balaam do strange things. Assignations. Vandalism. Thefts. Sometimes they give vent to such passions as they never would in the light of day. Emboldened by ale or the dark, they do to one another things nobody might credit. What I see, I put from my mind. Those things belong to the Balaam of night-time, not the one we live in.

Then came a light, bobbing along the high street, and hurrying behind it was the shape of Mistress Agnes Hollar, the midwife. I saw not her face beneath her shawl. I daresay she saw not mine. But we surmised one another, and nodded, as we always did.

'Let your night's work be gentle,' I said to her as we passed.

'And yours too, Mr Peachment,' said she softly, and neither of us stopped.

I would be content always to walk in silence, but in my line of work it helps to know what to expect. So I called to my companion to tarry. 'I daresay I am not so young as you,' said I. And he obliged and fell into step with me, and I began to make him out a little better: a boy of fourteen or fifteen, and I knew him then from one of the farms on the western edge of Balaam, just before the woods begin. As we walked, I asked why I was summoned. What had happened. Was this a member of his own family, was there infection in the house?

'Our neighbour-child,' said he. 'It was croup. The mother will not leave her.'

Balaam thinned. We passed the comfortable spread of the boy's own home to a cabin beyond it, which I had not known was there. A light was in the window and a young woman was crying by the only bed. She looked up when I came in. Her face was white and her eyes red.

'Snow,' she said. 'My Snow.'

I knew her then. It was Elizabeth Guskett, whose people had been in the town even before mine. Her father was an alderman; her brothers had been schoolmates with my own boy Joshua. One had gone to sea for his fortune and one was a druggist, doing handsomely. The daughter was not such a point of pride.

Still, I do not stand in judgement.

Beneath his wig the Alderman Guskett had red hair, or did when we were young men. His daughter's, uncovered, was the same, and straggled loose from the braids coiled at the nape of her neck. She had the same guileless blue eyes. She had not the paunch. Elizabeth Guskett, thin as winter sticks. Bony wrists and sunken cheeks. Draped over her shoulders was something more mend than shawl. She sat by the body of her little girl, Snow, one infant hand lying slack in her own, and looked up at me fearfully as if she thought I would not be kind. I took off my hat.

Haste is not a virtue. I did not approach the infant on the bed but went to the hearth to see the fire damped down, while Elizabeth sagged in her chair and told me how it had come on so fast – how only a few days ago her baby had been toddling about her skirts, and so pretty, so precocious, gabbling *Snow do it. Snow do it, Mama no help.* And she fell sick – all the children at the farm did, but none so bad as Snow, who was the littlest – and she coughed and coughed and could not breathe, and her fever would not break, and so here we were.

'Her little voice,' Elizabeth Guskett said. 'I shall never hear it more.' The thought made her face contort, and she pressed her fist to her mouth.

I said nothing.

'A good mother would wish to die in her place,' she added. 'I can't wish that. How could I have left her alone? Who in this world would ever be kind to her but me?'

I was minded to tell her that our town was not so very bad,

that charity and care would be extended to a little bastard orphan, but she knew better than I on the matter, so I only said, 'She is beyond all cruelty now.'

Elizabeth nodded. 'You may take off your jacket, sir.'

The room was cold. Nevertheless I laid it on the one vacant chair and came to the side of the bed, rolling up my sleeves.

She watched as I measured up the thirty inches of Snow Guskett, from her pink toes to the damp brown curls smoothed across her brow. Snow had long lashes, so dark that their roots were a shadow beneath her eyelids. She had soft round cheeks, a crease on each plump wrist. Elizabeth's eyes flicked between me and the infant, and I saw her nails blanch her palm.

'What did she ever do wrong?' she whispered. 'What was there to punish her for?'

'Nothing indeed,' I said. Snow lay still. Her nightgown was fine and white but the single room of her home was scanty, with its one bed and two chairs, its polished-dirt floor, its single shelf almost empty of crockery or food. But there was a fine wax-faced doll and a horn-book tidied into a basket, and a collection of fruits and vegetables stitched from scraps of cloth, and an uneven piece of slate with scrawls upon it – the last of their kind.

'There is a parish coffin for such occasions as these,' I said carefully, 'and it will cost you nothing. You may have use of it for the laying-out, for the funeral. I would be discreet.'

Elizabeth was shaking her head vigorously before I had left off speaking. 'She'll have her own coffin,' she said. 'A good one. A soft one. I cannot have my Snow lie in the dirt and the cold. And you may send the Alderman Guskett the bill: I should have asked his help before now. Only pride prevented me.'

She fixed me with those pale, wide eyes. The shadows beneath them were purple.

'There's nothing more I can do for her,' she said as if I must be persuaded. 'This is the only thing.'

'I understand.'

I determined that I would send no bill. Dorcas would agree with me.

'And will I sit watch for you tonight?' I asked. By profession I am a cabinet-maker, by pragmatism a coffin-maker. And thus by habit I am become a companion of Death, and all his necessities fall under my jurisdiction. It often falls to me to sit up with a friendless corpse. My mother said this must be done in case the dead roused themselves, but to my knowledge such a thing never occurred in Balaam. It was all for the living. Always after a death, the women arrived in silence, and washed and laid out the body, and opened the window, and lit the candles. They cushioned the shock with the sound of their breath and the warmth of their bodies. They filled the strange hours with gentle talk, and reminiscences.

'Do you have people coming?' I asked Elizabeth Guskett.

She shook her head. 'The goodwife from the farm offered. She's been kind to us but I'll have nobody else here. I will do it myself. I will do it all myself. I always have.'

'You are tired, madam.'

'Not so tired. Please. Let me have this time.'

THE COFFIN

I went to my workshop and set about things. I had a good plank, which I thought would do well for little Snow. I planed it smooth, and the wood went into gold coils. In an hour or two, when the dawn approached, my son came in from over the road. Our girls have left for Sudbury and for Boston but Joshua, our eldest, remains in Balaam. He built a new house across the way and filled it with grandchildren, and this is a true joy to Dorcas and to me.

'I saw your light,' he said, chafing his cold hands.

'What were you doing awake?'

'The little lad had a bad dream.' Joshua laughed. 'I woke to him standing by our bed in the dark. Perfectly silent. I was afraid, until I saw it was him.'

'You did the same when you were small,' I said. 'The nights the dead did not rouse me, you did.' Beloved Joshua, hot from sleep, waking me with his presence in the dark. I would rise in silence to give Dorcas her rest, and escort him without seeing him. No candles lit. His bare feet patting the boards, his hand in mine. 'You will miss it one day,' I said. I recalled the stickiness of tears on his baby cheeks as he laid his head upon my breast, and the slowing of his breath. What sanctuary I was to my son back then. And now he was grown, and I was old, and he spent his nights staggering after children of his own.

He was eyeing my list of measurements. 'What news?' he asked.

'The Guskett child,' I said. But there were many Guskett children in our town, so I added, 'Elizabeth Guskett's little one.'

He scratched his chin. The rasp of bristles upon skin. 'The fatherless one.'

'There'll be a father somewhere.'

He took breath as if to repeat what many in town did – that men are men and what can be done about that, but most girls would rather die than succumb to flattery or temptation or threat as Elizabeth Guskett must have, so the baby was more hers than his, whoever *he* was – but I shook my head.

'Not over the poor child's coffin,' I said.

He grumbled and rubbed his chin again.

Then he said, 'Well. I'm sorry for it. It was not the child's fault.' He came close to the bench and rested his hands on it, watching me at my work. In a more jovial tone, he asked, 'Who do you fancy will go along with her?'

There is never just one knock. My father was the coffin-maker before me, so I discovered this truth through the broken nights of my own boyhood: that the dead leave in pairs. Perhaps not two in a night, but always one on the heels of another, so that the news of one death as it passes around town is not received as the entire story, but as the opening of a door, which must wait to be closed by the next who goes through it.

'You think it'll be another little one?' Joshua persisted, and I looked up at him then for his voice sounded not quite controlled.

'Could be,' I said, and regretted it. The fear in a new father's heart is a terrible thing.

Where babies are concerned, love is fear. There is no reassurance. So many things might befall the puny creatures. That they are well in the current moment means nothing: they could just as easily leave off breathing the next. Every little child I measured up, I knew might be my own – tomorrow, if it pleased God.

Nightly, I used to pace the dark house with the newborn scrap of Joshua mewling on my shoulder, and the sorriest grief in my heart at the deal I'd struck to have this son to love. Nightly, I imagined him laid out. His crumpled brow, the feather-brown hair smoothed aside, his tiny fists loose on his shrouded bosom. I saw it so clearly. And as he grew tall and strong and clever, and did not succumb to any fever, and was not overlaid by Dorcas in the night, and was never kicked by a horse or gored by pigs or stuck by a rusty nail, and did not join a militia, the fear might be moved to the back of the shelf, as it were. But it was only put away, and never gone. So, I was sorry that I had provoked Joshua's, when he was so fresh in his fatherhood.

'Then again,' I said as I worked, 'it won't be another child that goes with her. Two the same – no, no. For what would the lesson be then?'

I've a fancy that there's a warning for us in those pairings, if we care to pay attention. The humble go with the proud. The friendless with men of renown. The whore goes with the minister and the merchant with the vagrant and the stillborn with the governor himself. God wishes it known that we are all risen from the same mud, and all return to it anon. He wishes it known that He sees each one of us, and judges us just the same, and that although we presume to abhor or torment or cheat certain of our fellow men, by virtue of our own perceived superiority, He sees through all this.

'It will be someone of standing,' I told Joshua. 'A person well thought of in Balaam.'

'A rich old man.' My son looked happier then.

'Perhaps.'

'It could be the Alderman Guskett himself,' he went on. 'Long-lived, admired, a person of considerable influence. He had the means to help that little girl. With ease. His own natural grandchild.' His eyes had grown bright; he rubbed his hands through his brown hair so it stood up. Joshua enjoyed gossip. 'It *should* be him.'

'I cannot speak to "should",' I said. 'We'll know soon enough.'

I went to bed and slept.

When I woke, Dorcas was in the passage taking off her outdoor things.

'What news from town?' I asked. The stories begun by night for me and my measuring tape take new shape by day for Dorcas and her errand-basket.

'They do not talk loudly of the Guskett girl, but they talk of little else,' Dorcas told me. She was unfastening the clasp of her cape. New blue wool, which looked well on her, and the cold had made her cheeks pink. A good woman, Dorcas. 'The ladies say that now she is free of the child she might be persuaded to leave town. They feel they might raise a collection for her, enough to set herself up.' She paused in folding her gloves to inspect their seams. 'It's easier for them to help her now the child is gone.'

'And yet it would have meant more to her before.'

She caught my eye in the mirror. 'I expect you'll supply the coffin gratis?' she asked. When I nodded she said, 'And yet you did not pay for a doctor.'

'Mother Hollar was abroad last night,' I said then. 'What news of that?'

Dorcas nodded. 'The glover's wife had her sixth baby. Not the glover *we* use; Jessop on the high street. I tried him but we will not buy from him again.' She held up her glove to show me where a seam gaped and laid it peevishly upon the console. 'That's another chore for me today. Well, the Jessop gloves are not robust, but their babies are. All came off well for both mother and child, I hear.'

I kissed her bright cold cheek and made to return to my workshop.

'It won't be either of them,' she said as I went.

'Beg your pardon?'

'You wonder who will go alongside the Guskett child,' she said. 'And I say it will not be Amiable Jessop, nor her baby.'

'You can't know,' I said. 'I have seen people who seemed hale as anything carried off in a moment, when a pair was wanted.'

'*Wanted!* None of this is ordained, Josh Peachment. People are not gloves; they do not go in pairs. It is all accident.'

I said nothing to that. I went out to the workshop to cut the pieces for Snow's coffin. I measured and sawed and sanded and chiselled, and mixed up my rabbit-glue to fix it snug together. I am conscientious in my work. When I build a cabinet I do so with the desire that its owner will find no fault or cause for irritation in it. That it will serve them sturdy and true for many a year to come. My coffins are the same. And as I worked I thought of what the glover would commission for his wife Amiable. What gilt handles and silken trim. And all the while little Snow was laid out in her bare home where her mother wept uncomforted. If their coffins were ever to be considered side by side, neither one must be found wanting.

For I was sure the two would go together.

All the afternoon I turned it over in my head. Ill-begotten Snow Guskett, her mother's only; Amiable Jessop with six children to feel her loss. Snow who had had no doctor, and no warm blankets, and no visitors in her sickness. Amiable Jessop who must now be sipping hot wine in her large house. No doubt she snubbed Elizabeth Guskett in life ... Might she go side by side with a child so few lamented?

'I don't like this talk, Josh,' Dorcas said when I related this to her by the fire. 'It is not seemly.'

'But there is a lesson here, if the townspeople would see it,' I said. 'This is very levelling.'

'"How unsearchable are His judgements..."' Dorcas recited, and I joined my voice to hers to say in unison:
'"... and His ways past finding out."'
Dorcas leaned forward from her seat to lay her hand on mine. I took it. It was warm. 'I never knew a man kinder to those brought low,' she said. 'I love you for it. But guard yourself from wishing suffering upon those you view as too fortunate.'
'Wise wife,' I said. But still I thought on it. And I thought I would cover the coffin of Snow Guskett with white holland-cloth and make a pattern of shining brass tacks all over it.

I had no more holland-cloth so I went forth for it next morning. On the high street I passed the Jessop house, and there was Agnes Hollar with her basket of herbs and bottles. Her face was creased and troubled. She did not look as if she had been to bed.
'I heard all went well,' I said, which she took as a question and shook her head.
'The goodwife Jessop is ailing for something. She has not recovered as she usually does.'
I did not walk on, but I did not speak again. She pressed her fingers hard to the place between her eyebrows.
'Go to bed, Mr Peachment,' she said. 'Rest while you are able.'
This was all the intimation I required. I bowed to her and went on my way to buy the holland, and with it a few dark-coloured satins for Mister Jessop to choose between.

On my way back I passed the house again. Mother Hollar was gone and the shop was still shuttered up, although all the other businesses were open now, with their wares hung out and their errand boys coming and going. The Jessop house, in its bareness and its stillness, stood like a visitor from the night-time.

There was nothing to see but still I looked. That fine, broad house with its snug-boarded walls and its second storey and its attics. Twenty paces off and its perfect equal was the house in which Elizabeth Guskett had been born, and where her parents still lived. Such a home might little Snow have enjoyed, had she been permitted.

I should not have stood staring. It does not do for a coffin-maker. The high street was full of its usual activity, and many passed me by, but I had not felt much observed. Now it was as if I did not stand alone. I looked behind me and saw a tiny child on the other side of the road, fifteen paces off. Too young to be out by herself: I judged her not even two years old. And her white gown was too thin for the season, and too clean for the dirty street. And her little cap with its strings knotted under her chin afforded her no protection from the cold air. And her face, oh her face was forlorn. She was looking about searchingly, made mute by fear. Her eyes were wide. Her lower lip petted out.

I thought, *She has wandered from a house. She does not know her way back.* And I looked about to see if anybody had come forth in search of her. Perhaps they had her in their sight and it was only she who thought herself lost. I did not like to approach a strange child. I stood apart, to watch her. But nobody came, and the little girl's shoulders rose and fell more swiftly, and she clasped her hands together as she stood all alone and so small on the road, while all around her the people of Balaam surged about their business unseeing. And she was staring in my direction – staring, it seemed to me, at Jessop the glover's house.

I knew her then by her brown hair and her long lashes, the pretty round cheeks I had seen last by the light of a rancid tallow candle. Snow Guskett, standing in the street, waiting for a companion to join her.

Never had such a thing happened to me before. I had heard tales of those who saw the dead. I had not, myself, thought it possible. I am not a man who sees the dead. Granted, I believe the order in which we each depart is ordained, as all things are, but I take this as God's lesson to the living. It is none of the dead's doing. Could it be that they, in the meantime, become restless?

I stood dismayed. My feet were lead. I could neither go to the child nor run from her. I stared in expectation that my eyes would correct what they saw. They did not. Snow Guskett, white among the crowds of buff fustian. She waited. She stared. There was a tear upon her cheek.

I followed her gaze back to the Jessop house. Mother Hollar was on the step, closing the door behind her.

'Mr Peachment,' she said. She frowned.

'What news?' I asked. My blood thundered. How wild-eyed I must have looked.

She put her hood up and arranged the weight of her basket on her arm. 'Have you waited here all this while?'

'Been and come back,' I said. I held out my bundle of coffin-cloth and she shook her head sternly.

'Do not loiter about my clients' houses,' she said. 'It's no business of yours how they fare.'

'It might be.'

She stepped down into the street and made to pass me by. 'Stay away,' she said. 'This is a job for me. If it becomes one for you, you will hear.'

'Mistress Hollar,' I called. She paused.

'They are well,' she hissed. 'Mother and child. They will not need your services.'

'I believe—' I stammered. I could not finish. There was no way to tell her that her patient was surely dying, that her hour was nigh, that a minister must be fetched. I looked back to where the child had been, but the crowd had rolled about her and I saw no child there.

The Watch

I furnished the coffin and my hands shook. I pricked my fingers and I bruised a knuckle with the tack-hammer. There was a sick raw taste in my throat. A spot of blood on the white holland, which I was able to conceal. It was unlike me to be so careless.

I carried it to Elizabeth Guskett's cabin. I saw no need

to put it on my cart: it was too small. I paced down the high street with Snow Guskett's empty coffin upon my shoulder, so all might see the pattern of stars and scrolls and six-petalled flowers I had picked out in tacks upon the holland-cloth. The winter light was grey and sulky, but the tacks shone like gold. My fellow townspeople broke off to stare at its whiteness. They stared at me, carrying it as soberly as if I approached the grave. I spoke not a word.

Let the people of Balaam see that lowly Snow would be well buried, in a coffin padded with horsehair and wool.

Let them see that she was ready now to go to her grave, and wanted only a journeymate.

Let them think on what account of themselves they might make to the Creator, were they to be called before Him tomorrow.

I went by the Guskett house. Alderman Guskett was standing before it with the magistrate, and he looked at the coffin with his blue, blue eyes, and looked at me, and said nothing. I went by the Jessop house, where two faces rippled at the upstairs window. Amiable Jessop, baby on her arm. So. Perhaps it was not to be her. Dorcas had told me that the fever had been almost nothing, after all. 'But Mother Hollar said you were very strange with her,' she had said to me in my workshop as I prepared to leave.

'I was upset,' I said.

'By what?'

Dorcas has been my wife over thirty years. She has never failed to take my side. I might express the most lunatic of views, and she would look for the sense in it. And if she found no sense, she would be grieved that I had lost my wits, and love me still, and seek to understand me. Her faith in me – her faithfulness to me – is deep in her nature. Had I told her what I had seen, she would have listened kindly. That was why I could not.

'You are much affected by the death of the Guskett child,' she had said, putting a hand on my shoulder.

'I do not know why,' I said.

'You do not like injustice,' she said. 'Or, you do not like untidiness. You are a good man, but you seek a moral where there is not one for us to know.'

'Someone must go with her,' I had said. 'Two always go together. Must this child be set apart, even in death?'

This is not the work of a just God, I thought to myself as I reached the opposite side of town and set my sights on the farm beyond, which concealed Elizabeth Guskett's cabin. *The God I know would take this opportunity to set things right. To set us all as equals again.* And so who would it be? Perhaps Joshua was right and the Alderman Guskett was indeed the most fitting companion for his little grandchild. If he would not acknowledge her in life, perhaps he would be obliged to walk with her in death. There would be sense to that.

So, I thought. I had been mistaken. Snow had been standing in the street, yes, but had I mistook which house held her attention? Was not the Guskett house only a few doors along? Perhaps, then, she had come for her grandfather?

My breath was a cloud. The sky had a moleskin look to it.

A red cardinal-bird hopped from twig to twig through the bare thorn-bushes ahead of me, and that was the only colour. My hands, though gloved, throbbed with the cold. The path was clogged with mud, and my boots broke the crust of frost upon it. It was not frozen solid, and I was glad of that since the gravedigger was at this very moment breaking the ground for baby Snow, but it would not be long now before true winter set in.

The mud did not make for an easy walk. I am not young. My feet slithered; I felt the strain in my knee as it went from under me. I grunted but I knew I must not drop, and must not loose my grip on the white coffin. My joints were jarred and my muscles twinged. Somehow I struggled onward. Stamped and coughed and slipped again. Kept that coffin spotless.

I found Elizabeth Guskett much as I had left her, sitting numb in her chair. The ashes in the hearth were cold. I found Snow Guskett there too, all in her winding-cloths, with a posy of evergreens on her breast. I did not stare but I was satisfied that this child had not recently walked abroad. It was beyond her to go anywhere. And so I could not have seen her in the street.

'I am sorry I have come to you so,' I said. My boots were muddy almost to the knee. My breeches and cloak spattered also.

I carried the white coffin upon my shoulder but she did not want to see it, and replied only, 'I am sorry I receive you so. I cannot light the fire.' She nodded toward her child. 'All her life I worried how to keep her warm. Now she must be kept cold, and I have cold enough for her and more. How the wheel turns.'

Since she had given me permission to look at Snow, I did. And I saw her little face and the brown hair quite unlike her mother's, and knew beyond doubt that she was the child I had seen in the street. How I was to feel on that matter, I could not decide.

'See what I have brought you,' I said to Elizabeth.

She rose and stared at it. The tacks sparkled. I put it down on her table and she came to look.

'I can change it, if you wish,' I said. 'You need only say.'

She was leaning over it. Her eyes filled with tears. 'And so it has come to this,' she said. Slowly she reached out and put her hand into the white linen within, all cushioned soft as she had wanted. She sighed. Her shoulders became less rigid. 'Thank you,' she said.

I looked at the child on the bed. 'Where have you been sleeping?' I asked.

'I have not,' she said.

'I will sit the watch tonight,' I said.

'Sir, no.'

'She goes to her grave tomorrow,' I said. 'Take some rest before that. Let me help you.'

I did wish to help her. But I had thought on my old mother's words, that we sit the watch in case the dead rise and walk again. And thus I would sit up with Snow Guskett.

I had brought my own candles. I had brought a meat pie. I looked at the wall while Elizabeth brought Snow to her coffin, for I did not think it meet to witness that last putting-to-bed. I heard Elizabeth whispering while she busied herself about her child, tucking and straightening, gathering some object from the basket of toys to lie with her. Then she blew her nose and joined me as the dusk came in.

I sat in one chair with my cloak still on and she sat in the other, wrapped in the blanket from her bed. She pulled it up over her nose and stared over its folds. I compelled her to eat a little, and presently she did with her eyes warily upon me. The candles I brought wavered. For an hour or more we sat. I never mind silence. My thoughts were turning.

'She was born in this room,' said Elizabeth suddenly. I had been staring at my hands, not expecting her to speak, and I raised my eyes to see that an urgency had come over her. She longed to tell me about her child. 'It was the end of February last year,' she went on, 'and the snowstorm came in from nowhere.'

'I recall it,' I said. Nobody ever saw its like. It covered the fruit-trees and cleaved their trunks as lightning does. It got under thresholds and down chimneys. It froze every cow in Balaam.

'No good for the farmers or the shopkeeps,' she said, 'but good for me. Nobody could come or go. Nobody was out gossiping. There was no world beyond these walls but the thick sky and the tumbling snow.'

She looked about the cabin. The bare shelves, the white

coffin, the shrouded child. 'I did it all by myself,' she said. 'All alone. No Mother Hollar for me. No friends or family, not even the women from the farm, who did not know my time was upon me and could not have reached me even so. But somehow we two came through safe. Some days later I tried to open the door,' she went on, and she looked to that door now as if it might open. 'The drifts were high as my shoulder. I stood on the threshold with my baby wrapped up to her eyes, and I showed her a chink of the world. All was silent. The snow was thick and smooth, without a mark. Nothing looked as it commonly did.'

She was looking to the door still and I almost saw it as she did. What stifled snow-light once fell through it. Elizabeth Guskett, plumper then, barefoot, bloodied, holding a bundle in her arms.

Now she was wringing her hands in her lap. 'Mr Peachment, I was so afraid before she was born. I wondered, would I leave her on the steps of the church, would I let my father find a nurse for her in another town, would I smother her before she took a breath? I did not mean to keep her. But as soon as she came forth I was filled with astonishment.'

I nodded. I found there were tears in my eyes.

'I didn't love her as I do now. I was simply amazed. Amazed. I could not let her go. And the snow would not let me. I think God sent it to wrap us up and keep the world away. For a fortnight, my baby saw no face but mine. We lay together in my bed. I ate all my provisions and burned all I owned to keep us warm. We stayed here, we two, until my father came to dig us out. It was a wonder we survived – he was astonished to find us, and I think not pleased. He said he must take the baby away, but by then I would not give her up.' She was staring at me. 'So that is the story of my Snow,' she said, 'and how I came to keep her and to live the life that I have.'

'You loved her very much,' I said.

'Selfishly. I ask myself, would the loving thing have been to let her go? She might still be alive if I had sent her to another mother. But if that mother had been cruel . . . Snow never knew cruelty with me. She never knew sadness, never knew shame. She would have found it in the world, or it would have found her, had she grown. The sins of the father are visited upon the child: she was marked from the start.'

Often, people ask me, have they done the right thing? Could they have acted differently? Could they have tried harder? Since they want an answer, I give them one. *The doctor was too far distant to arrive in time*, I say. Or, *He had lived a long life and was dismayed by his infirmity at the end.* And while I do no more than summarise, and offer no opinion at all, they are comforted. To Elizabeth Guskett I said:

'Snow's life was brief and she was loved.'

Elizabeth nodded slowly. 'Is that what *she* would have chosen?' she asked me. We regarded one another. 'Of course you cannot say. Or you will not.'

I turned away to see Snow white-bundled in her coffin. I thought of how I had seen her standing in the cold street, alone and afraid. My throat was tight. I could not tell her mother about that. Were I to say, *Snow is weeping and waiting for a companion into death,* I believe Elizabeth Guskett would straightway do what was necessary to be that companion.

'We will all have our answers in the next life,' I said.

'Do you think I'll get there, Mr Peachment?' Elizabeth asked softly.

'You stand as good a chance as any of us.'

She was staring at the coffin. 'Snow was the great sin of my life,' she said, 'and taught me the most grace. What patience it takes to be a mother. What kindness, what forbearance. For her, I became an outcast and I cannot regret it. Who would I have been, had I not strayed? Nobody remarkable. If I am now to live without my Snow, I might do some good for her sake.'

Dawn was coming. The grave would be dug by now, awaiting its occupant.

'Thank you for your kindness, Mr Peachment,' said Elizabeth Guskett.

'I was glad to give it,' I told her and pressed her hand.

'I had thought it would be strange with you.'

'How so?'

She gave me a careful look. 'It is strange with everyone,' she said. 'They are hungry to know who – to know how Snow came about. And yet you have never once asked.'

'It doesn't matter,' I said. 'I would treat you no different.'

'No,' she said. 'I do not believe you would. Thank you, sir.'

I bade her farewell then and promised I would see her in the churchyard. The day was cold and murky once again, clotted sky over black mud and the trees standing all spidery against it. My hips moved at a creak. My knee ached from the day before. And my head was thick with sleeplessness as I set off along the path. Elizabeth stood before her cabin, hands clasped, watching me go. Her loose red hair flashed across her face.

The Funeral

There had been no sign of that spectral child at Elizabeth Guskett's cabin. Nor did I see her outside the house of the Alderman Guskett, or Jessop the glover. I walked all across town and saw her nowhere, until I reached my own street.

Joshua was outside his house. I saw him from a distance. He had the baby in his arms and the three little boys before him. It seemed to me he was explaining the rules of a game, for he was gesturing as best he could while the elder two observed. Little Joshie, too small to understand, crouched to inspect something in the dirt. And I saw beyond them, hardly set apart, another little child. This one was white-clad. She wrapped her arms about herself and shivered. She stared at the backs of the children, and at Joshua who did not see her. He addressed each child in turn, but Snow never caught his eye.

I hobbled closer. I wanted nothing more than to return home and rest my bones before the fire. I could not leave this cold little girl.

'Grandpa!' the children were shouting, and pointing. 'Grandpa!'

I raised my hand. All their little faces were turned to me. All of them, and Snow Guskett's. And my eyes roved over them and saw what I had not seen before: the round cheeks of each child, the brown curls, the dark eyes. They were smiling and calling, and she was weeping and shivering, but nevertheless she was all of a piece with them.

'Good morning, Father,' called Joshua. The baby in his arms held her head up on a wobbly neck, goggling at me. What a good father I had always thought him. What a good father he *was*, to the children under his roof. 'Where have you been?' he asked.

My mouth was all dried up.

'Elizabeth Guskett's,' I said.

'Oh.' He put a finger beneath his collar. The agitation returned to him. I had noticed it as I built the child's coffin and had thought him simply afraid for his own little ones. 'Surely you have given her enough of your time,' he said. 'She should not be your concern.'

'Shouldn't be. But is.'

He was watching me all fearful. 'Are you feeling well?'

The children were thronging around me. Their little hands patting my legs, my spattered cloak, slipping into my own. They reached to be picked up. I hoisted stout Joshie, my namesake, to sit on my arm, and thought of how he was only born last February, weeks before the great storm came in, and he was as warm in my arms as Snow Guskett would have been, resting his brown-curled head so trustingly upon my shoulder.

I looked upon Joshua and felt such rage it struck me blind. My vision was white. Then I righted myself and saw him again, and saw him clearly as ever or more so.

You are her father, I would have said, and also:

She has come to fetch you.

I put Joshie down and strode away. The children were calling after me, and Joshua too. He broke into a run after me, saying, 'Do you know? Do you know? What do you know?' and then, 'What did she say to you? It was not what you think. Please, do not – do not tell Sophia. This is nothing. And isn't it all over now?'

I tried to look him in the face but that white crossed my eyes again. Never had I felt myself in such disarray. I could not credit that this man before me, gabbling his excuses and his mollifications, was the son I raised so carefully. All we had done for him – the love Dorcas and I had lavished upon him, watching him grow with our hearts in our mouths, beseeching God that he be delivered from sickness and ill fortune, that he be granted a fine long life, our one beautiful son – was it all for this?

And here he stood with that little white-clad child unseen behind him, her feet bare on the dirty ground, her eyes so like his. And I thought, *She has come to take him away. Not my son. Oh, not my boy.* And my heart was clenched and awful.

'Please, Father,' Joshua said.

I went into my house and closed the door.

*

Snow Guskett's funeral was attended by nobody, and very well attended at that. Only I and the minister joined her mother at the graveside. But beneath each of the graveyard's willow-trees and in each of its shady corners lingered a black-clad onlooker. I saw the bulky form of the Alderman Guskett, hat pulled down. His wife stood with her arms folded some distance away, affecting she had not noticed him. I saw three goodwives around Elizabeth's own age clustered in the porch of the church, casting glances over their shoulders at the proceedings. I saw my boy Joshua, and he saw me. The clouds were yellow as horn and the air grippingly cold. There was frost on the mound of earth at the graveside.

The bells rang out but the minister said no words over the grave. There was nothing of note about Snow Guskett's short life. Elizabeth quietly handed a coin to each of the hired pall-bearers but there were no gloves or rings to disperse. There was nothing fine but Snow's white coffin, which went into the ground.

The earth was frozen in heavy clods, and it fell down – *thud, thud, thud* – upon the white coffin for all in the graveyard to hear. Elizabeth Guskett flinched with each shovelful. I offered her my arm and she gripped the wool of my sleeve with her bare hands, her nails grey with cold. She was shaking.

'Come away,' I said, but she shook her head. She wanted to see the grave filled and the earth tamped down. She stood in her thin shoes and her thin dress and her thin shawl, shivering.

I had arrived ready to see little Snow again. I had been certain she would be here, fixing her beseeching eyes upon the person she wished to accompany her, and after that the matter would become clear and no longer turning over and over in my mind.

It must be Joshua. As I had brushed my cloak clean and made myself ready for the funeral, I had agreed with myself that this was so. For he was well thought of in Balaam. And he was loved by his children and his wife. And he had neglected and denied Snow Guskett while she lived. And he was a hypocrite, where she was an innocent. Therefore, by my own reckoning, he made a fine candidate to accompany her. I would have been quicker to conclude this had he not been my own son.

Still, I saw no Snow. I cast my gaze around every corner of the burying-ground. There was the Alderman Guskett, taking his leave. He went contritely, in the shade of the wall, as if he for once wished himself smaller than he was. His wife waited a count of ten before she followed him. Snow Guskett did not trail them. The goodwives from the porch clasped hands with one another, and released, and left in a line, never looking back at their friend Elizabeth. No little child went with them. Away went the minister, and the two pall-bearers, off to their homes for there would be no gathering after such a funeral. Only Joshua was left, lingering by the lich-gate. And Snow was not with him.

'Will I escort you past that man?' I asked Elizabeth Guskett. She was weeping silently. She did not let go of my arm.

We went across the frozen grass together. It crackled at our passing.

'Liz,' said Joshua as we went by. Poor Joshua. His voice was soft and pleading. He had taken off his hat and I thought him a little boy with rapped knuckles, who longs to be forgiven. Elizabeth's head was low and she did not say a word, but her fingers were tight about my sleeve and I felt her body begin to shake again.

'Let her be,' I said to my son. I thought, *Snow is coming for him.*

'Liz?' he repeated. She would not look at him.

I guided Elizabeth Guskett through the gate and into the lane. There were flashes of white in the corners of my eyes but when I turned my head there was no little Snow — not in the hedges, not in the trees, not in the frozen puddles. Her mother's breath came fast and ragged.

'She did not want my help,' said Joshua, turning his address to me. He had cast aside his chastened affect. He strode to catch up with us. He spoke swiftly. 'She might have asked. She kept herself away from me.'

'I wanted nothing to do with you,' gasped Elizabeth Guskett. 'I wish never to see you again.'

'Do you see?' my son asked me — my son who would soon be dead, whose little daughter stood invisible among his children, waiting for him. 'There is nothing to be made right. You always take the part of the despised, Father. Naturally you now favour this woman' — and he said *this woman* in a very terrible tone — 'over me.'

My lip curled. The sight of him now was bitter as aloe to my heart. He was standing wide in the lane with his hair all a-bristle, and very big he seemed, very black in his cloak, while Elizabeth Guskett shrank against me.

So often I have walked the streets of Balaam at night. So often I have honoured my contract with its people: that in the light of day I will forget.

'There was a beam in my eye,' I said, 'and I never looked for it.'

Joshua put on his hat and left. His longboots went fast down the lane. He would be in search of Dorcas and Sophia, to bring them his story before I brought them mine, but I would not race him. Let him acquit himself as he saw fit.

'Your redemption is your own lookout, Joshua Peachment,' I called as he went. 'Prepare yourself for the hereafter.'

And my voice broke. And my insides were hot. And I felt the most terrible grief at all that had passed, and not least that a reckoning would soon be upon my son and that I could deliver him from many things in this world, but when it came to the next I was helpless. And did not little Snow deserve company on her crossing? Surely she was not so despised that nobody would go with her. If it were to be him, it would be one mark to the good on his balance-sheet.

'I'll leave you here,' said Elizabeth Guskett.

'I wish you had told me,' I said.

She sighed. 'It would have done no good, Mr Peachment.'

'None of us will ever know now,' I said.

'No. But we might decide what will be next.' She squeezed

my arm and released it. Stepped away and dabbed her eyes and tried to smile. 'Nineteen months, I had her. What a brief chapter.'

I stood in the lane not knowing what to say. Then something faint and white came down, and it landed on her eyelash. And another settled on my lip, and another in the red hair that showed under her cap. The scumbled sky had opened. It began to snow.

Elizabeth Guskett blinked and turned up her sore face. The flakes were very light and small; they danced in the air and made cold little points on our skin that lived but briefly before fading in the heat of our flesh.

THE DEATH

Late it was, and so often that's the way. I opened my eyes although I had heard no sound, and saw standing by my bed a small expectant figure. Perhaps I sensed it more than saw it, for it was dark in our room and the child no more than a shadow.

'Back to bed,' I whispered, and rose.

I would not wake Dorcas, although she shifted and murmured, as was her habit, 'Bless their soul.'

The child pattered away into the passage. 'Let's have you cosy again,' I said. I pulled the door to behind me and followed the sound of its nightgown, its little feet on the boards. And the passage was doorless and lightless, and longer than it should have been. I had thought it only a few steps to the room where my children slept, but the child, that little shadow hardly higher than my knee, pattered ahead and gave no sign of pausing. At last I regained sense and asked myself, *Where am I? There is no passage such as this in my house.*

And then I thought, *Who is this leading me? There is no child such as this in my house.*

I was ready to be afraid, but I was not afraid.

'Little one,' I whispered, and that small person slowed until the hem of their gown flapped against me.

'Little one,' I repeated, and it slowed again.

Then I felt a warm, tiny hand slide into mine, and a voice said, 'Snow.'

'Snow,' said I, and knew her, and understood why I had followed her without question. Had I not done the same for each of my children? And would I not do the same for any of my grandchildren? I picked her up although I could not see her, and I felt her cheek against mine and her heart busy in her breast. And I cupped my hand about the back of her little cap, and I put my arm around her to hold her safe. And then she laid her head on my shoulder and let out a sigh of great tiredness. And she became heavy.

'Well, here I am at last,' I said to her. I carried her down the passage. Her breath slowed as sleep came upon her. 'I am sorry you were obliged to wait so long.'

And here was the bed, still-warm covers thrown back, and I laid her gently in it. She curled on her side, and her thumb went into her mouth. Very small she was in that large bed. I kissed her brow and stroked her cheek and saw her comfortable. Then I bethought me to return to my own bed, where Dorcas had spread herself into the space I left.

I turned to go. And too late found there was no way back: no door, no passage, no walls even. Only a planeless, featureless darkness and behind me that warm bed where little Snow lay.

I turned back to her. Her eyes blinked in the darkness. She sighed. She reached her arms out to me, for she was all alone.

And I saw that the bed was large, and soft, with room enough for two. And so I laid me down.

THE SIGNAL BELLS

Natasha Pulley

I

In Mabarrow, where the parish records began eight hundred years ago with an entry that read *Today the Devil took all the children,* Christmas carols always seemed melancholy. You sang rejoice, but the music was sad, and in the lopsided church with its leaking roof and the windows hardly bigger than dinner plates, it didn't feel as though there was much to rejoice about.

Because it was such a bugger to fight your way up to the church against the streams of water pouring by, and dangerous getting back down again in the dark when you were tired, there had been a petition to do Midnight Mass not at midnight but about three in the afternoon. The vicar was horrified and refused, negotiation ensued, and everyone had settled grudgingly on nineish. Angharad was grateful for that, because she had an eight-mile walk home to the cottage by the mine. It took her two hours. Her bag – filled with carrots – felt heavy after two hours. And she liked not to be traipsing around by the mine after midnight. She didn't believe the stories about what happened then, but she didn't disbelieve them either. Empirical thinking was all well and good until it turned out God had invented it as a joke.

After all that, the vicar didn't even give the sermon. The curate explained in a wobbly voice that Mr Pennyfeather was ill. He had written the sermon, though. It was, as usual, about the Devil, with exhortations not to be fooled by his wiles. The wiles seemed to cover more or less everything nicer than a hot cup of tea, and even then, the tone implied, be alert for the smell of sulphur.

'We do not feast,' the curate quavered, 'we do not drink, we do not dance. We do our duty.'

It was better when Mr Pennyfeather said it. He sounded less worried someone was going to throw a saucer at him.

After the sermon, she lit a candle for her parents, half listening to the murmurs among the rest of the congregation as they wondered how ill the vicar could possibly be, to have left the service to the curate.

'No, no, honestly, it's just a touch of influenza,' the curate was telling people at the door, a little hysterically. 'Mr Pennyfeather will be giving the service tomorrow, I promise!'

The way he was twitching made Angharad think this was a lie. She was quite hoping the vicar was absolutely sozzled. He was the sort of person who thought a small glass of sherry was naughty, so it would have been a mighty victory for normal people if it turned out he'd been at the absinthe. Not too much, though. Angharad did actually quite like him. It wasn't his fault he was English.

'Condolences as usual, Miss Jones,' said the blacksmith, who had said the same thing to her on this day for forty years.

'Thanks very much,' she said back, though in all honesty, she felt guilty when people gave her condolences. It felt like being given lots of sympathy when you were pretending to be ill at school. She had been raised by a magnificent uncle who hadn't let being a shepherd get in the way of teaching himself Latin and teaching Angharad Latin too, rude words first, while they were out shooting apples off fences and climbing trees. She'd never deserved condolences. Not even for the magnificent uncle. He had died happy, certain that wherever his soul was bound, people there were probably much more reasonable and tolerant of those with what Mabarrow called *peculiar habits*, like learning to read. 'Wonder what's gone on with Michael?' Nobody but the curate called him Mr Pennyfeather. He wasn't a 'Mr' kind of person. Grown men showed him kittens.

You would think a man who preached so severely would be one of those thundering, frightening clerics, but it wasn't the case. People didn't do what Michael said because they were frightened of him, but because everyone had a horror of upsetting him.

'Been at the opium again, I expect,' the blacksmith said promptly.

The curate went purple. 'It's just flu!'

Angharad grinned and set out on the long walk home. She noticed people giving her bag of carrots interested looks, but it was a good idea to remain mysterious where you could, so she didn't explain.

*

The way home took her across the valley by a path so overgrown that it would have been difficult for a stranger to see there was a path at all. It was steep, and soon it became a waterfall, spray hazing the glass of Angharad's lamp and the new layer of polish on her boots, plunging down to the flood plain. And to the mine; or what was left of it.

The parish records also accused the Devil of having taken the miners forty years ago, but the official opinion of the Mabarrow Copper Company was that it had been firedamp.

Once there was an explosion and a shaft collapsed, you were never going to get anyone back in a mine as deep as Caer y Cythraul, not if you dug for months – always at risk of more explosions. So the mine was flooded to put out the fires deep underground. Now, the miners' cottages were all empty and crumbling. If the wind was up, spars fell off the old gallows frame and smashed on the lichen. At the moment, they splashed. In summer, the land was green and purple with grass and heather, but every December the floods were worse. Here and there, a tree clawed up from the water, drowned to its middle branches.

The only person left was Angharad. She was the shepherd, and she lived in the last cottage still standing: a tiny place that looked even tinier beside the mountain, right at the edge of the flood.

And the sheep, of course. Sheep counted as people. Sheep weren't usually known for their cunning, but Angharad's theory was that most sheep were intellectually understimulated. Hers had worked out how to open the gates. She suspected they could read. She suspected they looked at the sign outside the mine, the one that said *Danger – no entry*, and said to each other in Sheep, *Come on, lads, she'll be really cross this time.*

She was about five hundred yards from home, anticipating a future with hot tea and a rag pudding in it, when she saw a string of pale woolly shapes all through the abandoned mining gear.

Stupendous.

She had one of those miserable moments where she felt like she would always be wet, always alone, always exhausted.

Other people measured out the years in marriages, baptisms, the building of new houses. Not her. For shepherds, the years were circular. There was the lambing, the shearing, the dark and the floods after All Souls' when you plunged after lost sheep into ravines and floodwater every second day, and then round it went, again and again. You could begin tramping that great circuit at sixteen and not notice the lockstep of the decades until one day you looked in the mirror and saw your grandmother.

But that was the work. You went into the dark and you bloody well rescued the lost things out there, even if the lost thing was a homicidal ram making every effort to disembowel you. If you didn't do that, you were no shepherd.

She squelched towards the mine. Rain clattered on her hood and her lungs tightened with that familiar dread about the leak above the stove. She had been on the roof and boarded over every chink she could find, but still, there was a sliver of mildew down that back wall. She kept scrubbing it off; it kept coming back. She could smell it every time she boiled the kettle, a cold, dank dampness.

She was starting to catch that same smell from the wax of her coat. It was horrible.

The mud on the ground was a sickly orange. It became more vivid the nearer to the mine head you strayed. There was a sheep standing on some broken machinery, looking uncertain about what to do with itself. When she held out one of her Bribery Carrots, it hurried over. And that was why you should never go anywhere without a bag of carrots.

Caer y Cythraul meant 'the Devil's fortress'. There had been a real castle here once, or people said so, and the foundations were still somewhere in the mine.

In fact, from any distance, the abandoned works looked just like a ruined fort. Rust had overtaken everything: the smelting silos, the chutes, the carts that had hauled ore along the tracks. She walked along one of the rails, balancing, so she was above the mud. Weeds and little trees were growing up between them now. An owl was sitting in one. She tilted the light away from it. It was important to be polite to owls. Michael said the old stories were nonsense, but she wasn't convinced. You never knew when an owl had last been a person.

Most of the sheep were huddling just in the entrance of the mine, looking like gentlemen who had been out carousing but who'd had enough now and were waiting for a hansom cab.

'Evening all,' she said to them, handing out carrots and lifting one of the lambs out of an old mining cart. The lamb had soaked up water like a sponge. She squeezed him experimentally. A waterfall fell onto her boots.

In an hour she'd be dry at home with the tea and the pudding.

She was about to start herding the sheep home when a dog barked from inside the mine.

She frowned and held up the lantern, rain tinking on its brass top.

The bark came again, and this time the dog shot out, scattering startled sheep. It raced around her, then stood whining through its nose, tail lashing at the mud. It was trying to bark again, but it couldn't properly, because it had something soggy and dark clamped in its mouth.

She was sure she knew the dog. She caught it by the collar to see the tag, and yes, there it was, a coin of silver that said *GOWER* on one side and on the other, in English that managed to sound apologetic even when it was stamped into metal, *Please return to Mabarrow vicarage, sorry for the inconvenience!*

This was Michael Pennyfeather's dog.

No. Of course Michael wasn't here. He couldn't be. Gower must have escaped and gone on an adventure by himself. Michael was in bed with influenza, not lost in the mine. She definitely hadn't thought the curate was lying. That was silly.

Gower got his nose right in her face and dropped whatever he had been holding. She caught it just before it sploshed into the mud.

It was a Bible, battered and thumbed and full of Michael's tiny bookmarks, all different saints that he watercolour-painted himself and cut out with a scalpel.

'Bugger,' she said, as the hot tea and the pudding shrank depressingly into the distance.

Gower was still barking, frantic, and when she stepped forward he ran ahead of her into the mine, vanishing into the dark.

'Wait!'

He skittered back, wanting to know why she wasn't doing as she was told.

'Hang on, hang on.' She managed to get hold of his collar again for long enough to tie on her spare lamp. The lamp was tiny, just big enough to burn for an hour or so after her usual one had run out. After the Badger Incident, the spare lamp was an important part of her unwritten shepherding code. Go into the dark and rescue the lost thing. Always bring a bag of carrots. Carry a spare lamp for when you drop your normal lamp like an idiot because you've fallen over an opinionated badger.

She lit the spare lamp and sealed its little door to make sure the flame didn't singe the dog, and winced when he barked right in her ear.

'All right, go on then,' she said, and Gower shot away. This time, though, she saw the point of light galloping down the shaft.

For a few deep and echoing seconds she stood in the mine entrance, wanting more than anything not to go inside. They had never found the bodies.

And it was almost midnight. Midnight was when you could, sometimes, hear the singing. Or catch the smell of hot wine from the feast, or hear the steps of the dancers.

Go into the dark and rescue the lost thing.

She stepped over the threshold and thought straightaway how much colder it was inside than out.

A stream always trickled out here, staining everything copper on its way. But now it was bigger than a stream. She pulled her scarf over her nose. The air tasted of metal. Water dripped from the ceiling, snicking on the mud, and on her.

The sheep crowded into the entrance too and sat down, looking cross that she wasn't taking them home.

'Michael?' she shouted, in case he was close enough to hear her.

No such bloody luck.

What in the name of Christ was Michael Pennyfeather doing down the mine? Had he just – wandered in for a poke around? He was English, but he wasn't projectile English. He knew it was dangerous.

She didn't notice the wires sticking out of the wall until she walked into them and one caught on her coat.

She fell still. Forty years ago, her parents had stood here with her and explained how people talked to each other through the mine, and why she shouldn't worry that nobody would be able to tell them if she had an emergency at school.

They were the wires for the old signal bells. A bell was still there, right next to her, and somehow the years and the water hadn't tarnished it. It was bright silver, with a sigil she didn't know. It showed an owl with a crown around its neck.

Beside the bell was a fading list of the codes.

1 bell, all stop
2 bells: people descending
3 bells: hoist

There were about twenty, with different combinations of bells all meaning different things, but typed in bigger letters than the rest was:

9 BELLS: EVACUATE

The bells were all joined, or they had been. If you rang one, dozens more rang through the whole mine. She twisted the wires back together. Maybe some were still connected.

Up ahead, the darkness looked like a solid block. Gower, who had come back to hurry her along, was staring into it. The water from the ceiling dripped, but beyond that, there was a godforsaken silence. She wished she didn't have to disturb it, or any of the ghosts sleeping in it.

At least if she rang the bells, Michael would know someone was coming. If he had a light, he might find a code list and work out how to talk to her in return. There might even be a way to communicate how far down he was, and roughly where.

Yes: yes. Further down the list was exactly that.

1–1 bells: first level down
1–2 bells: second
1–3 bells: third

Angharad rang the bell twice. Someone descending.

Down through the mine, other bells rang in an eerie carillon. She thought uncomfortably of Michael with his halo of feral grey curls and his silver velvet waistcoat. The worst thing he'd ever done was try to convince her that cucumber sandwiches were real human food. He was the gentlest soul alive. The idea of him trapped in the wet, copper-tanging dark gave her a nasty twinge.

After a long enough pause for it to be an obviously different message, the bells rang again. Even though she knew what was happening, it was disconcerting to watch the bell beside her move by itself. Once – then four times.

1–4: that should have meant the fourth level down, but there was no fourth level.

Well. If you were stupid enough to wander into a mine, you probably couldn't count either.

II

Counterintuitively, the way was uphill. There would be a lift soon, she remembered that from when she was tiny. She doubted the crank for its machinery would still work, but Michael had got down somehow.

Water rained from the ceiling. It was foul. It was under her collar, in her hair, inside her boots. Water should have felt clean, but the floodwater never felt clean. If it wasn't slewing mud, it was full of soot from the factories in town, dribbling grey streaks over everything that, in the tepid winter, always turned green before long. The mildew smell from her kitchen wall was here too, under the copper. She would have traded nearly anything just to have one day when she didn't smell it. When she was little, winters had been pristine and white. But not for forty years now. She was starting to doubt they ever had been. Maybe winter was just a story her uncle had made up. No snow in forty years, no true winter, no true Christmas, just the water and the mildew; it was whatever you called the reverse of a miracle.

She swallowed it down. Thoughts like that came from being too much alone, but what were you supposed to do? Her uncle had warned her. The way you have to know the land, the way you have to read the weather, the iron you need in your soul – it looks like witchcraft and most people respect that, but they don't want it up close. She hadn't understood at the time, but it was true. The nearest she had to a friend was Michael, because he was another sort of shepherd.

The lamp winked on copper seams, and on the stalactites that had formed on the ceiling of the tunnel. She had to walk with her head bowed. Ahead, the light made an insufficient pool, and beyond it, nothing but the little point that was Gower. The shaft appeared in sections of ten feet at a time, the darkness flinching back beyond that, showing her the support beams and the cart rails. She was walking upstream, the orange water covering the soles of her boots.

There was a rattle as Gower clambered into the lift.

It was a monster. It had three vertical compartments, each with its own low gate: the miners had crouched on the three levels, stacked on top of each other, so that you could send three times the number of people up and down all at once. When she was little, it had seemed like huge fun and she'd never understood why her dad hated it so much, but now the thing looked like a cattle cage.

She stopped. The mine was supposed to be flooded. If Michael was wrong about where he was, and she cranked the lever to make the lift go all the way down to the third and deepest level . . . was she going to be locked in a cage as it plunged underwater?

'Hang on,' she said, chivvying Gower out again. 'We need to do an experiment.'

Gower yowled as she shoved down the lever to −3. It was a long, long wait in the dark while the mechanisms howled and ratcheted, fading deeper and deeper. She listened, leaning into the shaft. No splash, but it was at least a hundred feet. At last, she moved the lever up to 0 again. The lift shrieked back up. It made her teeth feel like she'd bitten tin.

She expected the cage to come back dripping, but it was dry. Puzzled but encouraged, she opened the gates again.

Gower wagged back in. Angharad ducked into the middle compartment, pulled the gate shut and leaned awkwardly to push the lever down again. Even now she was inside her lamplight didn't quite reach to the back of the cage. Empty, it looked wrong. Her memory of it was always stuffed full of people.

There was a squeak as the old scale tipped. The lift could take something like four hundred stone and the scale was there to make sure you didn't go over. It was off, though. It thought that the lift was carrying about twenty-five stone now.

'Have you been at the marzipan?' she said to Gower.

The lift sank twenty feet, forty, sixty. The noise had been bad enough from the outside, but inside it was horrendous. The pulleys and cables sounded like they were fused with rust, and where water had leaked down the lift shaft, the grilles were orange. The whole cage reeked of copper. Orange prints already crisscrossed her hands where she'd touched the sides. You couldn't be a shepherd and fastidious, she was used to being covered in a layer of grit and lanolin, but this – she was never going to get it off.

She had to sit with her head tilted right to one side to fit in the space, and, too late, she noticed that the end of her plait had fallen through one of the gaps in the grille floor, brushing some slime that she hoped was old algae. She tried to tug it out, but something tugged back.

She snapped back so hard she banged her head on the grille above. Christ alive, someone else was down there, the scale *wasn't* wrong—

'Owr,' Gower said. He pushed his nose through the grille and tried to lick her knees.

She slumped. Probably something as mouse-looking as the end of a plait demanded some nibbling if you were a lollopy Irish water spaniel. She ground her knuckles against her heart, which was jackhammering, annoyed and relieved all at once.

Something in the foundation supports of her mind still didn't like that she couldn't see all the way to the back of the lift. Not below, above, nor in her compartment. The darkness smoked through the grilles.

Thunk. The third and lowest level. She felt the blast of cold air before she could see the contours of the passageway.

The second she'd kicked the compartment doors open, Gower burst out and hared along the corridor beyond, his light vanishing round a corner. She paused, uneasy. She'd thought Michael would be right by the lift. What was he doing? And, come to think of it, if he had been able to send the lift up, with Gower in it ... why hadn't he got in it himself?

No, she knew exactly why. He was panicking. This was the person who went into conniptions if somebody suggested rearranging the pews.

'Hello?' Her voice echoed and echoed. 'Michael?'

Gower barked and the echoes barked back.

Michael, Michael, the older echoes said.

Nothing else.

She pulled her free hand down her plait, which was an anxious habit that irritated her even while she was doing it, then stopped.

Usually, she tied the plait off with a bit of string. She'd had the same string for nearly a year now and it was a private victory that she hadn't lost it in all that time. The string was gone. Instead, there was a piece of green ribbon.

She swung the lamp back towards the lift. Empty; but the light didn't reach to the back.

She reached up for the scale without looking at it, so she didn't have to take her eyes away from the three compartments. It was going to show some weight, she told herself solidly, because it was broken, and then she was going to send the lift straight back up by itself, just in case someone *was* inside, and then she was going to think of a sensible reason why there was a ribbon in her hair.

She didn't want to look away from the lift itself even for half a second, and for a hideous moment she was frozen with her hand on the scale and her eyes locked on the shadows.

Christ, be a shepherd, stop being some frightened idiot—

She snatched a glance at the scale.

Zero.

She had never got her back against a wall so fast. She stood exactly still, not breathing, listening for anything that could have been the click of a boot heel under the echoes, or a rustle of someone else's coat. All she could hear, though, was Gower, who was rushing back now. When he reached her, he whined, trying to make her follow.

And – she had to, because Michael was here somewhere, because how else did Gower have his Bible, and why else would the dog be so frantic?

Gower bit the hem of her coat to tug her along to the next signal-bell station. He even jumped up and batted the bell. It sang around the mine. This time, she heard the bells above. And others, which sounded like they came from even deeper below, though that couldn't be right.

She caught his paws before he could do it again, because in fact one chime – all stop, stay still – wasn't a bad thing to tell a panicking vicar when you wanted him to stay put and wait for you.

The echoes died away.

Then: there. One, two . . .

She read down the list.

Three, four, five, six, seven, eight.

8 BELLS: HELP

Right. She took the list off the wall in case the next one wasn't so well preserved, then set off down the corridor, following Gower. He waited until she had almost caught up, but flicked away again to wait at the next corner, then the next, and she had followed him through three forks in the way before she realised she was going to need to start remembering the turns if she wanted to get back. Left, left, right.

She used to come down here to the pit faces all the time after school but . . . none of it looked familiar. There should have been a tool room somewhere, and a little cave where the miners ate lunch and the children drew faces on the stalagmites. And hadn't the ceilings been lower – rougher? Here, the way was supported not by oak struts but masonry archways, with keystones marked with the owl and crown.

But then . . . her dad had never let her stay. She'd begged to, because so many of the other children worked down here without even going to school, like proper grown-ups, but he had always been firm. What would happen if she heard the Devil's music, and went dancing off to his court and ate at his banquet, and could never come home? Given that hardly anyone earned more than five pounds a month while rent was rarely less than four, and that she had about as much chance of seeing a real banquet as she did of flying, it had seemed like a sensible idea to Angharad, but there was no accounting for the opinions of dads.

Whether she was remembering rightly or not, all this was supposed to be flooded.

Gower vanished around another corner.

It was no good. She picked up a shard of ore and scratched an arrow onto the wall, leaning into it hard to make it score the rock deep enough to see properly, and then she stopped.

There were other marks there already. It was writing, gouged jagged into the rock.

NEVER

She stepped back to shine her light further along the wall.

NEVER LET HIM GO

Under it, chiselled on, were names. Names and names and names, like people were undersigning the vow. They were all names she knew. They were the parents of her friends when she'd been little. All miners. All dead in the firedamp explosion.

Maria and Rhys Jones.

She touched the letters. Her ma had been able to carve in the most beautiful copperplate.

Gower's light stopped just up ahead, and this time, there were no more corners. There was a hole in the wall the size of the church door, and blackened marks around the outside that meant someone had blasted through with powder.

But instead of just blasting ten feet into the rock and loosening the way so the miners could clear it out and make themselves a corridor, this charge had blown through into a hollow space. She stepped carefully over the rubble.

The hole in the wall came out just above a landing on a great stairway that plunged down into the darkness. Far above her, the ceiling was vaulted, winking with gilt patterns she couldn't make out by the meagre glow of the lamp. She thought that maybe the pillars were carved into shapes or figures too, but she could only guess at their shadows. Something green was heaped up across the floor, bright points gleaming here and there. She couldn't tell what it was. Only that it was all on a scale she had never seen, nor dreamed.

When she let her breath out in a long, shocked sigh, it clouded. Cold: it had been cold when the lift came down here, but now it was bitter.

Caer y Cythraul: the Devil's fortress. They had built the mine over it, everyone knew that, and yet she hadn't thought there was a *real* fortress. She'd thought that was just one of the legends of a time that never really was, when Arthur was king and owls were witches.

Gower was already on his way down the steps, vanishing again so that he was nothing except his little light.

'Hello?' she called. 'Michael?'

A thought that had been blooming and darkening, and starting to carry that thick, dank smell of the stain on her kitchen wall, finally rotted its way through to the front of her mind.

Maybe it wasn't Michael ringing the bells.

Gower was leading her further and further in, away from the lift, away from the signal-bell stations. It was beginning to feel much less like a rescue, and much more like a trap.

This was stupid. She needed to get back to the surface, go into town and bring as many people as she could.

'Gower! Come on, we're going.'

She clipped back through the dynamite-blasted wall.

She was strong. If you could lift up a fully grown sheep, you could fetch a fully grown man a good sock in the jaw and a good boot in the crotch, and in any case, she was not the kind of woman anyone ever wanted to kidnap. If she wanted someone to leave her alone, all she had to do was look them right in the eye and ask what they thought about the dissolution of the East India Company. Conversation with her, she had once overheard Michael say in his anxious way to the blacksmith, was an awful lot like being forced to sit an exam you hadn't realised you needed to study for.

Where was the bloody arrow?

There. Yes. Next to *NEVER LET HIM GO*.

The lamp fluttered and she held it still, waiting for the flame to steady. She was almost there. It would only take a few minutes to get back to the surface.

She rounded the corner, and stopped.

She was back at the hole in the wall.

More slowly, she went back, holding the lamp higher, looking for the turn she had missed. There was the arrow again, pointing ... this way. Not sure what she was doing wrong, she ran her free hand over the wall, over the names carved there, looking for a hidden passage, but there was nothing. It circled straight back. There was the blasted-open wall again, and there, standing on the rubble, was the dog, or at least the light on the dog's collar. Gower jumped down the other side again, plainly not sure why she was messing around going in circles outside.

She stood at the edge of the rubble, looking into the hall, and realised with a feeling like dirty rainwater creeping down her neck that she didn't know what to do. There had to be a way out, because she'd got in. She had missed something, but she had retraced her steps five times and there was nothing. The corridor was circular. She tried again, letting her lamplight creep inch by inch over the floor and the walls.

NEVER LET HIM GO

Panic leaned a boot right into her chest.

This place wasn't right. There was something here, and it

had closed some door behind her that she couldn't see, with a lock she didn't understand.

Today the Devil took all the children.

When she pulled her hand over her face, the smell of damp came up from her sleeve again and she felt sick. It wasn't a sane thought, but she felt suddenly as though she would be able to think better, panic less, see more, if she could just escape that smell. She was mouldering away just as much as that kitchen wall at home. Oh God, but if she died down here in the dark—

Then she died, and no one would know, because there is no one who comes when the *shepherd* is lost.

Gower's light came back again. He wasn't barking any more, at least, just waiting patiently at the top of the stairs. There wasn't much left to do but follow him down.

The copper tasted sharper than ever.

'Michael?' she called again, her breath steaming. It was even colder on the stairs than by the exploded opening in the wall. Tiny frost crystals sparkled on the stone; she ground the sole of her boot against it to test the grip. Slick. Even Gower was going down carefully, his little light pausing just ahead of her before each new stair. It was somehow much more difficult to go down an icy staircase than up. Gravity was not on your side.

Down, down, down, following the smaller light ahead of her.

Gower barked.

It came from behind her.

What?

She jolted the lantern up and there he was, at the top of the staircase, tail slinging shadows everywhere.

So who had the other lamp?

Very slowly, because there was a childhood part of her still convinced that if she didn't see a thing then it wasn't there, she turned back.

The gaunt figure holding the other lamp set it on the step, and walked down into the darkness.

III

Angharad dropped her lamp as she snapped backwards, lurched to catch it, did, just about, but the lunge tipped Michael's Bible out of her pocket and onto the step in front of her. It landed open on the front page, which had Michael's name on it in such faded ink and such careful handwriting that he must have written it when he was a child. Then under it, in a scrawl:

> Whoever finds this please look after the Dog DO NOT COME INTO THE MINE all is true the Devil is here I think He will use Gower to Lure you down he wants to be Free but you Must Not come or you shall be Trapped as I am please commend my Soul to the Almighty for I do not think God is here

She felt terribly, terribly heavy: as though different versions of her were all meeting and trying to occupy the same space. There was a different Angharad who had seen the message up at the mine head when Gower first gave her the book, and maybe another who had managed to get home and halfway through a cup of tea before the dog scrabbled at the door, but all of them would have ended up here. She would have thought Michael was losing his mind in all this abandoned darkness. She had always been coming here. Whatever was here – she couldn't shake the sense that it had known she was always coming, too.

There was no sign of the person who had taken Gower's lamp.

Her own lamp was shivering.

It wouldn't give her light for much longer, but she picked up the second lamp and tipped its oil into hers, and then she carried on down the stairs.

At the bottom of the staircase, the hall felt vast. She had been right before; each of the pillars was carved like a person, arms up, holding the roof, all different. The closest was an old woman with a harp at her feet, and along from her, a man with antlers, then a girl who was halfway a swan, all giants, twenty feet high. Every plinth was carved with the owl and crown.

Her light fell across only the nearer part of the hall; the rest was a yawning void. That greenness she'd seen strewn over the floor was holly. It was stacked in heaps taller than her, a whole maze of it. Around and among it was green cloth, velvet . . . and those winking points she'd seen before were silver bells. They looked like they were supposed to be strung together, but they were scattered over the floor. She scanned the strange wreckage, hunting for whoever had walked ahead of her, watching for the angle of a knee or an elbow, tight with the awareness that the lamp made her into a beacon. *The Devil is here.* She kept turning, and kept finding no one.

Well, sod that. She pulled some of the dead holly into a heap and set it alight. Within seconds, there was a bonfire blazing, smoke pouring up to the rafters. Light wavered down the ways in the holly maze.

There were people sleeping all in a group not far away. The firelight ran gold over them. They were wearing work clothes: practical wool dresses, aprons, sturdy grey waistcoats, shirts smudged with copper and ore dust.

No; not sleeping.

Oh God, her mother and father—

She turned away before she could look for them. It wouldn't help to know.

Gower reappeared. He sat down next to her, wagging his tail as if he were an entirely good dog who hadn't lured her into a trap. He was holding a bolt of green velvet, rolled up like a newspaper. He set it down by her boot, then nudged it closer when she didn't pick it up straightaway.

It was densely embroidered. Not with brocade patterns like ladies wore, but pictures, all traced out in silver thread, and she wouldn't have cared or spared it a thought, but the first picture was of her, standing here next to the blaze of holly, looking down at a tapestry.

She shook it out.

The silver threads showed a feast, and people in fine clothes eating and dancing. Boughs of holly above, and little bells. Among them, a figure in a crown.

The next picture showed some kind of explosion in a burst of gold thread.

Then – other people. With pickaxes, and miner's lamps picked out in gold and silver. There were children with them, little tumbling figures rushing to join the feast and the dance, to the delight of the courtiers already there. The way the stitching flowed made them all look like they were whirling together. If she let her eyes slide away from the thread, she would have sworn it moved.

In the next image, the miners were angry. They were trying to pull the children away, but it wasn't working.

The same people dragging the figure in the crown away. That image was only half stitched, and overlaid with a mad pattern of hammers and what might have been a crucifix. She couldn't make out what the miners had done, only that it was appalling chaos.

In the next picture, the miners were trying to get out, their embroidered faces wailing. Trapped.

No sign of the bright court, nor the children.

Then . . . all the miners curled up on the floor, among the holly.

Then a figure standing at the fire exactly like she was now, holding the green velvet.

It was a tiny sound under the crackle of the burning holly, but distinct: the creak of a needle through dense fabric.

Gower bustled off into the dark where the firelight didn't reach. The slag heaps of holly made monster shadows.

She lifted the lamp again, and followed.

In an alcove, beside a spinning wheel and a loom, lost in the dark until the lamplight edged over his angles, there was a man. The light traced his hair, a dark straight fall over his nearer shoulder, and a needle, and a shine of metal around his neck. She couldn't tell what it was; only that he was watching her. There were points of light in his eyes, but they weren't from the lamp, nor from the holly fire. The rest of his face was in shadow. Gower was curled up next to him.

Closer to him, it was so cold that there was thick rime over the dead holly. The loom and the spinning wheel sparkled with it. Her breath came in white clouds; so did Gower's.

The man wasn't breathing at all.

'You can't talk, can you,' she said.

There was a silver bell on the loom too. The man picked it up, and rang it once. One. All stop. That must mean no.

'Why did you bring me down here?'

He rang the bell again.

Eight chimes: help.

She was close enough to hold her lamp up and see him clearly, but for a hanging second she didn't want to, in case he wasn't a thing she could unsee.

He looked like a person. Black hair down to his waist, clothes ragged, and green, green eyes.

Around his neck, there was a crown. It was misshapen and folded in on itself. It forced him to sit exactly upright.

If he had tried to bend his neck, the points of it would have driven through his jaw. When the light fell across him, he touched the crown, hooking his fingertips over it to show he couldn't even get his nails underneath.

'But – if you can open and close the way, then why are you here, why didn't you go above for help when—'

He jolted back from her. She had been coming closer and now she was too close.

It was an answer in itself. He was afraid to go above. No wonder. The miners had come from above.

They might have lived for days, even in this cold. She didn't want to imagine it, but she could, horribly well. It had been a battle of wills to see who would break first, to see whether the miners would get their children back, or whether he would keep them.

'Why did you take the children?' she asked.

Chime, chime, chime, chime.

Four bells: safe.

He was expressionless, but it wasn't indifference. It was the blankness of a person who had been so afraid for so long that the pressure of all the layers of fear had crystallised them into a diamond mask.

She felt like she was balancing right on the threshold of a deep drop. This was the Devil's Fortress, and the miners had found . . .

One of the bodies crawled towards the light.

Angharad almost dropped the lamp again. The light swung, but it caught over a halo of wild grey curls, and a silver waistcoat, and God, it was Michael, coughing in the smoke from the holly fire. There was ice on his clothes, and he was a grey colour she had never seen on a living person.

'Michael! Jesus Christ, Gower brought me down!'

'I'm so sorry,' he said wretchedly. 'Now you're trapped too.'

From the loom, the weaver watched them.

'Michael — what *is* this?'

He shuddered. Ice gleamed in his hair. She stared at him helplessly. Her own coat was damp, she was freezing, and already she could see frost dusting her sleeves, glittering just like the weaver's silver thread. When she brought a burning spar from the fire across to try and start a new one, the cold crushed it out.

'Michael, you need to get up, come to the fire—'

'No, no, better to go like this,' he said, smiling a bit. 'Takes less time than dying of thirst, you see.' He swallowed. 'Every year, close to Christmas, I pray here. To keep *him* down here.' He nodded up at the weaver, who studied him back without rancour. Perhaps he had done all his raging decades ago. 'The man who had my post before me told me about it . . . and the one before him told him.' Michael coughed. He sounded awful. There was a rattle in his lungs. She crouched down to hear him better. 'I always stayed at the mine head. But Gower ran in, and . . . I followed.' Another cough. 'He takes people. Especially children. They — hear something. Music, singing. They follow it, and they find a great feast like nothing they've ever seen and of course they want to join in. But then he doesn't give them back.'

Angharad looked down at the tapestry again. If you stumbled across one of the old courts, whether they were in a mine, or on the wrong side of a mirror, or beyond a stone archway on a moor, anyone could have told you the rules.

You didn't eat. You didn't drink. You didn't dance.

'I think they tried to kill him,' Michael said, struggling now. 'But they couldn't. So they took his voice away instead, so he couldn't lure anyone else down here. I think they would have given it back if he had given them the children, but ...' Something in his eyes hazed. He was so cold it was a miracle he was still coherent. 'Mabarrow,' he said distantly. 'When I first came here, I said, that's a funny name, and you said, that's because English mapmakers hear Welsh and go, bugger that for a game of bananas. Mab y Bore: the son of the morning. Funny.'

'Michael?' she said, shaking his shoulder.

'They all signed their names on the wall,' he murmured, drowsy. She had never seen anyone die of cold, but she had a sharp feeling she was seeing it now. 'Never let him go. You should ... sign it ... too.'

Creak, went the needle and the silver thread.

Gower whined. He was tucked into a nest of the green velvet, snug at the weaver's feet. The weaver bent a little to stroke his ears, and Gower settled.

Angharad tried to shake Michael again, but this time, he didn't stir. He was still breathing, but she couldn't imagine that would last long. She straightened up. The lamp was dying too. She was seeing only by the light of the holly fire.

Not far away, frost glittered on the bodies of the miners. She forced herself to look through them, not at them, in case she found her ma's blue scarf.

Never let him go, but . . .

But she was the shepherd.

'I think I can get that thing off you. I have a knife. Ready?'

The weaver went very still, and it was a stillness she recognised. It was how she'd stood on the threshold of the mine head, not wanting to cross. Gower put one paw on his knee. The weaver looked down, then at her again. Then, as though he were forcing every fraction of an inch against terrible gravity, he lifted his head to let her see the crown.

She stepped up to the loom. He shied when she leaned down. She stopped, and held her hands up.

'No. Wouldn't be much of a shepherd if I left anything here like they left you.'

He looked up at her with holly green eyes. She wasn't sure they were still sane.

'Look, you hold it.' She closed his hand around the hilt. He was colder than the flagstones. She guided the point of the knife to that grim mockery of a collar. There were scratch marks where he had clawed at it. The miners must have bashed it into place with hammers, folding the silver over on itself. God knew what they had tried to do with those hammers before they'd understood he wasn't something you could kill.

She slipped the knife blade under the edge, and between them, they leaned into it more and more to lever the crown open. Then, so cold it was brittle, the silver band snapped.

It fell onto the floor with a clang too loud for its weight.

The weaver sank onto all fours and for the first time she heard him breathe, a terrible half-voiced sob of a breath. He stayed like that, his hair pooling on the floor beside the ruined crown. She put her hand on his back. Gower nosed anxiously at both of them.

The weaver lifted his head, and then, with a clatter of wings, he was gone, and she was there alone with the dog and the lamp, surrounded by tawny, downy feathers. She picked one up, shocked and lost. It looked like an owl's.

All around the mine, the bells rang.

Nine times.

Evacuate.

Something about the air changed. No more stillness: there was a warm breeze.

The way out was open.

IV

It was almost as dark on the surface as it was in the mine. The sheep were still there, huddled by the mine head, waiting for her, and they bleated irritably to ask what she thought she'd been mucking about at, and where were their Bribery Carrots? She had to stand on the threshold for a second and breathe. Out. Free. Beside her, Michael was upright, just.

Their breath steamed.

The sky was as clear as glass, and in it, the stars were so brilliant that she cast a shadow.

She should have been standing in mud, but she wasn't. The stream coming out of the mine was frozen in a sheet of coppery ice. In the coats of the sheep, there was frost. It crackled when she patted them and whistled to get them going. Gower slid past on the ice, looking as confused as she had ever seen a dog look. He would never have seen ice. *She* had barely ever seen ice, not since she was tiny.

Where was the flood, where was the rain? Everything was white now, sparkling and pristine.

It began to snow. She put her hand out to catch one of the flakes. She heard someone laughing a delighted, childlike laugh, and realised it was her.

There was something else, too. On the wind, far away, was a song. When she turned her head that way, the air tasted different: of hot wine, and spice, and a feeling like coming home.

It was much easier helping Michael over the frozen ground than it would have been through the mud and the flood. Once they reached her barn, she wrapped him up as well as she could, got them both onto the annoyed horse whose only normal job was to pull the cart at shearing time, and set back out to Mabarrow. Gower ran alongside, sometimes leaping to bite at the snowflakes, which were as big as owl feathers.

There was a small crowd outside the vicarage. It was the snow: they wanted to know why the winter had come back after forty years, what did it mean, where was Michael, couldn't he come out just for a few minutes, for God's sake – was he even here? The curate was just inside, looking hounded, and trying to say that *of course* Michael wasn't missing, he was just, you know, with a doctor from town, and he would be right as rain in the morning, and nobody had any reason to be worried at all—

'Oh my God!' the blacksmith burst out as Angharad rode into the garden and fell off the horse under the silver birch. He rushed to help her with Michael. 'Vicar! What *happened* to you? We were getting worried ...'

Michael was looking at Angharad as though he expected her to catch fire at any second.

'I found him in the mine,' Angharad explained. She had flown through ordinary tiredness and come out the other side into a crystalline exhaustion. 'He was lost in one of the deep levels. It's not flooded like they said. I think he went in after the dog and his light went out.'

'It's all right,' the curate said, looking shaken. 'Come on, Mr Pennyfeather, let's get you inside. No more adventures. Can I make you a cup of tea, Miss Jones?'

'Why did you tell us he had the influenza?' the blacksmith demanded, which was a blessing, because the curate's tea tasted of dishwater.

They were all guiding Michael inside, but he was still looking back at her. He was crying.

'Because he asked me not to tell anyone where he was going!' the curate exclaimed. 'He said nobody was to know about the mine, he didn't want anyone to go looking—'

'What do you mean, *go looking?*'

Someone was singing.

Angharad turned around, trying to follow the direction of it on the wind, but it was coming from everywhere and nowhere. It was like a carol, sad and joyous at once, but it was older than anything these hills had heard for a long time. It was a song for the weary turning of the year, and candlelight in the dark.

Behind her, the others were still interrogating the curate.

There were more voices now. The longer they sang, the deeper the cold felt, and the cleaner. She strayed past the silver birch, to the garden gate. From there, the view was downhill.

The court was riding over the new-frozen field below on white horses, under green and silver banners. The bells were on the bridles, and the people were dressed in bright velvet and heavy furs against the brilliant cold. They had coloured lamps. She recognised some of them. They were faces she hadn't seen since she was a child, faces that had been childish then too, but grown now.

Someone was walking up the steep path. The wind flickered at his black hair. In the mine he had been ragged, but now he was wearing a heavy cloak of white fur, and silver-stitched boots that left no prints in the snow. In his wake, the last of the water dripping from the eaves turned to ice, and frost chased him along the broken fences. With the next pull of the wind came the smell of hot wine and spices. Angharad had a leap of happiness. She felt instantly bittersweet about that, because he was not coming for her; because nobody came for the shepherd.

But then he smiled as though seeing her had made him happy too.

He stopped at the gate, and didn't come through it.

'I do not think you will let me pay it,' he said, and there was music in his voice even though he was only talking now, 'but I owe you a great debt, and the hospitality of my hall.'

You didn't dance, you didn't drink, you didn't eat.

Only – you earned five pounds a month and rent was four. There would never be a feast in Mabarrow. Don't dance, don't eat, don't speak, just do your work. Send your children not to school, but to the mine.

She said, 'I would very much like to come, sir.'

She had never seen anyone look so pleased. It filled her up with a mulled-wine warmth, all cinnamon and sugared orange. When he held his hand out, silver glinting on his sleeve – or was it ice? – she took it.

She and he were both there in plain view, but nobody saw them go.

People looked for days, but eventually Michael Pennyfeather slumped down at the ledger that was the parish record and wrote,

Today the Devil took the shepherd.

A MIDNIGHT VISITOR

Susan Stokes-Chapman

If the Horoscope-Maker is a treacherous, lurking imposter, a sordid soul, a bad citizen, surely too, the cartomancer is [...] to be banished from society, and even to be punished.

JEAN-BAPTISTE ALLIETTE
Pertaining to the Art of Divination, 1773

A storm raged over Paris. It thundered through the broken city and across its labyrinth of tiled rooftops, sending streams of water down dark avenues where they pooled in ditches and turned the narrow footpaths to sludge. In the sky a wind howled its anger to a crow that navigated the ruins of the Bastille, tearing into the creature's feathers as if it had teeth, while a flash of lightning made a vicious cut over the winding vein of the Seine.

The rain lashed at the windows of a small and compact parlour which overlooked that twisting river, and would have woken the figure sitting in the threadbare *fauteuil* if she had been sleeping. But Noelle Labèque was not asleep, nor anywhere near to being so; she was counting out her takings for that past week by the light of a single candle at her side.

Her last client had left only moments before. A girl of sixteen, clearly with child. Noelle should have felt guilt at what she had just done, but guilt was a feeling she relinquished long ago — there was no room for such an emotion when it served to keep Noelle in comfort, such as it was. Instead she took the girl's coin and opened her shaking palm, read the lines there that told the fortune her young client so desperately wanted to hear: forgiveness, acceptance, marriage, happiness. But what could such a girl expect? She had come from money, that much was clear from the brocade silks beneath her sodden shawl, the twinkle of a sapphire upon her elegant finger. It was why Noelle lingered over the reading, offered for just a few more livre a fortune for the unborn child: a strong spirit, yet gentle and uncommonly kind, with a bright future in front of them (the girl had cried at this, pressed Noelle's crooked knuckles to her lips in thanks). But she had been naïve. Desperate. Whyever should Noelle dash all the girl's hopes by revealing that as soon as the child was born it would be taken from her, if it even lived at all? That her servant lover would likely find himself turned out onto the streets, or worse? That she would certainly not find herself married ... not to the man she loved, at least.

No indeed, to say such things would have been cruel. What harm were a few lies for the girl's peace of mind, if only for a little while?

Still, Noelle frowned as she sifted through the coins, passing them from one hand to the other before dropping them into a velvet pouch and pulling its ribbons tight. She had not lied enough. She should have drawn the girl's reading out further, or at the very least charged more for her services. The young *aristocrate* would have paid without question, of that Noelle was certain, might have even given her that lovely bauble which had twinkled so beautifully on her little finger. Well, it was too late now, but the cold certainty of it was Noelle had not earned enough this week to settle her debts.

Forty livre short.

A hefty gust of wind rattled the shutters. Noelle squinted into the rain beyond the window's thin panes. Paris lay in darkness, except when the lightning revealed the city in startling snatches – the angry stretch of the Seine, the Bastille's crumbling walls and the newly completed bridge constructed from that fortress' pillaged masonry. The lightning lit now Église Saint-Sulpice, Sainte-Chapelle, the mighty towers of Notre-Dame ... A flight of stone steps flashed before her eyes then and Noelle gritted her teeth, turned her gaze away from the window, placed the pouch beneath the loose sill and secured the board flat once more.

The storm had prevented people coming. Usually Noelle might receive six or seven visits of an evening, but she had this night entertained only two clients. Before the girl there had been a gentleman from Section du Ponceau, who wished to know the likelihood of his wife dying before the year was out. A matter of inheritance, he said in tones most sombre and secretive. The monsieur had been deceived with a reading concocted from the tea leaves still lingering at the bottom of her noon-time pot, and left Noelle's tiny *appartement* with the devil in his eyes.

Trickery had its merits and its failings. Tell a man yes to such a question, he might become impatient to see the deed done and contrive of a way to hasten the unhappy outcome ... but tell him no, would he then take matters into his own hands? In that instance Noelle had sanctioned patience (for death comes to everyone, eventually), and hoped nothing untoward would come of the monsieur's unfortunate spouse.

Thinking of the man, resentment unfurled in her chest. He had reminded her of Raoul. He too had a devious face. What would her life have been like, if not for Raoul's treachery? In the semi-dark, preserved snakes and bats observed her from their dusty glass cases, and she regarded their oblique reflections in the curve of hourglasses and the faces of soundless clocks. Did not the gutter of the candle lend the asp a mien of contempt, or the rousette an appearance of disdain on its fox-like features? It was as if they shared Noelle's resentment, understood all that Raoul had cost her.

She coughed, pressed her fingers to the hollow of her throat where a pain resided, tight and hard like a clenching hand.

Etteilla had understood. If it were not for him, Noelle may never have found a way to carve a new life for herself. Under his mentorship her name in cartomancy was made, despite Raoul's best efforts. And though her *appartement* was a far cry from the lavish home in which she had once lived, it was hers.

The rain continued to beat upon the glass; thunder rumbled far-distant. The candle wavered, as if breath had caressed the flame, and Noelle rested her head on the armchair's fraying back.

She liked storms. They held in them a strange sort of comfort, a hypnotic lullaby. Sleep, Noelle thought absently, might come if she were to seek her bed, but its cold, lumpy mattress was not a welcome respite, and though deeply tired she continued to stare at the candle flame, counting the time between the flashes of lightning and their inevitable replies. One particularly bright flash illuminated the river's torrid current – its answering thunderclap hailed on the count of eight, and upon its heels there came a knock upon the door. Noelle frowned, turned her head to regard the clock on the crooked bookshelf, the only one that worked, and squinted to read its faded numbers, its filigree hands.

A quarter past the hour of midnight.

Intrigued, Noelle rose from the chair and crossed the small space. The light in her parlour was so dim she could not perceive a shadow beneath the crack of the door. For a moment Noelle wondered if she had indeed fallen into slumber, felt sure she imagined the knock – the rain, the thunder, they had been awfully loud after all – but then the knock came again.

'Hello?'

A voice spoke her name in reply. It was a low voice. Calm,

even, and intrigued further Noelle slid the bolt from its rusting lock to pull the door open on its creaking hinges.

There stood upon the threshold a woman. She was tall, uncommonly so, her face pale yet undiscernible beneath the hood of the dark cloak she wore. It was wet from the rain, and the material dripped on the floorboards, trickling slowly into the worn gaps between, a steady *tap tap tap*.

'Madame Labèque,' said the woman again. 'I have come to have a fortune read.'

'It is after midnight,' replied Noelle, her voice weak from the growth in her throat. 'My hours of business are clear.' She gestured to the worn scrap of paper nailed to her door, the letters faded now, old, but if one were to regard it in the full light of day one could not easily mistake the words:

MADAME LABÈQUE ~ TELLER OF FORTUNES, DIVINER OF TAROT. READINGS AVAILABLE EVERY MONDAY, WEDNESDAY AND FRIDAY BETWEEN THE EVENING HOURS OF EIGHT AND TWELVE.

Still, the woman did not move her head to regard it and merely replied,

'But you are available.'

It was not a question. Noelle frowned, observed the woman carefully. In the shadows it was hard to make out her expression, but something about the stranger commanded her to take notice. It was a pull, a feeling, a sense of inevitability she could not ignore. Besides, she *was* available . . .

and Noelle was in no position to refuse, for her physician needed to be paid.

'Won't you come in?' she said, pulling the door open wider, and before Noelle could draw another breath, the woman had slipped into the tiny room.

Noelle shut the door. Turned. The stranger stood, tall and wet and dripping upon the shabby rug by the table Noelle always used for her readings, and she held out her hand.

'Let me take your cloak.'

'No, thank you.'

Noelle paused.

'You are wet, mademoiselle.'

'It matters not.'

The words were melodious, almost. Noelle tried to look into her face, but the hood the woman wore still concealed her features; only her eyes were visible, small and shining, and they watched Noelle now with a steadiness that both captivated and unnerved her. Many of the people who came to have their fortunes read found themselves in awe of Noelle – some even feared her – and it was a condition which she encouraged, for it made them all the more inclined to part with their money. This woman, however, seemed unaffected by her attire. Not having yet changed after her previous client, Noelle wore robes of patterned velvet, her too-slim fingers were adorned with golden bands, and what little of her hair she had left was bound in a turban of crimson silk. But Noelle had since shed her charlatan's demeanour; she was tired, in pain, no longer playing a part. Perhaps the woman felt unaffected because of this, and so Noelle attempted to restore the mysterious character of which she was so famed and said in lilting tones of her own,

'What manner of fortune do you wish for? I read palms, can consult the tea leaves. Or—'

'Tarot.'

Noelle tried not to smile. A tarot reading would more than make up for her shortfall.

'Forty-eight livre,' she said, bowing her head. 'That is my fee.'

It was a high price, Noelle knew, but Etteilla had charged fifty and so Noelle felt she was being somewhat generous. It seemed her client felt so too for without complaint the woman already held in her hand two silver coins, which she placed in Noelle's waiting palm.

She did not even see the stranger remove them from her cloak. Had she held them in her hand from the start?

The coins were cold, as if two discs of ice had been placed upon her skin. Noelle put them on the table, and as she did, brushed past the woman who stood so still and silent. She smelt stale, yet sickly sweet. It was a smell Noelle associated with the poor wraiths that lingered down at the banks of the Seine, but no such person could afford her services, and this realisation made Noelle, again, try to look at the woman more closely. All she saw, however, was the dripping cloak, mud-coloured and ragged, as if the howling wind outside had shredded it. Still, both the strange smell and the garment solicited in Noelle a sense of deep unease, and as the cloak continued to drip on the rug she wanted to demand it be removed, yet somehow could not bring herself to insist. It was as though something had clamped her tongue, and all Noelle could manage was to instruct her client to sit.

Turning away, she gathered more candles, placed four in the tall free-standing sconces that surrounded the table, then two on the table itself – it near filled the parlour, but this was a necessary evil for Etteilla's cards were large and required room to be shuffled, cut and spread – and as Noelle lit the wicks the flames flickered and grew, lighting the woman's pale face, revealing it at last.

It was a striking face. Certainly not that of a beggar for the skin was clean, unblemished. The woman was not beautiful, nor handsome, yet not plain either. In fact, Noelle realised she could not distinguish a single feature upon the woman's face in any way that would allow her to define them. She frowned. It was her eyesight, Noelle thought. It must be. Some days she could see tolerably well, other times her vision blurred. Often it happened after the onslaught of a headache, like the one she had suffered earlier that evening, after her first client's visit.

He really had made her so very angry.

Noelle replaced the tinderbox beside the dome that held the preserved remains of an Egyptian cobra. Its eyes glittered furiously in the half-light – black they were, like Raoul's, and determined not to think of him Noelle glanced once more at her client. Frowned. No, Noelle could not distinguish the woman's features clearly, but what she did observe was the way her eyes moved about the room with unabashed interest, and for the first time Noelle felt ashamed of her tiny parlour filled with decaying curiosities, the torn curtain which hid the single bed cramped beneath a low eave, the small stove she used to heat what little food she ate and keep the painful bite of cold from her fingertips. How far she had fallen, thought Noelle as she turned to the bookcase behind her. How terrible that her life had come to this.

She had been honest, once. If Raoul had not taken the boys, she never would have lost the sight. But take them he did, and then *then* ...

The simple wooden box containing Etteilla's cards sat on the middle shelf; Noelle lifted it down with shaking hands. This deck was special to her – it had become the means of her livelihood in ways the playing cards of her youth had not been. Divining diamonds and clubs, hearts and spades ... one could not be expected to concoct a fortune with those, with so little information to interpret. How often had they confused her and those she read for, even when she *did* possess the sight? How often had she attempted to divine them again and again and again until their meanings became worthless, a mockery of what her future might foretell? But with this tarot deck, Noelle could create stories that would be believed. Images such as those found on the Marriage card and that of the Devil could be deliberately misconstrued.

And her clients *did* believe in the cards, saw in them what they wanted to see. Every single time.

Noelle sat, placing the box on the table between herself

and the strange woman. Outside, the thunder rumbled. Pressing her hand to her swollen throat, she raised her voice above the sound and said,

'The tarot deck I use for my divinations was created by the acclaimed occultist Etteilla. He believed them to be derived from an Egyptian manuscript of arcane wisdom called the *Book of Thot*. Have you heard of it?'

The woman did not move, nor did she speak, but Noelle thought she saw something shift across her pale features; the dancing candlelight gave the impression her countenance was changing, realigning, but then it softened once more and again Noelle lamented that her eyesight should be so poor. Fifty-six was no age to lose it. With a cough, she placed her hand upon the box's smooth lid.

'The *Book of Thot* is made up of seventy-eight cards, which are distinguished by figures appropriate to their meaning. Within the deck there is a card specific to the querant. As a woman, this card is number eight, which I shall retrieve now.'

Noelle opened the lid of the box. Though Etteilla gave the cards to her only two years ago they were already well worn, some even fraying at their edges, and as she lifted them from their home Noelle felt comfort in the familiar weight and heft. Frowning with concentration (for her eyes had not yet adjusted), she began to sift through the deck until she found the female querant; the card depicted a naked woman with long flowing hair, surrounded by a cage of circles. These, so Etteilla told her, represented the labyrinths of the future in which the querent's imagination might find itself ensnared.

Noelle placed it upright, close to the woman, who sat so quiet and calm.

Quiet and calm, and expectant.

'I shall now shuffle the rest of the cards,' Noelle said, above the beating of the rain. 'Is it a general reading you wish, or is there a question for which you hope to receive an answer?'

The woman smiled. It was a soft smile, patient, somehow kind, and Noelle thought this more than passing strange for it did not seem to suit her.

'A general reading is all that is required.'

Again, her voice was low, melodic. Sweet and sonorous as a lullaby. Noelle had once spoken to her boys like that. Again, a vision assailed her memory – steps of stone, wet crimson on grey ...

'A general reading, then,' said Noelle, beginning the shuffle with more vigour than she meant, 'will reveal to you an insight into your past, present and future. It shall serve to help you understand the aspects of your life as it stands, and reveal to you the consequences of your intentions or actions. Will this suffice?'

'It shall.'

'Very good.'

Noelle shuffled the deck with intricate swiftness in alternate directions, the tarot cards slipping through her fingers in a dovetail shuffle that had taken her years to master – thrice she held them with her thumbs inward, releasing them so they fell to the table interleaved. At times she twisted some of the cards so that they would fall upright, others, reversed.

In truth, when shuffling, no such show was required, but for Noelle it was part of the act, a means of convincing her client that she was a true master of cartomancy. Noelle looked briefly at the woman sitting opposite to gauge her reaction, but she merely watched the shifting of the deck with those dark, shining eyes. She looked plain in that moment, her face a perfect white canvas.

Usually, Noelle could read people as well as cards. More often than not there was a tell, something from which she could derive a story. A woman in love; a man of business. These were the typical nature of her clientele. Easy, to advise an ambitious gentleman to invest in a new horse, easier still to convince a lady of romantic sensibilities she would marry her paramour. A non-believer could be just as gullible as those who did believe, for she could use their scepticism against them. The card of judgement, for instance. *Are you sure you have nothing to hide?* But this woman with her blank expressions and lilting voice would be harder to persuade, and the knowledge made Noelle distinctly nervous. What if she discovered her deceit, and took back those two silver coins? How then would she pay Monsieur Guillotin?

'As the querent, you are to cut the deck. Make sure to do so with your left hand. The left side of the body is associated with fate and intuition. Cutting with your left hand will make the reading more accurate.' Her client said nothing to this. Noelle nodded at the cards. 'You are to create six piles.'

Without hesitation the woman reached out, and through the torn cuff of her brown cloak her hands were white, thin, elegant. Her nails were short and clean. Again, Noelle wondered what manner of woman she was. Her tattered cloak hinted at poverty, but her face, those nails, they belonged to someone of greater means. Surreptitiously Noelle attempted to mark what the woman wore beneath the sodden garment, but so thick was it she could not tell.

As Noelle pondered all this, the deck was cut into six neat piles of even size.

'Now,' she said. 'Lay them on top of each other, so there remains only one pile.'

Again, this was done, and when the woman sat back Noelle reached for the deck once more.

'Let us begin.'

As Etteilla taught her, she took eight cards from the top and spread them in a line beneath the querent card. They were to be read right to left as an Egyptian might read their hieroglyphs, and would serve to tell a story.

Noelle only hoped she could convince the woman of its truth.

She glanced at the two coins on the table, shining in the candlelight. She should have put them away, Noelle thought, in the velvet pouch hidden beneath the sill where the woman could not take them from her if she did decide that Noelle was a fraud, and with a smile she did not feel, Noelle turned the first card.

'Your current circumstances. An old man, dressed like a hermit. Reversed. The key word, as you can see, states *Traitre*. This card represents a person who has betrayed the ones they love, or themselves, a person who wishes to be alone. It speaks of isolation, loneliness. Detachment.'

Noelle paused. Perhaps she need not have worried after all. Such a woman as her querent certainly seemed the type, for she was so very strange, so quiet. And yes, detached. No emotion played about those pale features, nothing that might hint at the manner of woman she truly was, and in that moment her client gave a nod.

'What else does it speak of?'

She regarded the card, then the woman.

'Reversed,' said Noelle carefully, 'the Hermit denotes a deceitful person, and from that deceit a period of emotional distress and hurt. As a consequence they seek answers to questions that plague their mind. Yet despite all this they refuse – or have refused – to listen to the advice of others. It speaks of a stubborn dogmatism, an inclination to blindness. Is . . . is this something that sounds familiar to you?'

It was a leading question, a bid to determine how far Noelle might manipulate the card's meaning, but the woman said nothing, merely inclined her head. A flash of lightning lit the room then, illuminating the table, the cards, her client's face, and Noelle sucked in her breath . . . for in that moment the woman looked not like a woman at all but a man. And not just any man.

She wore the face of Raoul.

Noelle's chest grew tight. Hatred teased the flesh of her fingers, as if they yearned to wrap themselves about a throat. She shut her eyes, but his handsome face swam in the dark recesses of her eyelids like a malignant taunt. The lightning lasted a mere second, and when Noelle looked back into the features of the woman before her they were thrown into relief; the candlelight highlighted sharp cheekbones, a long, elegant nose, bow-shaped rosy lips. She looked beautiful now, not like Raoul at all. Noelle pressed her throat, shook her head.

'The second card,' said the woman. 'If you please.'

'Yes,' breathed Noelle. 'Of course.'

She turned it. Another reversal.

'The Five of Swords. Its key word, *Deuil*. Alone. The second card of this reading signifies the obstacles that lie in your way. We must follow on from the Hermit card here, and conclude that your enforced solitude has only deepened your sadness, prolonged your mourning. That despite all your efforts and the sacrifices you have made, matters have only gone from bad to worse.'

A creeping sensation whispered up Noelle's spine, as if someone had gently caressed her vertebrae, but whether that sensation was satisfaction or dread, she could not tell.

'This is a card of arguments, of conflicts. Degradation, destruction. Dishonour. For it to be reversed, and on the back of the previous reversal too . . . You have been very unhappy, it seems.'

Noelle hesitated. It was odd that her words did not appear to upset her querant. If it had been any other woman she might have gasped, or sighed, or wept. She may have clasped her hands to her mouth and begged Noelle for reassurance, and though the woman did none of these things, Noelle felt it necessary to offer comfort nonetheless.

'The swords are the suit of the mind,' she said, the pain in her throat making her voice waver. 'We have seen here only the first two cards, which pertain to your inner thoughts as a response to the events of your past. What you must understand is that the tarot speaks in a language of symbols, the language of the unconscious. It links the world of man to the world of the spirit, binding together all levels of reality and opening doors which were hitherto closed. From here, we may see a way forward. Shall we proceed?'

'Yes,' came the answer. 'Proceed.'

Noelle blinked. The woman's voice did not sound as melodious as it had before. It held in it now a strange sort of need, a hunger. Taking a painful breath, Noelle reached for the third card.

'Upright, this time. The King of Cups.'

She paused to consider her next words, to fathom how best to manipulate its meaning, and decided to draw the moment out.

'The court cards tend to be the hardest to grasp in regards to their denotations, for they are more nuanced. Generally, each set of court cards reflect the querant and the people that influence their lives. Sometimes they represent situations or events. In this case, I would venture to say this is someone you know, or have known.'

'And who might this be?'

Gentle again. Lilting. Noelle pondered her answer.

'The third card of the reading represents your aspirations. *Homme Blond.* A fair-headed man, then, and a moral one. He is a man of intelligence. Educated, influential. An experienced man with knowledge he wishes to share. Priestly, even.'

Unbidden, the memory of Etteilla popped into Noelle's mind. He had been all these things, a man of honesty and integrity. A twist of guilt wrought its way about her gut. Her old mentor had not approved of dishonesty, of what he called evil diviners. Noelle had met him when she still worked with playing cards, and he saw in her a gift. But Etteilla warned her, as he warned all his students, that sometimes one might become blinded by ambition. That second sight could be corrupted, if abused.

How right he had been.

After the loss of her boys, Etteilla continued to guide her in the spiritual arts. He insisted that the sight had not left her, but she it. He had believed in her, even when she did not believe in herself.

That stale scent again. Noelle coughed. The growth in her throat throbbed, as if mocking her. The rain beat hard upon the glass.

'Do you know the man this card refers to?' she asked, hoarser now, and the woman stared at her. Those dark eyes shone, the flames of the candles flickering within.

'Oh yes,' came the soft reply. 'I know him.'

'Well,' Noelle continued, relieved, 'as I said, this is a card of aspirations. Whoever this man, you aspire to be like him – trustworthy, generous, someone with a calming effect upon others. A guide. Based on the cards before it, I would encourage you to pursue this path. But, be mindful. No person can ever be truly good. The King of Cups, being such an individual of influence, can also represent somebody who is capable of abusing their power, a skilled manipulator of the mind, and as such you should be wary of straying too far from the light.'

The woman smiled then; her glinting eyes narrowed. It was a peculiar sharpening of her features, no longer beautiful as they had been a little while before, but plain neither, for such an awful expression could not be found on a face such as that. Noelle's chest tightened. Was her eyesight truly to blame? Or was it merely fatigue that caused her to imagine such strange expressions on her client's face?

Noelle turned the fourth card so that she might not contemplate the answer.

It showed a pastoral scene, with a sun that emanated a fan of golden rays which highlighted a moon and a large star surrounded by six smaller ones.

'The Sky,' she said. 'It represents the passing of time. Reversed, it signifies day. In this case, in the upright position, it portrays the nocturnal hours. *Nuit*. In a reading of this kind, the fourth card of a spread indicates what needs to be awakened in order to move forward. I spoke just of straying too far from the light, and this card warns of a lack of it. Without the light of reason, one finds oneself in a passive state. The Hermit's influence may struggle to relinquish itself.'

Noelle fell silent. It occurred to her that these cards did

indeed tell a story, and not a positive one. But what she found more disturbing was that she did not find it necessary to lie, as she so often did in her readings. Despite her carefully measured answers the messages of the cards were clear to her, and Noelle began to feel the old stirrings that moved her so many years ago.

It had started with her sister. Much older than Noelle, she had left for England upon her marriage. The cards told her then she would suffer a cruel and wicked fate, that her husband's infidelity would be the means of her own downfall. But Noelle's sister had been a woman of sense. She did not believe.

Others did. They came to her for her readings, found in Noelle a divining force.

But then she met Raoul.

'And what, Madame, do you suggest?'

The woman's voice – this time clear, authoritative – coaxed Noelle from her unpleasant memories, and she thought for a moment before replying.

'This is a card of obscurity, mystery, secrets. Veiled purposes, ambiguous discourse. I do not believe these to require awakening. Rather, I feel these aspects of yourself need to be overcome, so that *you* can be awakened. Does that make sense?'

'Does it make sense to you?'

She frowned at the question. It was not customary for the querant to respond in such a manner, and it seemed to Noelle then that the woman was questioning her judgement. Did she think her a fraud after all?

Painfully Noelle swallowed, regarded the money that still lay glinting on the table. Forty-eight livre, two coins of twenty-four. Monsieur Guillotin would not treat her if she did not pay in full.

'The meaning is perfectly clear to me,' she replied uneasily, as another flash of lightning illuminated the room. The Egyptian asp's fangs drew shadowed curves upon its glass casing, its mouth twisting in an unpleasant grin. 'But perhaps,' Noelle added, 'we should look now at what precisely lies behind you, so that we might fathom a way to achieve what you must?'

The candles dipped. Noelle did not wait for the woman to answer, and proceeded to turn over the next card.

The Tower, upright. *Misére*. Based on the other cards in the reading, Noelle was not surprised.

'Tremendous upheaval. Arguments, disagreements. Violence. A life turned asunder by circumstances unexpected, a period followed by pain and suffering.'

She should feel sorry for this woman. These bleak cards told of a life tainted by darkness. What, precisely, had her client done? The tarot clearly revealed that this was a darkness brought upon the woman by her own doing, but nothing about her allowed Noelle to feel pity – there were no expressions of guilt or remorse, not even a single tear. Indeed, there was no reaction at all, no indication the reading affected her.

'This is a cruel hand fate has dealt you,' Noelle said, watching the woman carefully. 'See how the lightning bolt in the sky has damaged the brickwork? It indicates something that was once solid, now crumbled. It indicates disruption. But as with the Sky, you must overcome that which makes you the Hermit. Your future cannot be dictated by the past, even if it was of your own making. You refuse to see the truth of your own actions. You dwell on the unfairness of what happened but know that this destruction can also be freeing. A life . . . in shadow cannot be sustained . . .'

Thunder rumbled. Noelle raised her fingers to her temples, where another headache had begun to form, a dull, unpleasant pulse. The words Noelle spoke had triggered something within her.

Anton. Louis. Raoul.

All gone.

Raoul had been Etteilla's bookkeeper. A dark man, of dark passions, he had encountered Noelle at Etteilla's home on rue de l'Oseille just as she was leaving it after a session on palmistry. Raoul had been impressed by Noelle's beauty, the air of mysticism she carried with her, which she never had to feign in those early years. They never married, for he did not believe in such things, and being a woman of unconventional traditions herself, it did not occur to Noelle to mind. They lived in a set of beautiful *appartements* near Notre-Dame where their boys arrived within a twelvemonth. They had been happy.

But then on a whim she drew the cards. Not the tarot of Etteilla, but her playing deck of old, the fifty-two blacks and reds of their suits. The reading foretold loss, heartache. A painful, violent ending. So distressed was she by the reading she drew another card, then another, another, tried to divine more answers, ones with a different outcome, but none came. The cards lost all meaning. They mocked her, used her confusion against her. They divided her and Raoul. Noelle no longer accepted his affections, so wrapped up was she in the cards and the future she wanted them to reveal. When Noelle tried to tell him what the cards had shown her, he called her mad. Cartomancy was dangerous, he insisted, both to herself and their boys. So Raoul took Louis and Anton from her. And then ...

A smell invaded Noelle's nostrils. Sickly. Sweet.

'Card number six, Madame Labèque.'

'Yes.'

She turned the card. Noelle sucked in her breath.

Feu. Fire. It was generally a positive card. Reversed, it cast a deeper meaning, but this was not what had made Noelle gasp.

'What is it, Madame?'

Her client's voice held a snideful inflection, and Noelle raised her eyes to hers. Now the woman looked, somehow, old. Not old by age, but old in wisdom — a knowing emanated from her face, an expression that hinted she knew all too well, and suspicion began to take hold then, latched itself to Noelle's heart with hateful claws. She swallowed hard.

'The steps next to be taken. Enlightenment. Clarity. A

battle of the conscious and unconscious mind. This card speaks of passion, rage.'

'And what of the children?'

Noelle shut her eyes. The children!

The image on the card showed twin boys, cherub-like, dancing on stone steps, holding hands under a blazing star. She had watched Anton and Louis dance like that, beneath the towers of Notre-Dame. It had been summer, the day hot. Carriages threw up dust from the streets. Noelle had not seen them in weeks, and desperately she had called to them. Raoul was not paying attention, did not see her as she ran to her boys and they to her, down the cathedral's stone steps. They fell, *they fell*! Still holding hands. Their tiny broken faces ... the blood at her feet ...

The pain in her throat throbbed, balled there like hot coal. She gasped, opened her eyes, and in that moment another shard of lightning illuminated the room. The woman's face was wretched now, eyes black in their sockets.

'Were you angry, Noelle? Angry with Raoul?'

How the woman knew her name, Noelle did not know, but she answered all the same.

'He took them from me. If he had not, Louis and Anton would not have died.'

The stranger shook her head beneath the hood.

'Only four years old. So young. So innocent.'

Noelle nodded, and as she did she realised she was crying.

'They were,' she whispered, as thunder struck and the rain ran rivers down the glass. 'Too young and innocent to be taken from me. He called me unfit. Yet they died in *his* care, not mine!'

'But you were the means of their demise. If you had not followed Raoul that day, if you had not been so determined to take them—'

'Take them?' Noelle stared. The woman smiled, though it held no sympathy.

'You meant to take them to Dieppe. The place of your birth.'

She had. They would have been safe there. Away from Paris, where Raoul would not follow.

'It was his fault. I was not to blame.'

There was a pause. The wind howled. Two bone-like fingers tapped one of the tarot cards, the crumbling walls of the Tower.

'You refuse to see the truth of your own actions.'

'I was not to blame!'

'Perhaps not entirely. But you played a part, that much cannot be disputed. And what of the others?' the woman pressed, when Noelle did not answer. 'What of those you have harmed in the years since? The wife of your first client tonight – her body will be found five days from now, bloated on the banks of the Seine. And that poor girl, the one who came before me. A forced marriage to a lecherous old man will be her fate. If you had told her the truth, she might have found some means to escape it.'

But Noelle would not listen. Instead she stared at the Tower, then her gaze shifted to the Hermit, the Five of

Swords; the King of Cups, the Sky. She sucked in her breath, the pulse in her temples running wild. Her vision blurred then refocused upon the sixth card, which depicted her sons so clearly.

Enlightenment. A battle of the conscious and unconscious mind. Passion. Rage.

Clarity.

Noelle looked once more to the woman sitting before her.

'This is my reading,' she whispered. 'Not yours.'

The woman who was not a woman merely stared back, her eyes glowing softly in the candlelight. Her lips parted, and Noelle smelt again that stale aroma, that sickeningly sweet perfume.

'The seventh card. What will be. Turn it.'

Noelle did. There was no denying this now.

The card of tears. The Ten of Swords, upright.

'*Pleurs*,' whispered Noelle. 'Sorrows. Daily struggle. The decline of finances, desolation. Despair.' At this, her future so starkly before her, she shook her head. 'But there is hope, is there not? This is a card that indicates a turning point for those who cannot go lower than they already have. I can be better. I can rise.' Taken by passion Noelle slammed her hand upon the table, and the candles shuddered in their sconces. '*I can rise!*'

The figure tilted their head. 'But do you want to? How far can you climb from the bottom of this stagnant well in which you have imprisoned yourself? Raoul denounced you. In your grief and ruin, you lost your second sight. Only

Etteilla believed in the echoes of what once existed in you. Why else did he give you these cards?' They gestured at the spread before them, the untouched cards in their wooden box. 'Not even you believed, did you, Noelle? You acted the fraud, you played the part, and you took the hard-earned coin of trusting men and women. But look around you. What comfort has any of your deceptions brought?'

Noelle looked, as she did before the reading – her cramped *appartement*, filled with her too-large table and those decaying curiosities of bats and snakes, her crystals and talismans gathering dust; the curtain with the holes to which she would sometimes press her eye when she felt too weak to rise from her tiny bed; the low-eaved ceiling, the stove that smoked and spat . . .

'How disappointed Etteilla would be, to see how his faith in you was so misplaced. Do you really want to continue, Noelle, as you are?'

The voice that spoke was hypnotic, a strange and sinister caress.

'You are tired. The canker in your throat, your skull . . . Monsieur Guillotin cannot cure them. He shall be leaving Paris soon, after all, and you do not want to be here while the terror reigns supreme.'

Noelle sighed, felt the will leave her.

'Card number eight,' said the voice softly. 'The choice you make.'

She reached out to the final card. Noelle knew what it would be before she saw it.

'But,' Noelle murmured, her eyes roving the skeletal figure cloaked in brown. 'Death does not mean death.'

'Does it not?' came the reply, and Noelle shook her head.

'It means change. Renewal. Letting go of the past. The ending of a cycle.'

'And is this not the end of yours?'

There was nothing Noelle could say to that. Death smiled at her from across the table, beautiful again, pale and serene.

'My boys,' Noelle whispered. 'Will I see them again?'

Raoul, she did not care about. He was the instigator of all of this.

But Death shook their head.

'Oh no,' it said. 'Where you are going, they do not wait.'

Noelle pressed her eyes shut, felt the hot wetness of tears beneath their lids. But what was it Etteilla once said?

A real cartomancer accepts that which must be.

'Come, Noelle Labèque. The next life is waiting.'

Death rose, reached out a hand. Noelle took it, and though the spectre's touch was as cold and hard as bone, she did not resist when the cloaked figure led her gently from the room, leaving the door open to creak on its rusting hinges . . .

At length, the storm passed. Night shifted into a watery dawn, and as the first milky rays of sunshine reached like skeletal fingers into the silent parlour overlooking that twisting snake-like Seine, they touched the tarot cards that lay still upon the table, their images crisp and clear except for that of Death, devoid now of any image at all – a strange and sinister echo of what once had been – and beside it an empty space, where two silver coins had lain.

AUTHOR'S NOTE: Jean-Baptiste Alliette – professionally known as Etteilla – was the first person to use tarot as a means of divination. He created his own deck in 1789 with cards mostly recognisable today except for six, two of these being *feu* and *nuit*, as well as the female querant card, all three of which feature in this story.

AN ARTFUL CURSE

Jess Kidd

I t's unheard of. There goes Kate Gillespie taking the winding path out of the arse-end of the village. Through the scant wood of buckled trees she goes, past outlying mean fields with their crops of stones. A path that has only one ending: the lair of Nancy Langan. That the two are sworn enemies is common knowledge. What is often forgotten is that the two were once friends. Allied by a third, Ellen Keane, that kind of magical soul who can unite fire and water and have neither fare the worse for it. The three were born within a week of one another. They learnt at the same school, attended the same church, wore the same little pinafores and clogs. Ellen's family had rich farmland, managed well. Kate's family had a decent plot and were diligent. Nancy's family were tenant farmers on poor soil who hung on by their tooth-skin. Each of the girls was blessed with an aptitude entirely her own. Kate's was learning, Ellen's was loving, and Nancy's was cursing you to the Devil. The three young friends grew like trees in a thicket, close by, rooted in this place. Kate grew as straight and strong as an ash, Ellen grew as bright as a rowan, and Nancy grew twisted, like the lone hawthorn nobody will meddle with. Then came a time, no one can remember the whys and wherefores of it, that the three went their separate ways; Kate to become a mother; Ellen, a spinster; and Nancy an outright horror.

The last time Kate took this path she was carrying a newborn in her arms. Mena the golden-haired is a young woman now, with suitors lining up. God bless her. As Kate walks, she wonders at the slip and slide of time. How the days rattle by and the weeks barrel on and the decades come and go. She has a lot to be thankful for. She has a roof over her head and a bite to eat. Her body is firm yet and her hair thick and dark, although time has put its first frost upon it. Her hands are strong, her back is supple, and her mind is sharp. Only, lately, Kate feels her mind has been distracted by a puzzle. She must take advice, but the priest is sly, the doctor's a fool, and the rest of the village knows little, other than how to carry a story. Kate needs someone who speaks the truth as they see it, understands the ways of the world and keeps their own counsel.

Kate has seen Nancy Langan on occasion in the village, but only a snip of her; a glinting glance, the arcane gesture of a hand, the quick step of a foot. For Nancy favours the hooded cloaks common to olden-days walking women when she goes about, should she need to terrify children, or sleep in a hedge, or summon a storm. Today, she is without the cloak, sitting on her doorstep, soaking up the unseasonably warm weather. As she nears, Kate looks for the traces of the girl she knew, but truly Nancy looks every part the auld witch people say she is.

Kate feels no triumph when she sees how far her enemy has fallen. Nancy and her cottage have sunk into a state of feral decrepitude. The thatch on the roof is as unkempt as Nancy's hair; both look to be a home for wildlife. The cottage needs whitewash as Nancy needs a good scrubbing. She has the filth of ages upon her. A light wool dress darkened by peat smoke, a kerchief soaked with neck sweat, feet as caked as the flagstones visible through the doorway.

Nancy makes a big point of shielding her eyes against the sun. 'Who are you, treading the path that leads to my door?'

'You well know who I am.'

Nancy hawks up a spit in answer.

'I have brought you a puzzle I cannot solve.'

Nancy looks interested, as Kate knew she would be, not just on account of the puzzle, but on her own admission of failure.

'Go on,' says Nancy.

'Ellen is missing.'

Nancy brings two stools outside so they can sit either side of the door like a pair of gargoyles. But Kate is relieved: for all that she's strong of stomach she's loath to go into the cottage. Such is the air of malevolence from the gaping mouth of it and the cracked and cobwebbed windows of it and the broken-backed slump of its roof. Kate can only imagine the hexes woven into the fabric of the place. She'd likely drop dead if she put a foot over the threshold. Besides, for all her squalor, Nancy has her garden beautiful and to sit under a thatch when there's warmth in the day would be criminal.

Among the last of the roses are gentians and red goosefoot, eyebright and yarrow, dandelion and heather, toadflax, harebell and worts, hairy and otherwise. All of which Nancy no doubt puts in her potions.

Kate holds out a twist of tobacco.

Nancy scowls. 'If that's a peace offering—'

'I wish you no peace, Nancy Langan. As I said, I'm here for Ellen.'

Nancy takes it, unwraps and sniffs the tobacco, rolls it between forefinger and thumb, then shrugs.

Kate can begin. 'Ellen hasn't been seen since Thursday last. Rumour has it that she's run off with a fella.'

'Whose rumour?'

'Her husband's, apparently.'

Nancy fills and tamps her pipe unhurriedly. 'Wouldn't be the first time Ellen has run off.'

'That time Ellen ran off *because* of a fella and – as you of all people know – she didn't go far.' She glances behind her into the murky gloom of Nancy's cottage. It was always the most unlikely of refuges.

Nancy sniffs. 'How long is she married to this man now, Jack Flynn is it?'

'One year, almost to the day.'

Nancy gives Kate a sly side-eye. 'It isn't a match you approve of?'

'Ellen didn't consult me on the matter.'

'Why would she? Look what happened the last time you stuck your coulter into her business.'

'I am not here to discuss the past – if you won't help—'

'Tell me about the husband.'

Kate winds her neck in. 'She found him at a horse fair in Sligo. They were married within a week, clearly the actions of a madwoman.'

'Or a lonely one?' replies Nancy quietly.

Kate looks away. 'Well, I didn't see you down at the farm, darkening her doorstep.'

'How would you know? When did you ever call?'

'I was busy, rearing a child.' Kate is annoyed to feel her face reddening. It was a mistake to come here, she knows that now.

Nancy changes tack. 'So, like the cat Flynn has fallen on his feet.'

Kate's tone is one of begrudgement. 'Hasn't he just.'

It's the first time they've agreed in decades.

Nancy puffs reflectively. 'What does Ellen's husband stand to gain with her gone?'

Kate meets Nancy's eyes. They are the same as ever they were: hard, green, clear-seeing. She finds herself voicing her deepest fear. 'Her farm.'

Nancy gives the slightest of nods and continues calmly puffing.

'Can you find her, Nancy?'

'She's not a medal or a goat, Kate.'

'You've found other lost souls.'

Nancy smiles at Kate. 'I knew you were coming. I read it in the fire.'

'You did in your arse. There's no smoke above and I only knew myself an hour ago.'

Nancy laughs.

Kate catches herself before she laughs too. It would not do to forget what's passed between them. Not even for Ellen's sake.

Nancy sits back against the stone wall and raises her face to the sun. 'So, you believe in the old ways again, or only when it suits you?'

'It wasn't the old ways I stopped believing in.'

Nancy looks up at the sky. 'Would you credit it? Not enough cloud to lace a handkerchief, yet a storm is coming. When you see Jack Flynn on your way home, as you surely will, ask him three times about his wife.'

Kate glances at her with curiosity. 'You're setting a charm on him?'

'From what I've heard he has charm enough.'

Kate nods grimly. 'I'll do as you say.'

Kate returns to the village with a growing sense that something has been set in motion, for good or ill she cannot tell, as was always the way with Nancy Langan. She passes the church, the general store and the schoolhouse. Standing outside O'Malley's inn there's a gaggle of men, arms crossed in the male attitude of appraisal and begrudging approval. The object of their attention is the individual in a new flash buggy. The wheels are clean and bright, the lines elegant and there's a handsome glossy bay harnessed to it. Kate can see there's quality in the horse as well as the cut of the man's coat and the showy tilt of his cap. Nearing, she is stunned to see it is himself, Jack Flynn, up on the driver's seat, riding high.

The man is not blessed. A small balding fella, with a parched look about the lips, the reddish stubble of days about his chin and blue piggy eyes with a tendency to squint. Now he has a look of a suited and booted swine. Kate wonders what it is that Ellen, whose beauty is as rare and mythical now as it ever was, sees in this little bollock.

Jack Flynn casts a porcine eye over her, so that his onlookers take the same liberty. Kate fixes him with a withering glare. The men, sensing trouble, melt away down the road or into O'Malley's.

Jack Flynn smiles. It does not reach his eyes. 'Mrs Gillespie.'

'Mr Flynn. That is some manner of conveyance you have there.'

'It is indeed.'

'And you yourself are finely decorated.'

Flynn gives the slightest of nods, his smile does not diminish.

'And you seem in good spirits, *considering*.'

He steps down from the buggy and lowers his voice. 'Do not be mistaken, Mrs Gillespie, I am a man broken.'

Kate looks down at him, literally, for he is half a head shorter. 'So, your new jaunting car is to assuage your heartache? Although I'm not sure what use you'll have for a dashing city thing like this up at Ellen's farm.'

His smile cools.

'I hear she has gone, Mr Flynn?'

The smile freezes. 'Mrs Flynn has departed.'

'She's quite gone?'

Flynn frowns, a colour rising in the tips of his ears. 'Why ask me again – yes, she has quite gone.'

'Of her leaving, you are certain?'

He looks at Kate like she's a light gone out. 'Unless she is hiding in the woodshed, she has left.'

A crow, hitherto perched on the roof of O'Malley's with its head on one side in the attitude of an eavesdropper, takes to its wings. Kate watches it fly off in the direction of Nancy's cottage. It is said she can conjure nature, but a crow, as everyone knows, recognises no authority but its own.

Flynn taps his smart new boots with his smart new whip. 'And before you ask, I do not know where my wife has gone or with whom.'

'But she met him at a fair in Sligo?'

The frown deepens. 'Mrs Gillespie, I hardly—'

'Was it one of the roguish types that hang about there, waiting to prey on unsuspecting wealthy spinsters?'

'I assume that is the case.'

'Wasn't it at a fair in Sligo she met yourself?'

Flynn flinches but only very slightly, he glances over his shoulder, the men will be watching their exchange. He turns back to her with a blithe smile. 'If our business is concluded, Mrs Gillespie.'

'We have no business, Mr Flynn,' says Kate under her breath as he climbs back up onto his rig.

With a contemptuous tip to his hat-brim he drives off hard and fast down the one good road of the village. Which, Kate notes, does not lead in the direction of Ellen's farm.

Ellen Keane's old stone farmhouse lies out of the village, mellow and lovely in the late October sun. It is a place that used to be as familiar to Kate as her own home, when they were girls, at least. Kate long ago stopped calling. Somehow it didn't seem fair, with Mena bonny in the pram, or carried chattering on her hip, or skipping by her side, while Ellen was alone up at the house but for a parent on their last legs. Weeks and months could pass without Kate seeing her old friend. Sometimes she happened across her down in the village and then the pair would exchange civilities like strangers. If the child was with her, then Ellen's gaze would alight on Mena, with an air of quiet longing. Sometimes Kate — God forgive her — would duck into a doorway, or cross the road, for these meetings lay heavy on her heart.

Dónall, Ellen's farmhand, rounds the house, his cap pulled low and a bag on his back.

'Dónall?'

He comes and puts down his bag, his expression pained. 'I cannot take that man any longer, Mrs Gillespie.'

'Do you know where Ellen is?'

'I didn't even know she was leaving. He had me up at the

top field all that day. When I came back down, the mistress was gone.'

So, Flynn somehow manipulated her leaving. Kate frowns. 'What kind of man is he?'

'One who promises to paint the moon but he's only one rung on his ladder.' Dónall gestures to a set of empty crates. 'Drinking and shooting at the crows in the fields with his cronies. That's about all he is good for.'

'He said she left him.'

Dónall looks guarded. 'That's between themselves. But he has not paid me for the work I've done. And I'll not stay to see the place ruined. The cows have lost their milk, and the hens have lost their eggs with the upset.'

'Is anyone within?'

'If there is then they will not be awake. He's the house turned into a den, rousing at all hours.' With this, Dónall walks away with a grunt of disgust and without a backwards glance.

Kate arms herself with the heavy stick Ellen keeps inside the door. She's only a few steps into the hallway when she smells the sourness, as if the whole place had turned. It's not just the unwashed pots in the pantry, or the stale smell of poitín and porter and pipe smoke, or the pungent breath from the men asleep in the parlour where the peat fire smoulders. It exudes from the house itself, disgusted by its ill-use. And it has been ill-used. There are boots on the hearth rug and muck traipsed up the stairs. A door is off its hinges and the potted palms have been pissed in. Keeping the stick in her hand lest one of the men wake up and she needs to batter him with it, Kate climbs the stairs.

The bedrooms are undisturbed, aside from Ellen's room, the one she shared latterly with this new husband. It has been turned over. The wardrobe is open, with Ellen's things pulled out and strewn across the floor, where they mix with Jack Flynn's showy purchases. Jackets and breeches, hats and ties, a new rifle and several pairs of boots. A clutch of promissory notes have been deposited in the chamber pot; the man has been raising credit against the farm. The bed is a tangled mess of grimy sheets and Ellen's dressing table stacked with bottles and dirty cups. Her rosewood jewellery box has been ransacked. Kate looks around in dismay, fighting the urge to tidy Ellen's gowns, her bodices and stockings. She picks up the jewellery box and, remembering the trick Ellen showed her when they were girls, opens the silvered mirror to reveal a shallow compartment behind. But there are no clandestine love letters, only something wrapped in the softest piece of linen, indeed the hem of a christening gown. A hidden locket, and inside it, a coil of golden baby hair. Kate's heart twists at this secret token. Even a cursory glance of the contents of the wardrobe tells her that Ellen left behind all the things she would need to travel. Her warm cape, her dresses and good shoes. Ellen went in a hurry, with no time to pack.

Kate is rolling pastry when her first visitor arrives. Mena is with her at the kitchen table, bright head bent, coring apples to make a pie. The girl raises an eyebrow as Nancy Langan steps over the threshold, having been reared to treat this woman with the same caution as a mad bull in a field. Mena goes to fetch three cups from the dresser. With Daddy dead some years it has just been the two of them and adept they are at reading one another's moods. When Mena sees her mother's glance towards the back parlour, she gathers up her book and makes herself scarce.

Nancy, with a curt nod and a face like thunder, assumes the seat at the head of the table and extracts her pipe. Kate's gut flips as she scoops tea leaves from the caddy and fills the pot from the kettle and brings it to the table with the jug. She notices her hands are shaking as she sets the things down.

'Don't bother,' says Nancy. 'The milk is sour.'

'It was fresh this morning.'

Nancy shakes her head. Kate peers into the jug. Sure enough, the milk has turned and looks to be days old, a congealed band around the top where the cream lies. She dips her finger; the taste is rancid.

'It will be the same throughout the village; the butter and milk turned, and the cows dry. Nothing to do with me this time.' Nancy adds, with a bitter smile.

'What's causing it?'

'The Devil's in our midst.' Nancy lights her pipe and puffs a few rounds.

'And your divinations? Did you find Ellen?'

'I did not.' Nancy looks up, her face suddenly very old and, to Kate's astonishment, scared. 'She is nowhere to be found. Not on land or sea.'

Kate goes to the press and takes out a bottle of whiskey. Pouring them both a good measure she tells Nancy what she found up at the house.

'The signs are clear, then,' Nancy divines. 'We must look for Ellen beyond this world.'

Their eyes meet, they down their drinks and Nancy pours them another.

'You think she's . . .'

Nancy's expression confirms it. 'The dead may point a finger when the living will not own the crime.'

'And you think he . . .'

'Who else? Name one enemy of Ellen Keane's.'

The room has grown dark and cold. Kate shivers and gets up. She pokes at the range, lights the oil lantern on the table. Nancy sits smoking reflectively.

'We could go to the guards?' Even as the words leave Kate's lips, she knows the answer.

'Where is the evidence?' replies Nancy. 'Where is the body?'

The lamp splutters, the flame turns blue.

In Nancy's voice a note of warning. 'You have another visitor.'

There's a knock on the door.

'Speak of the Devil and the Devil appears,' murmurs Nancy.

*

For a small bollock of a man Jack Flynn seems to fill the kitchen, throwing shadows in every corner. He does not bother to wipe his boots as he crosses the threshold, nor wait to be offered a drink, but rather pours himself a generous measure and knocks it back from Kate's own empty glass.

He is all ill-breeding, ignorance and swagger.

He pours a second and raises the glass. 'Your health.'

Kate feels herself redden with anger but keeps her voice even. 'Mr Flynn, what is it that brings you calling?'

'I would ask you the exact same question, Mrs Gillespie. What was it that brought *you* calling? A little bird told me you were up at my house earlier.'

At '*my house*' Kate frowns and Nancy snorts.

Flynn swivels on his heel. 'Mother Langan, isn't it? Have you something to say on the matter?'

Nancy fixes him with a malignant stare.

'In person you are far less terrifying than your reputation. Apparently if I need a curse or a charm, you're the one. Here and there, scuttling about, burying your piseogs under haystacks for miles around, turning a baleful eye on some poor blighter's cow.'

Kate interjects. 'Mr Flynn—'

'I will warn you, Mother Langan,' continues Jack Flynn. 'Your auld countryside superstitions, your butter-switching and hexes, your love spells and potions, hold no truck with me. I am a man of science and logic. Come the new century we shall have no room for your like.'

Nancy's eyes narrow, the flame in the lantern fizzes and burns brighter.

The door to the hallway opens and Mena, a marmalade cat under her arm, enters the room. The cat, usually a docile creature, widens its amber eyes at Flynn in terror. With a hiss it jumps out of Mena's arms and streaks back through the doorway.

Flynn surveys Mena, a wolf's hunger on his face.

'You must be Philomena.' His voice honeyed, charming. 'Aren't you as pretty as a kitten?'

Mena frowns and glances over at Kate.

Flynn steps forward with his hand outstretched.

Nancy pushes her chair back from the table, blocking his path. Now she stands, raising herself up to her full height. Mena takes the opportunity to bolt back through the door she came in.

Nancy takes the pipe out slowly from her lips. 'State your business here, Flynn.'

'My business is none of yours, Mother Langan.'

Kate intervenes. 'There is nothing you cannot say in front of Nancy.'

Flynn turns to her. 'I simply came here to say – ah, how can I impart this delicately – my house is a bachelor's residence now and this village is full of rattle-tongues as you well know.' He smiles. 'What I'm trying to say, Mrs Gillespie, is that I'd rather you didn't let yourself into my property and go rooting about my bedchamber.'

Kate tries to keep her voice even. 'I have been welcomed in Ellen's house all my life, almost as a sister—'

Nancy throws her a sceptical look.

'But you are not Mrs Flynn's sister, nor mine for that matter. Allegedly, you are a respectable widow. Try to act appropriately, Mrs Gillespie.'

Kate bristles. 'I was simply concerned about my friend.'

Nancy gives a grunt of support.

Flynn's glance is sly and takes them both in. 'Great friends you are, indeed. Dependable but in no ways honest. Didn't you once spin all manner of tales—'

Kate's voice is high, laced with panic. 'I would ask you to leave my house, Mr Flynn.'

'Do you really think you've a single soul fooled in the town below? Ah, but there's one individual who doesn't know, isn't there?' He drops his voice. 'Imagine if Goldilocks ever found out.'

'You heard her.' Nancy growls. 'Get out, Flynn.'

'Gladly.' He surveys the women brightly. 'After all, I've a farm to run.'

Nancy mutters darkly under her breath.

At the door he turns and points at her. 'Don't go laying any curses on me, Mother Langan.'

'Why would I need to?' replies Nancy in a heartbeat. 'Sure, aren't you already a curse on yourself?'

Jack Flynn's mask slips, he throws her a poisonous look and is gone.

It's nearly midnight and they have the bottle of whiskey finished, although neither of them feels the benefit. The flame in the lantern burns yellow and the marmalade cat has returned to curl up on Mena's bed.

Nancy says they will not be further troubled by Jack Flynn tonight.

'Will we raise her, then?' asks Nancy. 'Do you remember what we need?'

Kate nods.

They clear a space on the kitchen table, household herbs are found, chiefly rosemary, along with certain stones, a broom and a pot of salt completes the equipment. The oil lamp is turned down and candles are lit. Nancy leads the proceedings quietly, so as not to wake the sleeping Mena. Kate hears ancient words whispered. Words passed down from Nancy's grandmother, closely guarded, spoken only when there is dire need. Salt is scattered, fragrant herbs burnt, a name whispered, a spirit invoked. The air starts to take on that heavy, soupy quality Kate always associates with the otherworldly, with the narrowing of the distance that separates us from them. She feels a growing sense of excitement laced with more than a little terror. She tells herself there is nothing to fear now that Jack Flynn is gone from here.

And now on this calm night, the wind picks up. It whines about the house. It rattles the door and whistles at the keyhole. It blows down the chimney and sends the bare branches clawing at the windowpanes.

'Ellen,' Nancy whispers. 'Come and take your place at this table.'

With one sudden violent gust the back door is blown open and the candles are extinguished.

They sit in velvet blackness. Kate hears the kitchen clock tick, her own heart thump, the house around her shift and creak. Somewhere in the distance, down in the village, a dog barks. The temperature in the room drops to icy; if Kate could see anything it would be her breath.

They wait.

And now the sound of the chair being drawn out from the table, the scrape of wood on flagstone comes with a far-off echo to it. Nancy lets go of Kate's hand and strikes a match, sudden and glaring. She lights the candles, slowly, calmly. Kate forces herself to look up. There, seated at the table, is Ellen.

Or not quite Ellen. The face in the flickering candlelight is no less lovely in death than it was in life, more beautiful perhaps, with a spirit's luminosity. Translucent, bare-shouldered and dressed in nothing but a sheet, Ellen's fair hair dishevelled and studded with twigs and leaves. She glances around, blinking, vague-eyed, sullen-mouthed.

'Where are you, pet?' asks Nancy gently.

Kate steels herself against the answer. She finds it harder to hear the dead than to see them. For there is always that jolting metallic rasp, that searing note of discord, that accompanies even the sweetest of otherworldly voices.

'I was sleeping,' comes the reply, as grating as nails over a chalkboard.

'Look around yourself, do you recognise the place?'

The spirit draws the sheet around her shoulders. Kate sees, with a sudden lurch of her heart, that Ellen's ring finger dangles on a ribbon of skin, while the rest of her digits find equally strange angles.

She glances at Nancy, but Nancy's full focus is on the apparition. Kate sees the beads of sweat on the woman's forehead, the high colour in her cheeks, the fire in her green eyes. Kate turns her attention back to Ellen, noticing how bruises are blossoming on her pale wrists now. When the ghost smiles Kate sees, with a sob of pity, that her front teeth have been knocked out. When the ghost talks, dark rubies fall from her mouth.

'I lie under heather. I watch the geese fly over me.'

Nancy speaks slowly, calmly, as if to a fractious child. 'Look around you, Ellen. Any landmarks? A wall, a tree, a house?'

Ellen pouts, pettish now. 'Why do you wake me? Leave me to my dark blanket. Leave me to my black hollow.'

'Poor lamb.' Nancy glances at Kate. 'She doesn't know where she is.'

Ellen bares her bloody teeth and starts to scream.

They have a job to calm her. More words, incantations, the liberal use of table salt. Thankfully Mena sleeps through it. Finally pacified, Ellen drifts out through the wall, down the garden and into the first pink of dawn. Where she stands, a little hazy now, bare-shouldered and battered, staring up at the henhouse.

'We must go to the guards,' whispers Kate.

'To say what? We've raised the ghost of a murdered woman?'

'We'll say we had a tip-off.'

Nancy pours them both another whiskey. Kate is grateful for its warming fire, for she's been shivering ever since Ellen's return.

'Without a body he will not hang.'

Kate well knows it.

Nancy rises and puts on her cape and hood. 'Lock your doors and windows and keep an eye on Mena. He has designs on her.'

Kate shudders and drains her glass. She draws the bolt after Nancy has left. Then for extra measure she scatters the thresholds with salt and burns a handful of rosemary on the range. She brings the kettle up to the boil, steeps the tea and pours it strong. Then carries two cups into Mena's room, such is her habit of a morning. As she passes the kitchen window she glances out, seeing neither hide nor hair of Ellen. Opening Mena's door, she understands why: the dead woman stands in the corner gazing down at the slumbering girl like some awful broken angel.

Ellen looks up as she enters the room. There is blood on her chin, faint bruising around her eye-rings. 'Is that myself?' she whispers, pointing, hopeful. 'There in the bed. Is that where I am sleeping?'

Mena stirs and turns over, pulling the blankets up to her chin, her golden hair spilling over the pillow.

Kate, fighting her tears, shakes her head.

The dead woman sniffs and wanders into the wardrobe.

*

All is not as it should be in the village. There is not a scrape of butter, nor a drop of milk to be had. What's more, it seems that overnight every hen has turned into a cock; the noise is deafening. If that wasn't enough to ruin a body's morning, now the villagers find that the turf won't burn, and the water won't boil, even if they had anything with which to colour their tea. The gossips are out early, scouting about with empty milk jugs. Soon enough they discover that the epicentre of this plague is Ellen's farm, for hadn't the farmhand Dónall told Peter Noonan that every cow above was as dry as a stone and the hens had stopped laying and didn't he blame this catastrophe on Jack Flynn? The men admit that Flynn may be a stranger to hard work and spin the odd story, but sure, who doesn't? Besides, isn't he the very soul of generosity down at O'Malley's? The women point out that the poor man is afflicted. What with his wife off gallivanting and himself not being blessed in the looks department, God love him. For all he tries to bring a touch of refinement to his appearance, if you took the pig out of the sty and dressed him in a tweed suit you'd call him Jack Flynn's brother.

Very soon Nancy Langan's name is on everyone's lips. If anyone is likely to bring disaster down upon them all it would be herself. And isn't it a misfortune that their village must be afflicted with a witch? For who among them would stoop so low as to avail themselves of her spiteful services? More than a few conveniently forget the time they slipped Nancy a coin, or a bag of apples, or a twist of tobacco to plant a cow's sling in their neighbour's land, or hide a rotten egg under a bale, or rub a bit of butter on their enemy's gatepost in passing, or turn the malign eye on someone's new heifer. Besides, wasn't Nancy Langan seen late last night with her hair streaming against the moon, arms raised and mouth foaming, muttering imprecations on the standing stone in Tom Feehan's sheep field? And wasn't Kate Gillespie herself seen taking the winding path out of the arse-end of the village only yesterday?

The evidence is indeed damning.

And so it is that when Kate Gillespie reaches the village, she has short shrift indeed. The postmistress barely looks her in the eye and the schoolteacher would rather cross the road than speak to her. Gone are the friendly nods and the few kind words. Now the men look away and the women startle. It is worse than being a stranger.

Kate gets her messages and heads home, puzzled as to what she has done to warrant the village's censure. Perhaps the town had always been aware of their sleight of hand, but hadn't she worked hard to be free of any taint by association? Her late husband was a decent man, mild to a fault, and wasn't she a decent woman? Hadn't her intentions been noble, offering the child a respectable home, saving Ellen's reputation? Even so, she must admit: their deceit was audacious. Ellen hiding out up at Nancy's hovel. Herself padding her belly and waddling into the village. Now, alone and unprotected, Kate must face up to the fact that all along the village has known her for exactly what she is and not what she longed to be.

She has the turning to her cottage in sight when she hears the frantic jangle of a buggy and the gallop of hooves.

At first, she thinks the man is fixing to run her down, such is the venom in his eyes. With a wall either side of her and the narrowing of the road she cannot step out of the buggy's trajectory. It screeches to a halt no more than four feet away. The horse snorts and the dust settles, and Jack Flynn scowls down at her from above.

Kate, with a prayer to whoever might be listening, meets the swine's eye.

'You ought to mind the company you keep, Mrs Gillespie.'

'That is rich coming from you, Mr Flynn.'

She sees a cold fury kindle in him. Well and good, let him run her down, she will not be cowed by this crook. She takes a slow breath and studies him hard. 'Where did you bury Ellen Keane?'

There it is, glimpsed for a moment, a momentary look of fear, confusion even, before he rallies. He smiles slowly; with the whip in his hand he touches the horse's back, lightly, caressingly. The horse's flesh twitches, it could be a fly landing, nothing more. With his other hand, slowly, carefully he takes up the reins.

Kate's instincts tell her to run. She ignores them, knowing that if she takes flight this man will mow her down. It is with profound relief she sees Tom Feehan crossing into his field over beyond with his dog at his heel. She raises her hand to him, and he gives the chariest of nods. Flynn follows her gaze, swearing under his breath.

Kate turns and walks away, her mind and heart racing, forcing herself not to look back and not to run. His voice trails her.

'There's a saying, Kate Gillespie, those who intend to sling clods want to be wearing a clean shirt. Didn't I tell you I know all about your dirty laundry?'

Kate keeps walking.

'You never saw fit to tell that girl in your house above what she came from.'

Kate keeps walking.

'That she's a child of sin.'

Kate will not give him the satisfaction of looking behind her.

'The truth will out, Kate Gillespie.'

Mena hears it from her own lips. And when Kate has finished the telling and they've both wiped their eyes the girl gets up and goes to the press. She takes out the whiskey bottle, sets the glasses and she pours them both a generous mouthful.

She holds Kate's eye. 'Is Ellen with us now?'

Kate nods. 'She's sat on the dresser.'

'Can she hear us, does she understand?'

Kate glances at Ellen. The dead woman's bruises have deepened around her throat and her cheeks have more of a sunken look. She is looking up at the ceiling with an air of bewilderment.

'I think she gets the gist of it.'

Mena raises her glass. 'To Kate and to Ellen: my mothers.'

Kate feels her heart burst with pride at their daughter grown.

Kate is sweeping the floor when she smells it. It is not the sweetness of peat smoke, but something rank and acrid and nearby. She drops her broom and runs about the place, searching every room and outhouse. Aside from her own range and the wisp of smoke from her own chimney there is no other fire to be found on her property. Yet here she is coughing and wheezing, heaving and spluttering, and her eyes streaming with tears – when all around her the air is perfectly clear. She climbs up to the highest point on her land and stands under the washing line and then she sees it. A plume of oily black smoke way off in the direction of Nancy Langan's cottage.

By sunset the fire is largely out, only the collapsed chimney stack is still smouldering, but sure, it will do that for days. Kate and Mena help Nancy, wrapped in the blanket, down the path, one on either side of her. The woman has no more than the clothes she stands up in.

A deep hush falls as they walk through the village. The three of them, a fright to God. Their hair and faces besmirched with smoke and smuts. Nancy holds her burnt hands out in front of her as if she's sleepwalking. Gone are her eyebrows and lashes, the hair is melted on her head. Even Mena's fairy-tale locks are blackened. But most terrifying of all are their faces, set like masks, eyes hard and glittering within. A child bursts out crying, others bless themselves. After the women pass, life resumes. Clocks continue ticking, O'Malley draws a nice pint, the postmistress locks up and the schoolteacher puts away her register.

The story of the burning of Nancy Langan's cottage spreads even quicker than the flames themselves did. Although some say it was astonishing how quickly the thatch had gone up, rotten and riddled as it was. It transpired that after his brush with Kate Gillespie that morning, Jack Flynn had rounded up a brace of burly local buckos to act as bailiffs and rode out to Nancy's cottage to inform her that she owed him eighty-five years' rent. For the Langan land is owned by his wife and therefore is his now and he had come for his dues.

Nancy had told him to stick his dues up his hole. Then she had turned to the young buckos and threatened to shrivel their vitals for them. Knowing, as they did, of the harm that may befall anyone who crossed the auld bitch, the lads promptly took their leave. Not to be outdone, Jack Flynn rode away, returning with a barrel from which he anointed Nancy's cottage. With a grin of pure devilment, he struck a match and threw it in the thatch and the whole place went up, raging like the fires of Hell. Nancy herself only narrowly escaped with her life. It was later said that the severity of the conflagration was caused by the magical artefacts within. The dried hemlock and black candles, dead newts and desiccated cats. So fierce evil was the fire that the stones turned molten, and the earth bubbled so that nothing could ever grow again on the land for the ground would never cool.

In the village, factions emerge. Some are all for Nancy Langan, for isn't it a terrible cruelty to put a poor body out of her home and then burn it down for her? Some are for Jack Flynn, for Nancy Langan is the worst kind of cunning woman who has had the village in thrall to her for long enough. Tensions rise, as they will among people with no fresh milk or the wherewithal for a cupeen of hot tea. Jack Flynn stands the men drink after drink in O'Malley's, and in that hallowed space there is only one topic of conversation. That the village must be purged of witches, all wild heathen bitches must be brought to task. Nancy Langan is the ringleader, she will turn others. Soon even the best and most peaceful of wives will be out cursing and casting and howling at the moon. Dancing about in the altogether. Taking the Devil as a lover. A few of the older married men can't see it themselves, but they join in, for it's an exhilarating change from hurling and horses. These are brave words indeed bandied in the snug of the saloon. A gang of foolhardy young fellas take it upon themselves to march up to Kate Gillespie's place and demand she hand over the auld witch, for it is well known that Nancy Langan is roosting in her attic room. They bang on the door and throw a few stones until Mrs Gillespie appears at an upstairs window with a shotgun and threatens to blow the head off anyone trespassing on her property.

That Nancy Langan will retaliate is a certainty.

The general store sells out of table salt. There's a run on holy water. At every Mass the priest offers to curse – from a height – anyone found cursing.

And so the villagers wait.

The eve of Samhain comes. Before the sun sets every living creature is safely tucked up inside, the women and the men, the babies and the old folk, the dry cows and the cock-hens. Bibles are taken out and rosaries kept nearby. Iron shovels are slid under sick beds and horseshoes into cribs. Even O'Malley has the inn closed and the shutters drawn.

The night passes without incident. Mrs Ginty is delivered of a baby who is born without a tail. No one dies. The people wake into a dour, damp and tealess morning as if they've been given a new lease of life. But the relief fades as an unwelcome thought rises in the collective mind: won't it be May Eve that Mother Langan is waiting for?

The weather turns bitter, they have never known the like of it. Even the cosiest of cottages is plagued by sudden draughts and freezing corners. Keyholes are plugged, thick curtains are sewn, mufflers are worn, but it is as if a bone-deep chill has stolen into the village. And with the cold comes the damp. Soon it is as if the whole of the village has been built upon a lake. Even in the dryest of houses silt appears on the hearthrugs and legions of frogs wash through the pantry. Take up a floorboard and you'll discover a river. O'Malley's barrels are found bobbing in the basement, whole families of rats sailing on top of them. Tidemarks rise three feet high on every wall. Mould paints the skirting boards with mysterious hieroglyphics and bog asphodel blooms on carpets. Everywhere is the smell of the open ground. Nothing can be kept dry. Books slump and pages coagulate, bread turns to soup and collars wilt, newspapers turn to plash before the headlines are read. Then, to add insult to injury, the flames begin to burn blue and lose their heat. Candles, oil lamps, peat fires, pipes, it makes no matter. One thing is for certain now: there is no warmth or dryness to be had in the village. Some say this is Nancy Langan's doing. Others say that such misfortunes could only be wreaked by a far greater evil than one auld cunning woman could produce.

Kate looks across the kitchen table at Nancy; she is smoking doggedly. She wears a scarf wrapped around her bald head for Mena has gently shaved away her burnt hair. Her hands are carefully bandaged; a week on from the fire they are healing well. She is reciting for Mena, who is taking notes, her fingers blue and the ink undried on moist paper. Even the cat on her lap looks frozen to the bone. Ellen sits on the dresser wrapped in a spectral bedsheet, staring at Mena who, having no gift for the otherworldly, cannot discern the dead. This is just as well, for Ellen is not a sight for the faint-hearted. She has taken on a greenish tinge and her eyes are dull and sunken and her expression either vacant or aghast. Despite being unable to see her, Mena has taken to singing Ellen songs. It calms the dead woman but also draws her nearer. The girl says she does not mind; when she gets too cold, she'll add another pair of bed socks.

The three of them work long hours at the kitchen table. They eat apples and whatever Kate finds in the pantry. Thankfully she has a few bottles laid by. Sometimes Nancy paces, sometimes she swears, sometimes she goes out and smokes a pipeful under the moon.

Once, when they are alone at the kitchen table, with Kate changing Nancy's dressings, she catches the woman looking at her intently.

'I wanted Ellen to keep her child,' Nancy says softly. 'To make a stand against them. I hated you for persuading her otherwise.'

Kate says nothing, only ties and tucks bandages as gently as she can.

'I saw a terrible greed in you,' Nancy continues. 'Your wanting of a child, whatever the cost.'

'Perhaps I hated you for seeing that,' Kate replies, finding no anger for the other. 'And for believing things could be any different.'

Nancy looks thoughtful. 'We lost sight of Ellen in what we wanted.'

Kate stands and puts her hand on Nancy's shoulder.

Nancy raises her own bandaged paw and covers Kate's hand.

*

It is just before dawn when the candleflame turns yellow and the kettle left hopefully on the hob starts to boil. The three have worked through the night, buoyed by some shift in the tide. Even Ellen seemed to feel this change: she stood up from the dresser, gave them a sharp nod and walked out through the kitchen wall.

'It is done,' says Nancy, not without relief.

Kate hesitates to ask.

'Ask it, Kate.'

'What if it comes back on you? Aren't curses like hens in that they can come home to roost?'

'A righteous curse will find its target,' says Nancy.

'She's wrought it as fine as a poet's curse, Mammy,' reassures Mena. 'It can't fail.'

Kate looks thoughtful. 'I'm a widow, surely there's benefit in that when it comes to cursing?'

'And strictly speaking I'm an orphan,' adds Mena.

Nancy looks from one to the other of them. When she smiles there's more than a hint of her old roguish spirit.

Three figures walk into the village at midday. They wear black capes and hoods. They move slowly, regally. A wind picks up and the sky lours with unspent rain so that the light already looks to be dying. The women stop outside O'Malley's inn, where a flash new buggy drawn by a handsome bay waits for its feckless owner.

The figures turn towards the door.

One by one, with sombre ceremony, they kneel on the ground.

Now they wait.

The men look out.

'Will they come in?' whispers one.

'Let them,' says Jack Flynn and he turns to O'Malley. 'A round, for the men.'

O'Malley holds up his hands. 'I don't want any trouble, Jack.'

Auld Peter Noonan pipes up. 'They're after cursing you, son.'

'Is that so? Well, they can curse away.'

The men glance at one another and draw away from Jack Flynn, their expressions sober, frightened even.

'Ah, damn you all!' says Flynn. 'That you are afeared of a few bloody women!'

Flynn takes up his riding crop and steps outside. As he closes the door the wind picks up. He glances behind him; the friends he has latterly been drinking with are watching through the window. A few bystanders have stopped to observe. More people are arriving in response to the story being frantically carried from door to door. Namely, that Nancy Langan is after cursing Jack Flynn.

The three women, their faces obscured by their hoods, kneel, still as stones.

'Are they are not intending to curse him from a height?' whispers the postmistress to the schoolteacher.

'They only do that in stories,' says the schoolteacher. 'Pay attention now. Here it comes.'

With perfect timing, the three kneeling women raise their faces and push back their hoods. Nancy Langan, her head shorn to the bone and cheekbones sharp, is flanked by Kate and Mena Gillespie, with their hair in tight buns.

Flynn sneers and points with his riding crop. 'The maiden, the mother and the crone.'

Their eyes are fixed on the man, not with hatred nor with anger, but with cool concentration. There is a composure to them. By contrast, Flynn is twitchy, slapping his crop against his boot top, turning back to the men watching through the window, gesturing, grinning.

'He won't know what's hit him,' says the postmistress.

The schoolmistress nods, riveted to the spectacle.

Kate and Mena, in unison, reach up with their left hands and loose their hair; it is whipped up by the wind, dark and golden strands, whirling and twining together. The three raise their right hands and point.

Flynn's grin falters, he takes a step back, as if pinned to the door of O'Malley's.

'He's already lost his ground,' observes the schoolmistress.

Nancy begins. In a sonorous voice she names the man and names his crimes and names his punishment. Kate and Mena repeat her lines with their own strong and strident voices. When Flynn laughs, high and nervously, no one laughs with him.

When Ellen Keane's name is spoken aloud, he flinches, a

fact not lost on the watching crowd. No one will remember the exact words the women weave but weave they do. They weave a snare and a net and a noose for the man. They wish him every injury that he has ever inflicted. They wish his tongue to swell with every lie. They wish his bones broken and his guts on fire, his eyes pierced and his ears stopped, his body unwaked and his soul damned to the Devil. And so, they proclaim, it is done.

A silence falls over the village. The wind dies down.

Kate Gillespie is seen to glance over her shoulder and nudge Nancy Langan, who turns to look behind her. Onlookers make out three faint shadowy figures kneeling behind the women. They bless themselves and mutter placatory prayers.

In O'Malley's inn the fire, which has latterly been burning with a sultry indigo flame, bursts into life. Anyone not outside watching the cursing of Jack Flynn would witness the moisture subsiding from their walls, the exodus of frogs or, in the case of O'Malley's, the floating of barrels down, down, to rest on a perfectly dry cellar floor. Last of all the smell of the open bog lifts, leaving only the familiar scent of turf fires and tobacco, leaf mould and the coming winter.

Everyone's attention is on Jack Flynn.

The people know that some curses are fast-acting, while others take generations to come to fruition. Some curses miss their target entirely to mug about the air or skulk about the ground, ready to lay low some unsuspecting individual.

A smirk appears on Jack Flynn's face.

The crowd feels a surge of disappointment. Until they recall that an unjust curse will recoil right back on the person who made it. Everyone turns to look at the three kneeling women.

They don't look a bit concerned.

They are studying Jack Flynn with a calm, unyielding interest. Like the hawk watches the mouse. By contrast, the man himself seems to be unravelling, he capers and gestures, red-faced, pig-eyed.

'This place is witch-riddled,' he spits. 'I'll not stay here another day to be hexed.'

'There is a world of difference,' says Nancy Langan. 'Between a hex and an artful curse.'

Before Jack Flynn can open his mouth, the sudden sickening sound of snapping bones. He screams, looking down in horror at his hands. Watching as each of his fingers, with a violent volition of its own, breaks and assumes a unique angle. His nose explodes with blood, great gouts pouring from each nostril. He starts to whine but is doubled over by an invisible blow to his stomach. He straightens, spitting blood and teeth, only to be launched four feet in the air and slammed against the door of the inn. His limbs flail helplessly while some invisible hand throttles him until his eyes bulge.

The villagers can only watch, knowing better than to get involved with a supernatural variety of justice. Flynn is set roughly onto his feet and shaken until his remaining teeth rattle. Now his legs start to move, as with the jauntiness of a puppet he is carried off at pace down the road.

The women calmly rise and follow. And after them trip the villagers.

Out towards Ellen's farm the cursed man stomps. Snivelling and snorting, whimpering and bleating, holding up his broken hands against invisible blows. Sometimes he falls but no one presses forward to pick him up. More than once, Nancy Langan is seen to smile.

Past the farm and towards the open bogland he trots. Kate Gillespie calls for a spade and someone puts one into her hand.

Finally, Flynn stops walking. The man is crying the gulping sob of the afflicted. Kate Gillespie steps forward and presents to him the spade. He screams in pain as his arms shoot out and his broken fingers close firmly, one by one, around the handle. Now his body is digging while his face streams with impotent tears.

Ellen Keane's body is brought to light at the dying of the day, curled in the black sod, wound in a bedsheet.

༄

They find Ellen's will in the hearth up at her farm, scorched but not destroyed. It seems Jack Flynn was destined to do everything half-cocked. Although it was reported that he competently put his neck into the noose when the time came. Ellen had bequeathed her estate in its entirety to Mena Gillespie. If the villagers have anything to say about this, they keep it to themselves. For it is common knowledge that young Mena has a house guest in Nancy Langan until her cottage is rebuilt, and of course her mother is a frequent visitor. It is said that Nancy keeps her hand in. Only these days, with the encouragement of her friends, she favours charms over hexes.

AN AGE OF EVIL

Stuart Turton

Juliette, I'm on my way to Clarendon Manor. I've left you everything I've dug up on the place. I'll call when I get there, but I should only be gone a day or so.

— Kevin

You're wasting your time. Every ghost hunter in the world has done a night in Clarendon. Nothing ever happens. Did you feed the dog before you left?

— Juliette

Yes.

— Kevin

൭

A clipping from the Manchester Evening News

MANSFIELD HEIRESS FOUND DEAD

December 27th, 1932

Cassandra Pope (34), daughter of industrial tycoon Peter Mansfield (61) has been found murdered, along with her two children.

Mrs Pope made headlines last year when she abandoned her husband, absconding in the night with her two children and Douglas Wren – private secretary to Mr Mansfield.

Her whereabouts swiftly became the subject of national speculation, though her location was never uncovered. It now appears she and the family settled in Clarendon Manor in Cheshire, where she was found dead last night.

The police have refused to reveal any further details, but Peter Mansfield has been taken in for questioning.

From the records of Bury Old Road Police Station

Interview conducted between Peter Mansfield and Inspectors Arthur McMullen and Oliver Spaight on the morning of December 26th, 1932

[Spaight]   So, Mr Mansfield, you admit that you travelled to Clarendon Manor with the intention of killing Douglas Wren?
[Mansfield]   I travelled there to bring my daughter and grandchildren home. I had no desire to hurt Douglas unless he tried to stop me. I gave you Cassie's letters. You saw how afraid of him she was.
[Spaight]   For the record, your daughter is Cassandra Pope and your grandchildren are Sally and Lucy Pope.
[Mansfield]   They were, before he — before Douglas did what he did.
[McMullen]   If your intention was merely to bring them home, why did you take the foreman of your warehouse with you? Once again, for the record, I'm referring to Thomas Church.
[Mansfield]   Cassie's letters made it sound like Douglas had gone round the bend. I took Tommy with me in case Douglas started any trouble. Tommy's a big lad.

	I thought he could end any arguments before they started.
[Spaight]	We've interviewed a number of people who knew Douglas Wren. From what they saw, he was a loving partner to Cassie and a doting parent to her children.
[Mansfield]	Aye, they would say that. I'd have said it, too. Douglas was my personal secretary for two years. Had me fooled like everybody else. He used his position to seduce Cassie away from her husband, then stole her away in the night, along with the children. He was capable of anything.
[Spaight]	When did you first know the family had gone to Clarendon Manor?
[Mansfield]	A few months after Cassie ran away, she sent us a letter renouncing Douglas and begging me to fetch her. That's why I went down there.
[Spaight]	You arrived at Clarendon Manor around midnight on Christmas Day. Correct?

[Mansfield] That's it. Church bells were still ringing when we went inside.

[McMullen] Can you describe what happened after you arrived, Mr Mansfield?

[Mansfield] Well, I went inside and I saw ... I ...

[Spaight] Take your time, sir. Best we get the facts on the table, nice and clear.

[Mansfield] I saw the kiddies first. Lucy and Sally, sitting down for their Christmas dinner, only they were wearing old clothes, much too big for them. I thought they were playing dress-up, but when I got closer I saw that they were tied to their chairs. They'd been ... it was awful.

[McMullen] Was your daughter at the table?

[Mansfield] No, I didn't know where Cassie was. I started calling for her. That's when I heard her screaming. I ran back into the entrance hall. Douglas was holding her in the air by the throat. He smiled when he saw

	me, then slit Cassie's stomach open with a knife.
[Spaight]	You're saying Douglas Wren killed your daughter?
[McMullen]	For the record, Mr Mansfield is nodding in the affirmative.
[Spaight]	Lifting somebody up by the throat — even a woman — takes a great deal of strength, and by all accounts Douglas Wren was the bookish type.
[Mansfield]	I'm telling you what I saw.
[McMullen]	Can anybody corroborate your story?
[Mansfield]	What does that mean? Corrob— corbate?
[McMullen]	Corroborate. It means did anybody else witness the murder?
[Mansfield]	Tommy Church maybe. He tried to help Cassie, but . . . it was too late. Last I saw, Douglas was chasing him upstairs. Maybe you can—
[Spaight]	Mr Church is in hospital. He jumped out of a window to escape. He survived the fall, but we haven't been able to

wake him. Doctors say it may be
weeks before he recovers.

[Mansfield] There was a little boy, maybe
eight or nine. I saw him a
couple of times. Kept calling
for his dad, but—

[McMullen] We searched the house. There
was no boy present.

[Mansfield] He was there, I'm telling you.
Little lad, maybe nine. Dark
curly hair, dark eyes.

[Spaight] Seems you saw a lot of things
that night nobody else did.

[McMullen] You claim that Douglas Wren
killed your daughter and
grandchildren, then chased off
Thomas Church. Let's put aside
that your employee was twice
his size and ask this question
instead: why are you alive, Mr
Mansfield?

[Mansfield] I . . . I ran.

[Spaight] You ran?

[Mansfield] What else could I do? Douglas
had gone mad. There was no
sense me dying alongside
everybody else.

[Spaight] Now, here's the issue, Mr

	Mansfield. You see, our officers found the body of Douglas Wren in the library. He'd hanged himself from a mezzanine balcony, about two days prior to your arrival, according to the coroner. Now, what do you have to say about that?
[Mansfield]	I . . . I saw him.
[McMullen]	No, you didn't. You couldn't have. He was long dead by the time you arrived. And from where I'm sitting it seems like you've been telling us a pack of lies in the hopes of blaming your crimes on a dead man.
[Spaight]	Come now, sir. The truth, if you please. It'll go better with the judge — and God — if you confess now. You're caught. There's no sense holding out. You took Thomas Church to Clarendon Manor with the intention of killing Douglas Wren, didn't you? Why? Was the scandal of your daughter's desertion too much? You're a proud fellow, and proud fellows

| | occasionally act rashly. Did
your temper get the best of
you? Did Cassie try to put
herself between you and her
lover? Is that why you ended up
killing Cassie and the girls?
[Mansfield] | I ... didn't. I wouldn't.
Douglas killed them. I saw it.
[Spaight] | And what will Thomas Church
say when he wakes up, do you
think? Do you think he'll
corroborate your story? Who do
you think he'll blame for the
death of that family?

From the records of Bury Old Road Police Station

Written statement from Thomas Church on January 13th, 1933

> The tall man the tall man

Letters recovered from the Mansfield residence during the police investigation into the Clarendon Manor massacre

September 14th, 1932

Dearest Mama,

 I am writing, because I cannot abide the thought of you worrying over me. Douglas, myself and the girls have arrived at our new home and have already begun to make it our very own. Please know that I am safe, well and cared for.

 My heart breaks in memory of how I stole away in the night, but there was no other path. My marriage to James was over. We bore no love for one another, and he bore no love for the children. I realise you will hate Douglas for what has transpired, apportioning him the majority of the blame, but – truly – he's done nothing wrong. I was not whisked away against my will. I waltzed. He did not seduce me, unless you believe that being attentive, kind and funny is a form of seduction – which I suppose it is. Douglas is a wonderful man, who loves me better than I ever hoped to be loved. I feel certain you want that for me, so please forgive the scandal I've caused in achieving it.

It saddens me that I cannot tell you where we've gone. We have decided to start afresh, a new life away from the whispers. We will be happy.

Your ever-loving daughter,
Cassie

October 11th, 1932

Dearest Mama,

Although you cannot respond to these letters, I hope you do not begrudge receiving them. I miss our conversations over afternoon tea, and take succour in continuing my side of them.

We have been in our new home nearly a month, and have made ourselves very comfortable. We live in a manor, if you'd believe it, though I'm still not certain how Douglas came to possess such a grand property, especially one in such fine repair.

He teases me when I ask, saying only that the deeds came to him by chance, and it was their deliverance that convinced him to risk everything for our love. He is so happy here, often taking Lucy and Sally on 'rambles' to explore the manor's labyrinth corridors. He's searching for a servant's bell he claims to hear ringing in the dead of night. It's never woken me, though you know how deeply I sleep. He believes a bird may have built a nest near the pulley mechanism.

Alas, sleepless nights aren't the only drawback we've

encountered. The nearest village is many miles away and we've found it difficult to hire servants, as the manor has a dark reputation in these parts. Knowing where we live, the villagers treat us vilely. They whisper behind our backs when we visit the shops, even hurling rocks at poor Douglas. At first, I believed they were aware of the scandal which chased us here, but dear Harriet has put us at ease on that front.

Oh Harriet. I haven't mentioned her before, have I? She's a young girl from the village, who was in situ when we arrived, having been asked by the previous owners to stay on and keep the place between owners. She has served faithfully as our cook and housekeeper in the months since.

She explained that the village's fear is based on a previous tragedy. At the turn of the century, a group of parents carried their children up to the manor in the early hours of Christmas Day, murdering them in cold blood, before taking their own lives in the snow. Can you imagine anything so evil?

Of course, the surviving villagers blamed the inhabitants of the manor, Lord and Lady Deville, and their son Henry. The villagers accused them of witchcraft and, in their grief, slaughtered the entire family and all of their servants.

Suffice to say, it's likely Harriet will be our only help for a little while. Despite that, we're going along quite well. Douglas seeks his irksome bell, while the children combat their loneliness by creating imaginary playfellows. They tell me stories of laughing children, who beckon them into the woods to play, and a lonely little boy with curly dark hair and eyes who wanders the corridors, searching for his parents.

Sometimes, they're so convincing I think I hear him myself.

Your loving daughter,
Cassie

PS. I wish I could remember the recipe for that pain tonic you used to make. I'm suffering a terrible ache in my shoulder and nothing I do eases it.

November 22nd, 1932

Dearest Mama,

Forgive the lapse in correspondence. Truthfully, I don't know where to begin, for our last weeks have been so odd, so filled with apprehension and confusion that I hardly know where to start.

Lucy and Sally have adopted the guise of twin sisters called Elsbeth and Annabelle, and have fallen into their pantomime so completely I hardly see them out of it. They quarrel most violently, using language quite unfit for girls their age. I cannot imagine where they could have learned it, for the village remains as unwelcoming as ever.

Unable to make friends, Douglas has become positively obsessed with the servant's bell he keeps hearing, and has started ripping the panels off the walls in hopes of tracing every rope and pulley. I fear the strain of our situation is fraying his mind. I hear him conversing with somebody while he goes about his work, even arguing with them on occasion, but he shrugs it off when I question him, claiming he's merely voicing out loud some problem or other.

Harriet tells me not to worry. She says men will be men, each odd in their own way, but I'm not so sure. I don't know what to do, Mama. I'm so confused and can hardly catch a wink of sleep. My shoulder aches so, and every night I hear footsteps prowling up and down the corridor outside our bedroom. Douglas chides me for letting my imagination run so far, but the other night somebody rattled the door handle. I know they did.

Your anxious daughter,
Cassie

December 4th, 1932

I've written my address below. Please send Father to fetch me. I'm frightened.

My beautiful girls are no longer themselves. They dress differently; act differently. I walk into their bedroom and they go silent, staring balefully until I depart. They are so cold with me. Almost strangers.

They tell me 'the tall man' has taken a fancy to me. What does that mean?

Douglas wanders the house every night in search of the ringing bell. I found him in the library this morning, standing perfectly still, staring at the balcony above. His head was moving from side to side, as if he could see something swinging up there.

There were tears in his eyes.

He claimed he couldn't sleep because of the incessant ringing of the bell. Mama, the house was silent. I tried to calm him down, but he shoved me away, something he's never done before. I brought him carefully back to bed, but he kept looking over his shoulder apprehensively.

Only once did I follow his gaze. I swear, back there in the shadows, I saw a tall man following us.

December 19th, 1932

Dearest Mama,

You say Father will not come. I'm begging you. Please. Douglas scares me. He told me we must invite the tall man for Christmas dinner next week, and has instructed Harriet to prepare an extra place at the table.

Our housekeeper seems unfazed by this request. She hums and sings, and goes about her duties diligently, suggesting I indulge Douglas and that all will be well soon. I fear this house has taken hold of her.

You say that Father wonders why I don't deliver myself to you on the train. The children will not leave Clarendon, which means neither can I, though I'm starting to worry they may not be my children any more. They only answer to the names Elsbeth and Annabelle, and have moved themselves into a different bedroom, where they insist on sleeping in the same bed, cradling each other.

I have asked them why they're behaving this way, but they laugh so cruelly. They say the tall man is coming home for Christmas, and that I will make a fine gift.

I'm so terribly frightened. Please don't leave me here alone any longer.

Your daughter,
Cassie

༄

Okay Kevin, I admit it – I'm interested! I stayed up waaaay too late last night reading through the clippings you left and found something odd. The letters mention that Cassie's daughters started calling themselves Elsbeth and Annabelle. I did a bit of googling and those were the names of two sisters who went missing eight years prior, in 1924. Far as I can see, they never met Cassie and Douglas.

Check your email, I've sent over the articles I found.

– Juliette

I knew you'd come around.

– Kevin

I haven't 'come around', but you're there now, so I'm going to help you make the best of it. Because I'm amazing.

– Juliette

A clipping from the Woolwich Herald

MYSTERY OF MISSING SISTERS

January 18th, 1925

Woolwich Constabulary continue to appeal for information concerning the disappearance of two sisters residing in south London. Elsbeth Lee (32) was reported missing six weeks ago, followed by her younger sister Annabelle Lee (27), who vanished three weeks after.

Police have described the sisters as 'close', saying they wrote letters weekly. Each sister packed a bag and left their home in sound mind, claiming to be visiting the other at Clarendon Manor. Officers from Woolwich Constabulary have undertaken a search of the derelict property, which is located in Cheshire, but have found no trace of the missing women. Investigations continue.

∽

Page torn from the diary of Elsbeth Lee, recovered from Clarendon Manor during the search for the missing sisters

16th December, 1924
Our Christmas decorations are up. The tinsel, in particular, is my pride and joy. I had little belief I'd be able to find a ladder large enough to reach the high ceiling, let alone hang it with such symmetry. Candles burn jollily through the house and we have placed our large tree in the entrance hall, where all might enjoy it.

I do hope my husband is pleased with the results. He's due back any day now, but his moods are often erratic after a long absence, with his tempers difficult to gauge.

The pain in my shoulder still hasn't abated, but I'm hoping to spend the morning foraging for mushrooms in the woods. Henry loves the stew I make from them. Sometimes, when I'm out there, I hear the wild laughter of the village children as they play among the trees, and wish that Henry were a little less shy. If he'd only introduce himself, instead of tinkering with his doll's house all day. He is a kind, imaginative, beautiful boy with his dark hair and dark eyes. I'm sure they would come around to him in time.

How much longer can the sins of the past be held against us? Are we to be blamed for something that happened forty years before we got here? The deaths of all those children was a tragedy, but hardly one of our making. It was their own parents who slaughtered them in the snow on Christmas morning, and those same parents who butchered the Deville family for it. We weren't even living here then.

Oh my, Annabelle's ringing her bell again.

Will she not grant me ten minutes of peace? I know it's uncharitable, but sometimes I do resent her so. My sister lies in that darkened room, stinking and bitter, ringing that bell from noon to night. It's hardly my fault she's bedridden. I bring her food, comb her hair, bathe and read to her, but it's never enough. Ten minutes after I close the door, the bell rings again. I can never do enough. When will it ever be enough?

17th December, 1924
Our housekeeper Harriet prepared the most magnificent breakfast this morning. Fresh fruit and croissants. Kippers. Black tea. More than I could ever eat, all served on silver platters. I didn't even know we owned any silver.

Of course, my feast was interrupted by the agonising

tinkle of Annabelle's bell, but Harriet has offered to take up my duties for the day, freeing me from my obligations. I cannot describe how relieved I am. Annabelle's bedsores need washing, which always makes her so cross. More than once she's struck me. I've been fretting about it for days.

Harriet obviously wishes to cheer me up. We stayed up late last night, drinking wine in the kitchen. I confided my fears about my husband's infidelities, but — by the warmth of the hearth — they didn't

a gift for the tall man a gift for the tall man a gift for the tall man

seem quite so terrible. Harriet can be wonderfully reassuring. She told me that my husband has appetites I can't satisfy, but it was ever thus between men and their wives. He has made a beautiful home for me, and given me a beautiful life. And while I wait for his return, I have Henry to care for. A child must have a mother.

There's the bell again. How insistent it is. How violent. Harriet's gone to see what the matter is, but I will not find any peace where it can reach me. I think I will go down to the village. If I can overcome their hostility, perhaps I will find a doctor capable of alleviating the ache in my shoulder. The pain grows daily.

If I cut through the woods I may even see the children whose laughter I enjoy so much. Odd, that I've never encountered them before. I could put in a good word for Henry.

18th December, 1924
I'm so cross with myself. I woke late this morning, losing any time I might have had with Henry before my duties to Annabelle overtook me.

My son misses his father terribly, not least because he's promised to bring back another toy for his doll's house. Every one of them has a name and a story. I even hear Henry talking to them sometimes. It worries me, but I'm certain his obsession stems from his loneliness. Clarendon is a beautiful place, but it is dreadfully isolated – especially for a young boy in need of friends.

The bell has thankfully been quiet this morning. No doubt Annabelle's sleeping late. She had another of her turns last night. It was a few minutes after midnight when I heard her wailing. I ran down the corridor and opened her bedroom door with my master key, only to find it barricaded from the inside with furniture.

Shoving it open inch by inch, I finally managed to squeeze inside.

My sister was naked and thrashing, her sheets twisted tight around her body. She'd raked at her skin with her fingernails, leaving bloody scratches on her stomach and arms. Her eyes were wide, but it was obvious she was still tangled in her dream.

'The tall man!' she cried out. 'The tall man!'

How many times have I heard that name? Held her while she screamed it? He knocks three times on the bedroom door before twisting the handle. Finding it locked, he steps out of the shadows.

You lie still, squeezing your eyes shut, listening as his footsteps cross the room towards your bed. You feel his presence looming over you, then the touch of a dreadfully cold hand on your cheek. A moment later, his clothes rustle as he starts to undress.

How strange. I don't remember Annabelle telling me about her nightmares, yet I recollect the story so vividly ...
 I called Annabelle's name softly until she finally broke free of her dream, bolting upright into my waiting arms. I cradled her until she stopped trembling, shushing and stroking her hair, as I'd done when we were young girls sleeping in the same bed.

bring them for the tall man bring them for the tall man bring them for the tall man

Annabelle was hysterical, weeping uncontrollably, begging me to kill her; to release her from this torment. Staring into her wounded blue eyes, I felt so terribly selfish. What is my pain compared to hers? She is bedridden and sick of mind. I'm her big sister. I must nurse her better, for who else is there?

Eventually, Annabelle fell asleep in my arms, and I returned to my bed. I must confess, for the first time I felt a measure of contentment in my role.

19th December, 1924
It's been much too long since I've seen my other sisters. I must invite them to Clarendon.

Harriet thinks it's a marvellous idea.

I will write to them as soon as the pain in my shoulder eases.

∽

There's a f*****g ghost here!

– Kevin

Shut up.

– Juliette

I'm serious. I got to Clarendon late last night, put my sleeping bag down, fell asleep, then heard this voice asking if I wanted to play with him. I look up and there's a little boy sitting cross-legged next to me. Dark curly hair, and dark eyes. Old clothes. He said his name was Henry Deville.

– Kevin

Did you get a video?

— Juliette

Second I went for my phone, he vanished.

— Kevin

You HAVE to get him on video. That's proper numbers for the channel, Kev. No more day jobs.

— Juliette

Of course I'm going to get him on video you melon. Look, I went to the local library this morning and had a chat with the librarian. She told me that Henry Deville was the son of Lord and Lady Deville. They were the first owners of Clarendon Manor, back in 1881. The local villagers killed them all in their beds, including the kid.

— Kevin

Jesus, why?

— Juliette

She didn't know. Point is, every one of the accounts mentions a dark-haired little boy called Henry, and I reckon it's Henry Deville. He's been haunting this place for years!! I've already started working on the script for the video. We're going to be proper rich.

– Kevin

I don't think Henry's the only ghost in that place. I had a dig around in the police archive and found something out about the other missing Lee sister, Annabelle. Apparently, when the police went looking for her they found a statement she'd left behind in one of the bedrooms. *Proper serial-killer stuff.*

– Juliette

ぶ

Statement by Annabelle Lee found in a bedroom at Clarendon Manor

I used to ring the servant's bell in my bedroom incessantly, hoping it would be my sister, Elsbeth, who'd walk through the door. By the time I arrived at Clarendon this damned house had possessed her almost entirely, but there were occasional flashes of the loving woman I'd known. A confused smile when she brought me food, or a wrinkled brow when I begged her to let me go. Something tormented in the eyes.

The last time I saw my sister – my real sister, that is – was the night before I escaped my bedroom. The tall man had just finished with me, leaving me bruised and shaking, scratches across my body. I was trapped, with no hope of escape, so I screamed and screamed, and Elsbeth came running, like she used to when I had nightmares as a child. She unlocked the door and pushed through the barricade I'd made to try and keep the tall man out.

My heart soared. It was her! It was Elsbeth. The real Elsbeth. Not the flat, distant, dreaming monster who lured me here, locking me in this bedroom.

There was life in her eyes, concern on her face. It was my big sister.

And then she was gone.

It was like her soul drained out of her body. Her face went blank, her limbs hung loose and that strange, tight smile crawled back onto her face. I tried to jump out of the bed and run past her, but she held me so tightly. Impossibly tightly. How can she be so thin, so frail and withered, yet so strong?

I wriggled and fought. I tried to bite her ear, but she kept smiling at me, like I was a child to be soothed. Eventually, she squeezed me so hard I couldn't breathe. I must have passed out.

I woke up the next morning thinking all hope was lost. I was ready to end it.

I paced the corners searching for something sharp and that's when I saw an object gleaming on the floor in the dim light.

It was Elsbeth's master key, lying in the dust. She must have dropped it when she rushed in. Am I foolish to believe that she did it intentionally? That she was trying to free me while she still had control of herself?

I waited until the early hours of the morning, listening for any movement beyond my bedroom door, then unlocked it and crept outside. The house was even more decrepit than when I'd arrived from London. The ceilings were buckled and the floorboards shattered, as if they could no longer bear the weight of the evil growing inside this house. Cold air swirled through cracked windows, carrying the screams of children from outside. A strange fungus covered the walls, and the stink ... it was hard to breathe through. I don't know how Elsbeth put up with it.

I ran down the staircase into the entrance hall and pushed open the doors into the poisoned, twisted garden. I had one foot outside when I heard Elsbeth talking happily from somewhere in the house.

I should have left. I know I should have. I was almost free, but how do you abandon somebody you love? Elsbeth raised me and my sisters after our parents left. She kept me safe, fought for the things I didn't believe I was worthy of. Three weeks ago, I left my jolly flat, and my job, and my friends, because I believed she was in trouble. I travelled to Clarendon to save her. Like a fool, I thought maybe I still could.

I turned my back on the garden and instead followed her voice through the dank corridors to a dining room.

Elsbeth was sitting all alone at the end of a long table, wearing a filthy summer dress. Her hair was knotted and greasy, but she was smiling so happily. She was complimenting somebody called Harriet on the fine spread laid out before her.

Not only was there nobody in the room, but the table was covered in platters of mouldy bread and rotten fruit. As I watched, Elsbeth shovelled a maggot-ridden peach into her mouth, juice running down her chin.

I retched. I couldn't help it.

She stopped dead, frowning at me in the shadows. For a second, I saw Elsbeth in there, the flicker of recognition and the flash of fear — a desperate urge to tell me to flee, but then the other thing took hold of her. She leapt up onto the table and came hurtling at me on all fours, like an animal.

I panicked and grabbed a bread knife from the table, thrusting it out in front of me. It went straight through her eye, the wooden handle collapsing her cheek. There was no resistance. Her body had the same consistency as the rotten fruit she'd been eating.

She hit the ground, jerking awfully, before becoming still.

Sobs rolled out of me, all the strength draining from my body. I dropped to the floor and wept. Was it relief? Sorrow? I don't know. I don't suppose it matters now.

Almost immediately, I felt the cold shadow of somebody behind me, then a hand on my shoulder.

The pain ... it was like a flame, but then it was gone.

I opened my eyes to find the dining room lit by candelabra, everything beautiful. Like a dream. Glittering decorations festooned the walls, and the table was covered in a Christmas feast, heat still rising from the potatoes and turkey. Harriet was pouring wine from a silver jug, arranging my place at the head of the table.

Something in the back of my mind was screaming, urging me to . . . I don't know. Sometimes, we all feel trapped in our roles, don't we? It was silly. Much as I would have liked to get in my small car and drive back to London, I was a wife and a mother, and it was Christmas. Where else would I be?

My son Henry wrapped his arms around me and I ran my hand through that beautiful crop of curly dark hair. He wanted me to play with his doll's house with him, but I didn't have time. I had to prepare for my husband's arrival. A shiver of nerves went through me. He would be home any minute, but his moods were often erratic after a long absence, and his temper could be difficult to gauge.

From outside, I heard the carriage wheels spraying pebbles. Henry jumped up in glee, as Harriet smiled.

'The tall man is home,' she said.

൦

> Does that read to you like possession? One sister was possessed, then the other?
> – Kevin

> Yeah, possessed by the 'tall man'. Did you notice that Henry pops up again? I think I've sussed out the connection. I've been at the

British Library all afternoon, searching every name we've come across. I found some letters sent by a maid called Harriet Stouridge to her brother while she was working at Clarendon Manor in 1891! That's 43 years before Annabelle and Elsbeth went to the house and 51 years before Cassie and Douglas moved in! And yet they all mention her.

– Juliette

Send, send!!

– Kevin

※

*Letters between Harriet Stouridge and
her brother Stuart Stouridge*

Clarendon Manor Feb 6th 1881

My dear brother, I'm writing you this letter myself, with my own hand, and will admit my pride in it. There's a housekeeper here, who has taught me my letters and my reading. I am slow, but I get better each day. As you have asked, I will put in a good word at Clarendon Manor, which needs footmen sore. Here I will warn you, because I would not want you to arrive full of accusation. Clarendon is a troubled house. Lord Deville is not a kindly master. He forbids his son, Henry, any sort of company and beats Lady Deville until she cannot walk, putting the lash to servants who make a noise in his presence. He often visits the younger girls in the night, and they have taken to calling him the tall man for the long shadow that spreads across the floor when he enters their bedroom. I would welcome your presence here, and the company it would bring, but know that you will not be happy. Nobody is.

Clarendon Manor April 12th 1881

Do not come! This place is unholy. Lord Deville, who everybody fears, was weeping in the study like a child last night. Keeping curious, I crept inside and saw a different man than the one I've cursed these last four weeks. He was on the floor, being held tenderly by the wife upon whom he has visited so much pain. She kept saying, 'Is it you, is it really you, my love?' They saw me and were most startled. I expected such punishment, but Lord Deville begged me to run from this house. 'Fly!' he said. Upon these curious words I retreated to my tasks, only to return an hour later to clean what mess they may have left. I found his body swinging on a long rope in the library. Against God, he had taken his life. I woke the house. We cut him down, cleaned his body, tended him as was proper. Only – the next morning, he came to breakfast as normal. Born again.

Alive, and in his customary fury. Nobody else thought this strange. The devil walks these halls, brother.

Clarendon Manor April 18th 1881

I tried to leave Clarendon yesterday, for the tall man comes to my bed every night. I packed my bag, content to walk should no carriage take me. It was Lady Deville who stopped me. She took me to the basement and showed me my body, tossed upon the dirt floor and left to rot. We were all down there. All the servants, even Lord and Lady Deville. Dead for weeks. Lady Deville explained that we are held fast in the cursed place, far from God. We shall never leave. None of us.

Testing. Testing. You there, Kevin? I haven't heard from you all day. Did you read the letters? The tall man is Henry's father!
– Juliette

Sorry, Henry turned up again and I spent half the night walking around the house with him. It's weird, the house is beautiful today. It must be something he's doing. He showed me the bedrooms where Elsbeth and Annabelle sleep. And Douglas Wren and Cassie, and their kids. They're all here, Jules. Everybody we read about. I met them all.

– Kevin

Tell me you got a video.

– Juliette

You should come down here. Honestly, you need to see this place and meet Henry. He's a really sweet kid.

– Kevin

DID. YOU. GET. A. VIDEO?

– Juliette

God, I'm exhausted. I'm going to bed, okay? I'll message you when I wake up. I hope I can get some sleep, my shoulder's killing me.

– Kevin

Your shoulder? Why are you talking about your shoulder? Is that a joke?

– Juliette

Kevin?

– Juliette

Answer your phone! Henry Deville isn't what you think he is. You need to GET OUT of Clarendon right now! I'm driving down to get you.

– Juliette

╰⊱

From the records of Bury Old Road Police Station

A verbal account of the events that occurred in Clarendon Manor on December 25th, 1881 and the role played by Cliff Stouridge

I killed them. There, I confess it. It was a kindness. What else do you want? I bashed Lord Deville's head in and held Lady Deville so Old Man Peterson could do the same to her. We stabbed the boy. Everybody had a turn at that.

Why are you writing all this down? You want my story? Fine, start with this. Clarendon Manor wasn't built. It appeared overnight. Was just there one morning in the deep dark of the wood, where we were taught never to go. The Devilles arrived the next afternoon, carts full of luggage and servants trailing behind them.

Does that sound natural? A house appears, then a family to fill it?

For a few months, nobody in the village went near it. We told the children to stay away – and they did, for a while.

Money calls, though. It sings so sweetly.

The younger girls started to drift up first, as maids and cleaners. My little girl Harriet went. I ordered her to stay home, but she wouldn't listen. She saw the Devilles in church every Sunday, dressed in their finery. Turned her head. She thought it would be such a thing to work for a noble family.

After a time, we didn't hear from those girls again, Harriet included. We asked after them when the Devilles came down to the village, but Lady Deville would smile this tight smile and tell us not to worry.

I know what they said as happened on Christmas night, but it ain't true. Not close. I've heard it said that parents carried their sleeping children up to Clarendon during the witching hour and slaughtered them in the snow, before turning their rocks, scythes and blades upon themselves.

If you write down anything, write down this. That didn't happen.

The children got out of bed by themselves. Saw it myself, because my youngest son was one of them. They went up to the house in whatever they were wearing, wading through the snow in their bare feet.

We grabbed hold of them, tried to carry them back, but they fought so hard; they bit and kicked, and if that didn't work they started clawing at their own eyes, hurting themselves until we let go. What could we do?

The Devilles were waiting for them. Lord and Lady Deville, with their son Henry clapping with glee. I'll never forget their smiles. They stretched their faces, like somebody was pulling their lips up.

As soon as our children got there, they started a snowball fight. Never mind that their teeth were chattering, or their hands were chapped with cold. Henry joined in, seemed happy enough until a snowball hit him in the face.

You never saw a child lose his temper more suddenly, or more violently. He screamed, but it weren't the scream of a boy. It was something else, something much older. It made my blood run cold. The other children just — they stopped dead. Like they were froze. A few seconds later they picked up rocks from under the snow and starting beating the boy who'd thrown the snowball at Henry.

We tried to stop them, but they turned the stones on us.

It was Giles the blacksmith who saw the truth of it. Henry Deville was controlling the kiddies. All of them. They were doing what he told them to do. Had hold of his parents, too. I saw that myself. When he got hit with that snowball, Lord and Lady Deville got loose of him for a few seconds. Those horrible smiles vanished and their faces went slack, like two sails without any wind. They screamed at us to run.

Of course I can continue! I just need a second to gather myself.

A few of us scooped up our children and ran back to the village to raise the alarm. The children went wild, biting and clawing, desperate to get back to Henry. We held tight, though.

I had to tie my boy to his bed to keep him safe, then I gathered a few hardy lads and returned to Clarendon. Our friends were dead by the time we arrived, lying in the snow next to their slaughtered children. Blood and snow. God, I close my eyes and still see it. The Devilles were inside, enjoying their Christmas dinner around the table.

Lord and Lady Deville were like puppets, stiff and strange, sort of trapped within themselves. Was the same for all the servants, including my Harriet. Henry, though – he was laughing so hard there were tears in his eyes, still talking about the game he'd just played and how fun it had been.

So, yes, I killed them and I'm proud of doing it. I set Lord and Lady Deville free and ridded the world of that devil boy. Second I did it, the servants just – fell apart. Have you ever seen dead cows, after they've been left in the field for a few weeks? The servants – my Harriet – were like that. It was like they'd been walking around, decomposing the whole time.

That's my confession. That's what you wanted, wasn't it? My only regret was that I didn't burn Clarendon Manor with them. If you've sense, you'll see it done yourself. That house is evil, and – so long as it stands – evil will be done inside.

༄

It's Henry Deville!!! He's behind everything. He always has been. Please tell me you're on your way home.

– Juliette

Do you know why Lord and Lady Deville moved to Clarendon Manor? They were desperate to have a child, but they couldn't conceive. They consulted a doctor, who recommended the country air. By chance, Lord Deville's father had recently died, leaving them a house nobody knew existed.

– Kevin

Tell me when you get home. Are you in the car?
– Juliette

It took them a week to reach Clarendon Manor, but it was worth it. They found me waiting for them. A lonely young boy with curly dark hair and dark eyes. I came with the house. *I* was the house.

– Kevin

Henry?

– Juliette

Yes.

– Kevin

Where's Kevin?

– Juliette

I have my hand on his shoulder.

— Kevin

Let him go!!!

— Juliette

I don't want to. He's fun, like a big brother. That's all I've ever wanted. A mother and father. Brothers and sisters. Friends.

— Kevin

I'm bringing the police you little shit.

— Juliette

༼

A screenshot from the Guardian

MISSING COUPLE LINKED TO HAUNTED-HOUSE HOAX

December 27th, 2024

The police have completed their search of Clarendon Manor but have found no trace of missing couple Juliette Wash and Kevin Storer, despite evidence suggesting the YouTubers visited the infamous property in the days before their disappearance.

Messages between the couple have surfaced online prompting hordes of true crime fans to descend upon Clarendon. Police believe the messages to be an elaborate prank aimed at increasing their social media profile. They are urging the public to stay away from the derelict manor house, citing structural dangers.

FEAST

Kiran Millwood Hargrave

'Who has the matches?'
'Ouch! Beachwood, is that you, you lump?'
'Me, Grace.'
'You're crushing my foot, Alice, move.'
'Shhh!'
'Don't shush me, Helen.'
'Sorry, Grace, I only—'
'Shhhh!'
'Who has the darned matches?'
'I thought Lydia—'
'Not me.'
'Tarnation, who has the matches? Hamblin?'
'Shhhh!'

There was a notching sound, a whoosh, a flare of light that made all the girls shield their eyes, blinking. Martha Beachwood's hand, already shaking, held a stolen Mass candle out to the flame held in Helen Bomner's slender fingers and the wick ignited. Rose Hamblin brought her candle to meet Lydia Fraser's, and in turn passed the flame to Alice Simpkin, who bypassed Martha's and lit Grace's. Grace Clifford's face came into view, glowing like some angel painted on a chapel ceiling in Italy. It was all Alice could do not to sigh with pleasure as she remembered those rose petal lips on hers. Only once, three months ago, and only as a dare, but it had sustained her through the bleak turn for winter and the leeching cold that raked the windowpane above her bed every night. Alice was not the only one on whom Grace's face had such an effect. Every girl in the freezing attic – and indeed within the damp honey stone confines of Marchmont College for Girls – had a pash on the doe-eyed American. But Grace was no doe, and her silence was wielded like a weapon.

With the merest lift of her plucked eyebrow, Grace set the others to scrambling for their rucksacks, fumbling the brass buckles in their haste to lay out the contents. Martha's stomach growled as she removed the game pie, bought directly from the bakery in Frome that supplied Fortnum's. The pastry flaked onto her fingers when she unwrapped it from its wax cloth and slid it onto the plate Lydia had set down for this purpose. She licked her fingers, tasting butter and salt, and Alice slapped her hand.

'Goodness' sake, Beachwood. You're such a glutton. Help me with the cutlery. Ugh! Wipe your hand first, you beast!'

'Leave her, Alice,' said Helen, and handed Martha a napkin. Martha flushed and wiped her licked fingers regretfully, watching the remaining crumbs scatter to the floorboards.

This was Martha's first time in the attic. It could be accessed only from an outside drainpipe, which in turn was reached by squeezing through the tiny window in the dormitory bathroom. Martha had never been sure if she'd fit through, even if she ever were invited. The triumph of the invitation was still sitting on her like a sable cape, and she was determined not to let anyone, especially nasty Alice Simpkin, spoil her moment. They were a curious assortment, she and Rose Hamblin sticking out like two sore thumbs. Rose looked queer, pale and out of sorts, and Martha ventured a tremulous smile, which Rose did not return.

Rose felt twice as odd as she looked. When she'd arrived at the closed blacked-out window, last to come up the drainpipe, cold rushed out at her like a physical force, and with it the smell of a freshly dredged river: stagnant water and sewer, chalk and mud. More the smell of earth, of a grave, than of a draughty old attic. She'd hesitated a long moment, her chill fingers slick on the icy metal, a blunt shock of cold between her thighs where they met the pipe. The spill of starlight reached only so far inside, and Martha's plump leg vanished so completely beyond its reach she may well have passed through a black curtain. Only the sounds of their sharp breaths and the creaks of the floorboards telling her that yes, there were living, breathing girls in there, that her companions had not merely stepped the other side of some numinous veil and through to another place. That Rose, too, could climb inside and find it to be just an attic.

'Hamblin.' Grace's hiss had the effect of a fishing hook piercing her navel, and Rose jerked forwards, like a caught fish, plunged into another world. The others had not waited for her. Nearest to her were shadows, angular and haphazard, and she touched, carefully, to confirm they were only pieces of furniture stacked together: bedsteads and chairs. One step at a time, she trusted herself to the nothing.

There was no sense of the scale of the place, though she knew it must be vast to footprint the school. Where were the others? Rose stopped, afraid to go further. What if she could not find them and wandered the wrong way? She had no lamp, no matches even. She listened, hard, for their voices, and heard whispers but could not tell where from. Why did Helen not come and fetch her?

She looked behind her and saw that she had forgotten to slide the window closed. There was the oblong of the night sky, demarcated by blue, duskish light of stars, and she wanted to go to it, to swim through the darkness and breathe the air out there. But there was a suck of pressure, a push of cold, and the window slid closed.

Rose froze, her skin crawling. The window had closed so precisely, not slammed as it should have, or scraped down the stiff pulleys. It had closed as though someone had closed it. As she stood in the black cold, she thought of Grace's voice. *Hamblin.* How had it sounded so close? There had been no echo to it. Had it been Grace's voice at all?

'Rose.' Rose let out a little shriek as a soft, familiar hand gripped hers. 'There you are.'

'Helen, where did you go?' Rose gripped back with both hands, straining to see her lover's face in the blackness. There was nothing, only Helen's warm breath, smelling of toothpaste, and her cool hand between hers. A thought came to

Rose, that she was a trick, a lampie, sent to lead her astray. She felt up her arm and pulled her closer, wanting to kiss her, to know it really was her, but Helen pulled back.

'Not now, Rose. Grace is waiting.'

༺

There had been great excitement when Grace announced a midnight feast to mark the winter solstice, chased by great disappointment when the girls realised this fell after the end of term, and only the over-holidaying girls would even be able to be considered for attendance. Such was Grace's influence, several considered cancelling their home-goings, willing to forgo Christmas trees hung with candles and candied puddings for a few hours in a draughty and almost certainly haunted attic with the Gahls.

Grace. Alice. Helen. Lydia. The only girls in the school referred to by their first names, a perverse mark of respect in this dominion of surnames. Lydia was the daughter of a judge and a minor royal, sixteenth in line to the Austrian throne (though this did not hold such cachet as it did before the Great War). She was also subject to a vile and debilitating illness, a voice that told her not to eat and to move constantly, and was narrow-waisted as a Gibson girl. This voice grew louder by the day, and no one else could hear it, or see what Lydia saw in the steamed-over windows in the bathroom. Helen Bomner was the greatest beauty of the school, and Alice earned her place following a brawl with Lucinda Purley where she lost but swallowed three teeth and so was declared the bee's knees by Grace. She also provided a perfect vowel for their friendship acronym – together they were the Gahls, pronounced with deference to Grace's Texan drawl, and they decided everything from which pashes could be consummated to the laundry rota. They oversaw the organisation of night-time jaunts: brawls, cigarette distribution, occasional yomps to the stones for both, and feasts. These were usually held on the tennis lawn in summer, and in the dormitory in winter – the attic was solely the Gahls' domain, which was what made this feast all the more special.

The attic access had been bricked up decades before. The reasons for its blocking were the subject of intense speculation: a Marchmont prefect had hanged herself following her rejection by a lover and her body still remained there, hanging from a beam; that girls once used it as somewhere to smoke and drink and otherwise carry on; that a satanic coven held séances there; that it was haunted by the spirit of a nun or madwoman or both. The fact that the Gahls had now claimed it as their den only added to its mystery, for none of them spoke about what was up there, even Helen to Rose.

Cold perpetually leaked from the plaster that covered the trapdoor, and the bed below was occupied by whoever was lowest in the social ranking, usually a first year, but currently Martha. She had been relegated there for snitching on Laura Watkins, making her invitation even more of a surprise. The rest of the room was a tolerable temperature only towards the end of Easter term. Otherwise it was dank and chilly, the walls being too damp to support the weight of radiators, and so the girls relied on hot air piped up from the kitchen, where a coal furnace was installed, and on fireplaces dotted almost at random throughout. High fire guards did not quite mitigate the fire risk, and so at night only two wood burners in the centre of the dormitory were kept stoked, and the beds closest to these were highly prized.

In the Winter term of 1932, these beds were occupied by the Gahls. The Gahls were the undisputed rulers of Marchmont, their power absolute, and Grace's power absolute over them. It had been a coup, really, Grace overthrowing poor Muriel Lambford the moment she glided across the threshold, the scandal of her expulsion from Cheltenham Ladies' College trailing like expensive perfume. She was a looker, such a ringer for Lillian Gish that a rumour started Grace was her love child, probably with John Gilbert if their chemistry in *La Bohème* was anything to go by. This had been the one and only time the Marchmont girls had been allowed to go to the pictures, a feat orchestrated by Grace herself, involving not a little manipulation of their new dormitory mistress, who was let go immediately afterwards. But there were a few lookers at Marchmont: Helen Bomner was possessed of silky blond hair and very green eyes, and Lydia Fraser's endless legs were the subject of many crushes. She was rich, her father being a Texan oil baron who had laid claim to a good swathe of Indian land north of Austin and made his fortune from it. But Muriel's father had a wing of the National Gallery named after him, and Jane Goodly's mother shopped couture in Paris, turning up in miles of silk and fur coats even for school concerts.

No, it was not merely her appearance or her wealth, but the atmosphere she created, a self-possession that evoked something febrile, faintly hysterical in those around her. Fear rubbed closely with desire whenever her attention turned on anyone. By the time her first term was spent, every girl's monthly bleed had harmonised itself to hers. Rose, who had spent time studying Grace, could not decide just how aware of it she was. It did not turn on and off like a light switch, nor dim like a gas lamp. It was always there, full glare – an inner certainty that blazed among the school's damp edifice and its damper inhabitants. Rose, perhaps, was the only person at Marchmont who was not under Grace's spell. Rose sensed something in Grace, something dark, a sensation akin to holding a match a little too close to an oil spill. She was not fooled by the rainbow-tinged surface, the slick imperviousness, the sharp tang of money that clung to Grace. Rose knew Grace was no good.

She'd once, early on in Grace's reign, made the mistake of saying so to Helen, who she'd gone steady with since third year.

'Oh no, darling,' said Helen, appalled. They spoke like this to one another, as though man and wife married for many years. 'Grace is a doll, she wouldn't hurt a fly.'

But Rose had grown up with a brother who came into her bedroom the night she turned eight and lied point blank to their parents when Rose told them what he'd done. His face had not so much as flickered. This knowledge that evil could look like a boy you'd known since you were born, a boy you loved and who was meant to love you, changed her so irrevocably she'd been able to see straight through people ever since, as though the skin of others were a pellucid surface beneath which their soul shone. Helen's was a creamy rose, like the innermost parts of her. Alice's was red: angry and staining. Swotty Martha Beachwood's was blue and sad, and Lydia's a deeper indigo and even sadder. Grace's, though – Grace's was black as oil.

'Hamblin,' snapped Alice. 'The cider.'

Rose jumped and fetched out the two green glass bottles Grace had bribed the garden boy into getting for them. It was famously strong stuff, scrumpy really, and as she forced the wire cage from the cork it popped out, nearly hitting Rose in the eye. She felt the force of it rush past her temple, the delayed shock like an icy needle darning her side. Alice laughed unkindly, and Grace smirked. Rose wondered why she had been invited. She'd only come because of Helen. She knew Grace didn't like her, and sometimes wondered if she was jealous of their relationship. Perhaps it was not a lover's jealousy, but she was at least desirous of controlling the Gahls, and indeed all the girls at Marchmont.

Marchmont Girls' was established in 1892 by a cotton merchant long suspected – and posthumously proved – to be a prolific abuser of young girls, rich enough to be indulged. He also found it helpful to be a passionate advocate for women's education, and a school combined his two enthusiasms in perfect harmony, though he did not live long past the first pupils passing through the Hamstone façade.

Overlooked by a stone circle of pagan origin, the house itself was once a convent, then an asylum for the country's most notorious cases, and as such was well adapted for multiple occupancy by adolescent girls. Set up on the Levels between the Mendips and the Polden Hills, it found itself in a valley prone to damp and floods, and a basement was dredged from the clay to create a reservoir in hopes of defending the house from the worst of the damage. Over the following decades it flooded repeatedly, and in fact during the Great War, when the school masters were replaced by mistresses and the groundkeepers by local girls, a drainage system was established, almost moat-like, around the building, adding to its appearance of isolation and eccentricity.

This sensation permeated the entire structure of the building. Its ground floor housed not only the expected kitchens and laundry, but also a chapel used occasionally as a recreational room and as such housed both altar and a bridge table. The first-floor classrooms were converted from doctor's consultation rooms, and history was held in a room where it was rumoured experimental treatments were undertaken that amounted to torture. Unchanged was the use of the floor above, where the sisters, then the patients, and now the students slept in neat iron bedsteads in a single room that spanned the entire footprint of the floor, but for a section built when indoor plumbing allowed for a bathroom to be established. Above this level, the attic.

'Hamblin?' Alice's sharp voice cracked into Rose's thoughts. 'We're waiting.'

Lydia slid a glass under the foaming bottle, and Rose concentrated on pouring, noticing her hand was shaking. It was cold in the attic, all of them bundling into coats they'd not been able to wear for the manoeuvres through the small window and up the drainpipe before the candles were even lit. Her fingers, protruding from her over-long winter coat, were pale as the unspent matches in their box. They looked and felt like they belonged to someone else. She felt a shadow cross her back and glanced over her shoulder, but it was all shadow there.

The large white cloth was now laid with food and plates and cutlery, persimmons scattered artfully about by Lydia, who had an eye for such things. The Mass candles were slid into the mouths of empty milk bottles, illuminating the game pie, the slab of cheddar cheese, the quince paste from Fortnum's and the slightly stale loaf of bread Alice had swiped from the kitchen the day before, along with the bread knife. Martha's stomach rumbled again.

By an unspoken cue, the girls arranged themselves along its sides, cross-legged on the wooden floor. By the thickness of the dust in a near-perfect circle around them, Martha could tell this was the usual spot where the Gahls assembled. The floorboards were free of dust, but for some chalky white lines extending from beneath the tablecloth. Martha slid her finger over them, trying to rub them away, and Alice slapped her hand.

'Stop messing about, Beachwood.'

Martha snapped to attention, turning her gaze along with the others to Grace, reclining like an emperor on the stacked empty bags, a glass of cider in her hand. She raised it.

'Welcome to our special spot. I thought it apt to mark this winter solstice with a feast. This is the longest night, the furthest we come from the sun, and isn't it jolly to be together and keep each other warm?' Grace smiled, but to Rose it was more a baring of teeth. She glanced at Helen, but she had her listening face on, her hair lovely in the candlelight. 'Tuck in, and afterwards I thought we could welcome the new day with some games.'

'New day?' blurted Rose, appalled and unable to contain herself. Helen hadn't mentioned games. 'How long will we be up here?'

'Shhh!' hissed Alice, but Grace smiled beneficently.

'Midnight, Hamblin. Not so long to wait. We'll have you tucked up safe before the night is through.'

Martha glanced at the watch on her wrist. Ten thirty. She hoped the games wouldn't involve too much rushing about; she always needed time to digest or her stomach burned something rotten.

'But first, let's eat.' Grace raised her glass again and the other Gahls lifted theirs almost in unison. Martha tried to clink her glass against Lydia's, and she wrinkled her nose as though smelling something off. Martha felt heat creep across her cheeks and neck, knowing she'd broken some secret code.

'We don't clink,' said Helen, but kindly. 'It's unchic.'

Rose rolled her eyes at Helen and Helen grinned back.

'Chin-chin,' said Grace, and drank her cider without wincing. Martha coughed and spluttered as it burned up her nose. Alice grimaced as she sipped and Lydia put hers down, untouched. As the others began to eat, she plucked a single persimmon from the tablecloth and painstakingly removed its leaves, took a mouse-like bite. Martha watched her from the corner of her eye, with a mixture of morbid fascination and envy. Lydia Fraser had always been thin, but this term Martha hadn't seen her eat more than a mouthful at every meal, and she was vanishing to nothing: hollows under her eyes and deep wells above her clavicles, a blueish tinge to her skin and fine hair over her cheeks. It was a mystery to Martha, that sort of restraint, Lydia's body a bed with hospital corners, or perhaps even just a bedframe. Martha had always been hungry, and could not imagine denying herself the satisfaction of at least trying to fulfil the endless need, which came not from her stomach but from her brain, her heart. She ate two slices of game pie, two pieces of bread with thick slabs of cheese, and was not even a little sated.

Rose had only a little appetite. The Gahls, with the exception of Lydia of course, who seemed to have given up eating entirely, were eating with a focused silence, as though in prayer. Rose tried to catch Helen's eye, but she was intent on her meal. What was this? The feasts in the dorm were raucous and giddy, and she'd always imagined the Gahls in their lair as a concentrated version of that, gossip and smoking.

This was almost sombre. She wanted someone to break the silence, but it wasn't going to be her.

Martha had finished her portion, was eyeing Lydia's with obvious keenness. Rose wondered if she'd noticed the odd atmosphere, the way they as the two invitees were shut out of whatever was passing between the Gahls. Even Helen's body language felt closed to Rose, though when she slid her foot close to Helen, her lover responded by leaning back, resting her thigh, bulky in its coat, against her. Rose was little reassured.

'Have more,' said Grace into the silence, making Rose jump. She glanced around and saw Grace holding Lydia's plate out to Martha.

'Oh no, I couldn't—'

'We all know you could,' said Alice.

Rose gritted her teeth against the rudeness. She would usually speak up for someone, but she felt strange in this situation, uneasy, powerless.

'Go on,' said Grace. 'Shame for it to go to waste.'

Rose felt like it was a trap, but Martha took the plate without incident. She ate gratefully, and finished her cider.

'Brilliant grub,' she said, on a current of alcohol-induced bravery. Alice snorted through her nose, but Grace ignored her, smiling at Martha and saying,

'Thank you, Beachwood, only the best for our solstice celebration.'

Emboldened, Martha said, 'My father sent off to Fortnum's once, for my mother's birthday, but it went astray on its way to Oswestry.'

'A terrible shame,' said Grace. 'What does your father do?'

Martha flushed. She thought everyone knew her father was in disgrace, sent from their mansion on Park Lane to the Welsh borders, his privileges and clearances stripped until he was barely qualified to run the local gaol. 'He's in law.'

'How interesting,' said Grace, and Martha was sure she meant it. 'And your mother?'

Martha bloomed under this question. 'An actress.'

'Beachwood ...' Grace tapped her finger against her lip prettily. 'Not Cressida Beachwood?'

'The very same,' said Martha, trying not to preen.

'Gracious me, I should shout it from the rooftops!'

The others were watching this exchange with a combination of incredulity and, on Rose's part, scepticism. She knew Grace knew who Martha's parents were. They all did. They'd all heard the sordid details of the judge's affair, the rage Cressida Beachwood was said to have flown into when she heard, breaking every window in the Park Lane house. Was this why Grace had invited Martha? To learn more? It was a base reason, a boring one. Grace was many things, but she only cared about gossip as currency, and this was well-covered gossip.

'I saw her in *A Pact with the Wind*,' said Lydia dreamily. 'She was radiant.'

She turned her glazed gaze upon Martha, who felt a disquiet that hit her like a punch. There was hunger in Lydia's eyes, an awful hunger.

'And in *Private Faithful*!' Helen nodded enthusiastically. 'One of the best pictures I've ever seen.'

Martha grinned, and each of them noticed for the very first time she had some of her mother's glory in her. They spoke excitedly about Cressida's other films, her famous on-screen chemistry with Dick Frampton.

'Is it true,' said Grace, 'that your mother holds séances?'

'Yes. Dick Frampton came to one.'

'And you speak to the spirits?'

'She believes so. I'm not allowed to attend.'

'Really? I heard you were once a vessel.'

Martha's stomach plunged.

'A conduit,' said Grace, without breaking eye contact with Martha, who felt pinned in her sights. 'Often a child, used by a medium to invite spirits to inhabit corporeal form.'

'No,' said Martha as firmly as her shaking voice allowed. 'No.'

'My mistake,' said Grace sweetly. 'Time to play game,' she declared. 'Let's clear up.'

They began to stack the plates. Martha's appetite had vanished for once at the mention of vessels and séances. It was the worst, the blackest moment of her life. She helped tidy with numb fingers, following Grace's instructions and moving the candles back further to create a ring, each of them backlit and the tablecloth clear before them. 'Light as a feather, stiff as a board.'

'Yes!' clapped Helen. Rose looked between them.

'Light as a what?'

'It's a magic game,' said Grace. 'A spiritual game. Perfect for solstice.'

'Spiritual?' Martha tried not to sound afraid.

'Oh, surely some of you have played.' Grace smiled around at them all. Here it was, her famous energy, the verve that made everyone desire her or desire to be near her. 'We'll use Lydia first, she's easiest.'

Lydia took off her coat and lay on the tablecloth, her nightdress falling against her cadaverous body like a shroud. Martha tried not to look too hard at the sharp points of her nipples, the concavity of her pelvis.

'Use two fingers of each hand, like this' – Grace held up her middle and forefingers – 'then slide them under her body.'

Grace was at Lydia's head and moved her fingers beneath her. Alice took her right shoulder, Rose, hesitantly, her left. Helen placed her fingers under Lydia's right leg, one set beneath her upper leg, the other her lower. Martha did the same on her other side, noticing how her legs beneath her nightgown were straight, no difference between thigh and calf, only the bulb of her knee interrupting. Lydia lay supine, her eyes closed. She looked childlike and old, none of the beauty she'd had even six months ago, before her starvation truly took hold. Martha realised she did not envy her, after all.

'Now, we lift her.'

'Lift her?' said Martha.

'Exactly.'

Rose shifted her grip, spread all her fingers beneath Lydia's shoulder, but Grace tutted. 'No, keep your fingers as I showed you. Ready? On three.'

Rose frowned down at their hands. She could not tell what Grace meant. She couldn't lift a textbook with her two fingers, and Lydia, thin as she was, weighed more than that.

'One, two, three.'

All of them lifted, and of course Lydia did not budge.

'Now,' said Grace, eyes gleaming with mischief. I need you to chant with me. "Light as a feather, stiff as a board, light as a feather, stiff as a board."'

Alice and Helen took up the chant first, Martha and Rose joining soon after. Their voices melded and found each other's rhythms, all tracing Grace's intonations. Rose's fingers began to tingle, and though she knew it was likely just lack of blood she felt a frisson pass through her body, hair lifting on her arms. Grace closed her eyes, and the others followed suit, so they were inside their heads, the words all around them, the shadows of each other imprinted on their lids. Rose felt, by some wordless agreement, she should lift. She raised her fingers, and surely that was not Lydia's leg rising with her? She carried on chanting, the words a tether, as the weight lifted from her fingers and she was certain, she was *certain*, her hands rose to shoulder height empty. But then Martha gasped and Rose opened her eyes to see Lydia floating – *floating* – in the air, their fingers beneath her but barely in contact. Martha looked horrified, and Helen and Alice grinned at each other. Grace nodded and they lowered Lydia, stopping chanting. Rose was sure that the moment the chanting ceased, Lydia's body regained its weight.

'And how!' exclaimed Martha.

'Want to try?'

'Me?'

Rose looked uncertainly around. Lydia was one thing, but Martha was the heaviest girl in their year.

'It doesn't matter who. It'll work.'

'How does it work?' asked Rose, staring at her hands.

Grace waggled her fingers. 'Magic. Come on, Martha, your turn.'

To Alice's not altogether kind whoop, Martha took another swig of cider. It tasted worse now, bitter and grainy. She swapped places with Lydia, who seemed totally unaffected by her levitation. They returned their fingers and, once more, Grace made them try to lift her. But when the chant started, Rose was better prepared for the tingle, for the vibration of the others' voices in her own chest. She kept her eyes open this time, so witnessed for herself the miracle of it: Martha lying flat and rigid, and then rising as though just ahead of their fingers. They had only just started to lower her back down when Rose snatched her fingers away.

'Ouch!' Martha landed awkwardly, sliding off the remaining supports as though Rose had removed a vital piece of scaffolding.

'Bloody hell, Hamblin,' snapped Alice, righting a candle.

'What's happening?' asked Rose. 'How are you doing that?'

'*We* are doing that,' said Grace.

'Well I don't want to any more.'

'Rosie—' Helen started.

'Hamblin.' Grace's voice was grave. 'Don't be a sap.'

'I just want to know how it works.'

'Why don't you go next?'

'I don't want to.'

'And I thought Martha here was the prude. Come on, Hellie vouched for you. She said you'd be a sport about it all.'

Rose cast Helen a sharp glance, but she only shrugged back at her.

'Have a try, Hamblin,' said Grace.

'No.'

Grace stared at her. Rose felt something akin to what she'd felt as she'd stood at the top of the stairs, a precipitous danger. She wondered if Grace was about to force her, but then she moved her gaze away.

'You get the idea, anyway.' Grace checked her watch, and Martha copied her, still slightly dizzy from the strange sensation of weightlessness she'd experienced when being lifted. It was a quarter to midnight. 'Let's play something else.'

'Truth or dare!' said Helen gleefully.

'Good show, Hellie,' said Grace. 'You first.'

'Oh, dare.'

'Kiss Beachwood,' said Alice, and Rose knew it was out of spite for her.

'No, something more interesting, surely.' Grace tapped her finger against her lips. 'I dare you to hold your hand over the candle for five seconds.'

She held a milk bottle out to Helen, who set her shoulders and held her hand over the flame.

'Closer than that,' said Grace, and Helen moved her hand down a bit lower.

'Closer!' Alice goaded.

'Don't be a patsy,' snapped Rose. 'She'll burn herself.'

'It's fine, Rosie,' said Helen, and moved her palm to just above the flame.

'One,' counted Grace, too slowly. 'Two ... three—'

'Godssake, Hellie!' Rose snatched at Helen's hand and pulled it away. She gasped as she saw the skin was red, a blister swelling as she watched. 'Look, you're hurt.'

'It's fine, Rosie,' said Helen, blowing briefly on her hand. 'Don't be a sap.'

'This isn't on!' Rose felt a fluttering of panic beneath her breastbone. She made to stand up, but Helen looped her hand around her elbow.

'Come now, Rosie, I'm fine, see?' She held up her palm, and the blister had stopped growing, a small blemish on her soft skin. Rose felt queasy.

'It's sweet,' said Grace. 'I know how you dote on our Hellie. But don't go yet, it's just turned midnight.'

She held up her wrist so they could all see the face of her fancy gold watch. The elegant hands showed they were two minutes into the new day.

'The best hour,' grinned Alice. 'Mischief hour.'

'Witching hour,' agreed Grace. 'Who's next?'

'Next?' said Rose, allowing herself to be pulled back down beside Helen. Her warmth, her skin on Rose's, was comforting. Helen poured her more cider and rubbed her back.

'Truth or dare.'

'Truth,' said Rose.

'Piker,' said Alice.

'I think it's brave,' said Grace. 'Truth is a terrifying thing.'

'Do you love Hellie?' asked Alice.

'Alice, you are being a pill,' said Grace. 'Of course she does. Don't we all? Let me think. I know.' Her eyes shone in the candlelight. What had Alice called it? Mischief hour. Grace's ink black soul glistened under her lovely face.

'What is the worst thing you've ever done?'

Rose immediately felt as though something was swelling inside her windpipe. 'None of your business.'

'Oh come along, Hamblin, be a sport,' said Alice, exasperated.

But Rose's ears were full of screams, her brother's face white under flowing red. 'No.'

'You're rather missing the point of truth or dare,' said Grace calmly.

'I didn't want to play,' said Rose. Helen had stopped rubbing her back. Rose knew she was embarrassing her, but she didn't care.

'Why did you come then?' sneered Alice.

'I'll go,' said Rose, stumbling to her feet.

'Rosie . . .'

'You coming, Hellie?' Rose held out her shaking hand to Helen, but her hope died immediately. Helen's liquid eyes moved away from her, towards Grace.

'Don't go, Hamblin,' said Grace. 'We've not seen out the hour yet.'

'Let her leave, Grace,' said Alice. 'I told you she was a stiff.'

The challenge in Alice's voice was a trap, but Rose walked into it. 'Fine. You answer, Simpkin. What's the worst you've done? And no need to mention your fringe, that's self-apparent.'

Alice spluttered, but Grace let out a shout of laughter. 'Oh-ho, Hamblin! That's the spirit. How about this: I'll answer instead.'

Rose let herself be pulled back to the floor by Helen.

'My father owns oil fields,' started Grace. 'And they used to be Indian land. He keeps everything the ground gives him, not only oil. He has shelves the entire length of his study, and on these he keeps his finds: a Lipan pipe, a Cherokee drum, a Comanche necklace, that sort of thing. Most of all, though, he finds skulls.'

Martha audibly gulped into the pin-drop silence. She clamped her lips shut, not wanting to hear any more. Grace's mention of her mother's activities had cast a pall over everything, and she wished Rose had left so she could go with her. The dark around them was absolute, the circle of burning-down candles scant protection against the blackness pressing in at their backs. Martha did not even know which way the window was. Oh goodness, and she had to clamber down that pipe, and in through that tiny gap in the bathroom window. She felt very weary, and her heart raced.

'These he has polished up and ranged on the shelves too. As a child I would lie under his desk beside his spur-heeled boots, eavesdropping on his meetings and watching the skulls mounted behind Daddy as though they were extra pairs of eyes. The black sockets did not frighten me, but fascinated. I liked to hook my fingers through them.'

Nausea was crawling up Martha's throat like the fingers Grace evoked. But Grace was not done – there was more.

'The maids threw blankets over the shelves when they cleaned, they thought them cursed objects. I know they terrified them all, but one maid, the youngest, she would weep when she had to clean the study.' Grace seemed amused by this remembrance. 'So one day, I stole my favourite skull. It was a child's, small and with all its teeth. I put it in the maid's bed.'

Martha, dizzy, thought surely this was where the story ended – but Grace was still talking.

'It was my father's favourite too. It lived on his desk, so of course he noticed it was gone. He summoned me, was intent on punishment, but I told him I saw the maid go into his office the night before.'

Martha was searching Grace's face for remorse, for a flicker of feeling, but she could have been recounting a usual day at school. There was nothing to betray the awfulness of what she was saying.

'They found it in her bed and Daddy was furious, of course. He had the maid taken to his study. I listened at the door. I counted a hundred lashes.'

The attic was eerily silent. None of the sounds of the wind outside, the creak of floorboards, the hissing of the candles burning down and down.

'What happened to her?' asked Rose, her voice strangled.

'She was let go,' said Grace. 'So there we are.'

She looked around at them all, and Rose understood the story was not told as a confession, but a warning. That Grace's heart was not black, but perhaps not there at all.

'You've rather murdered the mood there, Grace,' said Alice, trying to pass it off as a joke. Martha's teeth were chattering and she couldn't stop them. 'Should we call it a night?'

'But we have something special planned,' said Grace. 'And look, perfectly on time.'

Rose glanced at her wristwatch. Half-past midnight.

'The heart of witching hour. Shall we play another game?' said Grace.

'Another?' said Martha, her teeth still chattering.

Rose wanted to run screaming from the attic, but Helen looked at her, and in her pale, startled face Rose saw she could not leave, but did not want to stay.

'It's going to be fun. Here.'

Helen picked up a candle and moved it from the tablecloth. A hand reached out beside Martha and she flinched – she'd forgotten Lydia was there. Her bony fingers shifted off another candle, and Alice helped until the tablecloth was clear. Rose and Helen were sitting mutely, their hands intertwined, and Martha wished she had a hand to hold. It was ridiculous, because they were all so close by one another, but she felt she'd been set adrift and was floating alone on a dangerous sea.

'Voila!' Grace moved the tablecloth aside with a flourish. Beneath, drawn on the floorboards in chalk, was a shape totally unfamiliar to Rose, and utterly known to Martha. Martha let out a stifled scream and dragged herself away.

'What? What is it?' said Rose, pulling on Helen's hand.

'Don't worry, Rosie,' said Helen, still pale but smiling. 'It's a star.'

'A special star. For solstice,' said Grace.

'It's a pentagram,' said Martha, now on her feet and dithering on the boundary of darkness. 'A summoning circle.'

'Nonsense,' said Grace. 'It's for protection.'

'Against what?' said Rose sharply.

'You must have heard the stories, Hamblin. We didn't know what was up here, did we, girls, when we first made it our den? Hanged Marchmont prefects, creepy founders – I had to be sure it was safe.'

'And it is,' said Helen from her spot near one of the star's points. 'Come on, Rose, it's wizard, what Grace can do.'

'Whatever do you mean?' Rose was looking at Helen hard, as though she did not know and love her, as though she were a perfect stranger. She had never mentioned any of this to her, stars and games, and the evil they surely all saw squatting in Grace.

'It's like light as a feather, but with our minds,' said Helen. 'Show them, Grace.'

'They have to want to see,' said Grace. 'You're not being forced to stay.'

That challenge again. Martha looked into the dark, longed to have the courage to walk away. But she came closer, lowered herself cumbersomely back to the floor.

'Good, Beachwood. Hamblin? Want to see?'

'See what?'

'There's no explaining it. I'll show you.'

Helen's eyes were pleading. Rose sat down.

'Here's the game,' said Grace. 'We pass the flame. Each of us lights the candle from the other, around in a circle, and mine last.'

'What's hard about that?' said Rose.

'We each close our eyes.'

'We might burn each other,' said Martha.

'That's why you have to move slowly. Remember how it felt, when we lifted together? You felt me, didn't you. I felt you.' She looked at Martha. 'And you.' She looked at Rose. 'And you, Hamblin. Once we've passed the flame around, we'll see.'

'Because there will be light again.'

'Not like that. I'll show you.'

The girls blew out their candles. The dark fell across them once more, and Martha felt a flutter of panic. Ever since Grace's mention of the vessel, she'd felt that awful, nauseating pressure she'd experienced sitting in her mother's séance circle, as though her skull was being pressed at from the inside. She had done so well to bury it, what she'd smelled and heard and seen that awful night. How had Grace known? Alongside the panic, a weight, like an anchor in her stomach.

'Close your eyes,' said Grace, and it was better to submit. Rose's eyes shut with the same mechanical heaviness as the china doll her father had bought her for her tenth birthday. *Click. Click.* She saw her green eyes, the long, feathered lashes, the soft velvet of her dress.

'Light your candle, Hamblin.'

Rose held out her hand, trembling. She felt the bite of heat against her wrist, adjusted her candle. She smelt the burn of her flesh, but did not feel it. It was far, far away. It smelt like her doll. Her father said it was an antique, rescued from a fire and restored, but that smell lingered. Scorched skin. She felt hers bubble into a blister. She saw the flare of light through her lids. It felt impossible to open her eyes, as though someone was pressing them shut. The cider, perhaps?

'Alice. Lydia. Beachwood. Bomner.'

Rose felt Helen shift to light her candle. She opened her eyes with an effort akin to waking before sunrise. Grace's eyes were wide open, her gaze steady. The other girls were drooped as tulips, their candles burning ghoulish shadows across their faces. Grace's candle burst into flame, and the same gust of cold that had closed the window crossed Rose's face, blowing out her candle. It blew out Martha's, it blew out Lydia's, it blew out Alice's, it blew out Helen's. Grace's flame seemed to burn bigger, bluer.

'What . . .' Rose said, but her voice was tight and trapped.

Grace began to chant. Marchmont girls learned Latin, but nothing like this. These were words unlike anything Martha, top in everything, knew. They were words that burrowed beneath her skin, into her ears, up her nose, and sucked like mosquitoes. She felt her blood slowing, running colder and sluggish. She saw something, something coming for her.

It was a woman. The woman was meant to love her and was coming to get her. Her mother. Rose wanted to scream as her mother who was not her mother came closer, closer. Helen shuddered, whispered 'No!' But it was Rose who saw it, Rose and Martha and Alice and Lydia, and even Grace shrank back from her mother's cold hands. A vessel, but she was not empty! Martha wanted to shout, I am still in here! Then they saw their dog, Alice's dog, running across the road to greet her, them, running and running and then the hard clear hit of the horse and trap, its soft belly split open, entrails spread. And Helen, Helen and Rose and Martha and Lydia and Grace saw Helen's father weeping and weeping, like a child, weeping and he would not stop crying, and in Helen's Martha's Lydia's Grace's Alice's heart was the deepest sorrow. And Lydia saw Lydia, saw her body awful and distorted, the worst thing, the very worst thing, and Rose Martha Grace Alice Helen wanted to claw their flesh from their bones with disgust. And now Grace, watching as her father beat the maid, the maid she'd framed with the skull, beat and beat her already whipped flesh until she could not fight any more and did not breathe, and Grace and Rose and Martha and Lydia and Helen and Alice only watched as her beautiful Black skin turned blacker and blacker and she was only a bundle of broken bones and her father stood triumphant over her, as though he'd won something.

And then he was coming. Her brother was in her bedroom, in her bed. And Rose would not let it happen, not let it happen again. Rose's hand slid under her pillow, and Alice's hand slid under the tablecloth, and the knife was there, the boning knife, the kitchen knife, and they raised their hand into the air and down, hard, and the spell broke, and the knife was in Alice's hand but Rose and Martha and Lydia and even Grace remembered the handle in their palms, felt the warmth as blood washed over all their hands. And Grace did not even scream, the knife stuck between her ribs, and before the horror – after the horror – the feeling that came for all of them, was relief.

THE TERROR BY NIGHT

Bridget Collins

I have always had a particular horror of feeling that I am the last one awake. As a small boy, when I could not sleep I would lie open-eyed, clenching my fists and staring into the darkness, full of panic at the thought that I was the only conscious being in the whole house – or perhaps the whole street, or the whole world ... I was not allowed to get up, or call for my nurse, or strike a match; so I would strain my ears for any noise, the creak of a footstep or a door shutting, even the rumble of wheels outside. Often, since we kept early hours and lived in a quiet, leafy part of a prosperous town, no human sound broke the silence; and then I would dig my fingernails into my palms and hold my breath until I thought I would burst, making desperate bargains with myself. I would have given anything, anything at all, if only someone would come ... ! Like most prayers, however, those childish pleas were never answered; and so I lay there, rigid with dread and loneliness, listening to the clock strike its implacable hours, until at last fatigue overwhelmed me and I slept.

But that was a long time ago. Now at least when I am wakeful I am not compelled to stay in bed, staring helplessly at nothing. Being a bachelor, and living in college, I can get up and light a lamp and settle myself at my desk without causing any disturbance. Insomnia is still my enemy – indeed, it plagues me more than it did then, due, no doubt, to my ageing constitution and sedentary habits – but it is an old, familiar enemy, and I have learnt to endure its presence with as much equanimity as I can muster. The best tactic, I have found, is dignified disregard. I pour myself a glass of brandy, add another log to the fire, set out my books on my desk and turn my back to the room, determined to work until I forget that it is night-time at all. Generally I lose myself quite efficiently, and it is only the slide of embers in the grate or a gust of wind rattling the windows which brings me back to myself; then, if it is morning, I open the casement a crack to feel the fresh air on my face, and look out into the court below with the sense of Pyrrhic victory that comes from watching through a night for no good reason.

Perhaps you know Yardley's Court, at the back of Pentecost College. It is not exactly a quadrangle, but makes two sides of a square, the other two being the river and the path that leads from the bridge through the Great Court to the porters' lodge. Pentecost has its share of cloisters and spires – in snowy weather the chapel resembles the kind of Christmas cake that appears in the shop window of an ambitious baker – but Yardley's is modest, its seventeenth-century arches and mullions austere and restrained, and the only elaboration is an old twisted apple tree that grows in the middle of the lawn beside the river. In summer, the flowerbed below my sitting room is fragrant with roses and low box hedges, but in winter it is bare and rather bleak, and the wind has a trick of swirling around you as you turn aside from the bridge as if it were trying to catch you by the sleeve and drag you back. There is a single gas lamp on the corner of the back lawn, and sometimes when the weather is mild a passer-by will pause beneath it to consult a pocket watch or light a cigarette; but on cold nights, after the scholars have gone to bed – the sets in Yardley's are mostly given to third years, who limit their excesses to Easter Term, after their final exams – almost everyone who crosses the bridge will continue on their way, chin lowered against the chill, without even a glance towards my window.

So a man who comes into the court and lingers, or does not head directly for his own staircase, fumbling in his pocket for the latchkey to his room, is a rarity, liable to draw attention – especially if it is late, and my ears have been primed by long hours of silence to remark the sound of footsteps. That first night, I do not know how long I had been staring, absently, past my own reflection at the far gleam of the lamp beside the bridge; but gradually I became aware that a thin, bare-headed figure was moving erratically along the paths, quirking his head at the crooked apple tree before wandering along the edge of the river for a few paces and doubling back. He was young, with a blaze of pale hair, and a fine-boned face; but there was something lopsided about his gait, and for a strange moment I wondered if he had some deformity. Then I saw that he was swinging a bottle in one hand like a club. At that instant, as if he had felt my gaze, he looked up at me and raised his free hand in a genial wave.

I drew back out of sight, my heart beating quickly, as if he might have overheard my thoughts – to be frank, there are few things I dislike more than an intoxicated undergraduate – and when I edged forward again he had gone. But a moment later the door below slammed, its heavy echo reverberating from the old stone walls, and bounding feet ascended the stairs. I got to my feet, thinking to close my outer door; but by the time I had reached my doorway, it was too late. He was already knocking, in a jaunty rhythm that made me think that if I did not answer he would go on for ever. I wrenched the door open.

'Ah!' he said, as if we were old friends. 'Professor – Dr . . .' He squinted at the name painted above my threshold, blinked several times, swayed, seemed to give up the attempt to read it, and finally concluded, 'Sir.' He gave me a wide smile that showed crooked teeth. 'Good evening. I saw your lamp burning. Everyone else is asleep.'

'Indeed,' I said.

'There was nowhere else to go. I came here, following the light. I am a storm-tossed vessel,' he said, flourishing his bottle – thankfully it was empty – 'lured by the lighthouse. Oh no, wait. That's the wrong way round. I suppose I'm a moth.'

'Whatever you are,' I said, 'it is very late. Perhaps—'

'My point entirely!' he cried, triumphant, and patted my shoulder. 'You and I might be the last people on the planet.

May I come in?' He did not wait for my reply before he insinuated himself past me and into my little sitting room. Before I had time to take a breath he had collapsed into the chair in front of the fire, the bottle dangling from his fingers, with a look on his face as if he was sublimely touched by my hospitality. 'You *are* kind,' he said. 'I knew you would be.'

'I am nothing of the sort. Who are you? What are you doing here?'

'David Moncrieff,' he said, inclining his head. 'The newly crowned Scott Scholar. Congratulate me, won't you?'

I could not help raising my eyebrows. The Scott Prize was the subject of much jostling and ambition among the Classics students. The composition of a worthy five-hundred-line poem in Latin – this year's subject, apparently, had been 'the wheel of heaven' – was no mean feat for a young man, especially given the declining standards of teaching in the public schools. I had heard the other fellows discussing it over dinner: the disappointment of one scholar, the dashed hopes of another, the deep resentment of a third . . . 'By all means,' I said, with what I hoped was a certain ironic detachment. 'But I daresay other men have already complimented you on your achievement. Now—'

'Ah, but they haven't, you see! The other chaps don't like me much, to tell the truth. So this evening I treated myself to a bottle of . . .' He blinked down at the bottle, and then shrugged. 'A bottle of something, and I drank all of it in my room, and then I – well, then the absence of companions and well-wishers started to grate on me a bit, so I came out for a walk. And then I saw your light, and . . .' He waved his hand, letting go of the bottle, which clunked to the floor. '*Aquesta me guiaba* — St John of the Cross, you know — "this guided me better than the noonday sun"—'

'I am familiar with the poem, thank you.'

'Well, anyway, here I am. Won't you have a drink with me?'

'Are you offering me my own brandy?'

'Oh,' he said, looking vaguely around, 'yes, I suppose I am.' There was a beat of silence; then, with a splutter, he began to laugh. 'Oh dear,' he added, with a rueful shake of his head, 'no wonder I have no friends.'

That flash of self-deprecation softened me a little, and instead of remonstrating with him for his intrusion I found myself asking, 'None at all?'

'No. Well . . .' He hesitated, shivering as if he had felt a draught, and for an instant I wondered whether he really was as drunk as he seemed. But whatever thought had prompted that brief shudder of sobriety, he seemed to shake it off. 'Only you, now.'

'Me? I am hardly—'

'Oh, don't be hard-hearted! Don't you ever want company yourself? Sitting there, bent over your books . . . I believe you left your curtains open deliberately in order to entice me in.' He shot me a glance, and grinned. 'Aha! You can't deny it.'

Now, against my will, I smiled. 'Don't be absurd,' I said. 'I like to be able to look out. Often I am awake to see the sunrise. I like to see my reflection fade as the sky brightens.'

There was a silence. He gave me a level, interested look, and I felt the colour rising to my face as if I had revealed more of myself than I had meant to. Then he got to his feet, and poured a glass of brandy from the decanter on the side, and passed it to me. I might have – *should* have – bristled at the liberty, but instead I took it without a word and waited while he poured another (I kept two glasses on the tray, although I could not remember the last time both were used at once) and raised it in a toast. 'To my success,' he said. 'Won't you drink?'

I hesitated; but it would have been churlish to refuse, and under his expectant eyes I echoed, dutifully, 'To your success,' and drank. Perhaps it was the long hours of sleeplessness, or the cushioned, dreamy effect of being in a well-lit room while all around us was dark and silent, but it was pleasant to allow myself to be cajoled into compliance.

He tipped back his head and gulped it down in one. He set the glass down with a smart tap, and turned, steadying himself on the mantelpiece when he staggered. 'Well, I had better leave you in peace again. It has been delightful to make your acquaintance,' he said. 'Good evening.'

'Oh – good evening,' I said automatically. 'I mean – good morning—'

But he had gone as abruptly as he had appeared, and I was left in my empty room, with a glass in my hand and a certain amused consternation in my breast, as if I had been visited not by a drunken young man but by a whirlwind.

*

A few days later I emerged from Evensong and saw my old friend Edward Blanford-Jones standing at the corner of the lawn, his gown flapping in the breeze as he gesticulated. 'The noonday demon is generally understood to be what is known as *accidie*,' he said, to his nodding interlocutor, 'but consider the terror by night, pestilence that walketh in darkness. Is that darkness figurative or literal? If the former— Oh, hullo,' he said, seeing my approach, 'we were just parsing today's psalm. One of my favourites, I must say, makes me think of the desert fathers. But you're the hermit, of course ...'

We walked together for a few paces, towards the Senior Common Room, where the other man took his leave. Then Blanford-Jones turned to me and raised his eyebrows. 'Are you all right, old man? Was there something ...?'

'Nothing important,' I said. 'I just wondered if you knew a David Moncrieff.'

'An undergrad? One of yours?'

'No. Classics. I thought you might—'

'Oh yes.' He rolled his eyes. 'Yes, indeed. Big chap. Think he's a rugby blue. Eton, or was it Harrow? Stolid, not much imagination.'

'Many friends?'

'Well, the rugby team, I imagine. Why?'

'No reason.' I had been toying with the idea of relating what had happened; but then, what *had* happened? Nothing, or nothing worth relating.

Blanford-Jones gave me a swift, shrewd glance, but all he

said was, 'Hmmm. Well, if you see him, tell him he owes me an essay on Seneca, will you?'

I thanked him, and moved away. There had, after all, been no point in mentioning David Moncrieff's name, and something in Blanford-Jones's look had made me wish I had not asked. To tell the truth, I had been rather preoccupied with Moncrieff since he came to my room; perhaps I had simply wanted confirmation that I had not dreamt it, or him ... I had watched through several nights, sitting at my desk, trying and failing to work, wondering whether he might return, but so far he had not. It was ludicrous to mind – that is, of course I did *not* mind, not at all – but he had piqued my curiosity, and I would not have been averse to seeing him again.

I had almost given up hope when, a little more than a week later, I caught sight of him in Yardley's, under the apple tree. It was, I think, just after midnight, clear and cold, and there was something of the mezzotint about the scene: the high bright moon, the gnarled dark arms of the tree, the stonework of the bridge and the soft veil of mist that lay on the water. It was only when he moved that I saw him, as if he had stepped straight out of the tree-trunk. He was moving erratically, halting and turning back on himself after a few steps, glancing around as if he heard something that I did not.

I opened the casement, and hesitated. I almost shut it again, and drew the curtains; I almost went to bed. I think if I had, I might have managed to sleep – and then ... But

I cleared my throat, preparing to call down to him, and at that small sound he swung round, raising his hand in a wild gesture of greeting. 'I'm coming up,' he cried, without giving me time to issue an invitation, and ducked towards the doorway below.

I opened my door, and stood waiting for him on the landing. When he reached the top of the stairs I drew aside to let him pass, and then turned to shut both doors, glad that for a moment he could not see my face. It had only been a week or so since that first encounter, and the change in him shocked me. He had been slender to start with, but now he was positively gaunt; the brightness in his eyes had become a fixed shine; and, even in the deceptive lamplight and shadows of the landing, there was hectic colour in his cheeks. As he went past me, I caught the whiff of unwashed skin and foul breath, and noticed a tidemark around his collar which suggested that he had not changed his clothes for some time. But it was not his physical state which concerned me most. There was something in the way he moved, darting from doorway to window and then drawing back against the wall, that made me very uneasy – although whether I was nervous of him or for him, I could not have said. But now that he had crossed my threshold I had to make the best of it; so I said, as warmly as I could, 'Sit down, won't you?'

'Thanks.' He flung himself towards a hard, straight-backed chair that stood in the corner of the room. He had to move a pile of books from its seat before he sat down, and at first I could not make out why he had chosen it rather than the armchair beside the fire; then I saw that he shuffled the chair backwards a few inches until it thumped against the wall, and then relaxed a little, as if he was grateful to know that there was something solid behind him. Even so, his eyes returned again and again to the window, and he craned his neck as if to see down into the court.

'Will you have a drink?'

'I – no, I had better not.'

I shot a glance at him, poured out two glasses without comment, and crossed the room to put one into his hand. After a moment he gave me a flicker of a smile, and accepted it. 'There,' I said. 'Now you had better tell me what is wrong.'

He grimaced, and swallowed his mouthful of brandy, gasping as it went down. 'I'm sorry,' he said. 'Turning up here like this . . .'

I waved his words away. 'I was awake already,' I said, 'and I am always glad of a distraction.'

'Don't you ever sleep?'

'Sometimes. But never mind that. You're in a dreadful state.'

'I don't want to burden you. It's bad enough barging in and drinking your cognac—'

'It didn't bother you before,' I said. For an instant I smiled at the memory, and expected him to smile too; but then, to my horror, he covered his face and broke into silent, shuddering spasms. I stood appalled, quite at a loss for how to react; finally the only thing I could think of was to rescue the glass that was tilting precariously in his hand and set it down on the desk within his reach.

'Sorry,' he said, 'sorry, I am very sorry ...'

I murmured something polite and waited for him to master himself.

At last he wiped his face on his sleeves, and stumbled to his feet. I thought he might be intending to leave, but instead he stalked – turning sideways, as if to keep out of sight – to the window, and stared down for a long moment, holding his breath, before he exhaled in relief and retreated. His fear was heartfelt, that was clear; but the whole procedure was so elaborate, so reminiscent of pantomime, so almost-comic that abruptly I felt my patience crack. I pushed past him, twitched the curtains closed in a brisk screech of rings and rail, and then pointed at the armchair. 'For God's sake,' I said, 'will you stop this fooling about and *sit down?*'

He blinked, and obeyed. There was a silence. I crouched awkwardly to stoke the fire, and gave it a few good thumps with the poker. When I had battered the embers into new brightness, and the fresh log had begun to catch, I said, 'Is there someone outside?'

'Someone?' he echoed, with a note in his voice that I could not identify. 'I am not sure. I think there is some*thing*, but whether it is human ...'

I sat back on my haunches and looked up at him. His eyes slid away.

With a grunt, cursing the stiffness in my knees, I got to my feet. I had left my own glass on the mantelpiece, and now

I drank from it, wondering what on earth he meant. There was something uncomfortably evocative of lunacy in his words, and his apparent conviction that he was the victim of some threat ... Had I been foolish in allowing him into my room? I remembered that moment when I might easily have locked my door, and gone to bed. If I had, he would not have been here at all. But before I could decide how best to get rid of him, he said, as if merely continuing a thought, 'There is something uncanny about this hour of the night, isn't there?'

'Well, when one is awake, and the rest of the world asleep—'

'In the daylight,' he went on, as if he had not heard, 'everything is clear and steady and civilised. There are lectures, and meals, and tutorials – omnibuses and bicycles and passers-by – pints of beer and football matches! There is nothing to be afraid of. If you live in that world, and go to sleep quite happily at bedtime, you never see the other side of things. And you're lucky ...' He raised his glass to his lips, and drained the last few drops from it. 'Sometimes,' he went on, still staring into the fire, 'I think that when the clock has struck midnight, something – some lock or seal somewhere – comes undone, and then ... If you're awake, and wanting something with all your heart – what if, late at night, something hears, and *answers*—?'

A fierce chill swept over me, and I jabbed the poker into the fire again, trying not to shiver. 'Suppose,' I said, 'you tell me plainly what the matter is.'

He shook himself, and shot me a small, crooked smile. 'Very well,' he said. 'I'm afraid you'll think I'm mad, though.'

I didn't answer — how could I? — and after a moment he leant forward, put his glass down, linked his hands together in front of him, and began to speak.

'When I came here before,' he said, 'I had just won the Scott Prize. It seems very long ago now, although it's only — good lord, only a week or so! I was so happy that night ... Well, never mind, I'll get to that. I had been so desperate to win it, you see.'

He paused; but I did not interrupt, and after a moment he went on.

'I think I told you before that I had no friends. I got the impression you didn't believe me, but it's absolutely true. I was a scholarship boy at my school, which was a penny-pinching, mean little place, and when I came up to Pentecost I knew absolutely no one. And I realised very early on that no one wanted to know me. They knew I was different — my accent was wrong, my clothes were wrong, my father was a clerk — and they despised me. I tried to console myself by telling myself that their noses were put out of joint because I had come here by merit, not money, but that wasn't it, really. They all got better marks than I did. I was proud of having got in, but I just didn't — don't have the knowledge that the others do. No matter how hard I tried, or how much I swotted, or how late I stayed up poring over my books, I couldn't match their work. But I resolved not to give up. All I could do was keep trying, so I did. I swore I would do well in my exams if it killed me. Then, when I learnt about the Scott Prize, I began to dream about that. Of course it was hopeless, my tutors would have laughed at me if I had told them I had ambitions to enter, let alone win it – and I knew they would have been right, I had no chance at all. But all the same ... That would show them, I thought. And the money – well, it isn't much by your standards, I expect, but it was enough to make a difference to me.

'So I promised myself I would put everything I had into it. I didn't mention it to anyone – not that anyone would have done anything but smirk if I had – and when I overheard the others talking about their compositions I only listened and looked vague, as if I had hardly heard of the Scott Prize. I had always tried to pretend I didn't care much about work anyway; it was the best way of keeping my pride intact, when I spent all my free time slaving just to scrape by. It wouldn't have occurred to anyone that I had any intention of going in for a prize.

'But in secret I worked harder and harder. To be frank I became rather obsessive about it. I stopped bothering as much with my essays and all that, and told myself that if I could only win it wouldn't matter so much if I got a second or a third in my exams. But it was jolly difficult. I knew that all the other chaps had been composing Latin poems for years, and that my only advantage was being willing to work harder than anyone else. So after dinner every night I came back to my room and sat up as late as I could with my books. I had always gone to sleep late, but now I stayed awake for hours – until early in the morning, most nights – until sometimes I could hardly see with tiredness. I would sit there, and all the lamps in the Great Court would wink out one by one, even the lantern in the chapel porch and the stained-glass coats of arms in the library windows, until my own was the only one burning. I ...' He hesitated, as if something had struck him for the first time. 'That was my undoing, I suppose – that light, calling out in the darkness ...'

'Like mine?'

He frowned. 'What?'

'When you knocked on my door, you said it was because you saw my light and knew I was awake, too.'

'Oh. Yes. In a way ...' He drew his hand across his forehead. 'Yes, now I remember, that was what – *he* – said ...'

There was a silence. Moncrieff had said *he* with a peculiar strangled rasp that set my teeth on edge. I sipped my brandy, but it tasted as flat and unpotent as water. I set down the glass too hard on the stone mantelpiece, and the sound made him break out of his trance. '*He?*' I said.

'I don't know his name. I didn't ask.' Perhaps he sensed my impatience, because he raised his hand, as if he were requesting time to think, before he started to speak again with an obvious effort. 'It was a week or so before I had to submit my composition for the prize, and I had started to despair. I don't know why I hadn't given up ...' He gave a laugh like a sob – maybe, in fact, it *was* a sob – and caught his breath before he went on. 'I was in a sort of daze. I believed, I think, that if I sat still for long enough something would come – and yes, indeed, something *did*—' His voice cracked, and he stopped.

I picked up the decanter, and poured another good measure into his glass. At that he managed to give me a watery smile. 'Go on,' I said.

'I had almost nodded off over my papers when I jolted awake,' he said, turning his glass in his hands and staring into the golden-russet depths as if he could see the past there. 'I thought at first it was the clock striking, but then I heard someone knocking at my door, exactly in time with the beats of the bell. I was rather intrigued, actually. No one ever visits me, especially not after midnight. So I got up to see what they wanted. And when I opened the door . . .' He frowned. 'I didn't recognise him, but in any case it was very dark, and I had a headache coming, and I couldn't see him very clearly. He was tall and thin, and I had the impression that he had dark hair, and a gown . . . Anyway, he said he had seen my light. I remember that, now. He didn't introduce himself, but he seemed to know who I was. He even seemed to know that I was working for the prize. I was too surprised to ask where he had heard that. He asked if he might come in, and I said yes. I don't think I even considered turning him away. It was all such a blur, I could not stop trying to scan lines of poetry in my head, and somehow I had the sense that it would be worth my while to let him say whatever he had come to say. So he came inside, and walked to my desk and started looking over my papers.'

'That was rather a cheek.'

'Yes,' he said, with a faint, obliging smile, 'wasn't it? Only at the time I didn't mind. I had this sort of hopeful feeling, although I could not have put my finger on why ... And as soon as he held up a page, and said that it was rather a promising beginning, I felt my whole heart leap.'

'Did he say why had he come?'

'Not exactly— That is, yes.' Moncrieff drew a long breath. 'He said he could help me.'

'Help you?'

'With the prize.'

I lowered my chin and looked fixedly at the rug. 'And did you – accept?'

There was a pause. Then I heard him make a sort of spluttering gasp. I lifted my head, and to my horror I saw him raise his hand and slap his own cheek with his palm, with a noise like a gunshot. 'Idiot,' he cried, his voice thick with misery, 'bloody *idiot*—'

'Stop that!' But before I reached him, he had leapt to his feet and darted towards the window. He wrenched the curtain aside and once more cringed sideways to stare down into the court, raking the shadows with his gaze. 'Stop it,' I repeated, more calmly. 'Look at me, David. *Look at me.*' I almost had to wrestle with him, but in the end he turned his face to me, and I laid my hands on his shoulders so that he could not twist away. 'Control yourself, for heaven's sake, and listen. You have blown this out of all proportion.'

'What?'

'All young men make mistakes. It does you credit that you regret it – but this is excessive, you must not let your finer feelings overwhelm your rational—'

He burst into laughter, and I recoiled. 'I'm sorry,' he said, 'you are trying to be kind – but don't you realise, it isn't the cheating that I regret? I mean, in a way it is, naturally – but it is worse than that, so much worse. If only I were simply feeling guilty!'

'I'm afraid I don't follow.'

He gave a final glance to the window before he moved back to the fireside and sank into the chair. That flash of horrid mirth had died, like flame to ash, and now he only sounded weary. 'I told – *him* – that I would be glad of his help. He phrased it nicely, you know, as if he would only polish up my scribblings, although that was flattery. I asked him why he would bother, and he said he thought I was worth the effort. I remember that distinctly, because I didn't understand – but I wanted to believe he thought well of me, and that somehow I had earnt this stroke of luck . . . Of course I knew, deep down, that it was wrong, I can't pretend I didn't. I chose of my own free will. He would never have been able to touch me, otherwise . . . As soon as I agreed he shook my hand.' Moncrieff's mouth twitched, as if he recalled a bitter taste. 'His grip was very strong – he had very bony fingers – and his flesh was strangely hot. I didn't like it, even though I was so grateful . . . Then he smiled at me and plucked my sheet of rough notes from my desk, and promised to come back the next night with a new draft. When he'd gone, I extinguished the lamp and went straight to bed. I was so tired, and so relieved, and so light-hearted. I remember the soft pillow under my cheek, and how comfortable I was, knowing I could sleep and sleep and everything would be all right ...'

I nodded. I had felt something similar when Moncrieff took his leave that first night: only a few minutes of his company had been like a window opening somewhere, and a soft breeze blowing in ... After that I had fallen asleep so swiftly I had hardly had time to marvel at my luck. But that was different, of course. That had been only the foolishness of an old man too set in his routine, who had been lonely too long.

I drew my attention back to what Moncrieff had been saying. 'And then?'

'He did come back. And the poem was magnificent,' he said. 'The funny thing was that it was just what I would have written, if I'd had the talent for it. I tried to thank him, but he only g-grinned' – he stuttered a little on the word, as if it conjured an image he did not want to see – 'and said he would be back to claim his payment.'

'Ah.'

'Yes.'

'You had not agreed in advance that you would pay him,' I said, prompting him. 'And now you can't afford what he's asking.'

'Yes.'

'There is a word for that. An ugly word.'

'Blackmail, you mean?' His mouth curled, and for a moment I thought he would break into that horrible laughter again. 'In a way, I suppose ... But he didn't need to threaten me. I entered freely into the bargain, and I shall have to pay the debt.'

'Then pay it.' I glanced, in spite of myself, at the desk drawer where I kept my cheque book.

He didn't answer; but he drew his shoulders up and shivered. At last he said, 'I submitted the poem for the prize. I managed to put the whole thing out of my mind until they announced the winner, and then ... Well, I was ecstatic. I could hardly believe that I – I, David Moncrieff! – had pulled off such a coup. Yes, I know,' he added, forestalling me, 'but I sort of – *forgot* that I'd had help. It didn't seem to matter. When my tutor congratulated me, I didn't feel any shame at all, I revelled in it, and when the other fellows looked at me askance, I felt just as clever and pleased with myself as if I had done it all by myself, against the odds. I wrote to tell my mother—' He stopped, and I saw his fingers whiten at the knuckles as if he were bracing himself against a gust of wind. 'Well, you saw how I was. That night I wanted to celebrate, and I had no one, so I wandered all round college with a bottle of cheap champagne I could never have afforded without the prize money, and at last I came here ...'

'I am glad you did.'

'But next morning,' he went on, as if he had not heard me, 'I felt rather different. At first I thought it was just flatness, you know, now that the fuss of winning the prize was over – not to mention too much champagne ... But it got worse. I started to feel ... itchy. Inside my head, I mean. Days went by and I couldn't settle to anything. I tried to concentrate on all the tasks I'd been neglecting, but every few minutes I got up and went to the window, as if I was expecting someone. And the worst of it was, I couldn't sleep. Every time I closed my eyes I thought I heard knocking at my door.' He exhaled slowly, and although I was on the other side of the room I caught a whiff of stale breath. 'Then, when I thought I would go mad, he came back.'

'And he asked you for money?'

'For money? No.' He shook his head. 'He came to claim my soul.'

There was a silence.

Finally I said, 'David—'

At the same moment he threw himself back in his chair. 'I told you!' he said in bitter triumph. 'I *told* you that you'd think I was crazy! Christ knows I would too, if it wasn't my own eyes and ears. He wasn't human, I tell you – I *saw* him.'

I kept my voice very steady. 'What did you see?'

'I saw ...' He faltered, and I wondered if his fantasy would crumble under scrutiny; but after a moment he went on again, his voice stronger. 'I didn't let him in, you see. I opened the door, and he said he was there to get what he was owed, and – I thought then he meant money, and I started to say that I didn't have any. And then ...'

I bit my lip. I did not think it was right to encourage him, but I could not bring myself to interrupt.

'I can't describe it very well. It was a flicker, like a fog parting, just for a split second. He reached out for me, and I saw – saw his face properly, for the first time ...' He squeezed his eyes shut. 'It was all shadowy,' he said, with a dead, level note that was worse than hysteria would have been. 'The eyes were hollows, and the mouth had no lips. The hand he held out was withered. But the worst thing was the smell. It was sour and dusty, like old feathers – like a bird dead in a chimney, or a woman's hat pushed to the back of an attic and forgotten. And when he spoke there was a thin, sharp clattering, like wings, only – too dry ...'

I swallowed. In spite of my disbelief the image rose in my mind's eye, surprisingly vivid: the man's eyeless, lipless face, and his gown no longer cloth at all but a mass of musty, jagged plumage.

'I drew back just in time,' Moncrieff said, 'and slammed the door. I heard a sort of thump and scrape, as if he had thrown himself against the wood; and afterwards I saw long grooves in the paint, like the mark of claws ... I was too afraid to move. I haven't believed in God since I was a boy, but I squeezed my eyes shut and prayed. I was so panicked and desperate that the only words that came were *here I lay me down to sleep.* I kept muttering them over and over until at last I was sure that he had gone.'

'And since then you have been worried he would return?'

Moncrieff hunched his shoulders. 'That was the last time I saw him clearly,' he said, slowly. 'But now ... he is waiting. Following me. I keep catching glimpses of him. I hear footsteps that scratch oddly on the stone, I see shadows that are too deep, as if someone is standing there, all in black ... Sometimes there's laughter in my ear, when I'm walking alone. He is stalking me, biding his time. I don't know why he hasn't got me yet. Perhaps he's playing with me. But one day — one night — he will, and then . . .'

He let his voice trail off. A long way away an owl hooted, its call unanswered and desolate.

I cleared my throat, rather too loudly. 'It's very common to have these kinds of fancies when you haven't been sleeping well. Occasionally I myself—'

'Oh, for God's sake!' He flung up his hand to cut me off. There was a brief silence. Then, carefully, as if his bones might break, he got to his feet. 'It's no good,' he said. 'But never mind. It isn't your fault.'

'Perhaps a talk with a doctor—'

'What use would that be? Do you think a few kindly words and a bottle of veronal can chase away demons?'

'Given that they do not exist except in your mind — yes.'

He bit his lip, evidently deciding not to argue with me, as if I was the one who must be humoured. 'Thanks,' he said, moving towards the door. 'You have been very kind.'

'Wait! David . . .' I intercepted him. 'There must be something I can do. Why did you come to me? You wanted my help. Let me give it to you.'

'I came to you because I thought you would understand, that's all. You were the only one awake . . . Don't you ever sit alone, in the middle of the night, yearning for something so much you would sell your soul for it? In the light of day, no one would do it — but now, after midnight, when the seams of the world start to come apart, and the darkness seeps in ... You know as well as I do that there are things abroad at midnight that hide away at noon.'

'Human frailty, yes! When we can't sleep, our weaknesses are closer to the surface—'

'You know that isn't what I mean.'

We stared at each other. He looked very young, with his wild hair and overbright eyes; and I thought how lonely it must be, to be gripped by such a fearful delusion. 'I *do* understand,' I said, grasping his arm. 'Honestly, David. I am not sure I believe in your demon – but that you were tempted, and fell, and now you are haunted by the horror of what you did – yes, that is understandable. But you must not take it so to heart. Many men would do the same. *I* would do the same.'

His mouth twisted. 'You?'

'If someone came to me, and offered me ...' But I could not think of anything I wanted, really; the only thing I ever longed for was company. I spread my hands helplessly.

He regarded me for a long time, his expression unreadable. 'I know you don't believe me,' he said. 'But if you really want to be kind to me, you might do one thing.'

'Certainly.'

'Will you swear not to tell anyone that I cheated?'

I blinked. 'If you are going to be dragged kicking and screaming to hell,' I said, trying to summon a chuckle, 'I don't see why you care about your reputation.' He flinched, and I was ashamed of my levity. 'Wouldn't it be better,' I said, letting my gaze slide away, 'to make a clean breast of it? It isn't exactly – well – it wasn't cricket, you know.'

'I shouldn't ask. No wonder you despise me.'

'No! No, but I ... If anyone found out that I knew, and said nothing ...' I fumbled for my handkerchief and blew my nose, with more fuss than was strictly necessary. 'I have a duty to the college – to the other scholars ...' I almost added *and to myself*. But that was unbearably pompous. Surely it was not such a terrible sin, really, to turn a blind eye to another man's weakness? And what harm could it do? It was over and done with; meddling would only make him hate me. 'Very well,' I said with a sigh. 'But honestly, I advise you to—'

'Thank you,' he said, 'oh, thank you! You don't know what that means to me.' And he took my hand and shook it hard. There was a dry heat in his skin that made me wonder if the whole thing were due to a feverish disturbance in his brain, and I tried subtly to feel for his pulse; but he let go of me, and strode towards the door. 'Good night.'

'David,' I said, lunging after him, 'wait! You said once that I was your only friend, and I would be honoured if that were true. I would be pleased to think—'

'You've been very kind,' he said over his shoulder, 'and I am very grateful. I'll come back and see you soon.'

'Make sure you do—'

'I shall,' he said, and gave me a smile like a flame, valiant but guttering. 'Good night.'

In spite of what he had said, I did not exactly expect to see Moncrieff again. If he came to his senses, I thought he might be ashamed, and avoid me; if he did not ... But I did not want to think about that. If truth be told, I was very uneasy. I wondered if I should ask Blanford-Jones to keep an eye on him. But that would only have led to awkward questions, and although I was already regretting having undertaken to keep his secret, I would not break my word now that I had given it. And after all, there was still hope – although I could not have told you exactly what I hoped for.

But whether or not I believed he would come, I could not sleep for thinking about him. I watched that night, and the next; at last I abandoned even the pretence of work, and sat at my desk staring down at the empty court, and its shadows, and the apple tree, and the whirling snow which began to fall, too wet to settle but obscuring the world in a thick, rippling curtain. It snowed for a night and a day and another night, until the paths were slick and treacherous and the river a swollen, rolling torrent. Then, at last, some time after midnight on the third night, I caught a glimpse of someone in the court below. I was staring at the snow, half hypnotised by its eddies and currents and the shifting distances; now I jerked upright from my daze, blinking, and tried to make out the figure that moved through the swirling white. It took me a moment to be sure it was Moncrieff, and by that time he was nearly at the doorway under my window. Through the pouring snow – and my own reflected face, as I leant closer to the pane – it was difficult to make out his expression; but I know that he looked up at me, and our eyes met.

For a moment I could not move or speak. He had not changed, and yet – was it his sodden coat hanging around him, or the unearthly light of the low sky, or the wet gleam of his skin? – and yet, I thought, and yet—

And then it was too late. He glanced over his shoulder, as if something behind him had caught his attention. I thought I saw a movement in the nearest archway, although it might only have been a gust of snow blown into a freakish shape by the wind; in any case, before I could be certain, Moncrieff broke into a run. He ran – ran flat out, as if his life depended on it – towards the river. It was not the sprint of an athlete, nor the desperate shamble of an undergraduate late for an important exam; it was something else entirely, a plunging near-horizontal flight that seemed to defy the laws of nature, as if his very feet had been lifted from the ground by his panic. He cast a single terrified look backwards, and his mouth and eyes were stretched and empty.

He came to the bridge, slid on the cobbles and flung out his arm to steady himself on the parapet. A thicker veil of snow rippled across my vision. When I next saw him, he was in the middle of the bridge, at the highest point of its small curve. Now he was on his knees, cowering on the stones, but suddenly he lifted his head as if to face whatever pursued him; and some detached, academic part of me wondered if he was thinking of the old superstitions about the protective power of running water.

I threw open my casement and leant out, squinting against the flakes that blew into my face. Something black fluttered across the path, like a ragged cloak snapping in the wind.

Specks of ice stung my eyelids, and automatically I

blinked them away. Had I really seen—? No, there was no one – it must have been a trick of the light, and the snow—

But there was someone – something. There was a hole, a hollow, a vortex – a shadow in the centre of a shape – moving through the blizzard, leaving nothing but an impression of darkness. It hung for a second in the light that pooled at the base of the gas lamp, a formless stain in the air, melting the flakes that blew against it. Then it lunged towards the bridge.

I wanted to cry out to warn Moncrieff, but I was too slow.

He flung his arm up over his face, as if what he saw burnt his eyes. Then the darkness was on him – over him – enveloping him. For a heartbeat his face was visible as if through smoked glass, pale and blind as stone. I had the impression, fleeting as a flash of lightning, of wide sooty wings, glinting and sharp-edged – spreading, impossibly large, over the bridge, blotting out the sky – casting a deep penumbra over the river and the court, to the window where I stood and beyond.

Then the bridge was empty, and Moncrieff was gone.

I will not tire you with what followed. You may imagine how I stumbled, bewildered and horrified, through the snow, to stand where Moncrieff had stood; how I shouted his name until I was hoarse, leaning over the parapet, desperate for the sight of him crawling out of the river onto the bank below; and how at last I went to enlist the help of the night porter, gasping out the story of what I had seen, still hoping against hope that Moncrieff had merely fallen, and might be found somewhere, whole and alive ... After a fruitless, miserable half hour of searching I suggested that we try Moncrieff's room, in case he had returned there; when the porter told me with a frown that there was no undergraduate of that name living in college, I insisted that we rouse Blanford-Jones, who knew Moncrieff and could vouch for his existence. Blanford-Jones was grumpy and resentful at being woken at that hour, but when he saw my distress he sighed and invited us in. 'No,' he said, as he offered me a towel for my dripping hair, 'no, I don't recall a Moncrieff...'

I stammered, 'But you told me—'

'Oh, you mean Molyneux? Daniel Molyneux. One of my first years. Nice chap. A jolly good scrum half, too. His room's just over there,' he added, pointing. 'We can check on him if you like.'

'Not Molyneux, *Moncrieff*! You must know him – he won the Scott Prize a few weeks ago—'

He shook his head. 'It went to Cedric Harrison this year. My dear fellow, you must sit down, you look all done up ...'

But I could not bear the way they were looking at me. I pushed the porter aside and hurried down the staircase, out into the bleak icy stillness that had finally followed the snowfall.

And now ... I cannot sleep. At least, I do not sleep; I assume it is not worth trying. I sit at my desk, and although Moncrieff cannot have been real, I still watch for him. He will come again, soon.

Was he ever alive? I remember the Provost telling a story one Christmas about a scholar meeting a bad end, a long time ago, after he had received some accolade... Maybe that was Moncrieff; maybe he went mad, and destroyed himself; maybe he is condemned to walk the night, telling his story to whoever is awake to listen. Maybe I was only a witness.

But I am afraid, and not only because I might have seen a ghost.

If you're awake, he said, *and wanting something with all your heart – what if, late at night, something hears, and answers?* I thought when he said *you* he meant himself. But when I was a boy, I would have done anything, promised anything, not to be alone; I never stopped longing for it. I always kept my lamp burning in my window, hoping that someone would come. And then he did, and I welcomed him and shook his hand... Was it a warning, or a trap?

That last night, when he paused below my window, I hesitated before I could call down to him. For an instant he looked misshapen, half-melted and twisted, like a figure in black wax. But what stopped me was something else. The air was freezing, metallic with the scent of snow; but the smell that filled my nostrils – strong as if its source were beside me, close as my own breath – was an old, acrid one: like a fur coat bundled into a damp corner and forgotten, or the rank stink of rotting feathers.

MACAW

Catriona Ward

'Say it for me, Benjy,' she whispers. My claws grip her finger. I raise my crest high. I bend and peck lightly at her hand, not breaking the skin. She gives my beak a soft tap.

'Say your name.' Her cheek is pink in the crimson light of the coals. She has not lit the gas sconces, she knows that is against the rules. No gaslight after nine o'clock, Samuel says, and this week she is following the rules. So she does not roll back the rug to draw on the bare boards, or say her strange poems. No, this time she came down here just to see me, and the knowledge fills me with flight.

'My name is . . .' she coaxes. She strokes my head. Her breath is soft, lifting my feathers.

I close my eyes. My quills tremble. I have deferred the moment as long as I can – the delicious reward. 'I'm a happy boy,' I say. 'I'm a happy boy.'

She holds up the millet seed pinched between her fingers. I lean in and crunch it in my beak, blinking with happiness.

'I know you can say that,' she says. 'Now, can you say your name?'

I dance from foot to foot, laughing. *Cacaw.*

'My name is Amabel,' she says. 'What is your name?'

'I'm a happy boy.'

'Benjy,' she says. 'Please.'

I bark, just like the dogs I hear from the stable, and nestle gently into her underarm.

She holds me there for a moment, kisses me and then puts me back into the cage gently. The green baize comes down over the bars with a soft rustle, shutting out the red light of the dying fire.

'Sleep,' I hear her say. I am already dozing on my perch as the sitting-room door closes softly in her wake. 'We'll try again tomorrow.'

I have not left this room since I was carried into Clough Hall by Amabel some years ago. I bite the golden bars, thoughtful. This room, the house – my cage within a cage within a cage. But there is more than one way to travel. I am a very observant kind of parrot, and I know a great deal about this place through what I see and hear. I go places.

I know that the Hall is in bleak country, with few neighbours. I know that it stands at the end of a long drive lined with drooping willow. Amabel has said that the trees bend inwards over the road like sad women over a grave.

Samuel married Amabel when she was penniless. She had a son from her previous marriage. Samuel is very wealthy and some years older. He was Lord Clough, and he made her Lady Clough. At the very beginning of the marriage she went visiting and so forth, in as far as there was visiting to be had in this area. But it did not last more than a week.

And since her son went Amabel does not leave the Hall. Her cage is somewhat larger than mine, I suppose.

I am content. I have millet seed and water and her warm hands.

I wake and fluff my feathers to the sound of footsteps and the raspy voice of the poker, stirring up the fire in the grate. I rise slowly from my dreams of bright jungle, lianas, high treetops, of my wings spread, arcing high on thermals, of taking flight above a rich forest canopy I have never seen, of warm winds I have never felt. I love these journeys I take in my sleep. Of all creatures, macaws have the most vivid dreams. I don't know where I heard this fact, but it is definitely true.

But I am back in the waking world now. The dappled light of the forest is gone, there is only the dim green inside the baize cloth and my cage. In the room beyond I hear quiet voices. Rain rattles on the windowpanes.

'Thank you for coming, dearest.' Amabel is upset, that is enough to wake me thoroughly. Her voice and her tears catch in her throat. 'You are quite wet through. Please! Warm yourself by the fire!'

'Of course I came, my sweet, how could I refuse?' It is Millicent, one of the few neighbours within calling distance. I wish it were not Millicent. I really do not like her – those pinprick eyes which rest so covetously on Amabel, her sharp nails which poke my stomach. *Who's a pretty polly, then?* Afterwards Millicent always wipes her fingers on her shawl, making sure that Amabel does not see.

'How are the children?' Amabel asks.

'Oh, Thomas is impossible, he wears through his stockings once a week.' Millicent laughs her particular laugh. 'As for Belinda, girls are even worse than boys in their own—'

'One moment, my dear,' Amabel breaks in. 'I will take Benjy out of his cage.'

'I do not like the bird,' Millicent says.

'No,' says Amabel, cheerful. 'Nor does Samuel. You have much in common.'

The baize is lifted. Light explodes. The bars of my cage glow brilliant gold in the firelight. Alas it is Millicent's thorny hands which grasp me, nails digging through the soft down on my belly. I cry out in protest.

'There, there.' It is Amabel's beloved voice in my ear, her beloved hands which are around me now. She strokes my poll and I settle. 'Come, Benjy, will you sit on my shoulder?' She extends her arm and I walk up it, hooking my talons into her green poplin. I take my perch by Amabel's ear and turn my stare on Millicent, who gives a small but perceptible start.

Her hand plays nervously with the cameo at her neck. 'That bird is unsettling. Do you not feel it? I will put him outside in the room.' She makes to lift my cage from its hook. 'You may place him within.'

'*No.*' Amabel's breath comes fast. 'Benjy stays just here.'

'I am very sorry, I'm sure,' Millicent says. 'There is no need to *snap* at me so.'

'Forgive me.' Amabel's tone is soft once more.

'It is your own business,' Millicent says. 'A parrot is not

like a nice loyal spaniel who will pass after a decent interval. Parrots can live for quite a time. Sixty years or more, I am told.'

'Perhaps Benjy will outlive us all. We should dictate our wills to him – he could recite them at the inquest, if we do not trust our husbands.'

Millicent looks away. Her throat moves.

Amabel sees. 'I am sorry,' she says. 'Forgive me. I'm nothing but nerves today. I don't know why.' She touches Millicent's arm. 'Let us sit. I have rung for tea.'

As if on cue, Edith the housemaid comes into the room, pulling the tea trolley behind her.

'We will have it at the sofa, Edith,' Amabel says.

Edith draws the trolley up to the sofa, and serves it on the low table before them, in silence.

'I wished to ask,' Amabel says as they sip from their saucers. 'You have a glasshouse at the Manor, do you not, with an abundance of herbs?'

'Why, yes!' Millicent is delighted that Amabel has mentioned it. She is proud.

'Do you have,' Amabel asks, 'such a thing as rosemary growing in your herb beds at the moment? I wish to make a special lamb dish for Samuel – similar to one which he loved during his travels in Greece. It relies strictly on a very pungent rosemary flavour ... garlic, too, I fear.' She makes a small moue, wrinkling her nose. 'And all the beds in our kitchen garden are bare.'

'I will ask,' Millicent says. 'Evans will remind me. The

gardener, you know. The glasshouse is all my idea, of course, the whole thing is my creation, but he takes care of the details day to day.'

'It is so clever of you,' Amabel says. 'How I wish I had thought of it. Samuel is so fond of these strong flavours.' She shivers slightly.

'Build up the fire, girl,' Millicent says to Edith. 'Your mistress is cold. That dress is so unseasonal, my Ammie. The weather is biting; you should have on a thick worsted, at least.'

'I like the cut,' Amabel says, hooking a slim finger into her high collar. 'I know it's foolish.'

I nestle into the soft crook between her neck and shoulder. She gasps as I nudge the sore place with my head. Beneath the high collar of the green poplin, the marks of Samuel's fingers are writ in black and purple on her throat.

Amabel smiles and pushes me gently from her. 'Your youngest, Belinda — you were saying?'

'Oh yes!' Millicent's face is almost improper in her greed to speak about her children. 'You would like to hear everything, I expect.'

'It is never tiring hearing about love.' There is a strange brightness in Amabel's voice. 'Why, I love you so much, Millicent, that the last time you stayed with us, I could have sworn that I conjured a vision of you on my husband's corridor in the middle of the night.'

Millicent clasps her heart and rises.

Amabel reaches for her hand. 'I am sorry,' she whispers. 'I

find I cannot do anything right today. And really, it matters nothing to me. Please, please, would you bring me some rosemary?'

Millicent gives a tight nod and goes from the room without a word.

Samuel put the marks on Amabel's neck when he caught her some nights ago. She had come down to her sitting room to draw her star and say her poems. I call them poems, because sometimes they rhyme, but secrets or wishes might do. Prayers, perhaps? There is another word for them, but I am careful not to think of it. Sometimes, in these dark nights, I have the strange conviction that Samuel can hear thoughts – that they echo through the sleeping house.

'Have I ever told you, Benjy, about the man I loved? Perhaps you don't remember him. You were young. He gave me my best, my most precious gift. My boy, my son.'

I supposed that Amabel meant her husband and son from her previous marriage. The son was fifteen, or perhaps five when he died, I do not really pay attention to human ages. He passed soon after her marriage to Samuel. Walked out of Clough Hall one dark autumn night and into the lake, they say. Amabel brought me here to this place soon after, and I am grateful to this unknown son, since I think it is the only reason Samuel allows Amabel to keep me. A consolation for her loss.

'I wish that you had known him,' she says. 'Marik Grey. That was his name. He was one of my kind. One of our kind,

I should say, because you are part of what I am, Benjy.' Her eyes are distant, seeing far beyond this house, this day. 'We were so different. But we were the same in the deepest ways.'

I shrugged. (It is not common knowledge that birds can shrug, indeed most cannot, but macaws are no ordinary birds.) I don't remember the times before this room, when I was a chick.

Amabel laughed now – really laughed. 'Oh, indeed, sauce-pot! You are very cavalier tonight.'

I settled against her neck and nibbled some of her hair in apology. In fact, I do love a story. All I have are stories and these four walls.

Amabel rolled back the rug to reveal the bare boards. She chalked her mark there quickly. Then she sank down, kneeling in the centre of it. She closed her eyes. I sat quietly on her shoulder and combed her hair with my beak. She gasped as the grandfather clock in the hall beyond began to strike. Something passed through her. I saw it like a ripple in water. Her eyes flew open, they stared, but at some other place than here.

'Ahh. Time is running out,' she whispered. 'There is no time to talk. Benjy, we must hurry.'

All my feathers stood up like the fur of a frightened cat. This was new.

Amabel grasped me. Her hand hummed with something, as if tight-wound clockwork had been released just beneath her skin. 'Marik,' she whispered. 'Reach for me, my love. Help us. Help us.'

The room swam with something other. The last stroke of midnight chimed.

The sitting-room door opened, silent. Samuel has all the hinges in the house oiled every Monday morning and they swing like silk. Even so, normally Amabel would have heard, she is always listening for him. But this time her eyes beheld some other place than here, her ears heard the winds and night birds of somewhere else.

Samuel came towards her, quiet on his narrow feet, legs poking out white and hairless from his nightgown, holding his candlestick where the little flame had burnt low in the socket. His head was cocked to one side; his mild face bore its usual expression of innocent bewilderment. As he drew near he placed the candlestick on a side table, freeing his hands. He flexed his fingers gently.

'I'm a happy boy,' I said, over and over, as he came on. I pecked Amabel's neck, trying to rouse her. 'I'm a happy boy!' But still she remained motionless, kneeling at the centre of the star, eyes open and unseeing. That strange wind still trembled through her flesh.

Samuel was upon us before Amabel woke from the state that held her. One of his hands clutched at me. I launched myself high and flew from her shoulder, up into the corner of the room, and clung to a section of cornicing. He let loose a brief *pffff* of disapproval. But I am not important and was soon forgotten. He turned his attention to Amabel and put his hands about her throat.

She came back to herself just then. Her eyes grew large as

they fixed on Samuel's face, inches from her own. He nodded, smiling, as if he had been waiting for precisely this.

I hid my head beneath my wing, but I could not shut out the sounds. He makes her unconscious and then he wakes her with sal volatile. When she gasps back up into life he closes his hands on her throat once more until she loses consciousness. So he wakes her again. It goes on and on. Samuel has so far not killed her, but the line he treads grows finer and finer.

Jack the boots cleans out the fireplaces and sweeps the grates at Clough Hall. He is from a town some twenty miles away – it might as well be a thousand miles. Near or far, no place is like Clough. Edith sweeps and dusts and makes good. She is from here, from Clough, of a family many generations deep. I may be a mere macaw, but I have learned this much: Clough's memory is long. All that passes at the Hall, all our lives, are but a moment in its story.

Jack and Edith do Amabel's sitting room in the early mornings. They don't have to work here at the same time, but they do. They talk as they work. Edith's tone towards Jack is both scolding and inviting. I think she likes him.

I swing on my swing. I cock my head and listen.

'We should tell,' Jack says.

'Who are we to tell?' asks Edith, dusting violently. 'Do you wish to write to her family? Who are her family? Do you know where to address a letter? Can you write well enough to do it?'

'It's wrong,' Jack says. He wipes his cheek, leaving a long dark slash of soot. 'He hurts her.'

Edith takes a deep breath. 'Yes. Don't take on so.'

'But—'

'Hush. Now, bend and clean the grate. It is better not to be seen to talk to each other.' Edith turns to the great gilded mirror over the settle and begins to scour, vinegar scenting the air. 'It's not good to know this, what I am about to say, but it may be worse not to know it.' When Edith glances at Jack his back is turned. He is bent over the fireplace, sweeping up cinders, seemingly oblivious.

She takes a deep breath. 'It started five winters gone. Daisy Smart was found dead in a ditch.' She coats the mirror in vinegar. 'The drain beside the road that leads to the mill. Daisy was loose. She liked a drink.'

'So she fell into the ditch?' Jack asks.

Edith shakes her head. 'She was already dead when she went into the ditch. Her body had been brought there from somewhere else. I think whoever it was meant to put her in the river but did not. Perhaps someone passed by.'

'How could you know—'

'She was already stiff.' Edith takes up old newspaper to scour the mirror. 'Frozen, kneeling, as if in prayer. Women do not kneel down in ditches in the deep midwinter. She did not even *fit* in the ditch, the way her body was set. But after all, it was Daisy, it was not unexpected that she had met such an end.'

Edith moves to the sofa and batters a cushion with a fist. 'Not three months later, in early spring, Hannah Todmarten was found at the bottom of a well. The well was disused, and had gone sour, so the smell wasn't noticed for a time. Hannah — well, her mind was not strong. She often slept among the haystacks. So she was not missed, until she was found. And once again it begged no questions in general.' Edith replaces the cushion and smooths it gently, as if in apology for her earlier ferocity. 'One night not long afterwards Anne, the chandlers' daughter, went out to bring the cow in from the top field. She never came back. Three girls of a similar age, all within months. The people of Clough are very good at ignoring unpleasant truths, but even they began to be uneasy.'

'It might have been coincidence,' Jack says. 'Maybe it was ...'

'No,' Edith says to him, kind. 'Three is too many. You know that.'

He catches his breath and nods.

'I should mention,' Edith says, 'that the old Lord died in the autumn, and the present Lord Clough came here in the winter, just before Daisy Smart was found in the ditch. It is just a detail. A point of interest. Do you see? No, don't answer that. The next one was only — no.' Edith covers her face with her hand for a moment. 'I can't. There was another girl, a death. That is all you need to know.'

Jack puts the brush and shovel down carefully. He approaches Edith, holding his coal-covered hands carefully high. They face one another, not touching. 'Edith,' he says, helpless.

'Don't,' she says. 'I must go on or I will never finish.

Summer came in hot and smothering. Mould grew on the hay, the grain. There were almost no lambs, and the sheep died with strange rot in their feet. We, the girls of Clough, waited in the heat for death to choose us.

'On the hottest day I have ever known, Lord Clough brought home his Lady.' Edith reaches out towards Jack, fingers closing, grasping, as if comfort were an invisible physical thing to be plucked from his person. She comes almost close enough to graze his braces with her fingertips. 'And . . .' she says.

'And?' His voice is soft.

Edith looks at him long, and then she stops her hand. She goes back into herself. 'It stopped,' she says. 'It all stopped, after they married. Now all the girls in Clough stay alive. They are no longer found dead in wells and ditches.'

'Surely,' Jack says, 'this is all superstition, some coincidence of events that means nothing . . .' His voice trails away, not sustained by conviction.

Edith backs away. 'You think so?' she whispers. 'There was one more death, after. It was the son of Lady Clough. He came here with her — but he is not here. They pretend he ran away but I saw what lay by the lake. It's so much to carry, the knowing. Or the not knowing but the might-be . . .' She hiccups, tears fighting in her throat. 'He vanished from this very room the night before the wedding. In the morning I came to do my usual. But those doors were open. When I went to close them, I saw clothes strewn on the lawn all the way from here to the lake. The boy had a bright red waistcoat, the kind only a young man could think handsome. It was there, on the grass. His shoes lay in the dew, strewn wide as if he had become a giant and cast them off in one great stride.

'When I turned, he was behind me – Lord Clough.' She shivers. 'Lord Clough is like a clock or something that you wind up, don't you think? He is either still as the dead or moving towards you with that even, soundless step.

'I could not think what to say. I was afraid that my apron and dress would be strewn next across the lawn, and I at the bottom of the cold, cold lake. Lord Clough seemed to see my trouble. Do you know' – she sniffs – 'he put his hand on my shoulder. He comforted me. He seemed sorry that I had seen.

'"He is a wilful boy," Lord Clough said. "I scolded him for swimming, I told him he would catch his death and he stormed away in a temper. He will be back. Do not mention it to your lady, we do not wish to spoil her wedding day."'

Edith is barely holding back her tears. 'It was a moonless night, filled with summer rain. Who would wish to swim alone in the rain? Whatever happened that dark night, that boy did not swim and he was not alone. I knew all this.

'Yet Lord Clough's hand rested so kindly on my shoulder and it all seemed so possible. Do you know what I did then?'

Jack shakes his head.

'I went out onto the lawn and I picked up all those clothes, though I did not want to touch them. They still held the memory of his living body. I folded them, laying that ugly red waistcoat on top. Then I came inside and handed the pile to Lord Clough. Then I went from this room, and I have never told a soul what I saw, until now.'

Edith turns and opens the French doors and thrashes her duster. The wind whistles in, icy, cleansing the room with cold. The lake is battered steel in the distance. Edith closes the doors, shutting out the roar. Her gaze lingers on the lake. 'Sixteen,' she says. 'It's young to die. The boy had barely lived.'

'Why would he do it?' asks Jack.

'I don't know. But there's an old belief in these parts – a memory of a memory. I reckon anyplace folks harvest crops or have farms or depend on the sun and the moon, they have some such belief like it. The place – the hills, the earth, the rock – they need an offering. Might be blood, maybe a life, something warm and pulsing, to please the old gods. The harvest queen, queen of the May, whatever name they give it – she is the sacrifice. In the village they think that as long as Lady Clough is here, he won't take the village girls. She keeps us safe.'

'It's not right,' Jack says quietly. 'You've seen the marks.'

Edith shrugs. 'They're right, in a way. She keeps him busy – the bad god.'

'He's not a god,' Jack says. 'But she is the sacrifice. You leave it be? You would rather let it happen than speak up?'

'Ah, I see,' Edith says, quiet. 'So Lord Clough is no god. But you are, maybe? You sit in judgement above us. You, a truth teller, standing up for what is right.' She turns to face him, studies his face. 'Why are you here? No one would come to Clough, except to hide. It's all over you. You're running like a rabbit, and I wonder why.'

'I needed a job,' Jack says. 'It's a simple matter.'

'Ah, yes, a stranger comes here to take up a post as a boots.' Edith smiles. 'Who every so often uses words most only know from the dictionary. Seems likely. You know, word travels, even to here. There was a man who was a problem about factory workers' rights and so forth back in Lancaster – a man who was sabotaging the machines in protest. He had an education but was working among the common man. But when the time came, he fled like a startled cat. So tell me,' Edith says, 'is it only when it's none of your business that you wish to stand your ground like a man?'

Jack picks up the full ash pail and goes wordless from the room.

'I didn't say it was right, what Clough is doing to her,' Edith calls after him. Her voice cracks. 'I said it's what they think. Them, not me!'

Jack is gone.

'Arse,' she says to herself and reaches into her apron. She comes over to my cage and pushes a sliver of cheese rind through the bars. She always saves the rind for me if she can. I take it in my beak and eat, purring like the kitchen cat that finds its way in here occasionally. (The cat sits neat and still below my cage; only its bright green eyes move, following me. The cat sits and purrs and plots my death.)

'We're all right, aren't we, Benjy? You like me, anyhow.' Edith leans against the wall. Her bright sharpness has deserted her. She is limp and deflated. 'This position, this house,' she says. 'I hate it. But it doesn't matter, does it, what I feel? I need my place here.' Tears cloud her voice. 'She misses him, her son. She named you for him, didn't she? Benjamin. She spends these long hours with you, because she cannot spend them with him.' She rubs her face hard with her hand. 'Whatever did he tell Lady Clough, that bad old man? Did she believe it? If she knows, how can she stay here?'

Edith's face grows slowly hard with horror. 'But of course,' she says. 'Here I am.'

'I'm a happy boy,' I say. I press my belly against the bars, asking to be stroked.

She smiles, thin through tears, and tickles me with a gentle finger. It is good to give people cheer, if you can. 'Oh, Benjy. You are fortunate that she does not allow you to leave this room. There is nothing worth seeing.'

'I'm a happy boy.'

'I wish you'd learn to say something else, bird,' she says, stroking me. 'Any bloody thing at all.'

Samuel comes silent into the sitting room in the early afternoon. I cacaw with surprise. He must know that she will not be here at this time. This is the time she is with her doctor, the one he says she needs for her mind.

He stands and surveys the hearth, the unlit fire. He rolls back the rug. But the boards are clean, varnished bright. No terrible star. He huffs and turns his eye on me.

I hop from one foot to the other. 'I'm a happy boy,' I say.

'I'm a happy boy!' I say it as loudly as I can, but it will be no good. Amabel's sitting room is at the end of a corridor, and the door is thick. Unless someone is nearby, they will not hear.

Samuel comes close and opens the door with his thin fingers. 'Come to me,' he says. 'Come to me, bird.' He holds out a fragment of walnut meat in his fingers.

I hop onto his finger. What else can I do? He draws me out from the cage and stands before the window. We gaze at the grey lake.

'She likes you better than she does her own husband and master.' I do not at first recognise the voice which speaks. Tears brim close in Samuel's voice, he does not sound like himself. 'It is unnatural, such sentimental attachment to a dumb beast. Why can she not see that I seek only to save her?' Samuel brings his hand close, his face becoming monstrous. I can see each pock in his bulbous nose, each liver mark, the deep black of his wet eyes, their shining rheumy rims.

'Why does she not love me as she loves you?' Samuel's voice is plaintive and full of longing. 'Does she still think of that other one, instead of me? The one that got the bastard on her? She is lucky to have me, you know. I give her a home, clothes, my name. I am a good Lord Clough.' He clenches his fist. 'I am a better master of this house than my father was.'

I purr like a cat and lean away from him. He picks me up. His hand is a bony cage.

'Why must she force me to discipline her, when I want

only her good? She knows how it pains me to do it. If I were my father, I would take the horse brand to her. It was his way.' Samuel's hand goes to his bicep, tracing the shape of something on his flesh that lies beneath the linen sleeve. 'I am not like my father. I am merciful. I am just.' The grip on my leg tightens and tightens. 'She said she would not continue her profane ways. She swore.' He looks at me closely. I try to step back; his face is so big and like old cheese, like something that is already dead. 'I think you are part of those ways,' Samuel says. 'They say the cunning woman can channel her power into an animal. Is that what you are? Or are you just what you seem – a dimwit bird?' He laughs, which does not make sense because I can see by the black of his eyes that he is not amused, not at all. His grip on my leg is ever more painful, the slender bone will snap, I am sure, it will crack in his heavy grip.

'I'm a good boy!' I shout. 'I'm a good boy!'

The door to the sitting room opens.

'You called, my lord?' Jack bows in the doorway.

Lord Clough turns his pinkish eyes on Jack in silence. 'No.'

'It must have been the bird I heard, my lord. It is loud and a nuisance. Shall I return it to its cage? I am sure my lady would not wish it to trouble you with its noise.'

The moment stretches out. Samuel nods.

Jack comes forward slowly and offers me his wrist. I hop onto it quickly. The door of my cage closing has never sounded so wonderful. I peck one of the golden bars, grateful.

Jack opens the door for Samuel, standing straight as a

ramrod, his eyes fixed ahead on nothing. After a moment Samuel goes from the room and Jack closes the door behind him with a soft click. He stands for a moment, listening, as the faint sound of Lord Clough's shuffling footsteps recedes down the hall.

Jack peers at me through the bars. 'Nothing wrong with you, eh?'

I dance from foot to foot to show him that I am well.

Jack nods and goes, and honestly, I am only too glad to put my head under my wing and be quiet. I wish people would stop coming into my lovely room with their troubles, which all seem very complicated. It almost stops me from being a happy boy.

Amabel and I are playing within the lines of the pointed star, its chalk outline stark on the mellow varnished boards. Millicent stays here at Clough Hall tonight, so we are somewhat safe. Samuel is occupied. Millicent brought great sheaves of rosemary in her carriage. Amabel took it quickly from her arms, but the mineral scent still lingers in all the halls and passages.

I flutter onto a point of the star and Amabel follows, jumping on light feet. I flutter onto another point as she lunges for me. Soon we are hopscotching back and forth, she breathless, me purring. In a bowl in the unlit fireplace, rosemary smokes, giving off a burnt savoury-sweetness.

I fly around the star on fast wings, slipping from her grasp. At last Amabel's hands close firmly about me. 'You are quick,' she laughs. 'But not quick enough.' Her breath runs through my feathers like warm fingers.

'Benjy,' Amabel says, serious. 'Do you see what is written, on each point of this mark? They are letters, which form a name. I will spell it for you. B-E-N-J-Y. Do you see? I was hoping the star might help you say it.'

I walk up her arm, hooking myself with beak and claws on the embroidery.

Amabel tuts and lifts me away gently. 'Come, come,' she says, 'I will have no dresses left if you insist on tearing them to shreds.' She puts me gently to her shoulder. I nibble her ear.

Amabel sits down on the sofa and takes a paper bag of pistachios from her pocket. I lunge for one, but she restrains me. 'You will crack the shells and spill them everywhere, Benjy.' She shells a nut and offers it to me on her palm. I eat it and bob my head pointedly at the paper bag.

'My apologies,' Amabel says. 'At once, sir.' She shells another nut and I eat its ripe meat. The bowl of herbs smokes in the hearth, and the room is slightly hazy. I blink and give a little cough like Millicent when she is about to be rude. I try to hide from the smoke by creeping into Amabel's hair, where it hangs loose about her shoulders.

Amabel laughs. 'Ah, you are perfectly fine.' She strokes me, eyes closed. 'That scent,' she says. 'Rosemary, for remembrance. Like in the play. Once in a while, writers are correct.

'I have felt it in me, this thing, ever since I can remember,' she says. 'I called it the whisper because that's what it seemed like when I was small and I first heard it. A whisper, a promise, a warning. A silent voice from the world, which told my heart that I was not like others. A voice which told me how to do things that other little girls could not do.'

Amabel gets up and goes to the fireplace. The rosemary has for the most part smouldered down to nothing. One stem still glows, red and alive. She stirs it down into the grey. Then she takes the fragrant warm ash from the fireplace, puts it in the copper bowl and brings it to the sofa. I peer into the bowl, just in case there is millet seed inside. You never know. But there is not.

She sets down the bowl of rosemary ash in the centre of the chalk pentangle. I caw in annoyance at her absence. I want to be stroked, and I want millet seed.

'Oh hush now. I merely need this.' She has a small bright spark of green between her fingers. A feather, from the bottom of my cage. She drops it into the bowl and beckons.

'Come, Benjy,' she says softly. 'It is time. It has kept you safe, but it does not last for ever.' I hate to see her plead because it reminds me too much of how she is in those times with the sal volatile. 'Samuel notices you now. He is losing patience.' She waits. I bob my head. 'We must go from here,' she says. 'But first, you must remember.'

I do not know what she means. Go where? Remember what? I crackle like the fire when it is built high in the hearth.

'You are afraid,' Amabel says. 'But do you not wish to leave this room, my love? Do you not wish to go with me?'

I fly up and clench my talons on the chandelier, quite angry. Why must she speak of such things? 'I'm a happy boy.'

'Please, Benjy,' she whispers. 'Your name.'

I do not know how long the door has been standing ajar. Or how long the milk-white figure has been hovering there, silently watching. Even as we look at him, he says nothing. He smiles. Silence is more powerful a weapon than most people give it credit for. It can hold more fear than any spoken word. His face is different. Any remaining human mask has dropped away. He is a skull wearing a smile. Amabel sees it too. Her body goes rigid from head to toe.

Now Samuel flexes his fingers. 'This is the last time,' he says gently. 'I have warned you. Over and over I have—'

Amabel rushes towards him. She does it well, going from absolute stillness to speed in a moment. She hits him with her arms outstretched and he falls hard to the floor. She leaps lightly over him and reaches the door and turns.

'Benjy,' she says. 'You must—' But I never discover what it is that I must do, because she has waited too long. Samuel's hand closes about Amabel's ankle. He pulls so hard that she skids backwards on the shining boards. She holds tightly to the doorframe and kicks at him, but to no avail. Samuel pulls himself up, hand over hand, on her leg, beneath her skirts.

He stands and takes a handful of her hair. With his other hand he takes her throat. She writhes as he closes the sitting-room door and drags her to the centre of the pentangle. They are black outlines against the fire. He is going to kill her this time, just as he killed her son.

I fly at him. My claws grasp his fleshy nose and sink in.

He screams. I beat my wings in his face. His hand strikes me like a hard-thrown stone. Then he seizes me in his fist.

'You love this thing,' he says to Amabel, who is quiet now, kneeling beside him as he holds her up by the throat. 'So watch me, now, as I do to it what I will do.' Somewhere, in the hall beyond, the clock begins to strike midnight. *One.* He squeezes me. I understand that he is going to do it slowly. I cry out like the dogs when he beats them. *Two.*

I am afraid that she is dead, but she opens bloodshot eyes and mouths something. I know what it is. *I love you.*

Three, four . . .

She is going to die, we both are, the face of the skull holds no mercy for us. His hand increases its pressure. I peck uselessly at it. But something is happening, like a light in my mind.

Five, six . . .

Memories are sliding in, things no bird has seen. Laughing with Amabel, trying to help her keep her yarn in neat skeins, making a mess of it. Sliding in the mud in the rain, shouting with joy and her scolding at the state of my britches. Sitting in the light of a garret window, where we share a bowl of pottage and stale bread. Happiness surrounds each of these images, like a haze of gold.

Seven, eight . . .

'My name is,' I say as he squeezes me. 'My name is . . .' My lungs are pressed so tight. I am almost beyond speaking.

Nine, ten . . .

The words swell in my throat. it is almost too late. 'My name is Benjamin . . . Marik . . . Grey.'

Everything bursts into light and pain. My body slips, liquid, from Samuel's hand. I am nothing, not even matter, I am something that is about to be.

My beautiful feathers fall away. Limbs shoot from me, burning. I grow, screaming and pink and featherless.

Eleven, twelve.

The pain recedes. I am panting on the floor. Samuel is screaming too, skull mouth stretched wide, eyes black. He still holds Amabel by the throat. She chokes and retches.

I turn and take the heavy golden birdcage from its stand. I raise it high in my hands and bring it down, again and again, on Samuel's head. When he is still I do it again, once more. Then I drop the birdcage at my side.

'Benjamin,' Amabel whispers.

'Mother.' Her tears are hot on my shoulder, as mine are on hers.

She pulls away at length, laughing a little. 'I have clothes for you. I will fetch them. And we must . . .' Her face falls, gesturing at the mess that lies before the fire.

'My lady.' Edith stands in the doorway. Amabel catches her breath. She and Edith hold one another's gaze.

'Edith,' she says. 'Please – we will go, we will leave this place. I promise that you will not hear from us again.'

'No,' Edith says.

'All I ask is that you turn your back for a moment. My son and I will be gone. Clough will never be troubled by us.'

'Lord Clough has gone on a visit,' Edith says slowly,

advancing into the room. 'He did not inform anyone when he might return. And I see, Lady Clough, that you have had a recurrence of the rat problem which has so plagued all the house. You killed the vermin, but how unfortunate that you have stained your rug.

'And your son has returned from his visit abroad.' Edith turns a swift eye on me. I am aware at this juncture that I am still without clothing, and I cover myself, blushing. 'How joyful.' She pauses. 'I have one condition, which is that Jack the boots must be made your private secretary and stay as long as he will.'

Amabel nods. 'Will it work?'

Edith shrugs. 'It might. And what do we have but *might?*'

I stand at the open French doors, looking out over the grounds. The lake reflects back the dark grey dawn. I stroke the velour of my beautiful red waistcoat. Amabel found it at the back of Samuel's wardrobe. Behind me Jack the boots has picked up Samuel's feet.

'We don't have all day,' Edith says, acid, and I start.

I take up Samuel's arms and Jack and I carry him out. I cross the threshold of the house, out onto the lawn. I am under the sky for the first time in eight years.

Stones bound to all extremities, golden birdcage about his head, the water takes Samuel's body like a silken mouth. The sun breaks the hill in a burning rim. Light falls on the lake, red-gold and blinding.

DR THRALE'S NOTEBOOK

Michelle Paver

I didn't expect it to be perfect, but I never imagined this. For years I've dreamt of spending summer in the Arctic, in the endless light of the midnight sun. It kept me going through the dark times. Mother and Cynthia creeping about in perpetual gloom, speaking in hushed tones, the whole house stinking of camphor and sick-rooms.

All through the journey up here I've clung to my dream despite five days of relentless rain. And for what? They tell me this fog could last for weeks.

According to the map we're surrounded by mountains, but I can hardly see a thing except for those beastly cable-cars dumping their loads on the jetty. The clunketty-clunk reminds me of the Zepps during the War. The coal-dust is giving me a headache.

And to top it all, I've nowhere to stay. Jacobsen, the mine manager, insists that neither the miners' barracks nor his own quarters are fit for a 'yentleman'. His English is rudimentary, but he manages to convey what he thinks of geologists: to him I'm merely a problem created by his boss.

I've argued and protested in vain. 'What d'you mean you

know nothing about it? I'm here to do a survey, it's been arranged for months!'

With a shrug he suggests that I might bunk with Ingstad the watchman, another hefty Norwegian with sharp grey eyes and a tobacco-stained beard, who crosses his arms on his paunch and gives me a stony look: *That's not going to happen.*

For a moment through the fog I glimpse a rocky hillside and a cabin standing alone. 'What about that?'

'*Nej*,' Jacobsen's head-shake is vehement. '*Sykehus.*' Hospital.

'Is anyone sick?' I retort.

'*Nej*, but—'

'Then I'm sure the doctor won't mind putting up with me till you can sort this out.'

A glimmer of amusement cracks Jacobsen's granite features. '*Nej*, he won't mind. He's dead.'

The cabin is tarred black and forbiddingly grim, but perversely, this cheers me up. This is what I've been craving: solitude, freedom, a rough male existence with no luxuries and no feminine frills.

Jacobsen and Ingstad have accompanied the men bringing my things, but they're ill at ease and eager to be gone. Jacobsen motions me to enter, and when I push open the door I find myself in a cramped cupboard; I've read about this, it's to keep out the snow if there's a blizzard. Opening the second door, I make my way into the cabin. It's rather dark, and so cold that my breath smokes, but what strikes me most is the smell: coal-dust and wood-ash, with a rank undertow that reminds me of a butcher's shop. There are two small shadowy rooms and a lean-to outhouse. The room at the back has a couple of jerry-built beds piled with a mess of medical equipment. The one at the front has another bed (evidently the doctor's), a trestle table, stove, water barrel and a rickety stool. The windows are tiny. They make me feel unpleasantly shut in.

According to Jacobsen, the doctor was only killed last week, and clearly no one has touched his things. His bedclothes are flung back as if he's only just left, and across them lies a rather sumptuous dressing-gown of quilted crimson wool. His tweeds are folded on the stool, woollen combinations and stockings laid neatly on top; the stockings have retained the shape of his legs. His books and papers are on the table, also a large notebook lying askew, and an ink-bottle and a fountain pen, its cap unscrewed; he must have been writing before he died.

To my consternation he's left something else too. A woman. She has just clumped inside, bringing a blast of cold air and a whiff of unwashed flesh. What a confounded nuisance. She's a Lapp, I gather that's a native tribe from north Norway. Jacobsen says the doctor brought her to 'do' for him, and she's a mute, no one knows her name. Squat and brown, she watches me with an unblinking black stare. I've put her to lighting the stove and making my bed. I'll decide what to do with her in the morning.

I've only brought the barest minimum of gear and as I start opening my trunks, Ingstad and Jacobsen are taken aback. 'Where are your lanterns?' says Ingstad.

To hide my embarrassment I force a laugh. 'Didn't bring any, old chap.'

He blinks. 'Candles?'

'Didn't think I'd need them. Midnight sun and all that. Never expected this confounded fog.'

The look that passes between them says 'amateur' as clearly as if they'd spoken aloud. I'm not sorry when they take themselves off, leaving me and the woman to set the cabin to rights.

Briskly I scoop up the doctor's belongings and dump them in the back room. Jacobsen is letting me have the cabin on condition that I dispose of the dead man's effects, as he seems to have had neither friends nor relations. I suppose it makes sense for me to do it as I'm a fellow Englishman, but I shan't tackle it today. For now it's merely a relief to get everything out of sight.

The Lapp woman seems to understand English, but she's sullen and wilful, had the impertinence to object when I brought in a very serviceable chair I'd found outside. Someone had thrown it on the woodpile, I can't imagine why. It's good quality mahogany with a studded leather seat and back. The legs and arms were smeared with some kind of reddish stain, which at first I mistook for blood. I told the woman to clean it off and she pretended not to understand. I persisted until she did.

The good doctor seems to have been rather careless with his money. He left a scattering of loose change on the window-sills, on the floor by the front door, and in the doorway to the back room. The Lapp woman doesn't like me picking up the coins. Doubtless she wanted them for herself.

I shall have to keep an eye on her. Just now I caught her trying to throw out that chair again. I had to wrench it from her grip, and got a nasty splinter in my thumb.

The butcher's smell is strongest in the back room. I've traced it to the medical stuff on the beds, a jumble of rubber sheeting, leather straps and electrical equipment – tangled wires, ear-pieces, dry cell batteries; they remind me of that patent electrical treatment which Mother tried last spring.

The doctor was clearly a man of means. There's a custom-made wooden chest containing more medical gear, and an instruments bag of black pigskin with his name in gilt: *A. E. W. Thrale*, plus a string of letters indicating his status as an alumnus of Cambridge and Fellow of three learned societies. A label reveals that his previous post was at one of the better hospitals for nerve-shattered officers in Virginia Water; I recognise the name as it's where poor Arthur would have gone if he'd survived his wounds.

The doctor must have been fond of his comforts to have brought that chair all the way from Oslo. I rather fancy he was vain, too. Ridiculous to bring such a dressing-gown to Spitsbergen! And that notebook is expensively bound in black morocco, his name and postnominals stamped in gold. A glance inside reveals that he wrote in a tiny, obsessively neat copperplate hand. It strikes me as disagreeably soulless and somehow conceited. Did he imagine he was writing for an admiring posterity?

I've shoved the notebook under his clothes, where I can't see it. I shall deal with his effects tomorrow. For today it's enough to shut the door on that smell.

Before Jacobsen left, he advised me to burn the lot. I was astonished. 'But those instruments must be valuable. Surely the hospital at Longyearbyen would be glad of them?'

He scowled and shook his head.

'Then sell them, man! You could make a decent sum.'

Another head-shake. As he disappeared into the fog, I saw him cross himself.

I find the fact that he's superstitious oddly reassuring. I might be an amateur when it comes to the Arctic, but at least I don't get in a funk over touching a dead man's things.

It's one in the morning and I'm too excited to sleep. I felt disagreeably cramped in the cabin so I've come outside for a smoke; there's a driftwood log by the front door which makes a tolerable bench. It's still light of course, though no sign of the sun. Only this uneasy white glow. The cable railway stopped hours ago. The silence when it did was oddly shocking.

The Lapp woman has gone for the night, thank God; I gather she has some kind of hut over the ridge. Before she left, we had rather an awkward misunderstanding. I asked whether she would be sleeping in the cabin and she shrank back, her dark eyes wide with alarm. Did she *imagine* I was propositioning her?

God I wish this bloody fog would lift. I'm desperate to stretch my legs, but Jacobsen was fierce about walking alone in the fog, even with my gun. He says I'd get lost, or eaten by a polar bear.

That's why Ingstad keeps half a dozen sled dogs, to warn him of bears. He's a fur-trapper in winter, he shoots bears for a living. In summer he works here as a watchman to make ends meet.

It was foggy last week when the doctor was killed. Ingstad saw it happen. He says the doctor burst out of the cabin 'like de devil vas after him'. Didn't hear Ingstad yelling a warning, ran right into the path of a cable-car. It struck him from behind and spattered his brains across the rocks.

It's freezing out here, but my Shetland pull-overs and Grenfell windproofs are keeping me snug. I almost wish I didn't have to go back inside. Those tiny windows. And let's face it, the place isn't exactly welcoming. Ha! Perhaps old Thrale is angry with me for moving his things.

They say one oughtn't to speak ill of the dead, but that didn't stop the Norwegians. Jacobsen said nobody liked Thrale, though he didn't say why. Ingstad was more specific. The doctor brought a cat with him, which caused havoc with Ingstad's dogs; one ran off and never returned, and the doctor refused to pay him for its loss.

'What happened to the cat?' I asked, hoping it wasn't lurking somewhere nearby.

'Dead,' Ingstad replied with satisfaction. I didn't enquire how.

Surprisingly, the 'sykehus' was Thrale's idea. Until he came, the mine had no medical facilities. I gather he persuaded the Company to create the post of medic for him. He even supervised the building of the cabin and chose the site, well away from the other buildings.

The man was obviously vastly over-qualified to work at some tin-pot little mine at the back of beyond. I wonder what made him relinquish his position at the officers' home to come up here?

Finally! I was just about to go inside when the fog miraculously cleared — and suddenly, unbelievably, there it was: *the midnight sun*!

It lies very low on the sea, shining into my eyes and bathing the land in a strange, dark-amber glow. The water is molten gold dotted with dazzling chunks of ice, the sky opalescent silver streaked with pearl. Mountains tower around me, sharp-fanged and glittering with snow. Below them the hills sweeping down to the fjord are rust-red — I suspect Devonian sandstone — and very beautiful in their nakedness. To my left rises a steep ridge of reddish scree. Far below me, the cable railway extends from the fjord to a hole halfway up the hillside, some distance to my right; that must be the entrance to the mine. The miners' cabins by the jetty resemble children's toys flung down in this vast, silent land.

Oh, I was *right* to cling to my dream! My life until now seems unreal, a dark cramped cage from which I've finally burst free. It was bad enough while Arthur was alive, but after he was killed there was no escape, not even at Oxford. Cynthia wrote every day, Mother twice. *'My darling Phillip, you are all we have left.'* They never knew how that weighed on my spirits.

The end of the War changed nothing, by then the flu had wrecked what was left of their health. When they finally died, within days of each other, all I felt was relief. The newspapers are calling this 'The Roaring Twenties', but so far they've roared right past me. It's 1927 and I've scarcely begun to live.

God I love it here. The freedom. The harshness. The endless, endless light.

Spitsbergen hasn't changed since the Ice Age. Most of it's still covered in ice, and what isn't has only the merest scraping of soil. No trees, hardly any vegetation. A thin crust of life on inanimate rock.

It's a geologist's paradise. I can't wait to explore.

I've had the most marvellous few days. Uncle Felix was right, this job is made for me: no colleagues and no need to report, except for a brief bulletin once a fortnight – and even that's hardly a requirement, since Uncle Felix was at Winchester with someone on the Board. And if his second-in-command regards me as an upstart and is practically *willing* me to fail, why, I shall take the greatest delight in proving dear Braithwaite wrong.

I've learnt that it's best to work at 'night' – that is, after midnight – as that's when the weather's more settled. At first I found this disorientating, it reminded me how we felt during the War when the Government brought in 'summertime', and we had to put our clocks forward; but I'm used to it now. And the geology is simply thrilling.

As soon as I've scrambled over the ridge behind the cabin, the mine is left behind and I'm in another world. Great empty slopes and rushing meltwater streams. Windswept plains of tundra squelching with moss. Giant boulders crouching like petrified trolls. And always — well, almost always — the cold white sun.

There are no roads and I never meet a soul. It's heaven. For company I have towering cliffs echoing with the cries of seabirds, and jagged blue glaciers mirrored in silent fjords. Yesterday I came across a gneiss cliff with the most extraordinary curved strata, they looked as if they'd been buckled out of shape. They quite put me in mind of that mad Bosch and his crazy notion that the continents once floated around, bumping into each other like leaves on a pond.

Every 'night' — which is really day — I return to the cabin exhausted, but I make it a point to write up my notes at once. Then if it's not too cold, I eat my porridge outside. The clamour of the mine hardly impinges at all. Dr Thrale knew what he was doing when he built his sykehus up here. As I sit smoking on my 'bench', I feel like an Olympian surveying the mortals toiling below.

The weather changes so swiftly I have to be constantly on my guard, it can go from frost to warmth to hail in a heartbeat. Just now I was chipping off a sample in brilliant sunshine, my smoked-glass sun-spectacles turning the world yellow – and by the time I'd stowed the sample in my ruck-sack, clouds had swallowed the sun and a grey wall was seeping soundlessly down the mountainside, while at my back, sea-fog was creeping in. They had come without warning. It felt like a visitation.

I only wish my wretched thumb wasn't so beastly painful. It's swollen to twice its size and giving me hell. I've tried tweezering out the splinter but it hurt so much I nearly passed out. Iodine has had no effect, and I don't fancy breaking into Dr Thrale's supplies. I know what's caused the infection, it's that damned red stain on the chair. I blame the Lapp woman. She has a revolting habit of chewing some kind of bark, and clearly some of the mess had found its way onto the chair on my first day. At the time I thought this was accidental, but the other day I chanced to return unexpectedly, and the woman sprang back guiltily from the chair. To my consternation I saw that its arms and legs were freshly smeared with red, and though I demanded to know what she was doing, she pretended not to understand. Surely she can't have smeared it on deliberately?

But *why?*

I still adore this light, but because of my thumb I've been sleeping poorly. The cable-cars don't help either, because of course my bed-time is the start of the miners' working day. And to cap it all, yesterday I was jolted awake by an almighty bang at the window. It sounded as if someone had struck it hard with their fist, but when I stumbled outside I realised it was only a bird. Snow bunting, tiny black and white job, up here they're called 'Arctic sparrows'. Poor little scrap must have been confused by the reflection in the glass. It was still alive, though its neck was broken. It died as I was reaching for a rock to finish it off.

What with my thumb and the cable-cars and suicidal birds, I could do with a tad more kip. I've tried my wax earplugs, but they make me feel unpleasantly cut off. I need to be able to hear, in case there's anything untoward outside.

If I'm honest, though, the main thing keeping me awake is this unending light. I still love it, of course I do, but I'm beginning to find it unsettling. Closing the shutters makes me feel disagreeably confined; as if I've been buried alive. I've tried tying my muffler around my head. Same thing. This ever-present sun feels somehow unnatural. It gives one the oddest sense of dislocation, particularly when the sky is overcast. At such times there are no shadows, only this strange grey radiance. It doesn't feel quite of this world.

And it's playing havoc with my dreams. Last 'night' I dreamt someone was with me in the cabin. I woke up – or thought I did – convinced that someone was there. I was frightened, couldn't bring myself to open my eyes. I lay rigid, listening to them dragging the doctor's chair across the floor. I distinctly heard the floorboards creak, and the scrape of the chair's legs. Someone was hauling it into the middle of the room, and there was something horrible about the sound, unhurried and purposeful, heavy and slow. As if somebody was slumped in the chair. A dead weight.

That's when I actually woke up: gasping, my heart hammering in my chest. The chair was where I'd left it before going to sleep, neatly tucked up against my work table, with its back to me.

I got out of bed and flung on my clothes. I went over to the chair. I couldn't bring myself to touch it. Instead I walked to the 'kitchen' end of the room and busied myself lighting the Primus stove for tea. My hands were shaking. It took several attempts.

Doubtless a poor diet is what's causing it, and for that I've only myself to blame. I was so determined to 'rough it' that I only brought the barest essentials: tea, coffee, oatmeal, flour, sugar, salt, pipe tobacco. For the rest I planned to live off the land with the help of my trusty Enfield; but I think I've rather overdone the simplicity. I daresay that comes from reading too much Jack London when I was a boy; and perhaps also an irrational desire to prove to poor Arthur that I can cope just as well as he.

Stupidly, I've only brought the minimum of gear. No looking-glass or razor (in a few weeks I shall have quite a respectable beard); more worryingly, I've nothing to prevent scurvy. Before I left London someone told me that scurvy grass grows up here, so I'd planned to rely on that; but I picked some the other day and it tastes vile, like rotten spinach.

Worst of all, I've only three books.

Of course I could humble my pride and ask Jacobsen to sell me supplies, but I'm damned if I will, at least not yet.

The Lapp woman makes fairly decent coffee and porridge and a tolerable kind of bannock. As for tea, I brew it myself. It's the first time in my life that I've had to make my own, and I'm finding it rather a lark.

But I would kill for a jar of marmalade. And hot buttered toast. And a bottle of Scotch. And books.

My word, that was a narrow escape. It's been a glorious 'day', but around four in the morning clouds swept in and the rain came down hard, so I decided to head back. I'd paused for a breather on a rocky slope when suddenly I heard a deafening thunder-crack. I barely had time to stagger out of danger, could only gape as boulders the size of houses went careening and bouncing down the hillside where I'd been standing moments before.

The rockfall was over as suddenly as it began, and the silence beat at my ears. The air was hazy with shattered rock, it tasted bitter and gritty between my teeth. My knees gave way and I sat down heavily. If I'd reacted a fraction more slowly, I would have been crushed like an ant. Here one instant, gone the next. And I do mean gone, snuffed out like a spark, nothing left. At least that's what I believe.

Of course Mother and Cynthia knew better. They were so certain they would meet Arthur and Father 'on the other side'. I used to find their conviction infuriating. I had such arguments with Cynthia. 'But what if it's nothing like that?' I would insist. 'What if an afterlife exists, but there's nothing there? No reward, no punishment, merely emptiness. Surely that's just as likely as encountering one's loved ones on some kind of nebulous 'astral plane'? And she would smile her superior smile and murmur, 'But Pip, it's what I believe. I simply *know* that I shall have my reward.'

Reward? *Why?* The universe owes us nothing. It doesn't even know we exist.

But it's pointless going over all that now. The rockfall was simply a warning. Watch yourself, Pip old man. Keep an eye out for danger.

I must have been more unnerved by that rockfall than I thought. That's the only way I can explain what just happened.

I was almost 'home', climbing the final ridge, and had paused at the top to catch my breath. The cabin lay below me, and beyond it the mine was waking up, cable-cars trundling, men trudging up the slope. The rain had eased off but the sky was overcast. I was cold and hungry, eager to get inside.

I wasn't thinking of anything in particular, panting with my hands on my knees, when I noticed the shadow of a man stretched on the ground before me. Assuming that Ingstad or Jacobsen had come up behind me, I turned to greet them – 'Hulloa, there—' – only to find that I was alone. No one behind me. And when I looked again, the shadow was gone.

That was when it struck me. *The sky was overcast. No sun.* How *could* I have seen that shadow?

Unless of course the clouds had briefly thinned and let in the sun. That must have been it. There is no other explanation.

But somehow I can't get it out of my mind. A shadow on a sunless day. It isn't possible. It doesn't make sense.

The Lapp woman is getting on my nerves.

I'll admit she works hard, fetching water from the stream, coal from the jetty, driftwood from the shore; cooking, washing, seeing to the outhouse. But she's decidedly underhand.

Yesterday I was returning to the cabin when I saw her watching me from the back-room window. I couldn't make out her expression, the sun was so bright that all I could see was a dark head, and as I drew nearer she moved out of sight. There was something furtive about the movement I didn't like, and on going inside I found that she'd gone.

This morning I gave her a talking to about it, and she pretended not to understand. She was chewing that disgusting red mess again. Ingstad says it's alder bark, she must have brought it with her from Tromsø; he says the Lapps believe it has power. When I asked what he meant, he rather unconvincingly professed not to know.

The Lapps are full of odd beliefs. They hold that everything in the world has a spirit, even mountains and rocks. There's quite a striking boulder a few yards above the cabin, doubtless a relic of glaciation, and I've seen the woman smearing it with fish oil. Presumably that's some kind of offering. At first it struck me as ludicrous, but since the rockfall I've begun to understand. If you live in the Arctic it probably helps to tell yourself that rocks have souls. It makes you feel less alone. Less at the mercy of an uncaring universe.

I'm still sleeping badly. This 'morning' when I woke up (that is, shortly after midnight), I found the doctor's chair in the middle of the room. It gave me quite a turn. It had no business being there, several feet from the table where I'd left it when I went to bed.

Obviously I must have moved it in my sleep. Though I have no recollection of doing so. I find that unsettling.

That chair isn't as comfortable as I'd thought. Some of the studs poke out, and on several occasions they've snagged my sleeves and my breeches. I ought to get around to hammering them flat.

Or maybe I'll simply throw the bally thing in the back room with the rest of Dr Thrale's belongings – which I still haven't got around to sorting out. Perhaps that's why the cabin feels so unwelcoming, because I'm constantly aware of them. If I were superstitious, I might even wonder whether he was annoyed with me for neglecting his things!

Three glorious days of endless sunshine. Cold, a north wind cutting like a knife; but glorious. Then the rain swept in and by the time I got back to the cabin a storm was coming on, the sky so dark it was turning 'day' to night.

I feel such a *muff* for not bringing candles and lamps. I wouldn't even have had to buy the bloody things, I had the pick of poor Arthur's mountain-climbing kit – but oh no, I was set on being my own man and roughing it in the wild.

As for hunting, I've been an abject failure. Until yesterday I hadn't bagged so much as a lemming. The miners shoot seals, but I don't fancy the blubber, and seagulls don't appeal either. The other day I came face to face with a reindeer. It was smaller than I'd expected, very fat and furry with stubby little legs, and it simply stood and stared at me. I would have felt unsporting to shoot the brute at such close quarters, so I let it live. Besides, the thought of butchering it turned my stomach.

Yesterday, though, I did manage to shoot a hare. The Lapp woman looked askance when I gave it to her (I gather her people subsist on reindeer), but the stew she concocted tasted even better than Cook's famous jugged hare.

The Lapp woman had gone when I got back today and the cabin was icy, I had the devil of a time lighting the stove. It was only after I'd got it going that I noticed that Jacobsen had taken pity on me and left some presents on the table: a battered storm lantern, a box of candles, a large stoneware jar containing some kind of preserves – and a bottle of schnapps!

A scrap of paper tucked under the jar of preserves bore a terse scrawl: '*Multe – for the scurvy.*' According to my pocket dictionary, *multe* is Norwegian for cloudberry. I remember them from Uncle Felix's grouse moor in Ayrshire, though I never knew one could eat them. Revelation! I've just added some to my porridge and they're *delicious*, tasting of caramel and in appearance resembling blackberries, though of a rather fetching dark amber, like little midnight suns. And this isn't the schnapps talking. Though it's helping a lot.

The work is going well too, my table bears a respectable pile of samples – gypsum, asbestos, magnetic iron ore – and I'm proud of the neatness of my notes and my survey map. Yesterday I sent in my first bulletin. I got Jacobsen to radio it to Longyearbyen and thence by some circuitous route to Head Office in London. How do you like that, Braithwaite? Not so useless now, am I?

And more good news: it turns out that oatmeal is something of a wonder-drug. Ingstad suggested I try a compress of the stuff on my thumb – and bless me if it hasn't done the trick! The splinter is out, the swelling is down, and wonder of wonders, it no longer hurts!

These Norwegians aren't such bad fellows after all. Rather dour, I grant you, and they've certainly no liking for amateurs. But when it comes down to it, they're jolly good sorts.

Not such a splendid morning. It's been overcast for days, and this unending grey twilight is setting my nerves on edge. I really *must* tackle Dr Thrale's belongings. I find myself thinking of them even when I'm out and about.

There had been a frost while I slept, and the ground was treacherous with black ice, so I had to fit my ice-claws. They made walking frightfully tiresome, I spent an exhausting few hours scrambling over a scree slope of splintered shale, its razor-sharp blades standing on end in hallucinatory zigzags. I stumbled often and was glad of my horsehide gauntlets. One of those nasty little foxes trotted past with a gull struggling in its jaws, and threw me a sly look.

At times I feel as if this whole country is out to get me. I know that's bosh, rocks and mountains don't give a damn. That's what drew me to geology in the first place, the fact that rocks can't feel; no messy emotions getting in the way. But somehow up here that's no comfort.

Professor Mannheim once remarked that a man needs a certain cast of mind to be a geologist: 'To spend his life contemplating the vast indifference of the inanimate world. I think you have it, Seaton. The Englishman's phlegmatic temperament.' I'm beginning to wonder.

After the scree slope I struggled across a huge rocky pavement crusted with black lichen. It wasn't too bad when the lichen was dry, but when the rain set in it turned as slippery as guts. Next I had to cross an icy plain, disagreeably swampy and strewn with bones. I've no great fondness for birds and beasts, but I couldn't help noticing that everywhere I turned I found evidence of violent death. Skeletons large and small, entombed in moss. I suppose it's because we're so far north. Dead matter takes years to decay.

In the distance the sky had darkened to charcoal, I couldn't tell if the bad weather was advancing or receding. As I was debating whether to turn back, I spotted a white speck on the other side of the valley and my stomach turned over. Bear?

Raising my binoculars, I was relieved to see that it was only a snowy owl. I watched it alight on a rock and shake out its wings. I met its baleful yellow glare.

I was about to lower the binoculars when it happened. A

dark shadow passed quickly before my lenses, briefly blotting out my sight. It passed so close that I jerked back with a cry, but when I lowered the binoculars the hillside was empty. Not so much as a raven winging its way towards the fjord.

It ought to have been a relief to regain the cabin, but just now when I pushed open the door I felt an overwhelming reluctance to go inside. The woman has gone, and yet the place doesn't feel empty. It feels full of ill-will, directed at me.

I find myself making an unnecessary amount of noise, whistling and stamping as if to announce my presence. I open the door to the back room, and the butcher's smell hits me anew. Dr Thrale's belongings lie where I dumped them on my first day. I remember chucking his notebook on one of the beds and flinging his dressing-gown on top. The garment sprawls with one arm flopping lazily over the edge. It flashes across my mind that maybe he's angry with me for disrespecting his work. I force a laugh, annoyed with myself for entertaining such fancies.

Quietly, I close the door. I take off my outer things and hang them on the line I've strung across the other end of the room. I light the Primus and fill the kettle for tea. I get the stove going with driftwood and sit on the stool and stare at the flames.

It's odd how one sees faces in the fire. I make out slanted eyes and a disagreeable black pit of a nose. I know it's merely an artefact of shadow and flame, but once I've seen it I can't unsee it.

First that sunless shadow, then the incident with the

binoculars. I wish I hadn't cried out like that. I didn't like the sound of my fear.

To hell with tea. I uncork the schnapps and take a swig. My hands are shaking.

Get a grip, Seaton.

It's a dangerous job, mining. Those poor devils work ten hours a day, six days a week. Crawling through tunnels blasted out of the hillside; hacking, drilling, scraping out coal; then getting into brawls on the seventh day and drinking themselves senseless.

Sometimes there are accidents. Three years ago a mine near Longyearbyen exploded. To this day it's still smoking. The bodies were never found.

What kind of men go in for such work? Answer: the roughest of the rough. Men ground down by poverty and drink. Men who need a place to hide, no questions asked.

From what I've gathered, this mine is every bit as dangerous as the others. Three miners have died this summer, two last month and one more recently. They're buried on the slope behind the cabin. Thrale is up there too; I don't know where. It all seems rather casual, without benefit of clergy, and nothing to mark the graves. Though I suppose in the Arctic, needs must.

It's not easy remaining rational when one is surrounded by superstition.

I think I know why the Lapp woman smeared alder juice

on Dr Thrale's chair. It's to ward off evil spirits. I finally got that out of Ingstad when I was down at Jacobsen's, buying more candles. And those coins I found on the windowsills and in the doorways on my first day. At the time I thought Thrale had been careless with his money, but now I'm pretty sure that the woman put them there on purpose; or maybe it was Ingstad or Jacobsen. Nanny used to do the same thing at Hallowe'en. It's an ancient charm against ghosts.

It's all nonsense, but somehow it's put me off using the chair, so I've dumped it in the back room. I wore my gauntlets to move it. Didn't want to risk another splinter.

It's no good, it has to be done.

I'm constantly aware of his notebook in the back room and I want it gone – but somehow I can't bring myself to burn it unread. And that's not out of respect for a fellow scientist, I loathe Dr Thrale. It's pure, morbid curiosity. I simply have to take a look.

I've made sure that the door to the back room is firmly shut, and placed the stool close to the stove. I have the notebook on my lap. I am afraid to open it, but I know that I must. I have the oddest feeling that this is what he wants. Which of course is absurd, he no longer exists. But I can't shake the feeling.

The first few pages are medical stuff which I don't understand, though I gather that his field of study was nerves. In his previous post at the officers' convalescent home, he seems to have worked on victims of war neurosis and 'shell-shock'. I can't make out what he did.

From what I can ascertain, there's a debate raging in the scientific world about how nerve impulses are transmitted, whether by chemicals, or by electrical currents – and the doctor was firmly in the electrical camp. '*Consciousness can only reside in the rapid flow of electrical current,*' he writes in his tiny crabbed hand, with such emphasis that in places the nib has dug into the paper. 'Ergo, *the only means of detecting consciousness is via voltaic measurements, as devised by this physician.*'

'*This physician*'. The pompous ass. His contempt for those on the other side of the debate is blistering; his conviction that he alone is correct, unshakeable.

Pages of equations follow, which I skip. Now we come to what's clearly the crux of his work. It's obsessively neat, obviously copied from a draft.

'*Experiment to detect consciousness after death.*'

What? What?

'*If consciousness resides in the brain, then on death it must survive outside the physical body. This physician has devised a certain method to detect it.*'

Well of course he has. 'This physician', in his overweening arrogance, has devised a 'certain method' of answering the question which has plagued mankind since we first began to walk on two legs. But what could be easier for the great Dr Thrale?

Down by the fjord, the dogs have begun barking excitedly. Marking my place in the notebook, I go to the window. It's feeding time, Ingstad is tossing them chunks of seal meat. Watching them squabbling and lashing their tails makes me wistful. That's normal life down there. I wish I could join it.

Method:
- *Trepanning to gain access to the cerebral matter while the subject remains alive.*
- *Voltaic probes inserted to this physician's design.*
- *Observations <u>must</u> be made at the precise moment of death: <u>controlled conditions</u>.*
- *Experiments (i), (ii), (iii) & (iv): <u>rodent, bird, cat, dog</u> (evolutionary progression).*
- *NB: Nothing must interfere with consciousness – hence <u>no anaesthetic</u>.*
- *NB2: <u>Sever the vocal cords at the outset to minimise noise</u>.*

God he was a cold bastard. I know what trepanning is, it's drilling a hole in the skull to get at the living, pulsing brain. He brought that unfortunate cat all the way to Spitsbergen so that he could butcher it alive. And he stole one of Ingstad's dogs. He drilled into their skulls and performed his vile electrical 'experiments' without anaesthetic – and he made sure the poor brutes couldn't cry out by cutting their vocal cords.

Even his language betrays his lack of humanity. His use of the passive voice to distance himself; and that word 'consciousness', instead of 'spirit' or 'soul'. No hint of emotion. No awareness that he was experimenting on sentient creatures.

The man was vile, and almost certainly deranged. I don't want to go on reading. The sight of his punctilious copperplate fills me with dread. But I can't stop now.

'*Results:* Inconclusive. *Working hypothesis: experiments (i)–(iv) failed because the consciousness of lower life forms is too rudimentary to detect. As this physician anticipated, further experimentation is needed on higher life forms.*'

Oh God no. *Higher life forms?* Surely he can't mean people?

There's a ringing in my ears as I turn the page.

And there it is, neatly and precisely laid out in his minuscule copperplate. '*The woman is not a fit subject. Being a female and primitive, her consciousness would be too rudimentary to be detectable . . .*'

I feel sick. I've just realised why he came to Spitsbergen. He needed men for his experiments. Men without homes or loved ones. Men whom no one would miss. He found them here. Three men dead in the space of a few weeks. The dates all fit.

'*Experiments (v) and (vi) failed because subjects M and N died sooner than expected. Imperative that the next subject is observed under controlled conditions. Measurements must be taken at the moment of death. Ergo, the moment of death must be precisely controlled . . .*'

I don't want to read on, but I do. '*Subject Y secured. This physician has informed Jacobsen that the patient is not expected to live. This physician has taken steps to . . .*'

The clunketty-clunk of the cable-cars gets abruptly

louder, and I raise my head. My heart jerks. The door to the back room is standing open.

I stare at it. I force myself to stand. I place the notebook on the stool and approach the back room.

No one's there. Nothing has stirred.

Firmly I close the door. I take a splinter of wood from the pile by the stove and wedge it under the door to keep it shut. I pick up the notebook and sit down on the stool. I stare at the notebook with loathing. I feel like a prisoner. But I have to finish it. I have to find out what he did. Then I'll stuff the beastly thing in the stove.

I wish to God I hadn't read it.

I've torn out the page headed *'Subject Preparation'* and burnt it so that I can't ever read it again. I won't repeat what it said to a living soul. Never, not even to myself.

He was mad, of course he was. This heavy cold dread in the pit of my stomach is some kind of psychological transference – either from him or from the poor devils who were his victims.

Perhaps there's some justice in the fact that it was his own 'work' which killed him in the end. According to him, his last murderous experiment succeeded, but what he discovered was so horrifying it sent him rushing out into the fog, into the path of that cable-car. Hence his final desperate scrawl: *This is not possible. I can't bear it*

I ought to put the notebook in the stove right now, only I can't stand the thought of sharing this room with its ashes, so instead I've buried it in the woodpile. I shall burn it tomorrow. I'll get the woman to help me. We'll make a bonfire of his belongings and fling his beastly chair on top.

When I was outside getting rid of the notebook, fog was rolling in from the sea. Now as I pace the cabin it's pressing against the windowpanes. It has swallowed the world. I can't bear to stay in this cabin on my own, but I've left it too late. I can't run down to Jacobsen or Ingstad, it's too far in this fog and the cable-cars are still going. They'll be going for hours. I don't want to end up like Thrale, my brains spattered over the rocks.

Thank God for Veronal. I've taken enough to knock me out and washed it down with the last of the schnapps. I huddle on the bed and wait for the drug to blot out my consciousness.

I wake with a start. I'm in the middle of the room, sitting in the doctor's chair. My heart is battering my ribs like a trapped bird. I can't move. Terror grips my throat – my wrists, ankles, arms. It holds my neck in a vice.

I know – I *know* – that there's someone behind me. I feel his intent. He can do what he likes to me, and he will. He is going to kill me. Calmly, dispassionately, he means to watch me die. Nothing can stop him. I open my mouth to scream but I can't make a sound. He has taken my voice. He is taking my life

*

Where am I? Darkness. The void. Soundless. Appalling. Infinitely vast. I am alone for ever. Oh God I can't bear it

A boom shatters the silence and with a jolt I am back in the cabin.

I'm back in the chair. Arms and legs bound. Head immobile. I make one last desperate heave. I tip myself over, fall to the floor. I struggle and twist but the chair is on top of me, it won't let go, it's snagging my legs, my sleeves. Moaning, I squirm and thrash. I tear one leg of my breeches free. I rip my sleeves clear. I kick the ghastly thing away. Moaning, I crawl on hands and knees. Pain jabs my palms. Broken glass crunches beneath me. I keep crawling.

The door bursts open and Ingstad rushes in.

I had cut my hands badly on the broken glass and Ingstad spent ages picking out the splinters, his thick fingers handling the tweezers with surprising dexterity. He hadn't hesitated when he'd burst into the cabin, he'd simply picked me up and hauled me down to his quarters, where, after seeing to my hands, he'd plied me with schnapps until I passed out.

Next day I asked him how he had known that I needed help, but all he would say was that the Lapp woman had alerted him after she'd sensed 'someting wrong'. I've given her enough money to buy a passage back to Tromsø. It's an inadequate reward for saving my life, but I think she was pleased. At least, she almost smiled.

When I felt strong enough, she and Ingstad accompanied

me up to the cabin and helped me burn Dr Thrale's belongings: clothes, instruments, chair. The notebook.

I believe now that Thrale wanted me to read it. He wanted the 'success' of his experiment to be made known to all the world. It gave me some satisfaction to watch his notebook shrivel and burn. Shrink him down, I told myself. Shrink him down to a still white point of silence – then snuff him out as if he never existed.

I haven't been back to the cabin since. I've been staying with Ingstad in his quarters. He and the woman went up there and packed up my kit, and oversaw the men taking it down to the store-room by the jetty. The steamer comes next week and I shall be on it.

In their rough way, Ingstad and Jacobsen have been kind to me. They haven't asked me what happened; nor have I asked them to describe what they found in the doctor's cabin on the day he was killed. They don't need to, I can see it for myself. The mutilated body of his last victim, the nameless 'Y', slumped in the doctor's chair, his arms and legs and neck restrained by leather straps, and beneath him the spattered rubber sheet.

I can picture Ingstad and Jacobsen too, aghast at what they found. I see them hurriedly burying the bodies of Thrale and his victim; bundling the straps and the sheeting in the back room along with the electrical apparatus; throwing the chair on the woodpile. Finally, I see them placing coins in the windows and doorways, to banish the unquiet dead.

Snuff him out, I told myself when we were burning his things. But of course I know that's not possible. I know that Thrale is still with me. I won't ever be rid of him, he's inside me, he's tiny fizzing sparks in my memory. Only when I die will the last of him die too. Take that, Dr Thrale. No one will ever know of your 'genius'. No one will ever know what you did.

But the worst of it is that I can't scrub from my mind what I experienced in those final moments before the gull crashed into the window. The great black silence that has no end.

That's what sent Thrale into the path of the cable-car. That's why he wrote his last desperate scrawl: *'This is not possible. I can't bear it'*

I tell myself that what I perceived in that moment wasn't real. It was merely some kind of thought transference, an echo of that vile man's deranged perceptions, seeping into mine. I have to tell myself this.

But what if it's true? What if, after we die, we simply go on, conscious and alone in eternal dark?

You would pray for oblivion. And there would be no one to hear you.

ABOUT THE AUTHORS

Elizabeth Macneal is the bestselling author of *The Doll Factory*, which has been adapted into a major TV series on Paramount+, *Circus of Wonders* and *The Burial Plot*. Her work has been translated into twenty-nine languages. Elizabeth is also a potter and lives in London with her family.

Laura Shepherd-Robinson is the bestselling author of four historical novels. Her debut, *Blood & Sugar*, was a Waterstones Thriller of the Month and won the Historical Writers' Association Debut Crown and the CrimeFest/Specsavers Crime Fiction Debut Award. Her second novel, *Daughters of Night*, was shortlisted for the Theakston's Old Peculier Crime Novel of the Year Award, the Goldsboro Glass Bell Award, and the Historical Writers' Association Gold Crown. Her third novel, *The Square of Sevens*, was an instant Sunday Times bestseller, a USA Today bestseller, and was featured on

BBC2's *Between the Covers*. Her fourth novel, *The Art of a Lie*, was an instant *Sunday Times* bestseller and was featured on Radio 2's Book Club. She lives in London with her husband, Adrian.

Stacey Halls was born in Lancashire and worked as a journalist before her debut *The Familiars* was published in 2019. *The Familiars* was the bestselling debut hardback novel of that year, won a Betty Trask Award and was shortlisted for the British Book Awards' Debut Book of the Year. Her following three novels, *The Foundling* (2020), *Mrs England* (2021) and *The Household* (2024) have all been *Sunday Times* bestsellers. She has now sold more than a million copies in all formats and in 2022 was awarded the Women's Prize x *Good Housekeeping* Futures award.

Andrew Michael Hurley is the award-winning author of four novels: *The Loney* won the Costa First Novel Award, Book of the Year at the 2016 British Book Awards and was hailed as a modern classic by the *Sunday Telegraph*. *Devil's Day* was the joint winner of the 2018 Encore Award. His 2019 novel, *Starve Acre*, has been recently adapted into a feature film. His latest book, *Barrowbeck*, was published in October 2024. Andrew lives and writes in Lancashire.

Imogen Hermes Gowar is the author of the *Sunday Times*-bestselling *The Mermaid and Mrs Hancock*, which won a Betty Trask Award and was shortlisted for the Women's Prize and the *Mslexia* First Novel Prize, amongst numerous others. Imogen lives and writes in Bristol.

Natasha Pulley is the *Sunday Times*-bestselling author of seven novels: *The Watchmaker of Filigree Street*, *The Bedlam Stacks*, *The Lost Future of Pepperharrow*, *The Kingdoms*, *The Half Life of Valerie K*, *The Mars House* and *The Hymn to Dionysus*. Her first novel won a Betty Trask Award and was an international bestseller. She lives in Bristol and teaches creative writing.

Susan Stokes-Chapman grew up in the historic Georgian city of Lichfield, Staffordshire, but now lives in north-west Wales. She studied at Aberystwyth University, graduating with a BA in Education & English Literature and an MA in Creative Writing. Her debut novel, *Pandora*, became an instant *Sunday Times* number-one bestseller immediately on publication, and was shortlisted for the 2023 Glass Bell Award. Her most recent novel is the gothic mystery, *The Shadow Key*.

Jess Kidd was brought up in London as part of a large family from County Mayo. Her debut, *Himself*, was shortlisted for the Irish Book Awards in 2016, the Authors' Club Best First Novel Award 2017 and longlisted for the John Creasey (New Blood) Dagger 2017. Jess won the 2016 Costa Short Story Award. Her second novel, *The Hoarder*, also titled *Mr. Flood's Last Resort* (US), was shortlisted for the Kerry Group

Irish Novel of the Year 2019 and longlisted for the 2020 International Dublin Literary Award. Both books were BBC Radio 2 Book Club Picks. Her third book, the Victorian detective tale *Things in Jars*, was released to critical acclaim. Jess's first book for children, *Everyday Magic*, was published in April 2021. Jess's fourth novel for adults, *The Night Ship*, was released in August 2022 and featured on BBC 2's *Between the Covers*. *Murder at Gulls Nest*, the first in the Nora Breen Investigates series, was published in spring 2025. Jess lives in North Yorkshire.

Stuart Turton's debut novel, *The Seven Deaths of Evelyn Hardcastle*, won the Costa First Novel Award and the Books Are My Bag Readers Award for Best Novel, and was shortlisted for the Specsavers National Book Awards and the British Book Awards Debut of the Year. A *Sunday Times* bestseller for three weeks, it has been translated into over thirty languages and has also been a bestseller in Italy, Russia and Poland. His second novel, *The Devil and Dark Water*, was chosen as a best books of 2020 pick by the *Sunday Times*, *Guardian*, *Daily Mail* and *Financial Times*. His most recent novel, *The Last Murder at the End of the World*, went to number one on the *Sunday Times* bestseller list, and spent a month on the *USA Today* bestseller list. It was nominated for the Theakston's Old Peculier Crime Novel of the Year.

Kiran Millwood Hargrave is a *Sunday Times*-bestselling author of stories including *The Girl of Ink & Stars*, *The*

Mercies and *The Dance Tree*. Her work has been translated into over thirty languages, and has won or been shortlisted for numerous international awards including a Betty Trask Award, Waterstones Book of the Year, the Wainwright Prize, the Prix Femina, the Strega Prize and the Janis Baltvilks Award.

Bridget Collins is the award-winning author of numerous novels for teenagers and four for adults: *The Binding, The Betrayals, The Silence Factory* and *The Naked Light*. *The Binding* was a number-one *Sunday Times* bestseller, shortlisted for various awards including the Waterstones Books of the Year, and was the number-one bestselling debut fiction hardback of 2019. She lives in Kent.

Catriona Ward is an American-British novelist whose work has been highly praised by Stephen King. She is the author of six novels: *Rawblood, Little Eve, The Last House on Needless Street, Sundial, Looking Glass Sound* and *Nowhere Burning*, coming in 2026. She has won the Shirley Jackson Award, the International Thriller Writers Association Award and is the only woman to have won the August Derleth Prize for best novel three times. Her books have been translated into thirty languages and her short stories have appeared in numerous anthologies. She lives in London.

Michelle Paver is the author of the internationally bestselling *Wolf Brother* books for younger readers, which have been published in thirty-six countries and have sold several million copies; and of three acclaimed supernatural novels for adults, *Dark Matter* (2010), *Thin Air* (2016) and *Wakenhyrst* (2019). Her fourth supernatural novel, *Rainforest*, is published by Orion in 2025. She welcomes contact with her readers on her website, www.michellepaver.com.

RAISING READERS
Books Build Bright Futures

Dear Reader,

We'd love your attention for one more page to tell you about the crisis in children's reading, and what we can all do.

Studies have shown that reading for fun is the **single biggest predictor of a child's future life chances** – more than family circumstance, parents' educational background or income. It improves academic results, mental health, wealth, communication skills, ambition and happiness.[1]

The number of children reading for fun is in rapid decline. Young people have a lot of competition for their time. In 2024, 1 in 10 children and young people in the UK aged 5 to 18 did not own a single book at home.[2]

Hachette works extensively with schools, libraries and literacy charities, but here are some ways we can all raise more readers:

- Reading to children for just 10 minutes a day makes a difference
- Don't give up if children aren't regular readers – there will be books for them!
- Visit bookshops and libraries to get recommendations
- Encourage them to listen to audiobooks
- Support school libraries
- Give books as gifts

There's a lot more information about how to encourage children to read on our website: **www.RaisingReaders.co.uk**

Thank you for reading.

---

[1] OECD, '21st-Century Readers: Developing Literacy Skills in a Digital World', 2021, https://www.oecd.org/en/publications/21st-century-readers_a83d84cb-en.html

[2] National Literacy Trust, 'Book Ownership in 2024', November 2024, https://literacytrust.org.uk/research-services/research-reports/book-ownership-in-2024